the good parts

pure lesbian erotica

the
good parts

edited by
nicole foster

alyson books
los angeles

Celebrating Twenty-Five Years

MANUFACTURED IN THE UNITED STATES OF AMERICA.

THIS TRADE PAPERBACK ORIGINAL IS PUBLISHED BY ALYSON BOOKS,
P.O. BOX 4371, LOS ANGELES, CALIFORNIA 90078-4371.
DISTRIBUTION IN THE UNITED KINGDOM BY TURNAROUND PUBLISHER SERVICES LTD.,
UNIT 3, OLYMPIA TRADING ESTATE, COBURG ROAD, WOOD GREEN,
LONDON N22 6TZ ENGLAND.

FIRST EDITION: JULY 2005

05 06 07 08 09 a 10 9 8 7 6 5 4 3 2 1

ISBN 1-55583-879-0
ISBN-13 978-1-55583-879-9

LIBRARY OF CONGRESS CATALOGING-IN-PUBLICATION DATA
   THE GOOD PARTS : PURE LESBIAN EROTICA / EDITED BY NICOLE FOSTER.—1ST ED.
      ISBN 1-55583-879-0; ISBN-13 978-1-55583-879-9 (PBK.)
      1. LESBIANS—FICTION. 2. EROTIC STORIES, AMERICAN. I. FOSTER, NICOLE.
   PS648.L47G66 2005
   813'.01083538'086643—DC22   2005041068

CREDITS
COVER PHOTOGRAPHY BY NICOLA TREE/IMAGE BANK/GETTY IMAGES.
COVER DESIGN BY MATT SAMS.

contents

introduction

When you go to parties, don't you wish you could take the hostess right there in the kitchen as she prepares the hors d'oeuvres?

Skip the small talk.

At the library, don't you dream of leading that little hottie outside to spank her with her book?

Studying is so…*boring*.

While shopping, don't you ponder pulling that blond into the fitting room with you?

Try her on for size.

We know you; we know all your dirty fantasies. And we know you lead a busy life. Why bother eating dinner when you can skip straight to dessert without gaining an ounce?

So we selected the sexiest stories—from our favorite erotica writers—and squeezed the juice from them. The crème de la crème de la crème.

Nothing less than the very best for you, sweetie.

—Nicole Foster

driving
M. L. Renki

We never leave the house on time. It didn't matter where we're going or whom we're going to see, we're always late because we're always fucking.

It was her mother's surprise birthday party, and her sister had called us twice to make sure we left on time. Her sister is a control freak who relishes such family events, while my girlfriend detests anything involving a main course of finger sandwiches and too-sweet punch as the only beverage. Nevertheless, we're on our way...late of course.

Her cell phone rings. "Hello...10 minutes and we will be parked and in our places." She hangs up.

"Your sister?" I ask.

"Yes," she says as she leans forward in the passenger seat, cell phone still in hand. "Fuck me," she demands.

"I'm driving and we're already late."

"Fuck me now."

I look over and she's pulling her pants down to the floor, slowly rocking back and forth against the leather seats. I can hear her pussy sticking and pulling; a sound that always gets me wet. That sound of wetness: of soggy pussy being worked against something of substance such as a finger, another pelvic bone, or in this case, a leather seat of a Ford Explorer. We have had sex in the car so many times that there is already a permanent darkening of the leather. She gets so wet that the come just pours out of her. I often reach over and rub that spot, hoping to pick up some of her scent, when I'm in the car by myself. I can stick my face in the seat at any time and know that I had fucked her raw.

"I need you inside me." She reaches over, takes my right hand from the steering wheel, and places it palm up on the seat. She squeezes my three middle fingers tightly together and backs her wet pussy over them, saying "You only need one hand for driving, so put this one deep inside me."

At first she bounces slowly, deeply, moaning as I feel the soft walls of her pussy; that pussy that I had been known to put many things into at her request to "fuck me properly." My favorite is still my own hand; she doesn't come nearly as hard when we use dildos, vibrators, Coke bottles or whatever other item we have lying around. And I never hardened the way I did when my fingers slid through her opening into the soft, wet stickiness of that luscious, sweet pussy.

And it was sweet, like nectar flowing out of the darkest center of a rare flower. That juice drove me crazy and at times, acted as a hallucinogenic showing me signing giraffes and surfing monkeys while my face was buried inside her with her clit between my teeth. As much as I enjoyed going inside her, I really enjoyed pulling out afterward and sticking my come-soaked fingers into my mouth to suck off the juice. Oftentimes I'd rub the moistness around my mouth and have her lick if off my face only after she'd sucked it off my fingers.

I could never deny this woman any request, so I drive with my left hand and keep my right inside her, hidden by her ass as she sits back deep into the seat so as to have my fingers all the way up her. But I can't stand her just sitting, moaning; I have to pump her. I lean over and rest my elbow on the console between the two seats for extra leverage. The deeper and harder I finger-fuck her, the closer her head moves toward the dash.

"Fuck yeah, harder...harder..."

The Explorer is only going 20 mph on the freeway, but I'm fucking her at high speed. Harder and harder I thrust my hand against the back of her ass, at the rim of her pussy. First, just my fingers, but the longer I pump, the more I feel her tightening...I have to put another finger in, and then a third.

We had long been past finger fucking. She could take my whole fist as she spread herself open for me, wanting everything I could give her.

I grow hot when I remember that I'm fucking her on the way to her family's home.

"Is that what you want? You want my whole hand, my fist...you want to feel me all the way inside you?" I ask.

"Goddamn yes, fuck me harder!" She's now standing, hunched over with the side of her face flat on the dash, the top of her head against the windshield with her ass in the air. "Fuck me, baby. Fist me, you know how rough I like it. Spread me out...spread me more."

Her sticky come is streaming down the back of my wrist and pooling in the palm of my hand. "I cant' wait to rub this come all over the inside of your thighs and lick it off. I want to pull over and fuck you so hard."

"No...just keep driving. Oh, God, just keep driving, but don't you stop fucking me. You better fuck me until I come so hard. I need to be emptied by you right here, right now." Her head slams against the windshield in synchronization with my hand slapping against her ass with each arm thrust. She moans, almost crying. She spreads her arms across the dashboard, pivoting her ass closer to me. "Deeper...deeper, I want you to split me open. I need more." She was begging me now, tears of expectation caught in her voice.

I'm about to explode—hard and wet, the seam of my jeans rubbing against my clit as my body jolts with each push. I begin to see white spots floating in the air and feel like I might pass out. I need to hear that scream of hers as she lets go. I need to be on top of her, to have her under me so I can use all my weight against that pussy. She likes it hard and it usually takes all of me pounding against her to push her over the top.

She suddenly throws her cell phone on the floor and turns to face the passenger side window, draping her ass over the console. "Load me up...pump me harder!" I'm ramming her now, grunting and sweating as I try to hold my own load and fuck her as hard as I possibly can without swerving off the road.

"Jesus Christ, baby..." I say through my teeth, as if that would help me hold things together. "Come all over me... come all over me." My sleeve is drenched from my cuff to my elbow.

"I'm coming...don't you stop fucking me...don't you stop...oh, my God. Yes...yes." She slams backward against me, and I feel her tighten around my hand and then release as her body goes limp.

She rests the back of her head on top of mine. I quickly take my hand out of her and place it between my own legs. She has made me so hard that I can hear my heart throbbing in my ears. She turns to watch as I beat off through my jeans. It doesn't take too much friction before I'm groaning and saying her name. I'm thinking about that beautiful ass in my face, with her wet pussy dripping come down the back of her thighs, as I shoot a hard load against the inside of my jeans.

"Take the steering wheel." I manage to whisper before closing my eyes and letting the come flow over me. My body trembles in the seat and I double over for a little while, trying to catch my breath. The spots are still swimming in front of me, and I can't form any words. I'm weak and crazy, the position she usually leaves me in after fucking.

"Oh, yeah, that was a good fuck. You fucked me properly, baby," she says as she guides the Ford into her sister's driveway. She pulls up her pants, fastens the snap, and says, "Honey, roll up your sleeves to hide the come stains. We have to go yell 'Surprise!'"

convergence

Sacchi Green

Last evening, from across the river, I watched you lean with an intent face as you played the leaping trout. You stooped to deftly grasp and then release your prize, the lines of your body revealing what the multipocketed fishing vest and the baseball cap over close-cropped hair had at first concealed; but I already knew.

That glimpse was enough to fuel dreams that left me sweaty, slippery, and tangled in my sleeping bag. But you had seen me too, naked in the rushing water; and in the morning you came back.

So young! But old enough to know what you were doing. I offered coffee, and wordlessly offered more. We sat on a high boulder and talked of fish and rivers while I ached to lay my hand on your thigh and take your hand and press it between my own to show you how every inflection of your voice, every tilt of your chin above your strong, smooth throat, every shift of expression flashing across your angular face, made the crotch of my jeans get wetter. It seemed impossible that you couldn't sense—and scent—my arousal.

You grew quieter, leaning back on one elbow, your dark, narrowed eyes glittering under heavy lids, your body a blend of stillness and tension. My pulse accelerated until I had to either touch you or take to the river.

Then, just as I tensed to move, you said, "You looked like one of those goddesses last night, there in the river. That virgin one, Diana, maybe—or was it Venus? Are you gonna make up your mind which one, or do I jump down there into what passes for a cold shower?"

I lay my hand over yours where it rested on your thigh. A tremor rippled almost imperceptibly through your muscles; your watchful expression didn't change. "I knew what I wanted," I said, "when I saw you fly casting. Such good hands."

"Think so?" You lifted a hand and surveyed it impassively. "I've been told they're too big."

"Not for me." I fumbled to untie my knotted shirt, leaned

toward you, and raised your hand to my breast. "I think I can fill them," I said, as your fingers curved to cradle the fullness.

You sat up, and filled your other hand too. "Pretty good fit," you agreed, pressing just hard enough to make me feel the firmness all the way down to my cunt.

"Might be a good fit...in other places..." Talking was getting difficult. Hell, *breathing* was getting difficult. I pulled away with an effort. "Might be somewhere more comfortable than on a rock to find out." I stood and began edging down the boulder's side.

In a single motion you uncoiled and leapt six feet down the sheerest rock face, your landing spraying damp gravel into the river. You pulled me from my foothold and swung me around to face the water, gripping me tightly from behind. "Comfort," you growled into my ear, "is highly overrated."

I pressed back, rubbing against your crotch. You read my mind, or my body, and ran those strong, deft hands up over my breasts until you were stroking me so delicately, teasingly, that you forced me to strain toward your touch. Even when my swollen nipples jutted out like thumbtips, even when my breath came so fast and shrill that it drowned out the rushing water, you didn't relent, but kept luring me closer and closer to a peak I could never quite reach.

"All you gotta do is ask for what you want," you murmured against my neck, but I just whimpered, so you kept up the torture. I couldn't stand to make you stop, until finally I couldn't stand not to.

I squirmed around to face you, rubbing gratefully against the thigh you thrust between my legs as you pushed me back against the rock. "Come on, damnit, suck me, bite me, now!" I said, and pulled your head to where I had to have it; and, after a few teasing licks, you bit. Hard. When you shifted from one breast to the other I could see, as I already felt, the hot, sweet pressure your mouth had put on my nipples.

By now my clit was at least as engorged, and it pounded as I rode your thigh. I let go of your head and fumbled at your belt. You pushed my hands aside, in classic mode, an old-fashioned girl. I let it go—for now. You spread my jeans open and pushed them down, and I kicked them loose as you worked your mouth down my belly. Then you were kneeling. Your hands gripped my substantial ass; but you leaned back and grinned at me when I arched my hips forward.

"So, Goddess, what next?" Your husky voice was not entirely steady, but the challenge was clear. You were prepared to tease me for longer than I could hold out.

"Shut up and use your mouth for something better!" Then you did, with a skill and rhythm perfectly tuned to my compulsive thrusts. My clit spasmed against your tongue and teeth, and hardened again before the exquisite pangs could quite subside. The throbbing demand of my cunt shook me so hard I would have fallen without the rock at my back. "More," I said, "now!" and tugged at your arm. But you raised your head, just the hint of a smile on lips slick with my juices, and said, reflectively, "So that's how a Goddess tastes!"

I yanked at your arm again. "You'll find out how a Goddess curses if you don't...don't..." but you half-relented, and brought one hand around to probe into my aching crotch. Again, it was all I could do to breathe.

"Don't what?" you said. "Just tell me what you want."

You meant for me to beg, and why not? It was little enough to give you. "I want," I said between ragged gasps, "to hold your hand—all of it. Please. Right now. Please."

So you let me feel one long finger, and two, and three...too gently, too gradually, not just to tease but to be sure I knew how much I could take.

I knew. "More," I begged, demanded. "More, all of it, harder!" My cunt clenched around the maddening pressure, tried to gulp it further in, and then you were past the narrow point and filling me the way I desperately needed to be filled.

Your eyes were closed, your mouth firm and unmoving against my clit. All your focus, your movement, was inside me, your curved hand thrusting, pushing my ache to waves of intensity surpassing even orgasm. Until orgasm struck; nothing else had ever come close.

Gently, you withdrew, soaked with my flow. Gently you stood and wrapped your strong arms around me in support until, not quite so gently, I nudged my knee between your thighs. "Please, I need this too," I whispered, as you stiffened. Then you let me rub against you until there was no telling who rode whom. I worked your T-shirt up until I could press my full breasts just under your own high, tight peaks. You buried your face in my shoulder and let my flesh muffle your shuddering release.

At last I turned toward the river. Not that I wanted to wash away your touch, my response, even the sweet soreness. But I did get what I wanted. You pulled off your clothes and joined me in the water, and somehow I managed not to stare too overtly at the beauty of your lithe, naked body. *Later,* I thought, *I'll make you truly howl.*

We stayed in the river until the sun was high and hot enough to threaten sunburn. You asked about my camera and tripod, and the stone towers I'd constructed, and I gave you the grand tour, describing the uses and goals of my photographs.

"Light and dark," you echoed musingly. "Good and evil? Either-or? Is that what you're hung up on?" You fingered a smooth, flat pebble with distinct striations of quartz and basalt.

"More like yin and yang, solid and space, stasis and flow, each defined by the other. It isn't opposites I find compelling, but their convergence." It was strange to be standing naked in a mountain stream, trying to verbalize the unexplainable. "I keep trying to catch something on film that exists only in my mind, a sort of stark, transcendent beauty that flashes at the point where opposites meet."

"Sounds like a matter-antimatter reaction," you said, and sent your pebble skipping across the pool. I pretended to do a little of this and a little of that, while all I could really think about was the graceful strength of your body, the residual throbbing of mine, and how I might force your own matter-antimatter to the exploding point.

Later you moved your gear to my campsite. We shared provisions, and when the late-afternoon light was right I shot rolls of film. I even took a few of you, just for myself, I said, when you said you'd only let me do it from the back. "That's fine," I assured you, "You're just as magnificent going as coming." You looked so startled that I wondered how blind the younger girls could be these days, to take what you so skillfully give but never tell you how beautiful you are.

You fished for our supper. We watched the sunset clouds glow bright salmon and slowly fade to steel, while the cascading song of a wood thrush rippled hauntingly from the darkening forest. Then, by the firelight, we lay together on combined sleeping bags, and I challenged you.

"No hands where you don't want them," I said, "no tongue, just lie back and let me make you howl." Your slight frown turned to laughter when I leaned over you and pulled your hands to my breasts. "C'mon, how can you turn down a tit-fuck? How often do you get an offer like that? The harder you can make me, the better this will work."

You responded with such skill and zest I could barely subdue my own aching need for more. It was worth it, though, when I knelt between your thighs, my breasts steadied in my hands, and teased your sweet ache with thrusting nipples until you writhed and dug your fingers into my shoulders. If you didn't truly howl until after you flipped me and ground your crotch against my hipbone, you came close enough. And then, while you still struggled for breath, I drew your head to my breast and slid my nipple, still slippery with your juices, into your mouth. "That," I said, "is how a goddess tastes."

ice

Karen Dale Wolman

All I knew was that her name was Mariah.

I had heard people say it throughout the evening. *Hello, Mariah. What have you been doing lately, Mariah? Fun party, Mariah. Nice leather jacket, Mariah.*

Sexy leather jacket, Mariah. I have always loved women in leather jackets. Black leather jackets.

I look at a woman in a black leather jacket and fantasize about how her body looks underneath it. I can visualize it so strong that I'm almost seeing it. I certainly smell the leather and the sweat, the hard body.

But I'm getting ahead of myself.

Underneath Mariah's jacket, I imagined olive skin, muscles that looked smooth at first, but turned out to be rippled. And salty—Mariah would taste salty.

Her hair was a rich black, jelled so it looked like the sea had just run through it. The salty sea...the warm water...those strong shoulders.

Her swarthy skin, her dark eyes, the strong way she held herself was slightly foreign, made me think of Italy, Greece, maybe Brazil.

I hadn't heard Mariah speak, so there was yet to be an accent to disprove my theory. Everybody talked to Mariah, but she didn't talk back. She just nodded and smiled and looked you over with those eyes. I imagined she was saving her voice for me. I imagined silky, I imagined raspy, but I didn't imagine I would get to hear it whispered right into my ear so soon.

Her voice was husky, of course. This gorgeous, muscular creature in black leather could be nothing but.

I was standing in the kitchen, gaping at Mariah, when I smelled the hors d'oeuvres burning. I opened the oven door to take them out, but in my gallant attempt to assist the unknown hostess—and my fascination with Mariah—I neglected to think about oven mitts. I yelled out, less from the pain than the shock-shock at the heat, not at my stupidity. When my hormones take over, I go brain dead. It's embarrassing for someone with as much education as I have, but I get really stupid when I see someone like Mariah.

I guess Mariah noticed when I screamed. You see, I not only lose brain function around someone like her, I also lose confidence. It never occurred to me that she was eyeing me too.

So while I was busy getting wet and stupid, Mariah used one hand to remove my flesh from the oven while deftly using the other to procure an ice cube from her glass of Coke.

She held my hand palm up and ran the cube back and forth across the hollow next to my burned thumb. I noticed that her eyes were the exact same color as her hair. That probably isn't what most people would pay attention to after almost turning their hand into a french fry, but Mariah captivated me. Concentrating was the only way I could prevent myself from completely wetting my pants. Not that my jeans weren't already a little bit soggy.

But Mariah didn't stop, didn't speak, and didn't acknowledge my reaction to her. I knew she was aware by the amused glimmer in her eyes: the black ones that matched her hair and her jacket. Perfectly. I blushed. Mariah laughed then ran the ice cube up my forearm, not stopping at the inside of my elbow as I expected her to. I was embarrassed at how fast the heat of my skin melted the ice. Mariah paid no attention. She kept her eyes locked on mine and continued to run the rapidly diminishing cube of ice up my arm and into an arc that swung underneath the tight black running bra I had been wearing for a shirt, showing off my own muscled body. I closed my eyes as Mariah ran the ice cube underneath the bra and over my breast, where she circled until my quickly hardened nipple was surrounded by nothing but her fingers and the cold water that had recently been ice.

Since my brain had already shut down, it didn't occur to me that a complete stranger had her hand on my breast. It did occur to me that Mariah's fingers returned with two cubes of ice, which she positioned on both sides of my nipple, and chilled my flesh to the point of excruciating sensation.

I must have moaned when Mariah slipped her hard thigh between my legs as she ran the two cubes across the sides of my nipple, which was swollen to the point of bursting. The edges of the ice cut in sharply, and I thought I felt blood through the slice, but then Mariah passed over my nipple with her fingers, warming it, and I realized all I felt was ice water and explosions.

Somehow or another, the party in the living room had ended, the noise had abated and the other guests had dispersed. Feebly, I questioned Mariah about the hostess finding us in her kitchen and throwing us out.

Mariah laughed from deep inside her throat and announced that she was the hostess. Was I having a nice time? Was there something she could do for me?

I laughed, and Mariah took the opportunity to push me back against the counter, trapping my hands behind me. She unzipped my Levi's and maneuvered her hand inside my jeans. I would have fallen if she hadn't had my back against the counter, but she held me tight against the Formica as her fingers dug inside me. I was helpless—a position, I must confess, that I rather enjoyed.

Mariah clawed against my body, biting into my flesh, leaving teeth marks on my neck, long red welts on my back, stinging ice burns and rivers and gorges between my legs.

I didn't realize I had hit the floor until I felt Mariah on top of me, saw my jeans off in a corner and felt her fingers deep inside me, forcing explosions. It was during one of the explosions that Mariah reached for more ice. Using them like blocks, she framed my left nipple firmly between the two frozen cubes. When my nipple was as hard as the ice, it reached forward, begging to be touched. After an agonizing, exquisite wait, Mariah began to stroke. And lick. And suck.

I almost died.

Then the ice cubes reappeared, pressed firmly together, trying to reach each other through my nipple, forcing it to engorge until I thought it would explode. Her tongue danced over my ribs, and the freezing water ran down my chest. Mariah, knowing how to control the cold, caught the liquid before it ran over the sensitive skin of my stomach.

Mariah also caught the come that was, by that time, shooting between my legs. My thighs began to close, as they do when I climax, but Mariah used her legs to clamp mine open, then lowered her body until I felt the heaven of her tongue sliding across me.

I was just beginning to cross the precipice again when Mariah's fingers reappeared like magic, but they didn't thrust inside me like I expected. Instead, a cube of ice appeared between her deft fingers and worked its way around my swollen lips, searing my juices frozen. My body stopped moving in shock as Mariah slid the cube back and forth across my labia, causing deep shudders and deeper eruptions.

Mariah laughed as the ice cube skirted around in her fingers. The ice was slippery against my cunt, gliding across the lubrication until Mariah almost lost hold of it, but she pressed it harder, pushed her bare breasts into my chest and began sucking on my tongue and my lips. The pressure froze the ice against my labia and Mariah began a game of pulling the cube away until it almost tore from my skin in exquisite pain, then pushing it gently back against me.

I was just getting used to that, reaching out to try and touch the body that was as incredible as the sensations it created in me, when Mariah smothered me in one of her beautiful, brown breasts. I moaned into the flesh as I took it in my mouth.

Having diverted my attention, Mariah's fingers reappeared again with more ice. I was not surprised until I discovered that it was two cubes instead of one, and Mariah had managed to frame them around my clitoris. The sharp shards of ice dug into my clit, forcing an explosion that almost threw Mariah's body across the room. She held on and laughed.

I struggled underneath Mariah, but she dug the cubes into the base of my clit and slid the icy slickness against my swelling lips until my clit felt more akin to a blazing fire than the frozen heat that swept across the rest of my genitalia. That was soon followed by the quick wetness of Mariah's tongue, which lashed across me fiercely as Mariah herself dripped in wet swipes back and forth across my thigh.

It wasn't until we were panting together in our pool of sweat and melted ice that I realized how much time had passed. The house was absolutely silent now, except for our deep, heaving breaths and the wet slapping of our bodies as they met across the slick liquid.

I felt so good I wanted to laugh. I had come to the party barely knowing anyone, having vague fantasies about meeting another woman, talking, exchanging phone numbers and plans to call about dinner. Instead, here I was, on the kitchen floor, underneath a woman called Mariah.

A smile crossed my eyes, and as it did, Mariah lowered herself down my body, her hair trailing over my torso until she was between my open legs again. The top of her head pushed against my pubic bone, her face turned toward my thigh, and her tongue began gently licking. I wanted to make her move faster. I wanted her to draw every ounce of wetness out of my body. I wanted her to make me scream.

But Mariah ignored my protests and continued to lick. Her fingers slid oh so lightly inside my lips. I held on tight. The smile in Mariah's eyes when she looked up told me she knew. She increased the pressure slightly then distracted my attention by plunging her fingers in hard, deep, making me scream. I made her scream back.

Then I screamed again. But not because of what Mariah was doing to my body. Because there was another woman standing in the doorway, watching us.

Mariah saw me notice, and continued to stroke and tease between the lips of my cunt and around my nipple as we both looked at the other woman. She just stood there, most of her flesh, brown like Mariah's, bared against cutoff denim shorts, a tight, black tank top and red high-top sneakers.

My body, of course, betrayed my mind, and the wetness that ran over Mariah's hands overpowered the feeble protests that I cried out unconvincingly.

"Who is that?" I asked between gasping breaths.

"I don't know." Mariah took my nipple in her mouth and drove her fingers up my cunt, so it was a while before I could speak again.

"You don't know who is standing in your kitchen and you're not worried?"

"I don't live here. I have no idea who she is."

"You told me you were the hostess."

"I lied." The tone of her voice was teasing. Her fingers were very serious. "I didn't want you to be worried about being caught." Her fingers were grinding into me very deliberately as she spoke. "That would have been too distracting." I breathed heavily but could not speak.

We were both looking at the other woman. "Does it bother you?" Mariah asked me.

The woman was watching us.

"No," I answered.

The woman took a step closer. Mariah put her mouth to better use. Three seconds on my clit and I exploded.

The woman was only two feet away from us now. Mariah and I got up and jumped her.

Six seconds later she was on the floor, naked, and underneath us. Mariah's fingers and mine touched inside her cunt. She was very wet. We plunged in together. She screamed. We laughed. The ice was not far away.

smack!
Jessi Holhart

Smack! At times like this, it's distracting when you slap me like that.

"Don't you dare come!" your voice is fluid, smooth. It feels like acid, a subtle warning I might be smart enough to hear. "Don't you fucking dare." I don't.

But your weight, pressing hard across my hips is not helping. The wet, hot squeeze of your cunt tugging on the strap between my ass cheeks, your seductive hip rolls, these things make it nearly irresistible. I groan beneath you, rolling eyes up into my head. The groan buzzes, a dim echo of the vibrations of the egg carefully lodged between my labia, just short of the place where it would so easily slide in. I suppose you feel me flinch within you, mediated by my remarkably firm, large, and gently curved dick.

"Don't." Your voice is sharp; your eyes hot as you turn my face back to look into yours. And then, your hand hits hard across my cheek. I suck my teeth and release my breath in a small sound, half grunt, half sigh. You are swollen at the base of my cock. Your lips wet my hair around its wide base. "Don't you come," My head swims, my breathing becoming shorter, faster. You slap me again.

I'm feeling like it should be helping, but it's not. I growl, fearing and knowing what's coming. Then it does. You strike repeatedly, quickly until my growl becomes a whimper. I sob, once. I do not come.

You are glory above me. A tear runs silently into my ear. I deeply inhale your scents. You moan, and your smile shines down on me. Your breath quickens. You sigh. I writhe under you. You pound me with your sex. I thrust up, a mountain beneath you, bucking with subterranean passions, a volcano, just barely still dormant. You ride me like a...

Smack! The thought is gone. I am stiff within, beneath you, a pillar of strength and lust. I am the eternal phallus, solid as stone. My thrusts are sharp, intense, focused, and quick. You are rising to your peak. I ride along.

"Don't you fucking come!" you warn. I wasn't even thinking of that, but I moan at the thought. Your slap, solid and hard, steels me, positively galvanizes me. I breathe. I am furious, hungry with intent. You are pulsing life around me. You are moaning and rocking, water swirling around me, invulnerable to my violent motions. You slap me again, a tide rocking my shoreline of stone. It vibrates my whole self, rocking me into an unexpected and resounding crash.

"Don't!" But it's too late. You slap again. "Don't you fuck..." you shudder around me, I thrust and come, hard.

You scream. You flex and writhe. You pound my chest, and are still wringing me in your powerful clenches. At last, still shaking, gasping at intervals, your fingers begin to dig into my nipples with each spasm. I flex. I moan, soft and low, catching my breath. But the pain remains, is revisited. My face is hot. My nipples beneath your nails are completely victim to you. The spasms have stopped. I turn off the egg, dropping the controls to the mattress beside us. Now you are just digging into my breasts. It makes it hard to catch my breath.

"Please..." I say, licking my lips, as I try to twist from under your grasp.

"You did, didn't you?" Your voice and nails cut my chest and heart as one. My nod is barely perceptible.

"Yes. Please...."

"Please what, then? Please let you come?" It cuts, and guilty, I won't try to evade the pain.

"Please forgive me." I gulp, waiting.

"Try again." You demand scornfully, beginning to sit up.

I'm thinking, *OK, not the right request.*

"Please..." Your hand comes down hard and fast, even as you sit up. *Smack!*

"Shut up," your eyes are smoke and fire. "And try again." And your hips tilt and grind into the place where I am weakest, where I have surrendered. The buzz in my crotch resumes as you turn the egg's switch. It is almost a laugh, my breath and the closed-mouthed shout. I look sheepish, finally understanding, I am sure.

"Do you need another?" It is the sweetest thing you've said to me all day. Your hand cupped against my cheek is burning.

"Yes, please." I say through clenched teeth. And you give it to me. I grunt. My nostrils flare. There are volcanic sensations. You feel the earth move beneath you, and smile wickedly.

"And don't you dare come."

sunday afternoon

Shanna Germain

"Pancakes?" I ask. That's the only thing she makes when it's her turn for Sunday brunch, so I think I already know the answer.

"No pancakes today," she says, surprising me. She turns away from the counter and holds out a beater layered with batter. "Want a lick of my muffin...mix?" she asks, raising one eyebrow and shifting her hip so that her bathrobe falls partway open to reveal a slit of her pale, naked skin.

I grin at this bold move from my normally demure girlfriend.

"Yes, please," I say. I stick my tongue out and run it along the edge of the metal beater, catching the dripping sweetness before it can hit the floor. "Mmm...blueberry."

She smiles slyly, grabs the bowl off the counter, and sinks one finger into the batter up to her knuckle. Then she pulls it out and sucks off the batter, leaning back into the counter, letting her robe fall open all the way. I can't decide where to put my eyes: on her lips, as she deep-throats her finger as though she's lubing up one of our toys, or on her dark kinky hair that I know is getting wet while she watches me watch her. She's putting on a show for me, and it's all I can do to stand here and watch when what I really want to do is put my hands all over her.

Finally, she sinks two fingers into the batter and holds them out to me. I lean forward and cover her fingers with my mouth, slowly licking away every last taste of batter until I can feel her smooth skin beneath my tongue. She roughly pulls out her fingers and turns toward the counter. "Close your eyes," she says, and I do. I hear her mixing the batter and other sounds that I can't make out. Whatever she's doing seems to be working; I'm getting wetter by the second. My nipples ache beneath my robe. I don't know how long it's been since she's been this aggressive, but as I'm standing in the kitchen, clenching my thighs together around the ache, I realize it's been too long.

"Suck," she says softly, and I think she means her fingers again, but I open my eyes to see that she has strapped herself into a dildo.

The lower third of the toy is covered with a thick layer of batter. I drop to my knees and take everything into my mouth: the batter, the toy, the scent of her. At first I'm afraid I'll gag—it's too thick, too much—but then she moans above me and pushes her hips against my mouth, and I realize I don't care. I would do anything to hear that soft, aching I-need-you sound from her lips.

I cup her ass with my hands, drive her deeper into my mouth. I suck until she's bucking against me, her fingers digging into the counter, her bathrobe falling halfway down her shoulders. I can tell she's far into it because there's a window right behind her, and she hasn't stopped to pull the shade or move into the bedroom. I sneak one finger between her ass cheeks and run it from front to back, slowly pressing into the crevice, loving the way it makes her gasp.

Before she comes, she stops me, pulls out and slowly lets out her breath. "Whew," she says, unsnapping the harness while I wait on my knees in front of her. Then she brings the bowl down to the kitchen floor and tells me to lie down. She opens my robe and sits on top of me. She scoops out a handful of batter and spreads it across my skin like icing. At first, it just feels slimy and cold, but then she's running her tongue everywhere, lapping the batter up with slurps and *mmm*s that make little apron-strings of pleasure run down my insides. With one hand, she starts drawing circles on my clit, lighting against it like a moth then flitting away. I grab her nipples, using the batter as lubricant, tweaking them softly in the way that she likes. She moans and rubs her clit against mine. I start bucking on the floor. *Please, please stick your finger in me, your hand, the dildo, something, anything...*

She laughs, tells me to shut my eyes again. I do, although I can't keep my hips still as she slides off me. They rise off the floor, impatient to be filled. Suddenly, she's back and I can feel her pressing something against my clit, nosing it between my lips. I lean up on my elbows and open my eyes to see her easing me open with the end of our marble rolling pin, pressing the heavy knob into me, opening me up until all I can feel is pleasure and pain mixed into one.

"Suck," she says again, leaning over me as I start sucking the batter off her thick nipple, rolling it between my teeth. With one hand she's driving the rolling pin deeper and deeper into me, with the other, she's rubbing her fingers sideways across my clit. *Fuck me, fuck me,* I'm chanting, but she already is, and I'm opening so that she can slide the rolling pin all the way inside me, deep inside me, until I'm fucking the rolling pin and don't care that it's huge, that it feels like my insides are burning...the pressure builds until I feel like I'm going to explode, and then I'm fizzing all over, bubbling up and over, layers of syrup spreading through my body.

After a moment, she pulls the rolling pin out slowly, her sweet tongue deep in my mouth. She lays down on top of me, still sticky and wet, and I wrap my arms around her. "That was hot," she says with a sigh.

"Hot enough to have baked your muffins," I say with a grin.

"Yeah," she says. "If I'd actually planned on baking them."

silent love

Andrea Herrmann

I patiently wait for you in my apartment, already showered and shaved in all the right places, freshly clean for tonight. My pussy is already dripping in anticipation of your arrival. I haven't seen you in weeks, months really, and you're finally admitting to yourself that you miss me. I know you won't ever say it to me in person, but you're longing for tonight just as much as I am.

I hear my cell phone ring. You're calling to let me know what I can already sense—you've just pulled into a parking spot and you need me to come down and let you in. I leave my door unlocked and make my way down the stairs to the side door, looking out at the parked cars identified by the streetlights. I see a set of car lights go out and your car door swing open. You pull your backpack out of the passenger's seat, checking quickly to make sure you've got the needed supplies for our encounter. I wonder if you are as excited as I am.

I meet you at the door as you walk over from your car. Neither one of us says anything, but I catch a faint smile on your face. I turn my back as you follow me up the stairs to my apartment. We go in and head directly to my bedroom, and your bag hits the ground as I close the door. The lights are out; I light a match to a candle.

You're already on my bed, face down against the pillows, relaxing and stretching. You've had a bad week at work. You're exhausted and longing to be with me, although I know you can never say it. You don't turn over as I approach. You still lay on your stomach as I start to play with your hair, gently stroking my fingers around the back of your head, trailing to your neck and shoulders so I can pull your hair away to start kissing your neck. I slide my body next to yours, moving closer so I can slide my arm around you to begin rubbing your back while I kiss and lick around your shoulders and your neck. I like to tease you, caressing your skin with my lips and tongue. My hands circle firmly on your shoulders, and slowly make their way down your spine to your hips. I know I'll have that shirt off soon.

You finally turn to me and smile. I know you can't say that you want what we're about to do, but the look in your eyes tells me I can proceed. You turn to face me and I gain access to your chest. I run my hand back and forth from your stomach down to your thighs, stopping in certain areas to provide extra touches, giving myself the chance to tease you.

I stop. As bad as I want this, I want to make sure we're both relaxed enough to enjoy this. I don't want you getting nervous on me. I want you to explore and enjoy tonight, and I don't want you backing down or being nervous about being with me. I remind you that there's beer in the fridge and offer you a drink. You insist I have one as well. I go to the kitchen to get you a can and a glass and pour myself a glass of wine. I can tell you're still a little nervous.

Our last encounter flashed in my mind—how you stopped me because you got too "sensitive." I know you're questioning yourself and that you really want to try this, but you're afraid. You've been anxious and uneasy about every aspect of coming out, from being together in public to showing me your body in private. I have no plans to back off tonight. I want to show you everything you've been missing, and all the passions and pleasure of being with another woman.

We sit next to each other on the bed, you nursing your beer as I down my wine. I look at your face, scanning for the indication that you're ready for me, and lean to the edge of the bed to take off your shoes and then my own. You put your glass down as I lean over to kiss you again. Your tongue circles mine as our hands dance across our bodies. My desires are building up again; I can feel myself getting more turned on. We're side by side, still kissing, still touching, as my hand makes its way under your shirt. I trace the arch of your back and move to the side of your chest. I rotate my fingertips around your breasts, feeling that your nipples are hard. My breath flusters as you release a soft moan.

I pull off your shirt. My fingernails rake across your back and then slide up to the base of your neck, scratching your scalp as you roll your head back to follow my movements. My left hand drops to unhook your bra and throw it on the floor. I move to sit behind you and pull you back on me so that your head rests on my clavicle. I resume kissing you on the back of your neck where your hair starts down to your shoulders while my hands continue exploring your body. I pull up the comforter so both of our bodies are covered, and then take off my shirt, hoping you'll feel less vulnerable. You pull me close, holding me and resting your head on me. I tell you that this is already more than I had expected to happen, and that I would like to go on...to finally show you how incredible it feels to come from my touch.

I turn my attention to your jeans and unbutton them, slowly sliding them off. You help me navigate them down your thighs as they fall to the floor. I take off your socks; I'm leaving your underwear on for now. I follow by removing my pants. Once again you pull me close to you, which I appreciate. I also want to enjoy feeling our bodies pressed against each other.

We kiss again, wrapped in each other's skin, and sense each other's wetness. My hand makes its way to your legs again, dancing up and down your smoothness. I sneak my touch to your underwear, feeling the dampness gathering between your legs. My fingertips trace the edges of your underwear, from the inside of your thighs across your belly and back down to the center of your crotch. My hand cups to meet the arch of your pelvis and begins to circle around the center of your crotch, ever so slowly increasing in pressure and tempo. You sigh and push your crotch into my hand as if by instinct.

I can't hold back anymore. I need to feel you. I lift the corner of your underwear and slide my hand in, first to tickle the sides of the lips and then to slowly measure the length of your pussy. I feel you pull away from me. You don't say a word or look at my face—you just pull off your underwear and throw them on the floor, closing your eyes as you lay back down.

I climb over to your legs and spread them apart, pulling the comforter over my head to cover our bodies. I kneel between your thighs, balancing myself over you, pausing briefly to allow myself the chance to see your nakedness. I begin to feel you again, stroking your skin, keeping my hands just out of range of your wetness. I can feel your thighs tensing up, preparing for the sensations you'll feel. I move up, placing my elbows on each side of you, supporting myself so I can focus on your chest. I slide my head up to lick gently around your left breast. My tongue circles around your nipple, pressing against it. I plunge my mouth around it, sucking it into my mouth while flicking the tip of my tongue across it. Your body shivers, shocked by my sudden movement. My right hand moves to massage your right breast and nipple. I can feel your hips rotating slowly below me. I see your lungs rise and fall. I can hear your breath hastening. Your mouth quivers and your skin blushes, both reacting to pleasures never known before.

I give the same attention to your right breast with my mouth and tongue as my left hand moves back down to your pussy. You're wetter than before, and I can smell your wonderfully sweet scent as I slide my head down your stomach, kissing you along the way. I kiss gently, sucking and nibbling down to your hips, your legs, your knees, down and back up to your stomach, getting ready to lick your juices.

I glide my tongue from your hip down to your pussy and pause to feel the warmth coming from you. My breath tickles your skin. My tongue parts your lips and begins to trail up and down your slit, enjoying your taste and your feel. I stroke your clit gently with my tongue, adding more pressure and speed with each lick, as my finger makes its way to your hole. I explore the walls of your pussy, feeling your muscles react to my touch. I slide another finger in and begin pumping you. Your wetness covers my hand as your come glistens on my finger in the candlelight. I start moving, licking, fucking you harder, increasing my pace.

You try to touch in between my legs; I push your hand away. You ask why. I remind you that tonight's for you. You try to touch me again. I quickly turn you over, grab a bandanna from the floor and tie your hands together. I pull your body to me, resting your waist over my legs. My hand strikes your ass. My palm cracks on your left cheek. You're silent from both surprise and enjoyment. I spank you again, this time on the right cheek, telling you that I'm not going to stop until you come all over my face. I spank you again, cupping each cheek after I strike.

I keep you on your stomach but pull out to lie on top of you; your rear is still red from my punishment. I position myself on top of you, grinding my hips into your ass while holding your hands above your head. I know how much you enjoy this. My head leans up to your neck. I whisper that I'm going to fuck you deeper and harder until you come for me. You enjoy each movement of my hips just as much as I do. I can't take it anymore; I need to taste you again. I turn you back over and straddle your waist so that I can lick and finger you again.

Without warning, my two fingers thrust into you and my tongue resumes massaging your clit. You gasp at the quickness of my movements, and I increase the deepness of my thrusts until my fingertips smack against the back of your pussy. You're getting tighter with each thrust, and I can feel your wetness all over my face. Your body is arching toward me, driving my fingers deeper inside of you. I can feel you start to shake; I see you tense up. I yell at you to relax and just let it happen. I turn my fingertips up so that they glide against the top wall of your vagina as my hand plunges in and out.

You lean you head back and open your mouth to release a deep moan as the waves of pleasure begin. I keep up my pace, urging you on to come for me. Your hips rise and crash as your body starts to shake. I feel your pussy swallowing in my fingers as your body moves through the orgasm. You throb and tremble; you are so tight that I can barely move. I continue as long as I think you can until take it you start begging me to stop, pushing your tied hands against me. I collapse on the bed next to you, untie your hands and pull you close to me. I wrap my arms around you, feeling your lungs quickly rise and fall as you compensate for the rush of energy. I sit silently by you, allowing you to contemplate and react to your first orgasm with another woman. I'll give you as much time as you need to recover. I smile to myself, knowing you're satisfied.

silicone pony

Dawn Sitler

For the first time, I felt bad, dangerous, and dirty. I had never felt something so exhilarating and naughty before.

I think I had only been sleeping for 20 minutes. The sheets were still soaked with sweat when I got up to make my way down the hall. My pussy felt as if it had been through a full wash cycle from fill, to agitation, to spin. I was sure there would be bruises the next day, but I didn't care.

I had never been fucked by a strap-on before and I had no idea it could feel this good. A dick wasn't completely foreign to me. I had sexual experiences with men but hadn't found them tremendously enjoyable or satisfying. So I'd figured there was no way a lump of formed silicone could feel better than any live member I'd had before.

But from the moment we were grinding our bodies together on the dance floor, I wanted more. I felt the lump in her pants and I wanted her to steal me away to a secluded spot and have her way with me. Her apartment complex was just a short walk across the parking lot from the bar. Finally alone, we shared our first kiss and groped each other while climbing the two flights of stairs to her door.

We were inside after a hurried fumbling for keys and my breasts by her hands followed by a quick turn of the lock. She was already pulling my sweater over my head before I could close the door. She threw me against the wall, and I could feel the desire in her jeans. The panties I should have been wearing would be soaked by now. We'd been dancing around the issue for hours now, and I couldn't wait to feel her inside of me.

She unbuttoned my tight pants and smiled a wicked grin when she reached inside and felt smooth skin all the way down to my lips. Kneeling before me, she licked the seam of my pants all the way up my inner thigh. Light kisses and tongue flicks peppered my lower abdomen. Her teeth tugged at my belly piercing and her tongue probed my navel. Her mouth was so wet and warm. Her

27

fingers massaged my pussy through my pants and my frustration built with every passing minute.

I pulled her up and took her fingers in my mouth, teasing them with my tongue. Then I drew a wet line from my chin to the front closure of my bra and begged with my eyes for her to release me from the restraining fabric. She popped it open and my breasts came springing toward her. She took one in her mouth and she licked my nipple hard and erect with frantic strokes. She was doing the same with her fingers on my other nipple. I think it was about 104 degrees in the room. I thought I was going to spontaneously combust if we didn't get to the main event pretty soon.

I dropped my bra and pushed her away to free myself from the wall. She pulled me to her with the force of a magnet. My bare breasts rubbed against her T-shirt, further fueling the already burning desire in her chest. Her nipples were becoming swollen, begging to be taken in my mouth. I clawed her back, bit at her neck and caught my breath to deliriously whisper, "Fuck me in your bed." She ran her hands down my back, over my ass, and reached for the back of my thighs. With one move, she lifted me up, and I squeezed my legs around her waist. Her dick strained against her pants. My wet cunt was tight against my pants. She carried me precariously back to her bedroom. Our tongues surged into each other's mouths. She threw me on the bed, and I let out an unexpected squeal. Before I could recover, she pulled off my pants. They lay in an inside-out heap on the floor. She climbed on top of me and extricated herself from her beer-and-sweat-soaked shirt. I rolled over and took command on top. I wanted that dick of hers and I was going to make it mine.

I opened her jeans and released her swollen prick. She grabbed at the drawer of the bedside table to wrangle her condom stash. I grappled for it and ripped it open with my teeth. I rolled the sheath down the length and eased myself into a perfect perch over the tip. I rubbed myself, wet and hungry, over the knob. I couldn't prolong it any longer. Finally, I devoured the member deeply into my pussy. I took it all. The shock of the size sent a delicious pain surging through my stomach. She played with my clit while I rode the shaft and it wasn't long before I gushed sweet come onto her body.

We changed positions, and she moved between my legs to lap

up the sweet nectar, the fruit of our labor. Slow, steady licks with her flat tongue from deep in my sex sent quivers through my body. I held her head tightly, not wanting the pleasure to stop. Her tongue worked me over better than an ice cream cone. I rolled from orgasm to orgasm, surfing the waves of pleasure.

I kneaded her breasts while my tongue flickered at her nipples. I was completely intrigued by her nipple ring, and I tried to imagine the delicious pleasure that she felt when I tugged at it with my tongue. I played with it for a long time while she lay before me moaning and encouraging me. Her dick was still there, ready and able to please me. The best thing about a dildo is that it's ready whenever and however often I am. I mounted my partner and rode her once more. This time slower and more carefully. I let my wetness lead the way up and down the silky shaft. I was in control. I maintained the speed, slow at first, then faster and faster until I reached a last, volcanic climax. Once more, she lapped up my sweet vaginal honey knowing I was spent and overwhelmingly appreciative. We would have to meet again for me to repay her the favor.

Her face was wet with my essence when I pulled her to me and kissed the woman who made me feel so intoxicated and satiated. My sexuality was animalistic. She spooned my dizzy body and, expended, we fell asleep.

eating out

C. L. Brown

I flick a crumpled 10 on the table and weave through the tiny restaurant, trying to escape her contemptuous glances. Only ice cream can soothe my torment, so I practically stumble out of the restaurant, looking up the avenue for the glowing pink sign of Baskin-Robbins.

I'm hell-bent on vanilla. That is, until I'm faced with the countless other flavors I hadn't considered. I contemplate the curative qualities of rocky road and spumoni swirl, and if I'd seen her coming I could've armed myself with some semblance of disinterest. But she was already on me, her breast pressed against my arm.

"Follow me," she whispers, her breath brushing my neck. She doesn't wait for acknowledgment. She leaves and never looks back, confident that I don't need coaxing.

Just let her walk away, damn it. I can't help but sigh at the way she swaggers in her tailored suit and heels. Nor can I pretend that the invisible leash she has clamped on me doesn't exist. *Tramp.*

I had watched her back in the restaurant, and she had known it. The way she'd twirled each clit-like mussel on the tip of her tiny fork and pouted her lips around the meaty morsels said so. I had just wanted her to take one last sip, and she deliberately tortured me as I lingered over my own dinner across the room. I'd caught myself leaning forward in anticipation as she swirled her wine around the long-stemmed glass and lifted it almost to her lips. I held my breath. She inhaled the bouquet. Then pretending to be consumed by some errant thought, she put the glass back down. *Fuckin' tease.*

I had dared to steal a final glance at her as I left my balled-up cash and a plate of half-eaten pasta, and that's when I caught it, well, more like that's when she gave it to me. She closed her eyes and pressed her lips to the rim of the glass. Her sip was long and poised...her swallow long and deliberate. The idea of the thick liquid seeping down her throat stung me between my legs, and I ogled her like some shameless, captivated voyeur. That's when she stabbed me with her knowing look. Her eyes were twinkling daggers, and one side of her mouth curled up in a sexy smirk causing me to scurry away in search of my soothing dessert.

I can't help it. Her conceited indifference makes her more irresistible than it does cruel, and that's why I follow her.

She's walking fast and far enough ahead of me to lose me if she really wanted. Suddenly, still without so much of a glance back for me, she dips between two buildings. By the time I catch up, the narrow walkway is empty. It's an inviting play of burnished light and shadows cast by old-fashioned lanterns along the wall. I follow the walkway to the end where it bends into a hidden landscaped alcove the size of a table for two.

She's waiting for me. Her blouse is already unbuttoned and pulled from her slacks. There's an old stone seat tucked into a bed of sleepy lilies and sweet honeysuckle, and she's standing on the ledge, her hands on her hips.

My breath is short and fills, which suddenly seems oddly quiet except for the distant hush of traffic. She leans down and kisses me on the lips. Hers are warm and tinged with spiced merlot.

I accept her silent invitation and snake my arms around her thighs. I look up at her, and our eyes lock in an exchange of a million wordless thoughts. I tremble inside, but I don't drop my gaze this time. Hers doesn't waver even as she undoes her zipper in a deft, single-handed motion, while cradling my head with one hand and unleashing her pearled cock with the other.

She strips me into full submission in a one delightful instant, and I'm slain by my need to feast. I push the tip of her member against my lips and push the molded head inside. I'm accustomed to its metallic taste and roll my fattened lips roll over the rim. I see that she's not watching, even though I know she likes it. Her head is rested back, lengthening her neck and emphasizing her svelte, amber stomach that undulates above me like a desert, her lacy breasts rising full on a far horizon.

I work my lover with rhythmic thrusts. Her syncopated moans confirm that every lunge is a divine assault on her true flesh hidden underneath.

"Take it all," she insists, casting her eyes down on me like a gift.

I don't consider us quite even yet. She needs payback for tormenting me over dinner, and I know just what she deserves. So, without hesitating, I relax my throat, grab her ass and pull her full length into me, making her spurt meaningless obscenities.

No matter how many times I do "that thing," as she calls it, she groans and her eyes roll in a sort of perplexed worship. This time they flutter and twirl up into her head.

My insides are heavy and threaten to fall out. I can smell her pussy. I can hear it too. The lake of wetness that's pooled in her cunt speaks to me with every push. Its *schlicky* sound begs me to suck harder, to swallow deeper, to feed faster.

"Lick it?" Her commands are now whimpering pleas.

I pull off of her, long and slow, then lap my tongue around the buoyant, shimmery length. I flick its tip like a serpent then trace the two apricot-sized balls underneath. I give each one a tender kiss before grazing the edge of her pussy and tickling its downy hair with my breath.

She sighs with tears, and I steady her as she starts to sway.

We hear the approaching laughter at the same time and freeze, my face poised at her dick-cunt. Ice-water panic runs through my chest as shadows approach down the seemingly dead-end path toward our secret spot.

"Shh." My lover protectively pulls my head against her womb, but doesn't bother to cover herself. She squares her shoulders, juts her chin, and waits, unfazed that her slacks are piled around her ankles.

"Hey!" she barks before the shadows reach us.

There's a hiss of drunken whispers, then a giggling, clamorous retreat.

"Oh...sorry, dude," a jovial voice calls out, friendly enough.

My lover keeps me pulled to her warm belly while she listens to the merry troupe fade back up the walkway and disappear.

"Guess you better fuck me now," she says as if it's the resulting thought of some deductive reasoning, like almost being caught was the mandatory prerequisite for me doing so. Her eyes are on fire, and I know she wants to come now.

Panic and arousal still burn all over me, but I'm obedient. I moisten my middle finger in my mouth, spread her ass, and then ease my finger into her puckered hole.

"Oh, fuck," she spurts through clenched teeth. Her legs start to tremble again, and she guides me back to her dick.

Down the shaft, swirl the tip, up the shaft, off. Down the shaft, swirl the tip, up the shaft, off.

She sets the cadence palming my head, and I know that, if repeated without fail, she'll certainly come for me. *Down the shaft, swirl the tip, up the shaft, off.*

I feel the rising inside of her. My own heavy, blood-filled pussy itches with pain. Her throaty moans, the wet musk emanating from her pussy, and the cinching heat of her asshole around my finger is my entire being.

When I feel the gradual tightening of her body, I know she's almost there. So with a final swirl around her shaft, I push the fruitless organ aside and expose her clit, which is already swollen out of its tiny hood, glistening like a glazed cranberry.

I hover my tongue close to her open pussy. I warm it and cool it with quiet breaths, and the smell of her insides makes me want to crawl in and drown.

"Wanna taste?"

"Uh-huh," I manage quickly with my tongue still poised over her nodule.

"Can you smell me?"

The sound of her nasty words pierces all my senses. I inhale and grunt another affirmative, which sends her whole body into a still, tight quaver. Her ass seizes around my finger, then gradually relaxes until it's loose enough for me to fuck her with it, but still tight enough to heat her delicate opening.

I fight to keep my tongue off her pussy, even as I choke on my compulsion to lick the silky slit. It's close enough to taste, a tongue's length away, but I'm content to tend to her giving asshole instead. This task makes me barely aware of my own feral sounds that coincide with each plunge. I fuck her slowly until she grows distant and still. But she comes back to me after an instant, announcing her return with syncopated wails to the ink blue sky.

She steadies herself with her hands on her waist and she thrusts her hips forward. Swollen to its fullness, her clit, without provocation, lets delicate droplets of liquid on my waiting tongue. I don't dare swallow; I can't chance missing a drop as she jerks her hips, pushing out her last bit of orgasm.

That's it. That a girl, I think while finally swallowing her warm offering. She coos, letting me lap the folds of her pussy for anything left there.

She's mine and she knows it.

Filled with my own power, I plant my mouth over her cooled, flaccid clit and draw a final relenting wail from her deepest part.

I lick my lips and look up at her.

She merely frowns, comes down from the ledge, and kisses me again. I resist sucking the trace of wine still on her tongue. Instead, I pull back and turn away from her with no intention of looking back. I don't need to. I know what arrogant contentment looks like on her. It's evil and it's pretty.

I ease into the shadows wishing for something to say. Shit, she wouldn't talk to me anyway. I keep on going.

I make my way down the avenue and let the knot in my gut melt into my panties. It's easy to do while I replay the sounds of her pleasure in my head. My own release pools between my thighs, and I know what I need.

"Back?" the boy at the counter smirks. I peruse all 31 flavors.

"Um, vanilla...a scoop on a sugar cone, please."

I eye him closely as he scoops the perfect yellow ball of cream, but I see her pass by. My pussy pulses with promise, and I resist following her. *Just let her walk away.*

The boy offers me the paper-wrapped cone topped with cream. I hesitate and raise an eyebrow. He mimics me knowingly.

"How 'bout a scoop of spumoni swirl right on top. Just a teeny one," he suggests so I don't have to.

I beam at him. "With a cherry on top. Yeah...a cherry'll do it."

fast girls

Rachel Kramer Bussel

The club is moderately crowded, appropriately befitting an average Monday night, open bar notwithstanding. Tonight, for once in a long while, I'm not interested in the free booze; I am plenty distracted by the form of a lithe, little girl in front of me, who at 26 gets mistaken for 12 and is often told she looks like one of the Olsen twins. She does sometimes, but she's a chameleon, channeling a new celebrity at every turn—one minute she's Britney Spears, the next she's Elizabeth Wurtzel, and I'm not the only one who notices. Not a day goes by that someone doesn't stop and think they recognize her.

She looks so sweet and innocent, and she knows it, using her simple charms for devious means. Maybe that's why I didn't know she was hitting on me the other day, even though she'd dropped numerous hints. I like that she was bold enough to just ask if she could kiss me when I didn't pick up on her hints; it's a rare girl who'll go that far out on a limb.

But that was weeks ago, before we'd become totally comfortable pawing each other all over town. Tonight we ignore my friend who's in from out of town in favor of our own corner of the couch. Well, maybe not entirely oblivious. Before my eyes close as I go to kiss her, I see that the suited guy next to me is smoothly checking us out. I'm sure there are others around, but I lean over and pull her small body against mine anyway. She is such a wonderful combination of delicate and sinful, innocent and devious. She straddles me unexpectedly, her legs opening over me, that mischievous smile on her face. I'm sure that people are watching us now—I would too if I saw us across the room.

My skirt is a respectable length, slightly above my knee, my legs covered in thick grey tights. There's nothing improper about it, except when I'm trying to make out with a girl on my lap and stay relatively under the radar. She has no such concerns; she writhes nimbly all around me in her formfitting red jeans and a light T-shirt. It's like a lap dance, but much more personal.

I don't know yet that she will become my girlfriend, that I will fall for her so entirely that I stop having eyes for anyone else, but there is still something, even now, so early, that captivates me. And it's not just the way she squirms all over me. It's in her face, the intense look as she peers at me, trying to decipher my essence as her eyes mull me over, her smile sweet and mischievous, curious and playful. In many ways she is like a girl—she looks the part, and has an optimism that most adults I know have lost over the years. As I sit on the couch, she straddles me with that daring smile on her face, leaning back over the edge of the couch to show off her flexibility. I smile too, utterly charmed by this nymph who, despite all appearances, is even bolder and more shameless than I am.

I pull her toward me, arraying her long blond hair all around us in the hope that it will make us somewhat invisible. I'm sensing that there is only so much further we can go inside this club, but I don't want to leave, knowing that the magic will end if we break the spell too early. She pushes closer to me, and I can feel her heat through her clothes. I grab her ass and fondle it as she leans in close to me. Her breath is hot on my ear, and I can hear tiny moans escaping from her as I squeeze her ass cheeks, occasionally venturing lower, seeing how far I can reach, how much I can get away with. Each moan sends shivers up and down my body, knowing that I can do this to her.

We're out in public, as open and viewable as possible and yet this feels as intimate as anything we've ever done. We don't have to care about the prying eyes because we're now in our own world, communicating on a level so intrinsic and primal that we could almost be naked right now and not even care. She presses in closer to me, and I take a breath of frustration at what we can't do. She bends all the way back again, her hair falling to the floor, her yoga skills coming to life as she contorts on top of me. For one of the first times in my life, I wish I had a cock to press up against her, a concrete way to show my arousal, to taunt her with as it hit her right along her cunt. I'll have to make do with other means.

I pull her face toward mine and we kiss, hot and wet and needy, her tongue diving forward to reach as much of me as she can. I bounce her on my lap and pull her even closer to me. Again, I feel like some macho guy, despite the skirt, hair, and makeup, with my girl on my lap to do with as I please. I don't know that this will be the first of many nights we're told that we're causing too much of a stir, making guys' cocks hard—guys who have no clue what we do in private but like to watch the swirl of hair and lips and skin.

I don't know what will happen beyond tonight, when she gets home to her girlfriend, what future we might or might not have together, and I don't care. Nothing else is as important as the way that she looks both sweet and slutty sitting on top of me. It's tricky, challenging, and a turn-on to figure out how much I can touch her here, out in the open, how many times my hand can skim over her shirt, slyly brush her nipples, how I can grab the back of her neck and squeeze it, scraping my nails lightly along that delicate skin, her head tilting back at the contact. We keep bringing ourselves right to the edge where it almost doesn't feel worth it to stay, where we need to rip each other's clothes off as soon as possible, and then return, still on edge but manageable.

Here, in a too-cool bar where everyone is trying to out-hip everyone else, in a straight enclave in the gayest section of the city, we are too fast for the likes of those around us. We're too much— too much girl, too much passion, too unrestrained—even though we're quiet, even though we're minding our own business. Maybe they sense that underneath our long hair and public kisses, our roaming hands and blushing faces, is something more powerful than that, something that won't let us break away and sit and be quiet like everyone else. We don't care who sees us because we're not here for them, or maybe we are, partly. With her, I don't have to analyze each and every movement, calculate who is watching and who isn't, I just simply close my eyes and take her in as the DJ swirls Madonna all around us.

I look at her and feel so many things all at once—excitement, lust, power, hope, maybe a little bit of fear. She's unlike any other girl I've ever met, a beautiful and maybe dangerous mixture of sweetness and daring, pushing every envelope she can find. I know I like to think I'm bold, like to think I will do anything, anytime, anywhere, but this girl really will. And she wants me. She ducks her head down to my neck, then lower, peeling the already low ruffle of my velvet shirt down just a little bit more to reveal the bursting pink of my nipple. For all my wildness, I've never done anything like this before. Her hair mostly hides her face as her lips find my nipple and she licks and sucks it, with light and gentle teasing.

Maybe it's because I don't have a good poker face and can't look nonchalant while this totally fast girl works her magic on me. Maybe we've just caused too much of a stir, finally worn out our lukewarm welcome. Whatever it is, I hear a knock on the wall and am too embarrassed to look up. "That's inappropriate behavior, girls, and you're going to have to stop," says a deep male voice. I mumble something vaguely apologetic, stand up, and quickly grab my bags.

She is calm and cool and keeps talking, hugging me, not at all bothered that we're too fast for this place, too out of control. We walk out into the night and laugh, lingering, her hand on my cheek and a look on her face I don't know how to interpret. It takes us a while to say goodbye, even though the air is chilly and it's getting late. I'm not sad to go, just wistful as she smiles that mischievous smile that promises me even more trouble the next time she sees me. She bundles her long coat around her and skips off into the night. *My fast girl*, I think as I walk to my train, a smile lingering all the way home.

for the love of the fuzzy cup

Nicole Foster

"I don't think I can reach this tiny spot," I said to P.J., in a campy but sultry whisper. She'd given me a big bowl of melted chocolate along with a clean paintbrush to access all the difficult-to-reach places—one of which happened to be in my vulva.

"Well, I guess I'll just have to do it myself," she said flatly. I could tell by the empty Heinekens on the end table that she'd had a few beers before I'd come over. Which was fine by me. This was the loosest I'd ever seen Ms. I'm-Too-Scared-to-Look-Sexy-Femme.

P.J. got down on her knees next to me on the floor. She dipped a long index finger into the chocolate mixture, then whispered, hot and heavy, into my ear, "Open up, Christmas Cassie."

And open up I did. But then P.J. did something surprising. Instead of applying the chocolate to my swollen lips, she insert-ed her finger into her luscious mouth and sucked the stuff right off. "Mmm," she said. "Now, I wonder what's sweeter? You or the candy?"

When my eyes grew big as chocolate coins, P.J. knew what to do. She went down on me faster than you can ring a dinner bell. In fact, she ate me out like I was her last meal ever. In between the chocolate and my flowing juices, my hot pussy was sopping wet. She focused her attention on my hard bud, taking it into her mouth and licking under the hood. "Oh, girl, you are sweet," my hot butch cried out.

She continued to slurp under the hood and around my clit, then flicked it back and forth with her tongue. I ran my fingers through her silky dark curls as she sucked and licked my entire vulva, her saliva mixing with my juices and the melted chocolate.

"I think there's probably a little more sugar deep inside," P.J. cooed, and boy, was I raring to go after that. She slid two fingers into my hungry hole—though, truth be told, I could have taken her entire fist. (Another night, another calendar...)

"Fuck me hard," I whispered in her ear. She was riding my body as she penetrated me, her stonewashed jeans and black Tee sticking to the chocolate covering me from the neck down. My entire snatch was on fire as I gazed into those sexy baby blues. As she fucked me, she covered my mouth in sloppy wet kisses (just the way I like 'em).

"Fucking you hard is easy," she told me. "You're a goddamn goddess, Cass." With her left hand she ran her fingers through my long red curls, pulled my head back a little, and nipped me playfully on the neck.

"If I'm such a goddess, how come you never gave me the time of day before?" I panted while she fucked me like a jackhammer.

P.J. said nothing for a moment, then whispered, without looking me in the eye, "Just shy, I guess..."

I guess I'd hit a soft spot with her, because she pulled away a little then kissed a tender, sweet trail down my body. When she reached my plump tits and licked the chocolate right off my hard nips, I thought I was going to explode.

And man, did I explode! A huge, gooey, chocolaty-delightful orgasm traveled through my entire body—from my red-hot puss to my sticky abdomen to my breasts to my quivering lips. "Genius Chrysler!" I screamed out, my body hot and cold and shivering and burning and just plain ol' freaking out.

Afterward, I lay spent on her hardwood floor, a mess of chocolate and saliva and come covering us both.

"So, you think you'll be ordering in more often now?" I chuckled as P.J. ran a gentle hand over my well-worked snatch.

"Yeah, and with you I'll make sure I always start with dessert," she said, then went in for more.

a stiff neck

Jean Roberta

I didn't really know why I was waiting up for Raf. She was only a friend of a friend, and I was letting her stay with me until she could find her own apartment. Raf's fit, muscular body, dark eyes, smoky voice, and glowing, sand-colored skin had nothing to do with it, of course. I was just a Good Samaritan, even though it didn't surprise me that her girlfriend had thrown her out. Raf seemed like the kind of woman who would drive anyone crazy.

The door opened, and she tiptoed in. "What?" she asked, looking at me. A knowing grin spread over her face. "Aww, babe," she snickered before I could explain myself. In seconds she was standing in front of me, pulling me up and holding me against the firm cushion of her breasts under a silk shirt and a sports bra. "You want me, don't you, Laurel?" she cooed into my ear. Her breath in my face was hot, smelling of beer and fried food.

My knees felt wobbly, and I wanted to cling to her heat and her strength. Instead I tried to free myself. "You've been drinking," I complained.

Raf only held me tighter. One of her hands slid down to grasp one of my ass cheeks, and I couldn't help squirming. "I'm not too drunk to know what I'm doing," she promised me. "Hungry little pussy. I know what you need."

My awakening clit told me to ignore my common sense's urging to push her away. One of her strong hands slid over one of my breasts, found the nipple, and rolled it between two fingers. I gasped, knowing that both my nipples were growing hard enough to show her how much I liked her attention.

She grinned smugly, running one hand through my long brown hair. I had left it loose, flowing over my shoulders, hoping she liked it that way. Obviously she did. "You like bad girls, don't you?" I was aghast. "Come on, honey, admit it. You let me stay here because you think I'm sexy and dangerous." Her voice sounded amused, but I could hear an undercurrent of anger in it.

This time I found the willpower to push her away from me,

turn my back on her, and walk toward the kitchen. I had only taken two or three steps when she grabbed me around the waist, dragged me to the sofa, sat down, and pulled me across her lap, facedown. My jeans felt tight across my butt as my wet crotch pressed against her thighs. I struggled to get up as I felt her thigh muscles tense beneath me. She grabbed one of my arms and forced it behind my back, immobilizing me. The humiliation brought stinging tears into my eyes.

"I should spank you," Raf sneered. The thought of her hard hand landing on my vulnerable butt assaulted my mind, and I wondered if I could bear it in silence. A worse thought followed: What if she pulled down my jeans and panties so I could feel every smack on my bare skin and she could watch the visible results?

"Raf," I muttered, trying to control my voice. "Please don't."

By a miracle, she let go of my arm, shifted her legs, and helped me stand up. "You sure, babe?" she teased. "I think you want it." I prided myself on being an honest and decent citizen of the Amazon Nation, but for once, I couldn't think of anything to say that would be completely true. I knew that my clit was as swollen as a bee sting, and my wet cunt yearned for something to fill it. Even the skin on my butt felt sensitive under my jeans, as though she had really given me a few whacks.

"I took you in," I reminded her. "You're staying in my house."

Raf stood and reached for both my hands. "Come here," she urged. She sat and pulled me onto her lap. "I don't want to hurt you, Laurel," she sighed into my hair. The smell of her breath was strangely comforting. She kissed my neck and gently stroked my breasts with one hand while she slid the other down the back of my jeans.

Her hot fingers slid over my sweaty skin before I reached behind me, grabbed her wrist, and pulled her hand away. "Why are you doing this?" I asked, avoiding her eyes.

Her arms held me close as she pulled my face to hers for a long, hot kiss. Her tongue pushed my teeth apart and entered my mouth. Her strong, tasty tongue flirted with mine. I moaned in spite of myself, and she held me tighter. A musky smell rose from her armpits and from the crack between her legs, where her own pussy was hidden beneath my butt. I breathed in the smell of an aroused she-wolf on the hunt.

Raf slowly pulled away so we could both catch our breath. "Why?" she repeated thoughtfully. "I've noticed you watching me. I know you don't really want to sleep alone in your room while I'm here, babe. You want it and I want to give it to you, you hot thing." Her remark reminded me of the sweat that coated my skin.

Raf squeezed the back of my neck. "You need to open up," she advised me, brushing my hair aside. "Stop being so stiff-necked." I jerked away indignantly, and she snickered. "It's late, honey...or early. You must have missed me while I was out with Andy and Bruce. Were you jealous? They're just friends, and they're not into dykes. They wanted to cheer me up and hear all the gossip first-hand. You know how queens are." Her hand on my neck slid familiarly down my back, tracing the curve of my spine to the waistband of my jeans. I sighed.

"I bet you're wet, Laurel," she teased. "Did you play with yourself while you waited for me? Tell me."

"No," I moaned. "I didn't, um—"

Her hand slid down my ass. She was searching for the truth. "Go on," she warned me. "I could feel the excitement in the laughter that shook her lungs. "Or I'll spank you until you can't sit down." I squirmed on her lap as her middle finger pushed against my anus. Without thinking, I shifted to give her more room.

"Mm," she commented as the tip of her finger pushed into a puckered opening. "Tell me, horny little wench. You can't hide anything now."

I took a deep breath as my sphincter clutched the invading finger. "I didn't know when you'd get home," I blurted before I could lose my concentration. "I didn't want you to catch me."

Raf suddenly pulled her finger out of me and pushed me off her lap. "Caught you anyway, didn't I?" she smirked. "Take your pants off, honey." I obediently unzipped my jeans and pushed them down over my hips, showing her my pale sassy ass cheeks, my virgin butt that was waiting for the first thrilling, merciless slap from her hard hand. I then realized that she wasn't planning to spank me yet, and I was disappointed.

She briskly pulled my jeans and panties down to my ankles, then pulled my shoes off and lifted each of my feet out of their pant-legs. I pulled my T-shirt over my head. While my arms were raised, she unhooked my bra and slid both her hands over my shivering breasts. She pinched my nipples, making me squeal. I pressed my butt into her crotch as she tormented my hard pink buds, pulling and stretching them until I wondered if I would come from that. I could hear my own breathing.

"You bad girl," Raf scolded. "You've got a double standard." I was alarmed. "Drinking alone isn't good for you." I hadn't thought she had smelled the wine on my breath. A feeling of shame surged up from the pit of my stomach.

"Just a glass," I muttered.

"That's how it starts," she warned me, tracing my lips with a salty finger. I sucked it into my mouth, making her laugh. "A little booze helps loosen you up, honey, but I want you to promise not to drink when you're home alone." One of her hands trailed down my midriff, tickled my belly button and continued south. "I'll be your sponsor," she joked. "Call me whenever you want a drink and I'll take your mind off it."

Raf tugged on my short and curly hairs. I was sure her fingers were getting wet, and I sent them a silent message of welcome. "I'm not gonna do this here," she told me calmly. "Will you invite me into your bedroom, hostess lady?"

"Gladly," I answered. "Let's go."

"Go ahead," she ordered. "I'll come in and ravish you when I'm ready." She lowered her head to suck each of my nipples. When she pulled away, they were wet and cool. Raf slapped my butt to send me on my way and give me a hint of things to come.

Walking into my bedroom, I caught sight of my naked reflection in my full-length wall mirror. My shape looked as girlish as usual, but my lips and nipples looked red and swollen like ripe fruit. The black ink of the bracelet tattoo on my right arm contrasted with my moonlight-pale skin. My light-brown bush looked as innocent as a spring plant, but the dim light from the hallway picked up glistening moisture on my curly hair. I felt like a woman about to be offered to a deity in some ancient ritual.

I crawled onto my bed and stretched out on my back. I could almost feel invisible fingers stroking me all over. I wanted to be taken.

Raf appeared in the doorway, naked and holding something that looked like a weapon. She seemed to glow as the light lingered on her smooth curves. She was walking toward me with purposeful steps and a determined look. The nipples on her generous breasts looked like little plums. The hair on her head gleamed raven-black, and a silver ring flashed from her hairless crotch.

"Hi, babe. You ready for me?"

"Oh, yes, Raf," I asserted. I didn't really think I had a stiff neck, and I wanted her to know what a wealth of passion I could offer her.

I could feel her heat as she crawled over me, holding an empty wine bottle above us both. I felt myself blushing. She touched my cheek with its hard belly and laughed when I jerked. The smooth, cold glass against my skin felt startling but refreshing. Raf had taken the bottle from my fridge and poured out the remaining wine.

"Pillows," demanded Raf, my seducer. I had four within reach, including my decorative cushions, and I passed them to her. Raf piled them in the middle of the bed and pushed me onto them, facedown. My stomach pressed gratefully into soft fabric. I loved the suspense of waiting for her to surprise me from behind.

A possessive hand slid down the crack of my ass and spread my thighs farther apart. "If you lived in a dictatorship," mused Raf, "you'd get busted for breaking the law. You'd be handed over to women guards who would keep you handcuffed while they got drunk. Then they'd fuck you with the bottle." Two of her strong fingers slipped easily into my wet cunt as I groaned. "You couldn't stop them. They'd take turns." She pushed and withdrew in a gentle but persistent rhythm. "You'd still feel it for a long time afterward. You'd be so corrupted, my dear. They'd make you crave it."

She held my cunt lips open as she guided the neck of the bottle into me. She kept a teasing finger on my clit as she pushed the bottle steadily deeper, moving it in a subtle spiraling motion. The mouth of the bottle found my cervix and rubbed it hard. "Oh!" I burst out. I felt as if I could explode.

"Mm, you like that," she crooned in my ear. "Come on, my bitch, show me how much you love it. Come for me. I want noise."

Spasms ripped all through my lower body and erupted in my clit. I heard near-shrieks coming out of my mouth as if they were from someone else as Raf continued to wield her bottle in my over-excited cunt. "Oh, Raf," I begged, not sure if I wanted her to stop or continue.

"Until you're finished," she chuckled, speaking to me from a cool glass state of calm detachment. I felt like an animal, a bundle of uncontrollable sensations.

Time stood still as I came and came and came. Gradually, my spasms slowed and I slid back down to my normal state of consciousness. I became aware of Raf's hand on my hip, holding me in place. She gently pulled the bottle out and held it against my face, letting me smell myself and feel my own heat in the receptive glass. I could feel juice running down my thighs.

Raf pulled me off the pillows, threw them aside, and rearranged me on the bed. She curled up behind me, pressing her crotch into my ass. I could feel her ring nosing in between my cheeks. "Tired?" she asked.

"Yes," I sighed. "You wore me out. But I want to do you, honey." I wanted her to understand me. "When I have more energy." I took a deep breath. "I want to give it to you, not just to pay you back."

Raf grew softer and more compliant. "Cuffs," she mumbled into my ear. It took me a moment to understand what she meant. "I have cuffs for my hands and feet. And a strap-on I want you to use."

A fascinating image of Raf spread-eagle on my bed flashed into my mind. It was harder to imagine myself wearing the artificial cock and filling the role of a deliciously stern and greedy mistress. In a burst of confidence, I knew I could tame the wild woman in my bed, the one who had yearned so long to get as good as she gave. I wondered if the breakup had anything to do with unsatisfied needs. Whatever might happen between us, I didn't want to leave her empty.

We drifted into a deep, sweet sleep in each other's arms. I felt as if we were both rocking on an ocean of come, the lust of all women made visible. We could rest as long as we liked, knowing the ocean would still be there when we woke up.

Daylight oozed from between my venetian blinds when I opened my eyes and heard Raf snoring beside me. It seemed like the sound of her trust, and it made me want to protect her. I wanted to know everything about her that could be known.

Raf shifted, reached for my nearest tit and squeezed it. She grinned without opening her eyes. "Raf," I called her. "Is that short for something?"

"Rafaela," she mumbled thickly. "After my grandmother. Who gives a shit?"

This tickled my funny bone, but I controlled my urge to laugh aloud. "Me, Laurel," I answered seriously. "I give a shit."

I raised myself up and positioned myself on all fours over her, holding her shoulders down with my hands. She jerked once as her eyes fluttered open, and I braced myself for a violent push. Instead, she looked up at me with a serene smile that I had never seen on her expressive face before. "What are you doing?" she asked as shyly as a virgin bride.

"You'll find out," I promised as I lowered my head to give her a demanding kiss. *So will I,* I thought, since I still wasn't sure what I was capable of. I wasn't worried. I knew that Raf's body would be a trustworthy guide to her feelings even if she refused me in words. "You'll get what you need," I promised her. *And so will I,* I thought with growing delight, realizing how much I needed to possess the beautiful woman I had lured into my lair. For the moment, I knew we could both give each other all the shelter we needed.

breaking the girl

Sarah Finster

Her calves moved smoothly against each other, the faint *shuck-shuck* of rubbing black silk barely audible over the whirring ceiling fan. Her legs curved perfectly into the sheath of my palms as I slid my hands from her ankles to the warm velvety skin of her thighs and spread her wide apart.

"Heavenly," she murmured, her glossy black hair fanned over the pillowcase. "Is that frangipani I smell in the air?"

"Jasmine," I said, thrusting my fingers into her pussy and feeling, immediately, the heat and wet.

The Hyacinth Girl—still the only name I'll ever know her by—moaned out loud and tipped her chin to the ceiling as I ran my fingers slowly, rhythmically along those damp inner ridges, stroked my thumb against the hard nub of her clit. *No theatrics,* I thought, *none of that playacting she'd put on for hundreds, thousands, of enemy agents who thought they'd cracked her Mata Hari code.* Wrong. Espionage is like medicine: Mistakes get buried. I was her ally, damn it, a fellow MI69 operative with the same license to kill, the same fucktoy training at the hands of the legendary Special Agent XX, and I wasn't letting her off with a few faked spasms and screams.

"There's a Cold War on," I whispered, cradling her cunt against my hand and savoring her involuntary little jerk and grind. *Back in the saddle.* "And a hot one revving up, in case you haven't heard. I'm your Mideast liaison, not your gardener."

The Hyacinth Girl arched her lovely olive back, tilting her small brown-tipped breasts high enough to rub against my own as I knelt between her sprawled legs. The whole curve and sweep of her skin was bare but for those black silk stockings, black garters and sky-high heels. Her arms laced tightly behind her in a leather sleeve from elbows to wrist, all she needed was the tagged collar and ball gag to make her the picture of a brand-new MI69 recruit.

I thought of the trainee inspection I'd conducted just last week: All those lovely little would-be secret agents and their muffled gasps as they worked themselves against Q Division's merrily buzzing Daisy Chain, for Special Agent XX wouldn't take on anyone who came a mere once or twice in succession. That got me even wetter, and I reached for the gladstone bag lying by my bed and fumbled for the little pink-and-white delight Q liked to call the Carousel Horse, then thought better of it. Anyone could break the Hyacinth Girl with Q's fiendishly clever laboratory of tricks. A real professional requires only hands and mouth.

I rubbed against her in turn, my nipples jutting into her flesh like little dagger points, my pussy hot on the smooth, cool plane of her belly. She wriggled, bound hands pressed into her back at an angle that forced her to shift upward and brace her chin on my shoulder as I cupped and stroked her ass with sticky, shining fingers, working one slowly but not gently into the cleft. Further in. She left lingering kisses against my neck, slow-drifting feathers that burned at the touch.

"I love redheads," she breathed, hips cradling me as she spread herself even wider, lifted her ass to let me in deeper. Her eyes were berries bursting with poisonously sweet black syrup. "One dark-haired native girl and bottle-blond expat after another, I get—mm, yes, right there—I get so *bored*."

"Save it." I yanked my fingers out of her pussy and ass, grabbed a chunk of her hair between my teeth, and pulled. I bit her silky cheekbone and sulky upper lip until she winced, then did it again. I'd rather have been dusky or bleached. Five-foot-10 redheads with legs like mine aren't exactly a common sight in Morocco, outside the harems—but then I do most of my best work in harems and have the nuclear blueprints smuggled to me by a certain besotted Jordanian princess to prove it. The Girl was about to get a nice little lesson in how a good odalisque behaves.

I gave the thin, fragile skin of her collarbone a cursory taste, nostrils filling with cheap violet bath salt, talcum powder, and the faint, ineffable suggestion of hyacinth, the unforgettable scent that came from no known perfume. The smell was overwhelming between her breasts, at the declivity with its small, moist explosion of sweat. I took one dark nipple into my mouth and, enjoying her little squeal, nipped like a puppy and sucked like an infant. Her nipple tightened, puckered, and as her breathing became quicker I pulled away to drag my lips across her rounded abdomen and licked up the gleaming trail of my own juices.

She was golden and ripe as an apple and it was a surprise to find the flesh soft and yielding, not taut and crisp when I bit again just below the lacy band of the garter belt. I twined my fingers in the coarse black furze beneath her belly, settled myself on the once-pristine linen sheets now pungent with our smells and, parting her with exquisite care, put my tongue to her clit and let flicker. The light, teasing touches got her greedy and she writhed and groaned while churning her hips as energetically as a five-dirham whore. As if one of XX's top girls would fall for *that*, I sneered to myself, as I ran my tongue along the edge of her salt-sticky lips and felt a long, hot shiver starting in my gut.

"The Soviet double agent," I began, between lingering kisses on that damp delicate skin. "The one who tipped off you and the Ponygirl before the KGB caught up with her. What did she tell you?"

I licked her clit more slowly, more firmly, gripping her thighs in my hands so she couldn't play Venus flytrap with my head. Her stiletto heels tapped a steady, impatient staccato against my back.

"Long live Mother Russia," she spat, expression so furious and hips moving in such a slow, rhythmic grind I knew she wasn't putting on a show. "That's what she told me—"

I snaked my tongue into her pussy and licked and sucked until my whole mouth was acrid; no florals here, cheap or rare, just a flavor so overpoweringly raw and female that it made me rub my own thighs together. My face was drenched in her from nose to chin; her cries, the steady snapping press of her cunt against my lips, were real and helpless and melted my heart as effectively as a blowtorch turned on a glacier.

"The Soviet," I repeated, not raising my head. I pursed my lower lip, let it rub hard against her clit as she whimpered for more of my tongue.

"I don't know her."

"Veruschka," I murmured. I rubbed harder, abrading, and bit. She shrieked. I bit harder.

"I don't *know* her, you bitch!" she shouted.

The fans whirred and the heavy scent of jasmine wafted

through the shuttered window from the gardens where the old landlady, Fatima, makes her little Aisha writhe and moan in full view of her tenants. None of us turn a hair.

They call this ramshackle Tangier neighborhood in the heart of the Zone Internationale *La Ville des Femmes,* where the women do exactly what they please inside the garden walls and out, where veils exist not to shield the chattel of jealous men but to excite the lust of the highest bidder. The Hyacinth Girl was undercover at the notorious El Sah'r nightclub, those round little breasts and drum-tight buttocks fondled by one bored drunken expat cow after another. The night one started a brawl by grabbing the Girl right off an infatuated sultana's lap was my first night as the agency's point woman in Morocco. I shut cow and princess up by emptying my wallet into their laps—expense account drained in a single shot—bundling my negligibly dressed "purchase" into a burqa and smuggling her straight back to Fatima's. The debriefing, such as it is, hasn't stopped since.

"Veruschka," I repeated between long, luxurious strokes of my tongue from the sour drumskin of her perineum back to the wet clit and lips. The red flush of arousal that had started on her chest spread to her neck, her face, as her plum-mouth dropped open in loud, shallow breaths and my hands kneaded her hips.

"I don't know her," she whispered, in artfully pleading tones. "I—"

Three times, Saint Peter, and not a Pharisee fooled. "A little hint," I breathed, cupping the golden apple-flesh of her buttocks in my palms, "you don't set foot outside this room until you pony up. So tell me a story. Tell me all about sweet redheaded Veruschka, the Kremlin's secret weapon against the decadent West...they thought."

"Lick me again," she whispered. "Please."

"Talk. Or you'll get more teeth."

She growled and gave my shoulder blade a clumsy, unmistakable kick. A mistake, as it gave me all the excuse I needed to grab her legs, lethal high heels and all, and, with no ceremony, shove them right behind her head. Discourteous of me, perhaps, but between the binding sleeve I'd laced her arms in the second she was out of the burqa—an unhappy surprise, that, but my most elusive Mideast contact wasn't giving *me* the slip before my say-so—and the leg shackles now lying empty at the foot of the bed, she really should have had the good sense to expect it.

51

I gripped her thighs tighter, enjoying the change of scenery, and with the tip of one finger teased the tightened edge of her asshole. She flinched and gasped. Well, well.

"Some more of that?" I mused aloud, wetting my fingers on myself and stroking her with a gentleness she didn't deserve. "We'll see."

"We met Veruschka last spring in West Berlin," said the girl, closing her eyes. "The Ponygirl and I. She—ah. Again."

I bent my head down and put my tongue where my fingers had been, licking her asshole and nuzzling her cunt as if she deserved me to be sweet. "And then..."

Silence. I looked up, and saw her shaking her head. "You've got it all wrong, lover," she begged, cheek resting against one doubled-up thigh. "I pulled out my whole bag of tricks to get that double agent list, but she only wanted the Ponygirl—"

I slid my tongue into her and she groaned, fingertips scrabbling feverishly behind her as if they had a chance of grabbing hold. I went deep in her pretty ass, surfacing only for breath and a taste of her clit before heading back down again, feeling my chest tighten and my pussy clench against nothing so that my hips rubbed at the mattress in consolation. *Lover.* Christ. Pull the other one.

"Whatever she wanted," I panted, "all she got was you."

"No—"

Her high heel clanged against the bedstead and clattered to the floor as I yanked one of her legs back down to the mattress, strad-dled it, and thrust against her thigh while my teeth latched on a nipple. She pushed against my own leg as best she could, but she was in no position to maneuver. Or bargain.

"Put your fingers in me again." It was half a command and half a plea.

"No."

She moaned in frustration, squirming against nothing while I rode her blissfully hard. "It's the Ponygirl you want to talk to! Not me!"

"Bullshit," I groaned, letting one hand graciously tinderstick her clit as I humped myself raw. "You fucked the little Red blue in the face and got a whole Rolodex of enemy names, faces, cover stories—didn't you? Made a real..."

My fingers, just like my breath, were faltering, wanting to grab her frantically squirming shoulders and crush them into stillness. "Made a real Ninotchka out of her, and when they found her with her neck broken in a Casablanca alleyway, you were already selling all her secrets piece by piece to the highest bidders." I rubbed harder, faster, hoping that it hurt. "Maybe even back to the KGB, because MI69 sure as shit hasn't heard from you since..."

"The Brandenburg Gate!" she almost screamed, when I shoved my fingers inside her, touched her in a place that made her writhe for more and then pulled them out again. "She told us everything and it's all on a cache of microfilm, buried on the west side of the Brandenburg Gate, Agent Christa's girls in Berlin are all Stasi plants; it's all in there, *please let me come!*"

I thrust my cunt against the hard, whorled edge of her knee, pressing my clit down so that I finally reached the exact spot I'd been grasping at for frenzied, endless seconds. Finally, I was able to forget MI69, forget all questions, forget the Girl herself even as her nipples spiked into the press of my palms and I came, shaking, against a silk stocking that was now soaked to the skin with me. Unable to bite back the hoarse, gasping breaths, I graciously reached once more for her pussy and dutifully stroked away, taking a distant sort of pleasure in her little grunts and squeals, the way she pushed her shoulders against the mattress as though she could burrow away from my touch.

"Yes," she hissed, as her movements and mine grew exponentially faster. "Yes, it—I—now, please *now!*"

When she came she let out a long, throaty laugh of relief, of triumph, and as her cunt clenched my hand in hard, uncontrolled spasms of wet I saw something black and slithery in the corner of my eye. *A snake,* I thought foolishly, and by the time I realized my mistake the binding sleeve had hit the floor and the Girl's fingers were pressing at the bundles of nerves at the back of my neck. There was excruciating pain, and a flash of white light.

When I came to I had my face pressed into a pillow and my bare ass pointing skyward. The Girl had shackled my spread feet facing the bed's brass footer and then bent me over it, the garter belt's elastic stretched to its limit, keeping my wrists tethered to the headboard. Turning my head as best I could, I glared over the stockings stuffed in my mouth at the sneering face of the Hyacinth Girl, now wearing the most clothing she ever did: a pale violet chador rendered transparent by the sunlight. She stretched out a hand, incongruously sheathed in *hijab*-modest violet gloves, and dropped a single hyacinth blossom on the mattress next to me. My muffled growl inspired a very unkind laugh.

I knew I should have kept her fucking ankles chained.

"Have yourself a good time, Agent Doe?" she hissed, murder in her dark eyes. "Probe the *depths* to your satisfaction? I hope so, because that's all the information you're ever wringing out of me."

I growled again. She straightened up so quickly that I found myself addressing the veiled curve of her thighs, the dark shadowed triangle showing between them. I've had worse conversational partners.

"West side of the Brandenburg Gate," she repeated. "If you and MI69 get there before the Stasi, and frankly I couldn't care less if you do, it's bonsoir, Agent Doe."

The little silver bracelets she'd twined around her ankles tinkled gently as she walked away; the door slamming loudly enough behind her to knock a vase off the nightstand.

Not having any choice, I braced my feet—already buzzing with pins and needles—against the wooden floorboards and waited for Fatima to come around with afternoon tea and, with any luck, a hairpin for the fucking shackles. A fine way to greet my landlady, ass-to-door and cat-got-your-tongue, but knowing her she'd take one look and knock 10 francs off my room fee. Knowing her, as a matter of fact, it might be some time before she had her fill and graciously deigned to free me. I wouldn't weep. Three days and nights on XX's sawhorse make the most inventive of Fatima's degradations seem tame by comparison.

As for the Hyacinth Girl, we'd meet again; I was sure of it. This wasn't our first interrogatory session between the sheets. We'll always have Paris, and so will everyone else listening in a five-mile radius. As loath as she was to admit it, she had a sentimental streak wide as Q's size-30 hips. Also, last night I'd taken the precaution of drugging her and extracting Veruschka's ill-fated microfilm from...under her doormat, so to speak, and slipping it with a hundred-franc note into Fatima's trusty safekeeping. The Girl would be in Indochina before she realized she was smuggling a snatch of blank celluloid. And I'd be back in the glorious West, trailing clouds of Kremlin documents that MI69 would—and has—kill for. The little liar would be out for blood, but who knew—there might come a time when she was willing to pay a far higher price than a bit of pussy for me to keep the Russians, the Koreans, the Brits, the Ossis, and all of MI69 off her traitorous double-dealing little tail. As they're so fond of saying in this corner of the world, the enemy of my enemy is my friend, and the Hyacinth Girl makes enemies like Hedy Lamarr makes men.

all you need to know

Debra Hyde

Meg has waited long enough. She's pushed me to my knees and pulled my face to her. When she does that—without explanation, without any words even—I know that she needs it.

Meg's scent is ripe and it lingers on the wisps of her pubic hair, on the edge of her magnificent slit. It's intoxicating, and I eagerly go where she wants me.

She doesn't have to tell me what she wants or how to give it to her. My tongue goes to her clit. Hard and ready, it greets me and I thrum back and forth over it, looking to catch that one magic spot, just to one side, where nerves cluster, waiting for stimulation.

When I hit it, Meg shivers. I keep my tongue there, working that spot. Already, she arches to meet my touch.

My hands grip her outer thighs, but as her scent grows and fills my senses, I let one hand wander until it finds its reward when it reaches her inner thighs. There, a slick wetness tells all. It invites me to probe her. My fingers ease between her legs and climb upward. They meet the rich folds of her labia and pry them apart. I hear a wet slurp issue from her cunt and, more than anything, I want to dig into her with my tongue. I want to feel every ripple of her flesh and savor every drip of her arousal, but she likes my fingers better.

I work my index finger into Meg. Resistance meets my push, but it's only because of the angle. I know that I'd be able to slip two fingers right into her if I had Meg on her back with her legs splayed wide, yet I like this upright tightness. I catch her cunt before it spreads wide in welcome.

I pump my finger in and out, slowly, savoring the feel of her. I feel her clench me on the inside and shiver all over on the outside. She pants as I work her, tongue and finger.

I pull my mouth away from her clit and rise up from kneeling. She moans when I leave her clit, but I twist my hand so my thumb replaces my mouth. I pull her to me, crushing my breasts against her back. I pant in her ear. I want to be next to her, cupping her, embracing her, as she comes.

"You're incredible," I tell her.

Meg's eyes are closed and she looks like she's in some kind of wondrous dreamland, a daze of sex and sensation. She's lost in what I'm doing to her, focused entirely on every iota of arousal that my stroking draws from her. She is erotic and ethereal. Fairies must look like this when they come.

I slip a second finger into her. I can't stroke both her clit and fuck her slit, not easily anyway, but I have my tricks nonetheless. Every so often, I spread my fingers within her.

Which makes Meg squirm and moan. Which makes her cunt throb and clench and reach for release.

"That's it, baby, come for me," I tell her. "I'm watching you. I'm waiting for it. Give it up, girl."

Where she squirmed before, she now humps my hand. I feel her clit press against my thumb, her labia squash against my hand, and although it cramps my hand, I manage to slip a third finger into Meg.

"Give it up."

Meg moans, and her cunt tightens around my fingers. *This is it,* I tell myself, *she'll come.*

Meg explodes around my fingers. A sudden clench, a blast of release, then those seismic throbs. Her orgasm is like a sonic boom, rippling past my insignificant fingers.

Crazy thoughts run through my head while Meg comes. I want to shrink and crawl up inside her, to be a living thing, engulfed by her orgasm and buffeted by every roaring pulse that she emanates. I wonder what it would feel like, what it would smell like, what it would do to a miniscule me.

They're silly thoughts. Fortunately, my other ideas are of a much better quality, and I have it in mind to squeeze more from Meg. I press my fingers against that rough washboard of hers. Knowing how sensitive it is right after she comes, I know how easy it is to stimulate it to action. It isn't much of a reaction—it's too soon in all of this for a torrent—but Meg gasps, and liquid cascades over my fingers.

"You're not just incredible," I tell her now, "You're delicious."

And to prove the point I fall to my knees, turn her toward me, and put my mouth to her. My tongue slips by my retiring finger and it catches that sweet and thick liquid bounty. Meg is the nectar of sex and, at last, my cunt throbs, aroused by all she is.

Finally, she speaks. In gasps, she begs me, "More. More. More. Please."

Who am I do deny her?

I take her to our bed and lay her on her back. Spread there, she is gorgeous. Her hips and thighs, her belly and breasts, are things of rich womanly flesh inviting me to them, begging me to caress them, to take her.

I can't resist her. I will give her more.

I prop a pillow under Meg's ass and reach for the lube on our nightstand. Maybe I can't shrink, but I can get insider her.

There's a way I go about this, and it's not quick and dirty. Oh, quick and dirty is fun when she's horny and needs to get off fast, but this requires finesse. And finesse works best in a slow, teasing approach.

I lay alongside Meg, and as I dip toward her breast I tell her, "I'm gonna do you good, baby." I draw her nipple into my mouth and my tongue lounges over its erect nub. Gently, I suck.

Impulse tells me to grab her tits and rough them up while delivering a ravaging kiss, but that's greed talking, not finesse. Finesse is subtle and patient and it's in my fingers. Gently, I spread wet lube over Meg's plush labia and I watch her shiver as she's reminded of what lube can do and what it will do.

Meg's labia are like clasped and praying hands and they are sensitive as a stigmata's suffering. My fingers are like a saint whispering forbidden knowledge and, devotedly, her lips beg for more. They tremble and I know my touch is like a thousand revelations to them.

Again and again, I lightly stroke them, encouraging them. Meg moans and I know she wants a finger at her clit. Something on her clit, something at her tit, perfect complements. Not yet, not yet.

Instead, I tease her labia apart, slowly, as if I'm pulling open the petals of an iris. I want to feel every bit of flesh here at the precipice of her slit at my fingertips. I want to feel every nerve ending that shudders at my touch.

I unfurl her. I spread her lips and tip my fingers into her, just a bit, just beyond the nail. Meg moans and I know she really wants me to slam those fingers into her, to take her and ravish what I can immediately, without lube, without patience.

But that's too easy. That's too hasty. Finesse, fingertips, and fingertips, finesse.

Still, I suckle and work three fingertips back and forth. Her cunt smacks with wet delight when I pull out, then silently gives way when I push into her. Before I know it, the tip of my thumb joins the foray and I know it's time for more lube.

I leave Meg's tit. Sadly, one cannot suck tit and slather lube at the same time.

I squeeze lube where hand meets crevice and atop my fingers, then begin the rhythmic push-pull that will stretch Meg and let her engulf me. I go knuckle deep, letting my little finger slip into the mix.

Meg's cunt hugs me with cushioned flesh. I want to hold my hand there and feel her all around me, but the rhythm is crucial, and although her labia gape and beckon me to use them, use them, use them, I must keep the rhythm going.

More lube and I'm fist-knuckle deep. Now it's just a matter of steadiness. Now I can afford to look away from my handiwork and gaze upon Meg. Eyes closed, her face shines and her smile is magic. She's in heaven. She's beatific. She's irresistible.

And it's why I love her, adore her, and never, ever tire of her.

More lube, around my backhand, down to my wrist. I press the rhythm and another moan rises from Meg. I feel her cunt moan as well in one long throb. Exquisite, she feels exquisite.

I reach for a nipple with my free hand and I play with it briefly before I caress her body. As my hand roams, I tell her how beautiful she is, how beautiful she feels, how luscious she is. My words push her arousal, and she spreads for me. My hand slips in, my fingers curl around on themselves and she embraces me.

I find her cunt so incredible I can only whisper praise. It does what mine has never accomplished; it takes me in a way I have never been able to take her.

"You are incredible," I tell her, and I dip my mouth to her clit.

One touch of my tongue, and she's coming. Waves roll over my hand. All she needs is an undertow and I'd be a goner.

And then it comes; her tsunami comes. It washes over my hand like a wave breaking toward shore, flooding past me, and seeping out onto the bed.

Meg tells me that it's like milk letting down from the breast, only weaker. When it's teased and summoned, it gathers and releases. But I have to take her word for it; she is a woman in ways I've never been.

This is why I marvel at Meg, why I cherish what she's capable of and what she gives me. I adore her splendor and love her completely.

What more do you need to know, I ask, as every move of my fist sends her spiraling into another orgasm? What more is there, beyond love and lust and wonder and ardor? As I look at Meg and see her heavenly smile of erotic achievement, I know the answer. I need nothing more. I have Meg.

penny, laid

Kristina Wright

"Come on, baby," Carla said, leading her up the steps to the front door.

The dim interior of Carla's town house hinted at the well-heeled lifestyle of Penny's aspirations. Carla mounted the curving staircase without a word and Penny followed. The banister was cool under her damp palm. "Nice house," Penny murmured.

Carla didn't answer.

The master bedroom was straight out of a decorating magazine. It was lavishly furnished with antiques, dominated by an enormous mahogany sleigh bed. Layers of bed linens in pink, white and sage invited rest, not sex. But Carla's grin suggested it would be a long time before Penny got to sleep.

Carla stripped off her jacket and no-nonsense business shoes. Her eyes never wavered from Penny's as she undid the buttons on her blouse. For her slender frame, her breasts were surprisingly large beneath the silk. They swayed as Carla took a step toward her.

Penny swallowed, hard. Unsure whether she should take off her clothes, she stood as timid as a schoolgirl on her first date. This woman made her nervous—and hot as hell. She couldn't think, she could barely breathe. She just wanted. Wanted what only Carla could give her.

"Come here, baby," Carla said. "Let me get a look at you."

Penny took a few hesitant steps until they stood inches apart, breasts nearly touching. "I'm not sure..."

Carla put her fingers across Penny's lips. "Shh, little girl. It'll be OK." She stroked Penny's face. "So bright and beautiful. You have so much to offer."

Before Penny could question that comment, Carla was pulling her T-shirt over her head. For a moment, her face hidden in her shirt, Penny forgot how nervous she was. Then the shirt was off and she was staring into Carla's green cat eyes that seemed to see into her soul. She wanted to fall into those eyes. Then Carla leaned close and kissed her.

Wet, soft, sensual—kissing Carla was both familiar and foreign.

They came closer, breasts pressing, and she could feel Carla's hard nipples through her blouse. She cradled Carla's face, kissing her while Carla's fingers found their way under her skirt and into her panties. She moaned against Carla's mouth, swirling her tongue the way Carla swirled her finger around Penny's clit. She wondered what Carla's cunt tasted like.

Carla pulled back, eyes sparkling, lipstick smeared. "You're so wet, baby girl," she said, showing Penny the evidence on her hand before popping her fingers in her mouth. "Mmm...I want to fuck you. Take your clothes off."

Penny trembled as she stripped. Bra, skirt, wet panties: they came off quickly, awkwardly. All but the shoes; she kept her sexy, slutty pumps on because she didn't want Carla to tower over her. She wanted to please this woman but she didn't want to feel smaller than her.

Carla cupped Penny's tits, raising them to her lips. She suckled the nipples hard, harder than they'd ever been sucked, sending shock waves straight to Penny's clit. Penny whimpered softly, pressing her tits into Carla's hands, wanting more. She tugged Carla's nipples through her blouse, enjoying the nubby feeling between her fingers.

Carla pulled her mouth from Penny's nipple, leaving it wet and standing tall. She put her hands on Penny's shoulders and pushed her down to her knees.

"Don't be shy, sweetie. Touch me."

Penny ran her hands up the heavy fabric of Carla's trousers to the waistband. She slipped the button and pulled the zipper down. Something large and hard brushed against Penny's hand and made her tremble.

An enormous cock jutted from Carla's crotch. It was the kind sold in the back of adult magazines, the kind Penny had never felt inside her but always wondered about. Bigger than any she'd seen in the porn flicks, the cock strapped to this gorgeous, sexy woman looked like a six shooter nestled in pubic hair as brown and silky as the hair on Carla's head.

Carla adjusted the dildo until it was pointing at Penny. The look of pleasure on her face made Penny realize that the broad, blunt end was pushing against her cunt and clit.

"Go ahead, baby, suck it. Make it wet."

Penny grasped the thick cock and guided the tip to her mouth, never breaking eye contact with Carla. The tip popped between her lips, and Carla groaned as if she could feel the sensation. Penny stretched her mouth around the giant dildo as Carla stripped her blouse and bra. Her brown acorn-sized nipples made Penny's mouth water. At the same time, she wondered who this naked goddess was who stood before her wearing only a fake cock hung on a heavy black belt that crisscrossed her hips and thighs.

"Good Penny. Suck my big dick so I can fuck you with it."

It was Penny's turn to groan. The thought of this monster inside her had her trembling. She sucked the dildo as if it were the main course instead of the appetizer.

Carla pulled the dildo from her mouth and smacked it against her cheeks. "God, you're hot. Get over to the bed now. Let me get a look at the rest of you."

Penny let Carla guide her to the bed. On hands and knees, she arched her back and thrust her bottom up, feeling cool air blow across her cunt and asshole.

"Baby, what a beautiful ass." Carla's hands caressed and molded the tight cheeks while Penny moaned against the sheets. "Nice little hole too. I bet it gets fucked all the time, doesn't it?"

Penny shook her head. "No, never," she gasped as Carla's fingertips slid down her crack.

"I bet it does," Carla teased. "Who could resist this ass?"

Penny shook her head. "I've never..." Carla's hand cracked across her thigh and Penny jumped.

"We'll find out in good time what you have and haven't done," Carla said quietly.

Carla used fingers and tongue on Penny's wet slit, teasing and tormenting until Penny thought she'd scream. She wriggled under Carla's ministrations, imaging that huge cock inside her, wanting it, needing it.

"Please, fuck me," she panted, rotating her hips as Carla tongue-fucked her cunt. "Fuck me with your big cock."

Carla chuckled. "Little girl wants her ass fucked, huh?"

"No. My cunt. Fuck my cunt."

Carla smacked her ass hard. "It's my dick. I'll fuck you the way I want." Another smack. "Won't I?"

Penny nodded, hair swinging. Carla pulled away and she groaned. Waiting breathless, Penny looked over her shoulder. Carla stood stroking the big cock between her legs. Penny trembled and whimpered, pushing her ass higher in the air.

Carla nestled the cock between the cheeks of Penny's ass. "Everybody wants to fuck this ass, don't they?" she asked, giving Penny's bottom a sharp slap.

"Yes," Penny gasped.

"And you never let them, do you?

Penny shook her head, unable to form words.

"But you want it fucked now, don't you?"

Penny groaned. "Yes! Fuck me!"

"Easy, baby," Carla said, climbing on the bed behind her. "I'm going to give you what you want. Soon."

Penny felt the dildo nudge her cunt. She reached between her legs to grab it, but Carla pulled away and slapped it across her butt. Penny whimpered in frustration and clutched the sheets.

Carla gently pushed the cock between the swollen cunt lips. Penny pushed her hips back, wanting to feel it buried inside her. It slid farther in, bottoming out before she'd taken much more than half. She looked down between her legs and saw it sticking out of her, saw Carla's shapely legs and hips beyond it.

"Cock, Carla, cock," she whimpered, fucking back against the hugeness inside her.

Carla thrust into her. "Baby wants more dick. Baby needs this dick in her cunt, up her ass."

Their rhythm was hard and fast animal fucking, not gentle seduction. Penny wiggled on the cock while Carla slapped her two round globes. Carla thrust a finger past the tight ring of Penny's anus. She double-fucked her, hard and fast, until Penny was screaming "Cockcarlacockcarlacockcarla" as orgasm after orgasm wracked her body.

In one swift motion, Carla pulled the cock out of Penny's wet, clenching cunt and thrust it into her ass. A sharp sting of pain was followed by sweet pleasure. Penny felt herself stretch like she'd never been, being penetrated deeper than she thought she could handle. The orgasms didn't stop; they rolled over her in waves as Carla pumped her ass.

Penny reached to rub her clit, to keep the edge as Carla drove into her. Carla moaned, jackhammering into her ass so fast, Penny knew she must be coming too. Their damp flesh slapped together as Carla slammed into her, a fistful of Penny's long hair pulled tight in her hand as she screamed out her orgasm. Penny collapsed under the onslaught, her knees going out from under her as Carla's full weight sprawled across her back and the dildo stayed buried inside her. Her clit rubbed against the sheet, and she cried out.

As suddenly as it had begun, the rough sex was over and Carla was cradling her, Penny's back pressed against her breasts and thighs. They were both panting, dripping with sweat. Carla stroked her, soothing her, the dildo still deep in her ass, moving slowly now, gently. For the first time in a long time, Penny closed her eyes and let herself be held by a lover.

"Sweet girl," Carla whispered, nipping her earlobe. "Sweet ass."

role reversal

Andrea Herrmann

My girlfriend is the femme. I am the butch. I wear uniforms to work; she wears dresses. She uses makeup; I use Old Spice. I am on top; she's on the bottom. Always. So I thought.

I was glad to be home, exhausted after a long day at work. My heavy eyes and dragging body told me I needed an afternoon nap. I closed the front door, kicked off my shoes, and walked right to the bedroom. I changed into an old T-shirt and pair of boxers and collapsed. She came over, sat next to me on the bed, and kissed me on the cheek. I pulled a light blanket up over my shoulders, and she stayed to watch me drift off.

I knew I had fallen asleep on my side, but I woke up on my back. I couldn't move. I couldn't see. Was I still dreaming? No, I was awake. I was definitely still in bed. But I was tied to it. I called out for my lover, worried that we had been robbed, not even thinking of the possibility of what really caused my current predicament. I heard someone enter the bedroom and sit beside me. "It's about time you woke up," her fingernails scratched my head. "What's going on? What happened?"

I felt a finger trace the arch of my nose and land on my lips, silencing me. "Shh..." her lips purred. "Don't talk." I was shocked by her next words. "I'll tell you when you can talk."

"What? What are you doing?" Her lips smothered mine, silencing me. She pulled back, grasping my lower lip in her teeth. "I said, *I'll tell you when you can talk.* Don't disobey me again." Her voice was dominating, almost frightening me.

It quickly dawned on me that my lover longed for a taste of the control and power I felt as a top. She had reversed our roles. "What are you going to do to me?" She just laughed in response and walked away.

Her laughter bragged about her accomplishment. My hands and feet were bound to the bed railing. The cloth strips secured my wrists and ankles to the bed with my legs spread open. Another piece of cloth covered my eyes. I was vulnerable, exposed, out of control. I had always been in control, calling the shots. Now here I was, at her mercy. I could hear her walk back into the bedroom. She stopped in front of me.

I heard scissors. *Snip, snip.* I felt my shirt lift up. The cold air rushed in against my skin. My shirt was lifted from my body. She continued to cut, throwing the loose pieces on the floor. My nipples hardened from the excitement and exposure. She stopped, leaving my boxers on. Her fingers tapped against my skin, pausing, appreciating what she had done. I imagined her grinning before me, contemplating her next move in her mind.

She lunged onto me. Her teeth grazed my body, surprising me, jumping around from place to place, leaving marks in my skin. She bit my arms, my shoulders, my neck, my sides, and my stomach. I shook with each bite. "We're going to do this again, but this time, you're not going to move." She bit above my hip, tickling me and shocking me at the same time. My shudder met a quick response. "*I said, don't move.*" She bit again, harder, holding my flesh in her mouth. I forced myself to remain quiet. My hands slid into fists and my toes curled as I held in my reaction.

"Don't make me have to teach you a lesson. You're going to do everything I say, when I say it." She grabbed my boxers and yanked them down from my waist. "If you're good, you'll get rewarded. If you're bad, you'll get punished." She bit the inside of my thigh, pulling on my skin with her teeth. I complied. I didn't move. She got up and walked away again.

I was curious, shocked, stunned, and eager. I was seeing a new side of my lover. I didn't know what to expect. Yet every second that I waited felt like an eternity. Logic tells me she was gone just for a few minutes, but my body thought it was hours. I was getting wet. This was all so new. It felt like a woman was touching me for the first time. I was uncomfortable from the awkwardness, but turned on by her command.

She gently kissed me on my lower abdomen below my belly button. They were the quick fluttering kisses I was used to, starting as quick gestures of affection, slowing down to sensual embraces from her lips. I didn't notice her arm reaching down for something.

The ice cube was pressed against the large bite mark above my hip. I moved my hand as if I could reach down and knock her away.

Its coldness stung in comparison to her mouth's warm wetness. She held the ice in place as it started to dissolve against my skin. She raised the cube up the side of my body, up to my ribs, across my chest, up to my neck, and back down again. She colored my body with the melting cube, drawing circles and lines on me. The streams of water probably shimmered on my skin. Ice traced my toes, my palms, my knees, and my elbows.

She let the last piece of ice disappear between my breasts and began to lick the water off my chest. Her tongue dragged up and down, moving to circle my nipples. She paused just before her tongue reached the center of my left breast. My nipple pointed up, pleading for attention. I leaned my back up, pushing my chest up to her as an offering. Then she got up and walked away again. I dropped back down on the bed, frustrated. I wanted to untie myself, pick her up, and throw her on the bed to tease her as she had just teased me. But I also wanted to see what she had in store for me. I wanted to see what it was like to submit my body to another person.

She entered the room again and leaned over me. I felt something cold hit my breast, dripping down my skin. Chocolate sauce. It rolled onto my other breast, piling up on my nipple, oozing around the center. Her tongue started on my left tit, licking up the tasty sweetness. She moaned while closing her mouth around my nipple. Her lips hummed against my skin. She lapped at my body, licking up all the sauce and remaining there until she was content. She moved to my other tit, tasting it, hitting it from every angle. I contemplated if I were allowed to release the moans building inside me. I actually wondered what her reaction would be if I showed my pleasure. My body couldn't hold in what I needed to express. I sighed and let go, exhaling my enjoyment. She bulled back, grazing a nipple in the process, and got up again, frustrated. "I'm sorry, I'm sorry, I didn't mean to," I couldn't believe what I was saying "moan, without your permission." I could sense her leaning over me again. "I'm sorry I moved without your permission. It won't happen again."

"Good," she whispered to my ear. Her long hair brushed against my face. "I was about to gag you."

She was really getting into the role. I was mad at myself for putting my own pleasure first before hers. It became clear that this is something she really wanted. I was resolved to let her live this experience out to the fullest.

She picked up the scissors again. Her left hand traced along the elastic of my boxers. "Are you going to be a good girl? Are you going to do what I tell you?"

"Yes."

"Do you like what I'm doing to you?"

"Yes."

"Do you want these boxers off?" She had cut them before I could answer. She pulled them away, dragging her nails down my leg in the process. She left, leaving me once again in suspense. Now I really appreciated how intense role-playing could be. As the top, I'm used to planning, plotting, doing. The waiting and apprehension were killing me. I could feel my juices building up between my legs. She came back in, quietly, maintaining the surprise of her next moves.

I heard her squeeze something out of a bottle. What was she doing? I felt her hand curve up the left cheek of my ass and stop. The tip of an anal probe gently rested against my hole. My cheeks tightened in resistance. We've had anal sex before, but this was different. This was at her pace. She gave the plug a quick push, moving the head inside me. I held in my reaction, which was heightened by the eroticism of her entering me. The lube she layered on the shaft of the probe dripped down into the crack of my ass, wetting the hole that my dripping pussy had already lubricated.

The plug poked slowly in and out, igniting my nerves and electrifying my senses. She pushed further in with each pass, sending unique waves of pleasure through me. "Relax," she commanded, "relax and let it slide in. Don't fight it." I tried to loosen up but my body reacted naturally to this new experience. The combination of pain and pleasure was intense. Receiving felt so different from giving. "Relax. That's right, relax. That's good. I'm going to fuck you so hard."

She had never been one for dirty talk during sex, and her words brought me to an even hire level of arousal. "Would you like that? Would you like me to fuck you?" She pushed until the probe slid in completely. She changed her position on top of me. "If I fuck you,

you have to stay perfectly still. You can't hump, you can't move. If you do, I'll stop. Do you understand?"

"Yes..."

I couldn't tell where she was until I felt her breath on my thigh. She maneuvered herself to place her head between my legs but kept her hand near my ass so she could continue to probe me. "Beg me," she commanded. My pussy had been tormented long enough. I needed to feel her tongue. I wanted her to finish me off, to put out the fire that she had caused in me.

"Please, lick me..."

"Please what?"

"Please, lick me..."

"Mistress!" Her fingernails marked my thigh.

"Please, please lick me, Mistress!" I pleaded for her touch. I longed to shove myself into her face, to force her tongue into my hole. I could sense all the pleasure she was getting from watching me suffer.

Her tongue dived into me, violently licking and twisting, exploring every inch of my mound. She moved up and down, from the clit to the bottom of my slit, back and forth, again and again. Twisting, twirling around my clit, pressing down, flicking, fluttering against me—she sent shivers running through every inch of my body. Her licks were always so slow and gentle, building up to an explosion. This time all she gave me were explosions, striking me with each touch like lightening.

I did my best to hold my hips down and perfectly still, but my intentions soon failed. She didn't seem to care. I was getting close, and she knew it. She held on to my hips, straddling them down with her hands so her face could keep up with my body's bucking movements. She twisted her body so her weight could help hold me down, freeing a hand to glide up and down the length of my wetness while her mouth focused on my clit. She took my knob in between her lips, sucking on it, enveloping it, pulling gently. Her fingers quickly found my hole and slammed right in, turning up to massage my G spot with each thrust. She flexed and stretched her fingers inside my body, timing her movements with her tongue's attack on my clit. I was almost there, almost at the breaking point. She stopped, pulling out of my vagina and away from my pussy.

I felt her slip away again and heard her stand up. My frustration grew beyond any level that I thought I could ever handle. I could hear her adjusting something, doing something, but I wasn't sure what. She climbed on top of me, pressing her waist on my body. I felt a familiar texture. "I've always wanted to try this." She was wearing my favorite strap-on. It was 10 inches long, light peach in color, and it secured to your body with leather straps and buckles. It was the first strap-on I ever used with her. I remember hearing her gasp the first time I slid it inside of her, our eyes locked in a deep gaze, her mouth releasing orgasmic moans. Now it was my fingers that were curling in anticipation, my body waiting to be entered.

She kneeled above me in triumph. She removed the blindfold from my head. She wanted me to see this, to see her on top of me, to see her entering me. Her hips raised; the hard plastic slid against my crotch. The tip penetrated, the shaft slid in me inch by inch. Her initial movements were awkward and choppy, as she figured out how to balance herself and push the strap-on as deep in me as possible. My wetness eased the shaft. She studied her efforts, quickly perfecting her technique. Soon she was bucking rapidly, her hair bouncing with her movements, her eyes looking at me in disbelief that this was really happening.

She was fucking me wildly, slapping her hips against mine. The sweat was building on her toned legs as she conquered me. The muscle contractions held the anal plug in place in my other hole while she plunged into the depths of my wetness. I was filled, stretched to the limits. I barely had the control to ask, "Mistress, may I moan in pleasure?"

"Yes!" she cried out, and I soon followed her calls, proclaiming the extreme satisfaction I was experiencing.

When I thought she couldn't go any further, she thrust so deep that I could feel the tip of the dildo smacking against my cervix. I shuttered from the slight pain caused by each movement. She enjoyed watching me and seemed to revel in her new role. I imagined she was just as wet as I was, turned on by the activity as much as the act itself. Somehow, her thrusts seemed to get deeper and deeper, faster and faster.

The world started to spin for me. I was climaxing, exploding inside, eyes rolling in the back of my head from the pleasure. I was fighting to keep myself from passing out. My entire body tingled. My hips froze; my legs were numb. I could feel the dampness on the bed below me. She stared down at me as she gently pulled out. She saw the rewards of her effort—my heavy breathing, my trembling body; my complete bliss.

I wanted her to take me from behind. I wanted her to raise my legs in the air and fuck me until it hurt. But I wasn't ready to be untied, not yet. At least, not if my top didn't want me untied. She's in control now.

perks

M. J. Willamz

She must have been new to the club; I'd never seen her there. She hadn't taken her eyes off me all night. My interest piqued, I made my way through the crowd and took her hand, leading her past the dance floor and into my office. Managing a club definitely has its perks.

After closing and locking the door, I turned to see her sitting in my leather chair behind my desk. She was young, maybe early 20s. She still had the tight body of youth, clad in a miniskirt and a tight button-down blouse with buttons straining over breasts I couldn't wait to taste. Her eyes—an almost purple shade of blue—never left mine. They implored me, almost dared me to take what she had to offer.

I began to make my way toward her. She stood and walked to meet me, putting her hands on my chest. When I bent to kiss her, her full, perfect lips parted. I pulled away, teasing her. Obviously *not* in the mood to be teased, she pulled my face to hers and hungrily kissed me. I hadn't expected that directness from her, but the shock waves she was sending through my body were more than welcome. Her tongue made its way into my mouth and my tongue wrapped around it, needing to devour her, to possess her.

As I kissed her, my fingers worked at unbuttoning her shirt. Once it fell open, I slid my hands inside to wrap around those firm mounds covered in a satiny bra. She quickly unhooked the bra in front and let it slide open. I slid my hands over her, rubbing my palms over her nipples so that they hardened.

My mouth moved to her neck, determined to follow the path of my hands. I found that soft supple spot just under her ear that I was sure needed attention. Her head went back and my lips felt her pulse race. As I lightly sucked there, she arched against me. My hands slid around her back and pulled her close so I could feel her freed breasts against me.

Her taut nipples caused an instant wetness between my legs. My clit twitched, craving the release I was certain she could give. *Be*

73

cool, I told myself. *Give this woman what she needs. Ignore the pleading in your pants.*

Trying to remain focused, I continued kissing her neck and down the open front of her blouse. She arched her back more to offer me her breasts. I teasingly licked around the bottom and side of one. She let out a moan, and I knew I was getting weaker. I couldn't fight it. I tried, but Goddess, I needed her touch. As I continued to nibble on her breast, I took her hand and slid it down the front of my jeans. With no underwear there to impede her, her magical fingers found the spot that was so craving her assistance.

Her fingers worked deftly: pressing hard just above the swollen center of my needs, making me push against her, knowing release was close. I buried my mouth in her neck as her fingers slid lower and pressed hard against my swollen clit. She rubbed me hard and fast, just the way I liked it. No nonsense, just get the job done. And get it done she did. It was only a matter of seconds before I crashed into an incredible climax.

Slightly embarrassed that I hadn't been able to wait, I began kissing down her chest again while I lifted her onto my desk and stood between her legs. I could feel the heat radiating from between those shapely thighs. She showed no modesty, sitting with her skirt hiked up, exposing the glistening wetness I forced myself to tear my eyes away from. My mouth found a perfectly erect nipple and my tongue began to tease it, just as my hands worked their way up her thighs, my thumbs converging on a very slick button that was swollen with her need.

She leaned back on her hands and arched her hips for me. My thumbs gave up their release on her clit so I could slide a finger inside her beckoning moistness. She threw back her head and arched closer to me. As I moved my mouth to her other nipple, I slid another finger inside and felt her tight, hot wetness engulf me. The extent of how wet she was amazed me. I could hear my fingers working inside of her.

As she continued to arch, I realized that only one thing was going to do the trick for this young one. I slid yet another finger in her and knew I was right. I finally slid my whole fist inside of her so she could have the satisfaction she deserved.

"Oh...Yeah..." she moaned as she moved all over on me. She was so ready for me that her juices were running down my forearm. I repeatedly thrust into her, turning and twisting to give her maximum contact. We were at that perfect angle, where every twist and turn rubbed her clit against my wrist as my fist moved deeper inside her.

I was about to have another orgasm myself just feeling her writhing on me, urging me deeper, twisting against me. And then she was close; so very close because the writhing took on a distinct rhythm. I met her rhythm: in and out, deeper and deeper. We were all alone in our own world. There was nothing except my fist in her and her hot creaming flesh wrapped around it. Her movements got faster, my thrusts harder. Her arms were clasped around my back, her legs wrapped around my waist. She moved faster and faster.

"Oh, God," She whispered, "Oh, yeah...Oh, yeah..."

"Come on, baby," I egged her on. "Come on, my sweet baby. You can do it. Come on. Come for me, baby."

"Oh, *God,*" She whispered again. "Oh, yeah...Here it comes. Oh, God, *please.*" She was twisting and turning and driving me even deeper.

"Oh...my...God," She pulled me closer, and it was her turn to bury her face in my neck so she didn't cry out loud.

"Oh my, baby," I whispered as I felt her contract on my wrist. I loved being inside her.

"Are you OK?" I asked a few minutes later, once the spasms had stopped. She nodded, still unable to speak.

"Good," I said, kissing her softly on the lips. She was still breathing heavily.

"You sure?" I laughed.

"I'm sure," she managed.

"OK. I'm glad," I said as I reluctantly pulled myself out of her.

"I'm better than glad," She purred, getting her clothes back in place.

"By the way," I offered, "The name's Rainey. Can I buy you a drink?"

phone sex

Lynne Jamneck

You've probably seen pictures of London's little red phone boxes. Most of them have been painted black, but trust me when I say, they're still a tight squeeze.

But I'll give you a bit of an introduction first—I hear it's good manners.

She was pure French roast and toasted filter cigarettes, faded Levi's (which, really, were more fucked than faded because you could see right through the back that she wasn't wearing underwear), and a white T-shirt that looked similarly manhandled, yet still decent enough to wear out on a Friday night.

I don't do the club scene anymore because of the bunnies. I feel weird being surrounded by a bunch of 16-year-old horn toads. Kids their age should be reading books—how-to books.

She politely asked me for the time as she stood in front of Starbucks, sucking the life from a Camel. I'd recently quit that nasty but disgustingly satisfying habit myself and didn't realize I was staring until she cocked an eyebrow.

I gave her the time.

She admired my breasts and said, "Your face looks awfully familiar."

"I'm a writer."

She lit another cigarette. "No, that's not it."

"Bugger," I replied sexily.

"You always drink coffee out on the sidewalk?"

"Maybe I can think of having it somewhere else."

The arched eyebrow again. " I need to make a phone call. Walk with me to the park. I'll feel safer."

My butch sensibilities came alive with some satisfying finality, along with my libido. It dawned on me that what started out as a run-of-the-mill Friday night had rapidly turned into an open invitation for the significantly enjoyable event that was the Anonymous Fuck.

As she walked ahead, I could see she had one of those perfectly curved bums—and tight beyond belief. To quote Joanna Lumley, you could probably bounce her off the nearest wall. She glanced over her shoulder and beckoned me into a box at the far end of the park. An overhead light had gone out, shrouding the booth in shadow. *Interesting.* I wondered if she did this often—and with whom.

I followed her inside.

I immediately grabbed her tight ass and hoped the booth didn't shake as I slammed her stomach against the glass paneling. It made a fucking racket. She tried to say something, but I grit my teeth and instructed her to shut her mouth. There was no time to waste. I'm terribly paranoid and my fatalistic thinking already saw bobbies carry the both of us off to the nearest police station. If I was going to fuck her, I'd better do it quick.

I reached around and gave her jeans a good *yank.* Buttons popped. A sound cracked in her throat, making me grab a handful of her dirty blond hair while I stealthily thrust two fingers deep inside her. Her back arched silently, sending her perfect-10 ass into my crotch. My phantom dick rejoiced. She kept silent, save for the small and quiet little *uh...ah* sounds she made into the finger-smudged glass. Thank God she refrained from shouting something like "Jesus Christ fuck me!" or our gooses would've been cooked. I spun her around without removing my fingers from inside her and smiled at the thought of her naked cheeks pressing against the cold glass. I tried keeping an eye out for the approaching arm of the London law, but I was distracted by the way her lips only mouthed the words she truly wanted to say out loud.

Deeper

Harder

Slower

I wouldn't give her the last one, making her both harder and wetter in my hand. From the corner of my eye I saw the violently shuddering cup of coffee I'd placed atop the telephone. *Better watch it; one shouldn't waste good coffee.* This made me fuck her slower, but with some force and very little restraint. I noticed her jeans were halfway down her pretty thighs and I became further aroused. I grabbed her ass and pulled her into me while she rode my other hand like a cowgirl trying to prove something.

She bit my neck as her orgasm struck. I got the feeling she was normally a yeller, and would probably have alerted the whole goddamn block. She'd probably get off on it too. Hell, I know I would. Then an involuntary action of her hand smashed the coffee off the telephone and into the glass paneling at our backs. Coffee dripped onto the floor. Dogs began to bark.

"Pull up your pants, darling," I whispered fiercely.

"First you fuck me then you order me around? Isn't that what my girlfriend's for?"

Hi ho.

We stumbled out the booth in opposite directions. I headed into Burger King for fresh coffee and something to eat. A whole horse would do.

Thank God she never told me her name. Pity I never found out why she thought my face looked so familiar. Suffice to say—next time she sees me on a sidewalk, she'll remember.

trying it on for size

JT Langdon

The blond reached for the lavender peasant top on the sale rack at the same time I did, our fingers lightly brushing together. We shared a laugh, but underneath that laugh was something intense, urgent. A jolt of desire flowed between us like an electrical current. She took the blouse off the rack and held it to my chest.

"This would look good on you," she said, but she wasn't even looking at the garment. Her eyes were locked with mine.

I said, "It would look better on you."

"Let's find out."

We found an empty stall in the fitting room and slipped inside. She was all over me the moment I had the door closed. She slid her hands across my hips and pulled me tight against her, lowering her mouth to mine. Her lips were soft, but the kiss was hard, eager, desperate even. I grunted and opened my mouth to her, letting her tongue dance over mine until we were both making needy, impatient sounds. The hands on my hips were determinedly sliding upward, pushing up my polo shirt until it was bunched under my arms. We broke apart long enough for her to pull the shirt off me then we were kissing again, her hand at my breast, my fingers tangled in silky flaxen hair. She groped my breast through my simple white bra, using the heel of her palm to knead a whimper. My fingers tightened around her mane.

Then the blond pushed me off her, breathing hard, cheeks flushed. Her lips curled into a smile that I returned. She took the peasant top off the hangar and helped me into it, slipping it over my head then turning me around so that we were both facing the full-length mirror on the wall.

I considered our reflection. The blond was a little taller than me, with blue eyes that sparkled under the fitting room's florescent lights. She had on a short-sleeved knit top that seemed to perfectly match the color of her eyes and a pair of loose-fitting khakis that I was eager to peel off her. Her gaze met mine in the mirror. The desire I saw in the reflection was mutual. She put her arms around me, one hand pressed against my belly.

"You look good," she said. Her voice became a breathless whisper in my ear. "Good enough to fuck."

I whimpered, pitifully, like a puppy wanting attention. Watching us in the mirror, I covered her hand with mine and guided it between my legs. The blond hummed in approval. She ground the butt of her palm into me, and I moaned in answer, leaning back into her.

The blond smiled at me in the mirror. "Are you wet for me?"

"Find out for yourself," I replied.

Hunger flared in her eyes. She unsnapped my black denim jeans and opened them just far enough to get her hand down the front. Fingers brushed over the crotch of my panties and I whimpered again, thrusting my hips at her, begging her to touch me. She laughed in my ear and eased her hand under the waistband of my panties, reaching in so that her fingertips glided over my slit.

"Mm," the blond purred. "You are wet."

The mirror let me stare into her eyes. "Please...please, go inside."

"Like this?"

The blond slid a little bit of her fingers into me, but I moaned like she had thrust in her entire hand. She slowly, gently moved her fingers in and out as if I would break. I sagged against her a little, eyes rolling back in my head. She panted in my ear.

"Open your eyes," she whispered. "Watch me fuck you."

I did what she wanted, staring into the mirror as she sunk her fingers into me. My face had turned a rosy pink. It was hard to breathe. I bit my lower lip with every thrust. The blond grinned, a playful, wicked grin that made me shudder with need. She plunged her fingers in deeper, moving harder, faster so that her thumb bumped against my clit. I wanted to shut my eyes, to lose myself in the warmth that crept through me, but I kept my gaze on the mirror, on the blond with her fingers wrenched up my cunt. Heat blossomed low in my belly, an almost painful twinge that made my cry out.

"You're going to come." It wasn't a question. "Watch yourself come for me."

I nodded. The blond smiled and started to nibble on my earlobe, her gaze never straying from our reflection as she pumped her fingers deeper, harder, faster, her thumb pressing down on my clit. I stopped breathing for a split second then my insides tightened and in a bursting surge I came all over her hand. My knees buckled. I would have slumped to the floor if the blond didn't have her other arm around me.

When I could stand on my own I turned in the blond's arms and kissed her, hotly, flicking her tongue with mine as if to give her a preview of things to come. She moaned against my lips, the arousal I heard making me want to flick my tongue over other places even more than I had before.

My hands went for the hem of her knit top. I hiked it up a little at a time until I had no choice but to rip my mouth from hers. We parted, gasping, and I lifted her shirt over her head just like she had done with me. She had lovely breasts, pale as cream and so inviting and on display in a frilly light blue bra. I buried my face in her cleavage, breathing in the scent of her until I felt lightheaded.

I managed to pull myself away from her and stood up, meeting her eyes briefly before stripping off the peasant top and handing it to her with a wry smile.

"Your turn," I said.

The blond smiled back at me. She put on the peasant top and modeled it for me, turning so I could get the full view. But I wasn't looking at that top the few minutes that her back was turned. She faced me again and looked at me expectantly.

"Well?"

"You are very beautiful," I said. It had nothing to do with the top.

The blond pulled me to her, and we were kissing again, hungrily, hands moving over each other at a frantic pace. She reached down and grabbed my ass. I answered by cupping her breast and giving it a gentle then a not-so-gentle squeeze. The blond moaned softly. The sound of rustling fabric and tiny gasps was all that filled the cramped little stall for the longest time, then the blond pulled back with a hard grunt and stared at me with such total want that I shivered like the temperature had suddenly dipped 20 degrees.

"I need your mouth on me," she rasped.

I nodded and sank to my knees in front of her. She started to open her pants but I finished the job for her and pulled down her khakis. The crotch of her cotton panties had a wet spot about the size of a quarter. I leaned into her and pressed my lips to the damp fabric. The blond groaned above me. I licked her through the crotch of her panties, dragging the tip of my tongue up and down the length of her cleft, teasing her. She sighed in obvious pleasure, but with an even more obvious frustration just under the surface.

I pulled aside the crotch, getting it out of my way. If I wanted to know if she was a natural blond, then I would have to ask because her pussy was perfectly smooth. I savored the musky scent of her arousal for a moment then pressed my mouth to her slit, kissing it, sucking on her puffy folds. The blond squealed with delight, hips moving against me as I went down on her. I dragged my tongue over her hairless slit just like I had done through her panties, but now I could dip my tongue into her, pushing inside. She gave a soft, muffled cry.

I lapped at her meaty folds, fucking her with my tongue, burrowing deeper and deeper until I was up to my ears in her wetness. Her whimpering little cries sounded distant. I could feel her cunt spasm around me in fits and starts, could feel the pressure of her climax building like a kettle on the boil. I used my fingers to peel back her cunt lips and exposed the glistening pearl that was her clit. I swirled my tongue around the hard little nubbin then pressed my lips to her clit and sucked it until her thighs quivered around my face.

I wrapped my arms around her legs and rested my cheek against her belly with a sigh, listening as her deep, heavy breathing slowed to normal. "I think that top looks good on both of us."

Fingers threaded in my hair. "Then I guess we'll just have to share it."

I liked the sound of that.

serena's return

M. J. Williamz

I sat back in my hot tub and looked at the stars. It was a clear, warm night, and I was so lost in my thoughts that I didn't hear my gate open.

I didn't even realize Serena was there until she began her descent into the tub. Damn, she was fine: tall, lean, athletically tight; yet so soft. As she slowly walked down the steps of the tub, each foot calculated, she allowed me to view every one of those soft spots that I had come to know so well. It had only been two weeks since we'd split up—two painful weeks without calling or seeing her.

She made her way toward me as lithe and graceful as a cat, not once taking her eyes off of mine. I could feel their piercing stare as I lustily took in that incredible body. It had been too long. I missed making love to her.

She waded across the hot tub and climbed onto my lap, facing me. My breath caught at the feel of her on me, of how at ease she was with the situation.

Somehow I managed to find my voice. "Are you sure about this?"

She took my face in her hands, pulling me to her, kissing me. Her lips opened, beckoning me. My tongue entered her mouth and hers immediately wrapped around it. She moved further up my thighs, pressing herself against me. I began to kiss down her neck, loving the taste of her, the feel of her skin under my lips. She arched her back as my mouth moved lower still, allowing me to claim her full, firm breasts. These breasts helped make her name as a model. And they used to be mine. Hungrily, greedily, my mouth moved over them. Kissing, sucking, nibbling. She arched further, pushing her secret paradise into me. She cupped her breasts together, freeing my hands for further exploration.

My arms slipped under her shapely derriere and slid her closer so her legs were straddling my waist. Her knees were bent, and I could feel her slick against me.

My hands enjoying her shapeliness, I held her against me and rubbed my curls against her as I took both nipples in my mouth. I was kneading and squeezing her and craving more. My hands moved up her underside until I found where I wanted to be. Spreading her lower lips, I easily slid my thumbs inside her. She released her breasts and grabbed my head, kissing me hard on the lips, her tongue dancing all over mine as she moved around on my thumbs.

The feel of her silky wetness wrapped around my thumbs only served to tease me. I had to have more of her. I removed my fingers and took her by the waist. Turning both of us around, I placed her on the hot tub's ledge. She lay back and dangled her legs over the edge—until I placed them over my shoulders so I could suck my way up her thighs until I found where they met. She was more than ready for me, her clit swollen in anticipation of my mouth on it.

I took her clit in my mouth and briefly sucked on it. I relinquished my hold and gave it one last little lick before my tongue moved on in search of the source of her milky nectar. I needed to be inside her, to taste her, to tempt her. My face was buried between her legs, my tongue deep inside her as she moved against me in a rhythm that was all our own. I pulled her closer yet, giving anything to be able to be deeper.

Her breath came in short gasps, letting me know I had her close. I was about to lose control myself, but I needed to take her to the edge first. I reluctantly moved away from my delicious snack and began to tease her clit with my tongue. It was so swollen and wet. I took it in my mouth again and sucked on it—hard—while my tongue lapped at its silky underside. My mouth released its grip and my tongue began its work in earnest.

She was bucking against me, holding my head in place, begging me for more pressure.

"Harder," She whispered.

"Oh..." she cried, closer still.

"Please," she whispered then, pleading for release.

My tongue worked at a frenzied pace. I knew exactly where she needed to be licked and I gladly did it as she got closer.

She was lost in the pursuit of orgasm and didn't notice that I had shifted positions slightly. I was so close to coming myself, that I had to do something to help. Since I was kneeling in the hot tub,

I figured the only way for me to get us both taken care of was to position myself in front of the jet. She didn't realize that my clit was being pummeled at the same time I was pleasing her.

She was writhing against me, hands firmly twisted in my hair, pushing me harder against her.

We were both frantic by then. She moved against me faster and faster until suddenly she jerked upward and cried out as the jets accomplished their mission on me, sending me crashing into an orgasmic free fall.

Slowly her movements against my tongue eased up. She released her grip on my head and lay there, satiated. I looked at her—legs spread, chest heaving—and I was in heaven. I climbed out of the hot tub and kissed her hard on the mouth, sharing her sweetness with her. My pulse raced as our tongues danced together once more, and I realized our evening had just begun.

vive la france!

Therese Szymanski

I had warned the tall blond what would happen if she went into the restroom before her girlfriend showed up. Her willing body and those private French embassy enclosures were too much for me to resist.

I watched her float across the room. She didn't look my way, but she lingered a moment at the open door, one shoulder rolling back in blatant invitation. I followed.

She went into the last stall, almost managing to close the door before I wedged my arm in, stopping it. She turned back in shock as I stepped through, sliding my arms around her waist and pulling her in close.

A shock of electricity flared between us as our tongues danced in each other's mouths. She feasted on my mouth like a woman starved. My hands enjoyed the feel of her curves, sliding over them before moving up to catch the zipper at the back of her dress and slowly pull it down. I put my beer on the floor by her feet.

Her skin was soft, and I caressed it for a moment. We didn't have much time, and I needed her naked. I raised my hands to catch the clasp on her bra between my thumb and forefinger and undid it with a single snap.

I threw her back against the door of the stall, which was more like a private toilet. The solid walls went from the floor to the ceiling, and the door was nice and thick. She would have to scream quite loud before anyone would hear her, especially since this room wasn't too popular at this almost entirely all-male gathering.

She stood at least a half-foot taller than I, but it didn't really matter. I wore the tie, and she wore the panties. I ground my thigh up into her crotch while I sucked on the luscious skin of her incredibly long neck, surrounded by the faint yet distinctive aroma of White Shoulders.

"Oh, God, no..." she moaned, half-heartedly trying to push me away.

I pulled her dress down, taking the bra with it, exposing her beautifully sculptured shoulders. I enjoyed the veritable banquet of soft flesh with my mouth before I reached up to cup her pale breasts, each topped with an already-hard perfect pink nipple.

I squeezed both nipples at once. She gasped in pleasure, breathing heavily into my neck.

I twisted them even harder.

She groaned even louder.

I kept squeezing one nipple, as hard as I could, and leaned down to take the other in my mouth. I was gentle at first, arousing the already hard nipple even further. My other arm was between her legs, my forearm pushed up against her cunt.

I could feel her wetness through my suit jacket.

I teased her nipple with my tongue, then started nibbling it, working my way up and down the hardened bud, gradually increasing the pressure of my teeth.

She moaned and arched against me, pushing into my mouth and against the hard muscles of my arm. I ran my arm up and down between her legs, rubbing against her.

She tangled her hands in my short hair and tried to push me down to my knees. I pulled my arm from between her legs and stood facing her. "Behave." I took her wrists in my hands and held them against the door over her head. She whimpered. I pushed my leg between hers, giving her the pressure she craved. She rode it like a pony.

I ran my hands down over her naked chest and pushed her dress to the floor. She wore panties and thigh highs underneath.

"Not here..." Her hands were again tangled in my hair.

My fingers found their way around her satiny underwear and into her wet, and she *was* wet. No matter what she said, she wanted it—hard, fast, and now.

Her knees trembled as she fell against me, but I knew she could stand for now, so I fell to my knees, pulled my switchblade out and cut her sodden panties.

I tossed them aside.

I stood, pulled her into my arms, and led her to the commode. It would break the mood if she were to fall onto the hard floor. I wanted to use my hands for things other than holding her up.

She sat, staring up at me. I pushed her back against the tank so her incredibly long legs stretched out in front of her. I ran my hands down over her naked, exposed form and knelt at her feet, as if worshipping her sex.

She was embarrassed and shy—after all, she was naked and I was still fully clothed—but she wanted it too much to let that stand in her way. She let her knees fall open so I could have my way with her.

I kissed her deeply again and pulled a sample package of lube out of my back pocket, opened it, and spread it all over my right hand.

I pushed her legs open further.

I reached between her legs and teased the swollen flesh there. I put first one finger, then another, into her while she sucked and bit my lower lip. I began caressing her clit with my thumb and she gasped, breaking off our kiss.

I attacked her neck with vehemence, biting and nibbling it all over. She wanted it hard and fast, and she'd get just that. I deliberately bit, wanting to mark my territory. Wanting her lover to know someone else had been there.

I grabbed her mouth again with mine, pushing my tongue in to caress hers, biting her lip...and then I pushed another finger into her wet pussy. And then a fourth.

She was warm inside. So warm. And accommodating. And she wanted me inside of her. Desperately.

I shoved my fist into her. She gasped in shock.

I twisted my fist around, clenched and unclenched it, feeling her warm, sweet flesh pressing against my hand, tightening around me...

I traced my tongue across her sweet collarbone, then down between her breasts...

My right fist was still trapped inside her, but my left hand was free to reach up and pinch a nipple, inciting yet another moan from my luscious blond fox. I released it to start caressing her entire breast, and I brought my mouth to the other.

I ran my tongue all over her breast, gradually drawing nearer and nearer to the erect nipple, until I grabbed it between my teeth and gave it a gentle tug. Up and down the nipple I bit...growing more intense with each bite.

She liked it rough and hard.

At least this time.

I yanked my fist out, and shoved it back in. Then I did it again, and again, and again, growing in ferocity with each push.

With each thrust she tightened, making the next thrust more difficult. With each thrust I increasingly thought she might break my hand.

It made it even more exciting.

God, she was fun to fuck.

I knew I could make her come the first time from just my fist alone. Well, my fist and my tongue and teeth on the rest of her body.

But when she was gasping for air and water after that, I knew she needed more. I brought my head down between her outstretched legs. I brought my tongue to her swollen clit with my fist still buried deep in her welcoming pussy.

She was sweet and heady and all the things my beer was not.

I licked up and down her hot cunt, enjoying her taste, reveling in what I was doing to her, and what I had done to her.

And what I was going to do to her.

I was not gentle.

I licked her clit gingerly, gradually increasing the pacing. Her moans were music to my ears, and I loved how she reacted to what I did to her. I sucked and licked the hardened apex of her clit, and pulled it into my mouth. Then I did it all over again, harder and faster and harder and faster, while still fucking her with my fist.

I loved that she gave herself to me. That she opened herself up to me. Let me do whatever I wanted to with her.

And, OK, fine, yeah, I loved her too.

But that wouldn't stop me from fucking her brains out.

And that I did do.

I pushed her thighs open even further. She was willing, and she liked it.

"Oh, God, yes! Yes!"

And I shoved my fist in again even further...almost crying out myself as she clamped down on it, squeezing me hard...

I kept on fucking and licking and sucking while she writhed and squirmed and called out my name. I kept on fucking and licking and sucking until she tried to push me away.

I gently removed my sore hand from her, and then I attacked her with my mouth again, taking her wrists in my hands to hold her in place while I ate her. While I went down on her again.

I loved the taste of her, I loved how her thighs squeezed my head tightly when she was about to climax, and I loved the way she ripped at my hair and frantically tore at my back.

I put my hands between her legs again and spread her lips open, giving me better access and making her feel impossibly more exposed.

I knew she had a few more orgasms in her for now.

I left the restroom before she did; after all it wouldn't do any good for anyone to see us leaving together. Especially not with the way I smelled of her. I killed my beer and went to get another. The French embassy really was a very nice place for a private group to rent for a party—there was lovely artwork on the walls and a wonderful grand piano in the foyer.

But this wasn't exactly my sort of shindig. There were only five other women present. I loved fags dearly, but I felt like a womon outside of Michigan at this party. I was only at it for my girl and her butch...

I saw the other butch enter and I greeted her: I gave her the official butch mode of greeting, actually—I tipped my head toward her and grunted.

But it was just after I got yet another beer that I noticed something even more interesting: She and the tall femme were now gone. So I looked for them. Oh, believe me, I looked for them. I went through the entire first floor of the embassy searching for them, with nary a clue—they were nowhere to be found.

Which meant one thing.

I rushed back to that solid door and pushed through.

All of the stall doors were open but one. I went to that one and listened for a moment. When I heard the familiar voice raised in a moan, I knocked.

Her dress was in a heap on the floor again, and she was

naked but for her thigh highs and heels. Shakily, she stood, as if trying to cover her nudity.

I met the other butch's eyes briefly, then turned to her. "I was hoping I'd interrupt the party." I closed the door behind me with a reassuring click and then locked it.

She was a lovely sight to behold, so tall and graceful. So feminine and alluring. So naked.

I leaned back against the door.

"Glad you could make it," butch said, pulling the tall blond into her arms. She kissed her.

For a millisecond, maybe, the sight was disturbing. Seeing my girl being kissed by another, being touched and held by another.

But I got over it.

I had been invited into their private party, and I wanted the same thing the other butch did: to please the blond, to make her moan, groan, and come. We both wanted to please her, give her pleasure.

And she had shown time and again that she could take it. She was made to be touched and stroked and caressed.

I stepped forward and touched the femme, running my hands lightly over her naked body. I felt her breasts, and then ran my hands over her inner thighs.

Both of us found her wetness at the same time. Together we caressed her pussy. She was still wet from me earlier, and I knew she was getting wetter by the touch now.

I glanced over at my big butch bro' and that was all it took. She pulled the blond up against her, away from the toilet, and I pressed against her back. She was sandwiched between us. As one, we pushed against her, hard.

She gasped, apparently realizing for the first time we were both packing. And maybe she also realized what we were about to do.

Her breasts were nice and full, and her legs so easy to push open even further. I kissed her sensitive neck and shoulders while the other kissed her mouth and collarbone.

She was moaning, pushing up against the other, drawing my hands up to her breasts and squeezing.

I loved giving her pleasure. I loved hearing her moan and squirm. We were in a public place, which made it all the more exciting.

I realized we were holding her up between us. She would fall without us.

I opened her even more. We both needed better access to her.

Her flesh was warm. Her pussy was hot. She never knew how much she could take, but we knew. We knew how far to push her, how many places we could take her when we took her like this.

What started off as a fling three years before had become so much more. She liked seeing her girl pleased, liked knowing she was happy—and maybe she even liked watching me fuck her and take her to the brink.

As one, we both undid our flies, pulling out our hard packs.

As one, we lubed ourselves, though she didn't need us to.

She trembled in my arms.

We both loved her.

She must've realized by now what we were going to do. She had made it quite clear that one area, and one area alone, of her body was not allowed.

I knew our clothing was rough against her skin, and that was part of the thrill for her. (Besides, we'd never let each other see us naked.) But I knew being in a threesome was a thrill for her, even still. Even after the half-dozen or so times we'd done threesomes.

I held her feet apart with my feet. I held her open for both of us. I caressed her ass and slowly felt down to her tight opening. Almost as one, we guided ourselves up into her.

I did it slowly, inching up into her ass, oh-so-slowly. She gasped. Her body writhed against the two large dildos entering her, as if trying to decide which was less of an intrusion, or which she wanted more.

She was naked and exposed, available, to whatever we wanted to do to her. I could stick it anywhere I wanted, and she couldn't do anything about it.

I pushed up further, causing her to gasp louder.

I could tell that another dick was also slowly working its way up into her. She was being slow and careful because she knew what I was doing.

I pushed.

As did she. We looked at each other, and then she pushed all the way in, causing the blond to groan out loud. "Oh, God, yes!"

So I pushed in all the way. "Oh, my fucking God!" she screamed.

I reached around her to run my fingers over her pussy. Then I plunged deeper to feel her wetness, to feel the tender flesh.

She was bucking under the steady thrum she was receiving from the other side, from the dildo being thrust into, then pulled out of, her pussy.

We braced her between us, holding her up, as we both fucked her.

We were as one, fucking her hard, riding her while we caressed her cunt, pinched her nipples, felt her stomach and breasts, pushed her legs open, held them open...

I ran my hands up and down her body as I pushed into and out of her, knowing that the other dick was pushing into her at the same time, knowing that at times we were both inside of her at the same time, totally filling her from both sides.

"God, God, yes, please, oh, God, fuck me, please, yes," she was moaning like a chant, practically delirious. Her ass was tightening against me, I could feel all her muscles tightening as I ran my hands over her body.

She had no idea what she was in for that first time she invited me into her bed.

I was hot and wet and sweating. Her skin was slick with her sweat. My hands slid easily over her.

"God, God, God..." She set our rhythm for us. One in, one out, one in, one out...we worked her body as one, as we always did...always taking her one step further...each time, something more...even when she pushed in and held her, I pulled out, then pushed in, reaching down to finger her...

Simultaneously, we fucked her then—in as one, out as one, more time in then out...fingering her and feeling her up...

We fucked her.

Good.

Deep.

She was ours.

down in back!

Heather Towne

One evening last week my girlfriend and I decided to blow off another dull night of studying by catching a cheap movie at the art-house theater just off campus. They were showing an uncut version of *Caligula,* and we thought, *Hey, what better way to learn about history?*

After snagging some popcorn, we plunked our tight little butts down in the back row of the almost-empty theater, and then watched with mounting wetness as sex scene after sex scene exploded on the screen in front of us. And when two gorgeous babes started tonguing each other, I felt my girl's greasy fingers slide under my tube top and squeeze my titties.

"Why, you horny little slut," I whispered at Carrie's darkened face, then slumped down lower in my seat so that her greedy hands could really feel up my tingling tits. We both had boyfriends who were also college students, but that never stopped us from an occasional lezzy session when the mood struck. Besides, our bods were too hot to be reserved exclusively for males.

Carrie is an energetic blond with green eyes, a pretty face, a pert set of tits, and a trim, athletic body that looks good clothed and better naked. I have dirty blond hair, hazel eyes, a curvy body, and medium-sized jugs. Put it this way: she's Britney and I'm Mandy Moore.

She pushed my tit-wrap up to my neck and fondled and groped my exposed boobs in earnest. I quivered at her touch, and heat spread from my cunny all the way through my body, as she kneaded my tits and rolled my nipples between her fingers. I moaned, my eyes glued to the big screen where the two well-endowed honeys were sixty-nining each other for all they were worth.

Carrie started sucking on my swollen nipples, slurping on my nubs, kissing them, tonguing them, biting them. I gripped the armrests and hung on. No one can do a girl's boobs better than a girl, and my bestest babe could suck orgasms out of my tits if she wasn't careful.

"You like?" she whispered, looking up at me and grinning, her hands on my tits, her tongue stretched out to tickle my nips.

I smiled shakily and said, "No one told you to stop, did they?"

She giggled, fed on my burning boobs for a while longer, then tugged off my shorts. I spread my legs, and my lips, and she brazenly shoved a finger inside of me. I yelped with joy. Ten rows down, a couple of heads swiveled around to see what all the commotion was about, but they soon turned back to the screen when the blond goddess getting cunny-spanked by her lover's tongue squeezed her gargantuan tits together and let out a riotous moan that filled the lusty theater.

Carrie shoved another finger into my bare, soaking wet cunny and started finger-fucking me. While her talented digits flew in and out of my steaming cunny, she grabbed my right tit with her left hand and pulled it back into her mouth. She swallowed almost my entire tit, her tongue slapping hard against my rock-hard nipple, her cheeks billowing in and out in a sucking motion.

"Mmm," I groaned, my head spinning, my overheated body going rigid as I careened way past the point of no return.

I stared glassy-eyed at the screen, as the two hotties faked mutual orgasms of mind-bending proportions. For me, however, it was no show. My body jerked and I bit down hard on my lip, muffling a scream, as a blazing orgasm tore right through me. "Yes!" I hissed through clenched teeth.

Carrie's fingers became a blur, her pussy-pounding intensifying to the frenetic, and her teeth bit into my nipple as I was ripped apart by multiple, white-hot orgasms. Pure, fiery, sexual joy flooded my body and turned me to jelly so that I was left trembling like a born-again lez.

Carrie pulled her dripping fingers out of my drenched cunny and stuck them in her mouth, slurping up my juices. "How 'bout giving me some luvin', missy?" she asked.

I shrugged. "Maybe sometime, bitch."

She pinched my nipple and we both burst out laughing.

More heads turned around this time, but we were slumped too low in our seats for anyone to see anything really good. I quickly got dressed and slid out of my seat and kneeled on the sticky floor in front of Carrie. I pulled off her shorts and tossed them down the aisle. Then I pushed her supple legs apart and buried my head between her thighs. I eagerly dipped my tongue into her slick cunny lips and tasted her wetness. She tasted good. I began lapping at her.

"Oh, yeah, sweetie," she purred, squeezing her tits with her left hand, while her right rested lightly on my bobbing head.

I started as far down as I could go—her tiny little asshole—and then licked all the way up to her clit in one long, flattened tongue motion, over and over and over again. Then I spread her puffy lips apart with my fingers and attacked her swollen bud with my mouth, licking, sucking, biting her ultrasensitive clit. In a mere matter of minutes, the poor girl was whimpering in sexual agony, begging me to bring her off.

"Fuck me with your tongue, you little cunt-whore!" she moaned fiercely, talking dirty like she always did right before she exploded.

Sure enough, she soon threw back her head and moaned the moan of exquisite orgasmic release. I gripped her thighs and fastened my lips onto her blossomed clit, sucking hard, grimly hanging on to her bucking body as she shuddered with orgasm after orgasm. She drenched my face with girl-juice, and I joyously drank it all in.

When she finally calmed down, just as the credits were rolling, I hastily kissed her lovebud one last time and then scrambled back into my seat. Carrie crossed her legs and pulled down her T-shirt, nodding an embarrassed yes when the usher asked if the shorts in the aisle belonged to her.

wham! bam! bam! bam! thank you, ma'am!

M. Damian

My predator instincts surfaced the minute I saw her come into the bar, laughing at something her friend was saying. I sauntered over and immediately knew I was going to fuck her that night.

We left the bar after one drink, my powers of persuasion easily detaching the woman I learned to be Taylor from her friends. We went to her apartment because it was the closest, but it was still far enough to make passion erupt as soon as I closed the door behind us. It took me less than five minutes to get her backed against the wall with her dress up, panties tossed aside, my fingers reaching as far as they could into her very core. Guttural moans escaped her lips, telling me how much she was enjoying the probing. Head thrown back, eyes closed, lips slightly parted as I churned my fingers around inside her, she whimpered, "Fuck me. Oh, please fuck me!"

Silently, I pulled my fingers out of her cunt and gently turned her around, making her lean with her hands against the wall, ass angled up and out behind her. Sexual anticipation was making my heart thud heavily in my chest as my hands roamed over her ass, her smooth skin like warm silk beneath my fingertips. She began wiggling her hips, her derriere swaying provocatively under my hot gaze.

Her teasing gyrations aroused me. I could feel my clit grow and swell to twice its size, its insistent throbbing urging me on. Eyes heavy-lidded with lust, I sucked on my middle finger until it was slick with saliva and slowly slid it down Taylor's ass crack, letting the tip linger briefly on her puckered hole. A throaty groan issued from my partner. "Oh, you're a back door gal, are you, darlin'?" I purred. "Well, your tight little rosebud is gonna have to wait because right now, your cunt has my full attention."

At my words, she angled her ass higher into the air, presenting her wet opening. I slid my finger in—she was wide open. Taylor moaned deep in her throat as I sank my digit inside her grotto. First with one finger, then with two, I fucked her with short plunging strokes, quick jabs in her pussy. Once or twice, I felt the walls of her vagina contract around my fingers, trying to imprison them. But my arm was pistoning in and out and her hungry snatch couldn't quite snatch my fingers.

My throat thick with burgeoning desire, I led her to the bed, sat her on the edge of the mattress, and then dropped to my knees in front of her. I ran my hands along the outside of her tanned and toned thighs, savoring their smoothness. "Mm," I murmured appreciatively, stroking, "as smooth as butter." I looked up. Taylor was hungrily staring down at me, lips parted, the tip of her pink tongue caught between her pearly whites. Wickedly, I teased, "Butter's made from cream, baby. Got any cream for me?" In answer, she lay back down, pulling her dress up over her hips with both hands.

And there it was in all its glistening glory.

I. Love. Pussy. Love to touch it, look at it, savor its aroma, and eat it. Taylor's was decidedly inviting—shaved, with pink pillowy outer lips splayed open to reveal pink-petal inner lips. Salivating, I lowered my head between her legs and my tongue became a cunt-seeking missile. Taylor thrust her hips slightly forward when she felt the first contact of my lips on her delicate skin, pressing her pussy against my mouth to ensure I got a mouthful of muff. My searching tongue bumped against a hot fleshy pebble; I gave her clit a teasing flick, gratified to hear Taylor's quick intake of breath, followed by her strangled groan of desire. My own clit was pleasurably torturing me, relentlessly pulsing against the seam of my jeans.

Cunnilingus—good cunnilingus—is an art. And I consider myself an artist. With long broad tongue strokes, I licked Taylor's gash up and down its entire length, thrusting into her moist, warm cavern. She grabbed my head and held it between her thighs, her hips convulsively starting to buck as my lips enveloped her engorged clit. Her sexual frenzy grew apace with my own as I sucked on her ruby teardrop. Sucking led to beating it up, down, and sideways with my tongue, inexorably bringing Taylor closer to orgasm. Sweat was pouring in my eyes—it was hot between her imprisoning legs, but my mouth kept working until with a last convulsive arch of her back off the bed, Taylor let out a wail, "I'm coming, baby, I'm c-o-o-o-ming..."

Her thighs slowly relaxed their hold, and her body grew limp. Satisfied with a job well done, I gave her satiated cunt a final kiss before leaning back on my heels. "Whew! That was quite a workout you gave me, girl. I hope it was good for you too," I chuckled.

"It was incredible," she gasped. "I can't move."

"Don't worry, darlin'," I quipped. "We have all night."

She took me at my word, and we shared a night of pure debauchery. Her strength returning, she got up from the bed, casually stripped off her dress and walked over to her bedroom closet. What she pulled out delineated how the rest of the night was going to be spent: an exquisite leather harness with a magnificent 'tool' dangling from it. It was a big cock, one with big veins and a velvety looking head that's designed for maximum pleasure. The thought of plugging her with that instantly made my clit stiff.

Crooking my finger, I beckoned her to where I sprawled lazily in a chair. Obediently, she came and stood before me, brandishing her weapon of pleasure. Knowing what I wanted, she handed me the harness and then undid my jeans and tugged off them and my Jockeys. She looked at me, her emerald green eyes sparkling. "Go for it," I invited softly. I slid down on my spine and opened my legs wide as Taylor sank to the floor. Her soft lips teased me as she kissed my lower belly, leaving a trail of fire as she dragged her tongue down to my cunt. I lost myself in the moment, savoring the feel of her face between my legs, her tongue lapping at my stiff clit.

After I came, Taylor licked me clean, making sure she didn't miss an inch between my legs and inner thighs. Now that she had gotten me off, my libido focused on her again. I wrapped my fingers around a handful of her thick chestnut hair and gave a gentle tug. She looked up. "Help me get this on," I said, nodding at the harness in my hand.

She responded with alacrity, securely strapping me in. The long, pale, thick stalk stuck out obscenely from its black tether. Wrapping her fist around its girth, Taylor simulated jerking me off as her tongue tangled with mine in burning kisses. After a few minutes, she knelt down and sucked noisily on my borrowed spear. I

99

watched as her head bobbed back and forth, deep-throating. When she left off, she got up and looked at me, commanding, "Here, right here. I want to ride you right here."

She climbed onto my dick, impaling herself on its length; her oral lube job letting it easily slide into her hole. Wrapping her legs around me, she slid up and down on her rubber joystick. I cupped her ass and felt the muscles in her cheeks tense every time she rode up, only to slide down and put its full 10 inches deep inside her. Pretty soon she was moaning in ecstasy. "I want to be fucked in my ass," she gasped, unwrapping her arms from around my neck. "Over the back of the couch."

We changed venues, leaving the bedroom and going back into the living room, but not without yet a different dildo from her closet. With practiced fingers, she slipped the big dildo out of the harness and replaced it with a smaller, smoother gel cock, lubing it with a generous amount of K-Y. Then she took a pillow and positioned it on the back of the couch, draping herself facedown over it. "Do it slow," she murmured. "I like it slow." Her puckered rosebud was my bull's-eye: Carefully, I opened her cheeks and nuzzled her bunghole with the head of the lavender-hued dildo. She let loose with a throaty groan when she felt that teasing gambit. "Fuck my ass, baby," she panted. "Slow. Make it last." I did as she requested—holding onto her hips, I slid the back-hole plunger up her asshole inch by inch and then plowed away, pushing in and pulling out slowly so she could enjoy every delicious centimeter of its length. I was getting so turned on by thrusting into her that I unconsciously began pumping faster.

"Stop," she suddenly gasped in a strangled voice.

"Too fast?" I asked, slowing down.

"Just stop," she said in the same voice.

I didn't know what was wrong as I pulled out. When we were disconnected, she got up and grabbed me by my horn, leading me back into the bedroom. Like a magician, she pulled yet a third toy out of her magic closet. The idle thought, *How many does she have in there?* skittered through my brain as she held this third appendage up to my view. "Use this one," she said. "This," emphasizing the word, "is my absolute favorite."

I could well believe the monster she held in her hand would be her especial pet. A generous thick nine-incher for her cunt, a sweet five inches for her ass and a clit tickler guaranteed to get her off. The thing had so many things sticking out of it that it looked like a mini-Medusa. "And I only use it with women who can handle it." She paused provocatively. "Because I get absolutely wild."

Clever bitch—her words were both an enticement and a veiled challenge. "Strap me in, baby," I confidently riposted.

"I like this," I breathed into her ear several minutes later. "I like fucking you this way—face-to-face."

She was underneath me, my triple-endowed dildo working simultaneously in her front and back holes with the tickler stimulating her clit. Her hands were above her head, languidly resting on the pillow as our bodies fused together. I moved slowly, wanting her to really feel what I was doing to her. *I* wanted to feel what I was doing to her. Never had I experienced such eroticism, such power, or such dominance. My clit jumped each time I surged forth, my arousal adding to my enjoyment. I kissed her neck, sucked on her earlobes, breathed lightly into the delicate shells of her ears, and rubbed my hard nipples against her stiff knobs as my hips undulated slowly, the three-headed pleasure-monster gliding in, out, and smoothly against her.

She gasped with pleasure when I pushed the triple-prong into her, uttering small moans of despair every time I eased out. "You like this, baby? You like what I'm doing to you?" An appreciative sigh was my answer. My own cunt was running with juice; I could feel it seeping out. I kept up a small patter of dirty talk: "You want me to fuck you, baby? You want my cocks as deep as they can go? Huh? That what you want?" She nodded her head at my words, her silk hair whispering on the pillowcase.

I was crazy with desire to fuck her brains out. Rising up, I supported myself stiff-armed and started thrusting deeper, faster. I could hear the sucking noises as the dildo's two heads went in and out of her pussy and ass. Taylor wrapped her long legs around my hips, her arms around my neck. I strained to push as much of my cocks as far as I could into her. I started pumping faster, and Taylor moved her pelvis upward to meet my thrusts. I could feel the veins in my neck standing out like cords as I used all my strength to give this bitch under me the fuck of her life. My grunts blended with her sharp cries. I heard her cunt squish with juice every time I plowed into her.

A burning sensation suddenly seared my back—Taylor was dragging her claws across my skin, flaying me alive. Her passion was at its zenith: There was no release for her except to explode in orgasm. I kept up my relentless rutting of her cunt and ass, knowing the clit tickler was doing its job by the way she began thrashing about under me. I screwed my eyes closed in intense concentration as I screwed my dicks deeper inside her. In, out, in, out, in...

A long low-pitched wail rent the air as her body writhed in climax. Words were beyond her. I stayed where I was, triumphantly savoring her orgasm with her, the orgasm *I* had brought to her. Being with her had been my most intensive fuck session ever. When I was able, I pulled out of her and slid my sweat-slicked body off hers. She turned into my shoulder and rapidly fell asleep.

blonde on a harley

Teresa Noelle Roberts

The first time I saw Aria she was leaning over her Harley to get something out of her saddlebag. All I saw were leathered chaps and jacket, a gorgeous butt and a long blond braid. That was enough to make me want to do her on the spot, leaning on the big purple and chrome beast. But it took a while to set up, even after she proved to like little femmes with big attitudes and a penchant for whips as much as I liked using my whips and attitude on leather-clad butches. First I had to borrow a friend's mountain cabin, then convince Aria to take me up there on the back of her bike.

When we got to the cabin, I left her fussing over the Harley and went in to change: black leather bustier; short, flippy black skirt; and under it, her favorite big blue strap-on.

Aria was wiping off every speck of dirt, mud or dead bug that had hit the bike during the ride. Her meticulous cleaning served me well. I waited until she was looking away and bent over, and then grabbed her from behind, cupping her breasts and biting down on the sensitive spot on the back of her neck. She dropped her chamois in surprise, made a noise somewhere between a purr and a growl, and tried to stand up to press herself closer to me.

I took one hand away from her breasts long enough to gently push her back down, leaning on the seat. "Oh, no," I said, speaking deep in my throat, "I like you in that position." She drew in her breath sharply, and she made some changes in her body language to suit the way things were heading. From a tough, capable woman working on her Harley, a woman who could bench-press me, she became a supplicant at an altar of metal and leather. Her back arched, she spread her legs more and bowed her head. I could imagine her cunt blossoming with anticipation, as I know mine was. If the strap-on were a flesh-and-blood cock, it would have been pointing to heaven.

"Very good," I breathed, and pinched a nipple hard. Sometimes a slow build is good, but sometimes we both liked it if I treated her more abruptly. Her reaction told me that it was one of the latter times, so I began pulling and twisting the other nipple. After a bit of clothed torment, I opened her flannel shirt and unhooked her bra. I thought of having her stand long enough to get them out of the way, but decided that the shirt, pulled forward and inside out past her head, made a decent makeshift bondage device. I wrapped the ends around her hands and tied them. She could have wiggled out of it, but I knew she wouldn't.

One of nature's ironies is that I have Victoria's Secret-made cleavage, but Aria, who lives in baggy shirts, has full, delicious breasts with big nipples. They were still marked from earlier play: a few bite marks from the night before, an almost-healed bruise from a mock punishment. I'd used the crop on her breasts that time to see the combination of fear and longing on her face. They weren't my primary target today, but I thought they could use more attention.

I drew a set of tweezer-style nipple clips from their hiding place inside my halter and put them on her. "Damn, you look great in those. I should keep you in them all the time."

"Sounds good to me," Aria said, an insolent gleam in her eye. That's my darling—she sounds cool right up to the point when her brain melts and she can only scream. It makes her eventual surrender even more exciting.

The fact I enjoy her insolence didn't mean I didn't respond by giving her breasts two sharp slaps, setting them jiggling and making the clips pull even more. She would have been disappointed if I hadn't.

"Ye-s-s-s," she hissed through clenched teeth, and I knew that the jolts of erotic pain were making her hot and wet. This was a notion that required further investigation.

I will spare you the details of peeling her jeans and underpants off while leaving the chaps in place. Suffice to say that after a little struggle and a lot of giggling, I had her how I wanted her: wearing chaps and blond hair while bent over 500 pounds of Harley. I circled the bike several times, enjoying the sweep of her now-unbraided mane as she leaned forward, her dangling breasts pulled down by the weight of the silver clips, her defined arm and leg muscles flexing as she maintained position, and best of all, the contrast between the pale heart shape of her ass and the black leather surrounding it. Normally, even in bondage and feeling her most submissive, Aria looks about as physically vulnerable as a Clydesdale. Maybe it was being naked and objectified outdoors, or turning into a stereotyped Fantasy Biker Babe instead of the person in charge of the gleaming hunk of Harley, but something opened in her. She was trembling, not exactly from fear, yet there was a little fear in her eyes. Her pussy gleamed with moisture in the afternoon light, the tufts of pubic hair I could see darkening and clumping from her juices. She looked so good, wet and vulnerable like that, but she wasn't far enough gone yet. I wanted her utterly helpless with desire before I fucked her.

I put back on my black leather riding glove and slapped her ass. Her reaction was instant and gratifying—she hissed and arched her body up even more to meet my hand. I continued slowly and steadily at first, a sensuous warm-up until her butt was a uniform pink. Then I followed with a quick flurry of blows that made her squirm away and quickly wiggle back to meet my hand. Her noises were equally confused, either pained gasps or deep, throaty moans depending on whether her brain or her body was in charge. Her body knew what it wanted, though; her juices were oozing down her legs by the time I deemed her ass was red and hot enough for the next step.

I didn't have a crop or cane with me, but the nearby shrub sacrificed a branch for the cause. I tested it on my thigh—stingy but not deadly. Then I made her kiss it. Her eyes widened and, incorporated with the reddened, ravaged face and the blond hair falling around her, she looked like an intoxicated angel. Shame I couldn't watch her face as the blows fell, but I'd seen her ecstasy faces often enough that I'd be able to imagine. "You're doing great," I said, and kissed her. The wave of lust and tenderness almost undid me, but I knew it would be worth finishing out the scene for the eventual payoff. "Ten stripes," I said. "You'll count them for me, and if you're brave and don't whimper, you'll be rewarded." I knew I'd reward her in any case, but I wasn't about to tell her that.

I moved into position and let loose with the first blow, a very controlled, light one. It left a faint line, nothing that would last. "One," she said with a pretty quiver in her voice.

Again, at the same level. "Two."

Three, four, and five were a little heavier, leaving a clearer stripe behind and making her voice sound both shakier and more excited.

"The last five will be harder. Are you ready?" She nodded as if she were too overcome to speak. The silvery trail of moisture headed down toward her knees.

The cane whirred. "Six," she yelped as a fierce stripe formed. That one might last. Number seven was harder yet, right at the edge of what I thought she could take, but she surprised me. Her "Oh, God—seven!" was not in the voice of someone about to safe-word.

"Are you going to come from being caned?"

"If it pleases you, unless you'd rather I didn't," she whispered, and I knew from the whisper and the ultrasubmissive response that she was at the peak of heat, ready to fly if I let her.

"Oh, it pleases me all right, when I tell you to." I whistled the cane down with great, cutting force—about an inch from her butt. Her reddened skin jumped and twitched, and so did her cunt. "Next one is on your ass, sweetness," I said. And it was, although I pulled the blow so she got the full impact of the whistling, but not of the cane. Nine and 10, almost as hard, fell in the sweet spot where her ass and thighs met. "Come for me now," I urged with the last one, and she roared wordlessly to the blue sky, throwing her head back, breaking position for the first time. She came so hard I swear I felt it too.

I gave her a quick hug and told her I loved her, then told her, "Bend over for your reward." We were both still riding the waves of her orgasm as I slammed into her with the strap-on.

It amazed me, as it always does, how wonderful her burning ass felt against me. Between that sensation and a bucking, twitching, contracting pussy, I wondered absently how male tops managed to stay in control long enough to ride their subs to the finish. I could gauge her reactions through the movements of the dildo as she gripped against it, and just knowing how hot she was, how much she was enjoying being fucked didn't do much to change how it rubbed against my clit, but it certainly affected my brain.

I'd wanted to play it out, but the long buildup had gotten me just as excited, and I found myself pounding into her, stroking her clit with one hand to make sure she didn't stop coming and grinding with each thrust to bring myself off.

I came with a cry that probably startled every bird for miles. I don't think Aria had ever stopped coming—she certainly hadn't stopped moaning—but as I built to my own finish, she made a few noises I'd never heard before from her.

It was pure dumb luck that the Harley didn't start to wobble until we were slumped against it trying to get enough energy back to move somewhere more comfortable. We got energized at that. In fact, I moved about as fast as I ever have in my life to help her steady it before it went over. When it was stable, she looked at me and said, "You know, it would have been really bad if it had fallen. Worst case it might have broken the faring, and at best it would have been hell on the paint job. You should have thought of that before we started jostling it like that."

I was about to make a reasonable answer, such as, "I should have known? But you're the one who knows about motorcycles!" but she stopped me with a kiss.

"But since nothing bad happened, I'll just see to it that you make some restitution for the risk to my bike." Her smile suggested that my little sub might just be a switch after all.

It's been a long time since I played on the other side. I imagine that will be another story.

library licentiousness

Rachel Kramer Bussel

I notice her as my eyes survey the avid readers seated at my home-town library. I've come here for a brief respite from the endless parade of familial concern and comestible offerings, figuring that innocent books can't possibly drive me as mad as my family. But just as I settle down in a chair with a beloved classic, I'm distract-ed by this girl, who seems like the answer to one of those "Which of these things is not like the other?" puzzles.

I can't help but check out her extreme buzz cut, studded belt, white T-shirt that clings to her breasts, short plaid skirt, and most of all the look of defiance on her face as she scans a local magazine and imbues the act of reading with all the hostility she can man-age. She looks nothing like the other patrons in their white shorts or flowered shirts, their suburban ease and casual browsing. No, she looks like she has a purpose, a mission, that transcends our lit-tle library. Her thoughts are radiating out into the world, and it's clear that she'd rather be anywhere else, preferably far, far away from this stifling little suburb.

I stare at her for another moment, then look away. I settle into a chair, settle in with my naughty novel, but after several pages of incomprehension I stop, realizing the futility of my attempts. I can't concentrate with this vixen in the room. She is reading a mag-azine and writing in a notebook alternately, mad fast-paced scrib-bles that blanket the pages in angry ink. I leave my bag and my dirty book and casually stroll over toward the magazine section where she's sitting. As I skim the bland, mainstream titles, I hear a voice ask, "Excuse me, do you have a cigarette?"

I turn and stare into that impish face close up. Now that I'm close to her, she looks incredibly young. She could be in high school, or just out of it. And, unfortunately, I don't have a smoke for her, haven't smoked since *I* was 15. I rarely miss it, but at this moment I sure wish I had one.

"I'm sorry, I don't. But if I did, I'd give you one," I say, hoping I'm not making a total fool of myself. She smiles back, a bit shyly it seems, and I keep browsing. I try to spy unobtrusively over my shoulder at her notebook, but she turns around and stares back up at me with her big blue eyes, seeking some hidden meaning, a covert approval.

"Do you want to take a walk and get some smokes? I could use a soda." She just nods, gathers her bag, and saunters after me. As we round the corner of the library, her ass twitches under the plaid as she walks, taunting me. I grab her backpack to stop her walking and then push her further along the walkway so we're in a secluded area against the side of the building. Her back is against the dusty brick, her thighs revealed as she squirms slightly. "So, just how old are you, anyway?" I ask, leaning in so my knees are pressed against hers.

"Old enough," she says. "I'm in college," with just enough bratty pride that I believe her.

I lean forward and tug on her ear with my teeth before whispering, "And what is it that you're learning there?" I don't give her time to answer before my tongue finds its way to her neck, licking back and forth while she squirms under my attention. My hand reaches up to cup her breast, and her nipple is already hard and ready. "How to flirt with older women in front of the whole town? Or how to wear clothes that are much too sexy for a library? Like this belt, for instance," I say, fingering the metal studs as I undo the clasp. I finally get it undone and hold its weight, swinging it lightly in the air. I bring my hand under her skirt, feel the wet warmth of her panties against my knuckles. "What am I supposed to think about a girl who wears a belt like this?"

I pull back to look at her, to make sure she really wants this. She stares back, blue eyes steady, desiring. "I think what you're trying to say with this belt is that you want someone to teach you a little lesson. Turn around for me." She turns so quickly I know I've pegged her correctly. That used to be me, staring after all the older girls I was dying to get into bed with, waiting plaintively until one of them noticed me, too shy to ask for what I really wanted but thrilled beyond belief when someone saw my need lurking just under the surface. I don't seek them out, but these kinds of girls seem to find me, strutting their queerness on the outside but shaking on the inside. Facing the wall, she turns her head and presses her cheek against the hard surface, her ass curving out toward me. I reach around her, bringing my hands up under her shirt and stroking her nipples again. She presses back against me, squirming, eager.

I lift the skirt to peek at her perfect ass, molded against her thin black panties. There is something so gorgeous about a woman's ass, the way it curves and bends, rises and falls, seemingly begging to be touched. Hers certainly is. I grab a chunk of this heavenly flesh and squeeze, feeling a tingle run through my whole body. "You have such a beautiful, sexy ass, it just makes me want to feast on it." She moans in response, and I squeeze harder. I run the nonstudded side of her belt over her curved flesh, and I can practically feel the need radiating from her skin. I drape the belt over my shoulder, and then, while keeping her skirt lifted, bring my hand back and spank her. She lets out a little whimper, and I do it again, harder this time.

I grab her by the back of her neck, turn her head slightly toward me. "Is that what you want, little girl? Is that what you write about in that little notebook of yours?" I see something change in her eyes, some kind of respect, a bit of fear that I've read her so well. I don't say anything else. I let go of her hair and reach down for her backpack, pawing through it till I find what I need. I pull out a slim hardcover library copy of *The Story of O,* heft it back, and bring it crashing onto her ass. It's not quite the best implement for the job—it thuds and doesn't have the stinging effect I'd like—but I don't mind. Another time we can try the belt.

I keep spanking her for what seems like a long time, with every other smack glancing around to make sure nobody sees us using library books for rather unintended purposes. I stop when her ass is a shiny red, like an apple, then lean down for a juicy bite. My teeth leave tiny marks that I'm sure will be gone very soon but for now they glisten there amid my saliva. I bite and lick, covering every red inch with my tongue, letting the skirt drop around my head but too far gone to care if anyone were to see me.

I finally pull myself away from her delicious ass and lean my weight against her, the belt, dangling over my shoulder, pressing lightly into her back. I blow on her neck, nuzzle my cheek against the fuzz that dusts the back of her head. "If you liked that, meet me back at the library, same seat, same time, a week from today, and we can try it again." I lean back and then start to walk away. Curiosity gets the better of me and I sneak a look behind me. She's trying to look cool and suave, like this happens to her every day, but I see the smile hinting around her lips, waiting to burst forth and let the world know just how bad she can be.

And I know my mom will be happy. I'm going to be coming home a lot more often from now on.

just the three of us

Nicky Donoghue

When the cab arrived outside the bar, we piled into the backseat and gave the driver Kelly's address. "You can crash on my couch," she said. "I'll make sure you get home in the morning." My head was spinning a little, so I agreed.

It was about a 15-minute cab ride to Kelly's, so we three drunken fools made idle chitchat, talking about the women at the bar and how I'd been single way too long. Kelly and Cathy were groping each other a little, caressing each other's thighs and such, and I was getting turned on watching them. "Like what you see?" Cathy said through a big smile. I just nodded, then Kelly started stroking the inside of my blue-jeaned thigh. If I hadn't been drunk, I probably would have protested, but I'm not sure. These girls were both gorgeous: Cathy a high femme with shoulder-length red hair and Kelly a soft butch with short golden-brown curls. I fell somewhere in the middle: an average-looking tomboy with short dark-brown hair. Kelly shoved her hand up the back of my shirt and massaged the skin there. I felt a puddle of wetness between my legs, and I was glad when the cab pulled up to Kelly's apartment.

Kelly paid the driver, and we all tumbled out. When we got inside her place, Kelly and Cathy just grinned at each other. They both grabbed my arms and led me to Kelly's bedroom. "We've been wanting this for a while, Nicky," Cathy purred. "Mm-hmm," Kelly echoed.

They wasted no time getting my clothes off, pulling my sleeveless Tee over my head and unfastening my bra. Kelly helped Cathy out of her little black dress, and Kelly pulled off her own clothes in no time. They hopped onto the mattress with me. There we were: three naked women in a bed, the smell of whiskey and cigarettes surrounding us. Kelly started sucking on one of my tits as Cathy went down on me. She circled my clit with her tongue and probed my hole with two fingers. Kelly bit and nibbled on one of my breasts, groping the other with one of her large hands. I looked up at the ceiling in disbelief as I gripped the sheets beneath me. As

Cathy ate me out, Kelly moved up to my mouth and kissed me hard on the lips. She took off my glasses and set them on the nightstand, then ran her tongue down the length of my body. When she got down to my crotch, which Cathy was still going to town on, she lifted Cathy's head gently and kissed her. "I can taste you on Cathy's mouth," Kelly said to me, which made me so hot I thought I would come right there.

Just then, Cathy repositioned herself and put two fingers inside me. She slid them in and out, then added a third. "I can tell you like this," she said. "You're so hot and wet. It's like a waterfall in there." She pulled out her fingers and put them in her mouth, licking off my juices, and then ran her fingers over her full, gorgeous lips. "And you taste so good." She put her fingers back inside me and increased her speed and force. Kelly sat on the bed and watched, groping one of her breasts and furiously rubbing her clit. I didn't know who to look at: Cathy who was fucking me hard and fast or Kelly who was masturbating and looked just beautiful in the lamplight. So I alternated my gaze between the two, getting wetter and more turned on by the second.

"Fuck this," Kelly said, then climbed on top of me, straddling my face as Cathy slid her fingers in and out of me. I felt my pussy clench her fingers, and there was a wonderful, sweet pounding in my clit and cunt. As Cathy fucked me, I ate Kelly out like she was my last meal ever. Her pussy was sopping wet, and tasted sweet and tangy. I focused my attention on her hard bud, which I took into my mouth. I licked under the hood and around her clit, then flicked it back and forth with my tongue. I slurped on it as I continued to flick it, then moved down and licked her hole. Kelly gripped the headboard as I tried to jam my tongue in, but I couldn't get it in all the way, so I just licked the perimeter of it, then moved my mouth back up to her clit.

Just as I did this, Cathy went down on me again and licked and sucked me into ecstasy. Kelly and I cried out in pleasure at the same time. She climbed off me, and as a huge orgasm traveled through my body, I watched as Kelly shivered and shook with the effects of her own climax. It was a sweet sight to watch this beautiful butch in so much pleasure.

Kelly and Cathy and I went at it for a couple of hours. But

toward the end of the night Kelly seemed to get a little jealous because Cathy was paying me so much attention and practically ignoring her. So after a while, she asked me if she could call a cab to take me home. Cathy protested, though, so we all fell asleep in the bed together, in a drunken haze, smelling like pussy and cigarettes and bourbon.

in hot water

Anna Avila

I crammed my stuff in my locker and locked the door. Chris led me to one of the showers, and we both entered and drew the plastic curtain closed. Thankfully, the locker room was fairly empty, so I don't think anyone saw us go in together.

Immediately Chris peeled off my sweaty tank top and sports bra. She swooped in on one of my nipples, which was hard and begging for her hot mouth. Without any words, she worked that nipple good and hard, taking it into her wet mouth and feasting on it, licking it all over, making little slurping noises. Just then she pulled back and grabbed both of my breasts in her hands, kneading them like bread dough. She gazed straight into my eyes, and the look on her face was like that of an artist concentrating on her work, admiring its beauty and form. She continued to caress and massage my breasts as she leaned in and kissed me hard on the mouth. She was full of urgency, of lustful need, and I was obliging her with no qualms. "You're so fucking hot," she said between kisses. "So fucking hot."

Her tongue was forceful and wanting, and I opened my mouth even wider to let it in. She ran it over my lips, my tongue, bit my lower lip playfully.

I helped her out of her wifebeater, then grabbed both of her small, firm breasts in my hands. (She wasn't wearing a bra.) Her nipples were dark brown and very hard and erect. I pinched one of them, teased it with my fingers, and she cried out softly before I licked and sucked it. Then she rammed her hand down my sweat-drenched shorts, teased my clit through my underwear. It was hard for me to tell how wet I was, because I was so sweaty. I remember a definite sweet odor in the air of sweat and come and saliva, though. The air was tinged a little with chlorine, which wafted in from the pool that was adjacent to the locker room.

Through my underwear, I felt Chris locate my clit and tease it with her fingers. My clit was throbbing now, so much so that I couldn't stand it anymore, so I grabbed her hand and shoved it under my panties. She rubbed my drenched pussy—up and down, up and down. I positioned her hand over my shorts so that it was right on my clit and moved her hand in circles. As she continued to work my red-hot clit, I looked at her body: sculpted, tan, and hairless. She was absolutely gorgeous, with rock-hard abs and firm biceps. "Yeah, baby, like that," I groaned, and I heard a light smacking sound of her fingers and my pussy juice and my clit all moving in rhythm together. "Faster, faster," I said as quietly as possible, so that no one would come in and bust us.

Just then, Chris yanked down my shorts and underwear and turned me around so that I was facing the shower wall. I knew where this was going, and I was thrilled: She was going to fuck me from behind. I braced my hands against the wall and stuck my ass out toward her. She grabbed my left thigh and slowly put what felt like two fingers inside me. I felt my cunt walls expand and then contract around her fingers, and I heard a slurping sound as she fucked me hard and fast. Her left hand moved up to my ass, squeezed it, then slapped it lightly. "Yeah, that's it. Oh, my God," I told her.

"You're so wet. You feel so good, like silk," Chris responded. She moved her mouth down to my ass and nibbled and kissed it forcefully as she slid her fingers back and forth. I looked over my shoulder and saw her get down on her knees. As she kept finger-fucking me harder and faster, she buried her face into my ass and started to lick my asshole. I'd never had a woman do that to me before, but I eagerly welcomed her warm, wet tongue there. My entire body was electrified, and I swear I saw tiny stars before my eyes. Just then, I guess she located my G spot, because I felt like I was going insane. Blood filled my hard clit, my entire cunt, and my fingers and toes were tingling. Chris massaged my G spot forcefully. "I wish I had my dick with me," she said. "I'm not properly equipped."

I could only grunt in response. But then I mustered up some words: "Right there. Please. Keep doing that."

My hole was gushing now, and I kept hearing those wet smacking noises—which turned me on uncontrollably for some reason—and felt Chris's strong hand grip one of my ass cheeks. Just then, she brought me over the edge, which was like wave after wave hitting a sun-drenched shore. Hot ripples coursed through my body, and my cunt was pounding in a combination of exquisite torture and pleasure. "Oh fuck, oh fuck, oh fuck," I moaned, and my entire body shook with release.

Just then Chris slowly pulled out her fingers, stood up, and turned me around. I grabbed her sweaty head and pulled it toward mine, ran my fingers through her wet, dark hair, and kissed her passionately. I kissed her neck, her beautiful collarbone, placed tiny sweet kisses on her forehead and the bridge of her nose.

"Are we still on for tonight?" Chris smiled as she took my breasts in her hands again.

"Yeah, but instead of going out to dinner, let's eat in."

"My place?"

"Exactly what I had in mind," I said with a devilish gleam in my eye. And that's just where we went.

my personal touch

Marla Carter

"Follow me," Jackie said, and went into the ladies room. She locked the door, then turned her gorgeous face toward mine. She reached into her purse and pulled out a fat blue dildo. "I'm sure a stud like you knows what to do with this."

"No problem," I said as I reached for her beautiful body.

"You got it wrong, girl," she said, pulling away from me. "I want to watch you use this on yourself."

"What? You've got to be kidding me." She was so tasty I wanted to eat her up, and what did she want from me? She wanted me to put on a damn show for her.

Just then she pulled out the WNBA tickets I wanted so badly. "Remember these? Come on, baby, show me what I want to see and they're all yours."

I was so turned on just looking at her that the thought of that big blue prick inside me sent shivers all over my body. *All right,* I thought. *I'll give her what she wants.*

I stood against the wall and pulled down my shorts and underwear. I left them around my ankles. Then I spread my pussy lips apart and slowly pushed the cock inside. The dark curls near my labia were glistening with my juices. I started out slow at first, taking the long dick inside me centimeter by centimeter. I looked over at Jackie as she stood there with a milewide smile. Then she licked her bottom lip and said, "Yeah, just like that. Now finger yourself too."

I did as instructed, placing two of the fingers of my left hand on my warm, hardening clit. "Push it in farther," she demanded, her voice a little huskier now.

Again, I followed her order and slipped the dildo in farther and deeper, the whole time circling my clit with my other hand. Jackie kept licking her lips, then she put her hand down her panties and started jacking off while watching me get off. I had no idea watching someone do that could get me so horny. My vagina was throbbing, my clit pounding, and I could tell she was totally turned on. She kept groaning and moaning and saying things like, "Yeah, that's it. That's the spot. Sweet kingdom come." I didn't know if this girl was crazy or just a horny bitch, but right then I didn't care, because that cock was so far inside me, and I felt powerful knowing I could drive a woman wild without even touching her. But man, did I want to reach out and touch her, grab those juicy tits in my hands, lick her sweet pussy, dine on her whole body.

I closed my eyes and thought about doing just that, as I kept pounding myself with that dirty little dildo and rubbing my hot love bead over and over. I thought about doing this fine woman from behind, poking her hard with the very same cock I was using on myself. I thought about taking her titties in my mouth and licking and biting her dark-brown nipples. I imagined burying my face in her sweet, sweet cunt as she straddled my face and cried out, "Marla, oh, God, Marla."

I opened my eyes and saw her with her hand still down her pants; she was up against the wall, writhing and moaning, and her hand was moving quickly. Just then she cried out, "Woman, you are too much," and her body shook with release. That was enough to bring me over the edge. I felt blood flowing hot and heavy throughout my body; my nerve endings were on fire. I was sweaty and my pussy was practically squirting out juice. As that powerful orgasm rolled through me, I pulled out the dildo. Jackie grabbed it from me and put it in her mouth, giving it a hot and heavy blow as I kept circling my clit with my fingers. Just then it was too, too much, because I cried out, "Oh, shit," then practically fell into a heap on the floor.

Jackie pulled me up with her strong hands, then kissed me tenderly on the neck. "Here you go, doll." She handed me the tickets as I pulled up my panties and shorts. "And there are plenty more where these came from."

I didn't regret hooking up with Jackie one bit. And, truth be told, the sex with my girlfriend that night was hotter than I'd imagined possible. Still, when we were doing it, I kept thinking about Jackie watching us. I envisioned her sitting in the corner of Trina's bedroom, looking on as I pumped her pretty pussy, saying, "Yeah, that's it. That's the spot."

I guess that's why I came back to her for more.

a very good morning

Melinda Johnston

Molly awoke to feathery kisses on her cheek. Still half-asleep, her eyes closed, she turned her head to meet Jane's lips. They kissed deeply, and Molly tried to wrap her arms around Jane.

She couldn't.

"What the?" she mumbled, still disoriented, and tried to squirm around. It took a moment before the situation penetrated her sleep-addled head. She was tied up, spread-eagle, and completely at the mercy of her lover.

Molly squeezed her eyes shut, shook her head slightly and opened them again.

Then gasped. In the moment she'd taken to figure out her situation, Jane had shifted position. She was now kneeling over Molly, her knees on either side of Molly's shoulders so that her wide-spread cunt was just inches above Molly's face.

"Mmm," Molly moaned and inhaled her lover's rich, delicious scent. God, she loved that smell. She never wanted to shower after sex with Jane. She loved to keep that aroma on her body as long as she could. When they went out, she always wanted to dip her hand down Jane's leather pants and dab her scent behind her ears. Now her senses were filled with it.

She could see how wet Jane was, and her own cunt stirred and began to drip in response. She looked into Jane's eyes.

Jane trailed her hand along Molly's cheek, then gently ran her fingers over Molly's mouth. Molly's tongue reached out and licked her index finger, which Jane promptly inserted into Molly's open mouth. She sucked on it, tasting the slight salt of Jane's flesh. Jane withdrew her finger, ran it through her own slit, and licked it off. Molly's jaw dropped and her mouth watered.

With a disdainful look on her face, Jane twined her fingers in Molly's hair, slightly pulled her head back, looked deep in her eyes, and growled, "Now get to work." With that, she lowered herself onto Molly's waiting mouth. Jane tasted a little like pineapple. She licked deeply, running her tongue along Jane's slit, briefly entered her, went up to Jane's clit, circled it, slid back down, entered her again, pulled it out, and licked Jane's clit hard. Jane groaned. Molly licked her in rhythm, from clit to vagina and back. Jane was getting wetter, and Molly gladly drank her down.

Jane hadn't touched Molly at all, and Molly was aching for it. She could feel the throbbing in the tips of her breasts and cunt while little shoots of electricity spread across her body. She writhed, trying to rub her legs together, against the sheets, anything to get stimulation. But there was nothing. Jane had done a good job of tying her up; she could barely move. But she knew Jane was enjoying watching her squirm. Molly took her tongue away from Jane for a second to moan, "God, Jane, please touch me, please touch me, baby!"

Jane abruptly grabbed her hair, tilted her head back, and looked down at her with ice gleaming from her cold blue eyes. "Now, why did you stop?"

Jane's voice was low, husky, rough. "That was very bad of you." She pulled Molly's hair. "I was going to play with you after I came, but now I won't. Now I have to punish you. Get back to work, and you better do a good job, or I'll punish you more." Jane released Molly's hair with a contemptuous toss and lowered her cunt back on Molly's open mouth.

Molly bent her head to her task with a renewed vigor. She focused on Jane's clit, licking it hard, sucking it into her mouth, softly biting it. Jane's words had started an ache deep in her womb. Jane was pretty good at tormenting her—especially since she always said it was Molly who came up with the kinky ideas. Molly feverishly licked and sucked, harder and faster, just the way Jane liked it as she was about to come. She could sense that Jane was close, and frantically sucked her, ignoring the fatigue in her tongue and jaw. There was no way she would stop now.

Jane's cries built, and finally she released, coming with a low groan, her whole body swaying, grinding onto Molly's mouth. She fell to the side, sighing with pleasure and fatigue. "Mm," Jane's voice was a low, purring growl. "That was good, baby. Now I need a nap, though. You be a good girl, and be quiet while I sleep."

Molly cried, "No, baby, please touch me, please. I'm so hot for you, baby, so wet. Please touch me."

"Well, you should have thought about that earlier, shouldn't you? But there's something to keep you occupied while I sleep." Jane said as reached into the drawer under the bed where they kept their toys and produced a pair of nipple clamps. Molly whimpered. Jane put them on Molly's already aching nipples. "Now, be quiet and let me sleep, or I'll punish you even more," she warned Molly before turning over and snuggling against Molly's side. Soon, Molly could tell that she had drifted off into a satisfied, post-coital sleep. Molly lay there silently, trying to relax, but her body wouldn't let her. The clamp bites made her nipples ache and her cunt was hopelessly swollen. She worked her vaginal muscles, as they helplessly ached to be filled.

It seemed an eternity before Jane stirred, stretched, turned back to kiss her.

"Now for your punishment," Jane whispered.

Molly gasped, her eyes wide. "You mean that wasn't it?" What was Jane going to do to her?

Jane smiled, the light dancing in her deep blue eyes, her whole face crinkling into an expression of wicked glee. "Oh, no, I've got much better punishments in mind for you." Jane got up, and strode, naked and assured, into the kitchen. She came back with a glass full of ice. She picked up an ice cube and started rubbing it all over Molly: her arms, stomach, down her legs, her inner thigh, back up her sides. Molly writhed with the sensation. Jane circled the cube over her sore nipples, soothing them at first, and then making them ache more intensely. She held it in her fingers, poised for a moment over Molly's cunt. Molly could feel a drop of cold water hit her clit and she jumped. Jane's hand descended swiftly, and swept the cube through Molly's slit. Molly gasped with the sensation. Just as fast as it started, it was over. Jane popped the cube, dripping with Molly's juices, into her mouth. "Mmm," Jane breathed, "tasty."

"God, you tease!" Molly moaned.

"What was that?" Jane's voice was harsh, the tone of a schoolteacher at the end of her patience.

"I, um, nothing." Molly felt a stab of fear. She didn't know what Jane would do next.

"I think that was an insult to me." Jane's blue eyes were icy. "We can't have that. I was just going to take mercy on you, but now I have to punish you some more."

"No, please, Jane, please," Molly could barely talk. Her lips had never felt so dry. It was an effort to unstick her tongue from the roof of her mouth. All the moisture in her body had flooded south and was seeping from her cunt.

"Shoulda thought of that before." Jane got off the bed and disappeared into the living room. Molly wondered how long she would stay out there. Jane had always threatened to tie her up and go off for hours. Maybe she was doing that now. But no, Jane came back with a ball of twine in her hand and a pair of scissors. Molly eyed them suspiciously. What was Jane going to do?

Jane bent over, her fine back and magnificent ass exposed, and rooted through their toy trunk until she came up with a vibrator. Molly eyed it hopefully, but Jane just threw it on the bed between her legs.

"What are you going to do, baby?" Molly gasped.

"Hmm" Jane looked thoughtful. "I think I'll keep you in suspense a little longer. She picked a black T-shirt off the floor and drew it over Molly's head. Molly now couldn't see, but she could feel Jane climb on the bed and heard her fooling around with something. Jane was whistling softly under her breath. Soon, Molly heard the snick of the scissors, and Jane pulled the shirt off Molly's eyes.

Molly gasped.

Suspended about two inches away from her cunt was the vibrator, hanging from the twine. The twine was suspended from a hook they'd put in the ceiling during an earlier adventure.

Molly looked at Jane with wondering eyes.

Jane switched on the pearlescent, goddess-shaped device. "Go to it," she said. Molly gasped and tried to swallow. It would be agonizing to try to contort her body so she could rub against it with Jane's eyes on her the whole time, seeing her struggle. As humiliating and horrible as the idea was, it also sent a wave of longing threw her cunt. Jane's hand jerked the chain that joined her nipples. "Go ahead," she ordered.

Molly's back arched with the jolt of pain that zinged through her nipples.

She really had no choice. She was at Jane's mercy. And she wanted it no other way.

She raised her head and tried to contort so she would contact the dangling vibrator. She writhed, arching her back. She was tied tightly, but the little movement she had allowed her to graze the vibrator. The sensation sent shock waves through her and she moaned. The vibrator, lightly suspended on the cord, swung away from her as she twisted, then swung back to gently bump against her cunt. It swung erratically, so she couldn't control it, and the more she writhed, the more it swung. She couldn't get it to rest on her clit. She collapsed back against the bed, moaning helplessly. She waited, gasping, until it stopped moving, then tried to very gently lift herself up. It worked, the tip of the vibrator rested ever so lightly on her clit, sending waves of pleasure through her. Molly moaned helplessly. She needed more. She tried to rock against it, but it swung away again, sweeping back to bump between her clit and her vagina. "Ahh," Molly cried, tears of frustration springing to her eyes.

Jane sat back in the chair she had pulled up to the bed, enjoying the show. She was wet and aching, and every moan Molly made caused her uterus to contract and throb. Finally, she couldn't take it anymore. She grabbed a double dildo from the box, pushed it inside herself, tore down the hanging tool, and plunged into Molly.

The sudden sensation of being richly, roughly filled, was enough to send Molly over the edge. Her back ached, her body convulsed, and she came, hard, her cries hitting Jane's cunt like a sledgehammer. Molly's helpless writhing, coupled with the delicious sound of her cries, sent an explosion through Jane. She came against Molly, grinding against her, joining her cries to Molly's.

Jane collapsed onto Molly. Molly's eyes were closed, and she looked completely relaxed. Slowly, Molly's eyes fluttered open. "Going to untie me now?" Molly asked, her voice hoarse.

Jane smiled, "Maybe."

more

Barbara Pizio

Her blue eyes flashed wickedly at me, but somehow I knew that I would have to make the first move. I held her smoldering gaze as I stood and motioned with my head toward the back of the club. She immediately stood and followed me. She never even had a chance to order a drink. But neither of us had come here for the liquor.

I'd noticed her the second she walked in the door: milky white skin, long shapely legs and honey-blond hair tumbled over her shoulders in soft waves. Her small breasts rose and fell with each breath, her tiny nipples pressing insistently against her cotton tank top. It seemed to me that she gasped slightly when our eyes met, parting those perfect pink lips. I knew just the use for those lips.

It was late and the club was nearly empty, the restroom completely vacant. Resting my hand on the small of her back, I ushered her into the stall farthest from the door. In one smooth motion I locked the door behind us and pushed her up against the tiled wall. I pressed my body against hers, and our breasts mashed as our lips met in a lusty kiss. Our tongues wrestled in a sudden release of pent-up lust. There was no sense of tenderness, just the desperate hunger of two strangers who seemed to have found exactly what they needed.

I threaded my fingers in her silky hair and held her head as we continued to kiss. We quickly became a jumble of sighs, moans and sweaty flesh. One of my hands was still tangled in her tresses as I broke the kiss and began nuzzling her neck. The subtle scent of her perfume overwhelmed my senses as I kissed and nipped her neck and shoulder. She moaned appreciatively and brought her hand underneath my jacket to stroke my back.

As much as I enjoyed her touch, I needed to see her naked. I quickly worked her shirt over her braless breasts. She moaned when my hands cupped the delicate mounds, running my thumbs over her erect nipples. I squeezed the pink nubs between my fingers, and my little blond gasped and bucked her hips toward me. Her skin was soft and smooth, and her supple flesh seemed to radiate heat. I wanted her to melt in my hands.

Reaching between our writhing bodies, I slowly unsnapped the button fly of her short-shorts and slipped them down her hips. They fell to the floor, and she stepped out of them. She wore no panties, and her sleek, hairless pussy was mine for the taking.

I held her up against the wall by keeping my left hand on her breast. With the other, I tricked my fingers along the soft flesh of her thigh before bringing one finger up to her shaved cunt lips. Teasingly, I ran my fingertip along the moist length of her pussy. Using two fingers I spread her puffy labia so I could dip just the tip of a finger inside her opening. She sighed in my ear and play-fully nibbled the edge of my lobe. Her knees buckled slightly and she thrust her hips against my hand as I traced the outline of her hole. I delved between her cunt lips, all the while denying her real penetration, loving the sound of her ragged breathing as I toyed with her.

Although my heart was racing and my own cunt wanted some attention, I continued her slow torment. I circled the swollen nub of her clit with my fingertip and she whimpered sweetly. With the lightest touch that I could manage, I stroked her clit and felt her pussy grow even moister with desire. I varied the speed and inten-sity of my movements, wanting to keep her on the edge of orgasm as long as possible.

Finally, I slipped a single finger inside her hot cunt and caught my breath as I felt her pussy walls quiver at my touch. I worked a second finger into her, and she moaned out loud as I gave her a taste of the penetration she craved. She squeezed her muscles tight-ly around my fingers, and I let out a moan of my own. I knew that at any moment someone might enter the restroom, but until then we were alone. And although we didn't have much time, I just knew that, somehow, it would be enough.

Her sex was hot and slick and her luscious wetness quickly coated my hand. Her snug tunnel surrounded my fingers with vel-vet warmth and I kept wriggling them inside her, caressing every inch of her silky flesh. Her legs were slightly bent, and I straddled her thigh, pressing up against her slender leg. The pressure forced the thick seam of my jeans to ride up between my swollen cunt lips and made my pussy ache with arousal.

I finger-fucked her tight cunt, delighting in her shimmying hips and tender moans. Reaching up inside her as far as I could, I gently nudged her cervix and made her gasp. I continued to toy with her dripping sex while I rubbed up against her leg. I was so turned on I wouldn't have been surprised if I was soaking through the fabric of my jeans.

She looked at me with eyes filled with need when I removed my fingers for a moment. *Good thing I come prepared,* I thought, and reached into my jacket pocket to pull out a latex glove and a small tube of lube. I could have sworn that I felt her shudder when I snapped the cuff of the glove around my wrist. She leaned her head against the wall and bit her lower lip in anticipation as she watched me squirt some lube on my rubber-covered fingers. I slid two digits back into her ravenous cunt, thrusting them a few times before working a third inside her.

"More!" she panted. I chuckled as I realized that was the first word she had actually said to me.

Pulling out slightly, I tucked my thumb inside my palm and pushed forward again, gradually working a fourth finger inside her. Her eyes fluttered and her lips parted, and she began to breathe more deeply. Man, she was tight, but the way she moaned and bore down on my fingers, I knew she wanted nothing more than to feel my whole hand balled up inside her. With gentle, insistent pressure I pushed in deeper, until I felt her cunt swallow the entirety of my hand. I folded up my fingers, then carefully turned and twisted my wrist, moving my hand as best I could in her tight confines.

She frantically fingered her clit as I churned my hand. Her fingers slid this way and that, gliding over her clit and bumping right into my wrist as she struggled to work herself to orgasm and hold herself upright. In mere seconds she found her rhythm, working her fingers in small circles over her sensitive button, her eyes shut tight in concentration. She suddenly burst out in a mantra of "oh, oh, oh," and I felt her cunt clench around my wrist. My free hand rested on her taut stomach, holding her up against the wall as my fingers fluttered inside her, my fist opening and closing. Her honey mixed with lube dripped down the cuff of my glove as her pussy contracted around me. Her whole body started to shake more intensely as she rode out her orgasm in a series of cries and moans that echoed off the bathroom walls.

I carefully slipped my hand out of her quivering cunt and stripped off the glove. She looked at me, still panting between parted lips, as I pushed down on her shoulders. She instantly dropped to her knees and helped me lower my jeans. She had to work a little to strip me of my panties, though. Riding her thigh, I had worked the sopping fabric in between my slick labia. Her lips curled into a smile as she tugged the wet panties down my thighs.

I had no idea who this little minx was, but I didn't care. The stall smelled sweetly of pussy, and her cries of orgasm were still ringing in my ears. Fucking her tight cunt had gotten me so hot I could barely wait to get off.

She brought her mouth up to my dripping slit and her hot breath puffed over my aroused clit, making me shudder. Now it was my turn to lean against the wall for support. I bent my knees slightly—just enough to let her kitten tongue reach me. It skidded over the length of my sex, and I let out a contented sigh when she made contact. She continued to run the flat of her tongue over my entire cunt, making me hotter by the second as she hungrily lapped up my juice.

As I writhed above her, she shoved two fingers into my dripping pussy. I gasped at the sudden intrusion and tried to buck my hips forward to fuck her fingers. She continued pistoning them in and out of my sex as she flicked her tongue over my clit in a maddening rhythm that had me on the edge of sanity.

She suddenly pulled her fingers out of me and I could see them glistening. Before I had a chance to utter a word, she worked one of them between my ass cheeks, wriggling it into my tight back hole. I squirmed and gasped as her juice-slick finger popped inside my ass I began breathing through my mouth as she worked her finger deeper into me and slipped another wet digit back into my desperate pussy. Slowly, she fucked both of my holes with her slim fingers, the double penetration nearly working me into a delirium.

She had a look of intense concentration on her face as she finger-fucked me. I closed my eyes to savor the sensation of the penetration that was stimulating all of my nerve endings. As good as it felt it was even more incredible when she brought her mouth back to my clit. She circled that little nub of flesh with her tongue and then sucked it between her lips. The suction made me gasp, and she backed off for a moment before continuing to tease me with tiny tongue flicks.

With both of my holes filled, it only took the touch of her tongue to my sensitive clit to spark my orgasm and cause it to smolder deep inside me. She must have sensed the erotic electricity flowing underneath my skin because she sucked on my clit once again. My stomach muscles tightened as I strained to capture the intensity of the feelings that were beginning to course through my body. It began as a slow burn deep inside my cunt, and then a tingling numbness seemed to spread outward to my trembling thighs. I grabbed the back of her head and ground my sex against her mouth while squeezing my thighs against the sides of her face. My orgasm rushed over me in a great series of waves. I was barely aware of where I was and how it was happening; I was simply lost in a swirling world of sensation. No matter how much I squirmed, she continued to suck and fuck my quivering cunt until I let out one last cry and released her head from my grasp.

Wordlessly, we straightened up and slipped back into our clothes. Once we were presentable, she exited the stall before me and headed for the door.

"See you around," I said. She turned and flashed me one last smile before strolling through the swinging door, disappearing from my life just as quickly as she had entered it.

coach-able moments

Mo Jensen

When I look up, she is standing at center court as if she's about to jump for the ball...or maybe for me. She played center in high school, but that was many seasons ago.

Flashing me a sly smile, she slowly unzips her nylon warm-up jacket and drops it to the floor.

I am sitting on the home team bench. The only illumination is from exit signs and safety lights. A moment ago, I'd been holding a basketball on my lap, visualizing what my first practice as a college head coach would be like next week. Yet she has now captured my complete attention.

So, the softball coach wants to give me a few pointers?

She pulls off her T-shirt, revealing a fire-engine-red "soccer shirt" à la Brandi Chastain. After deftly twirling it over her head, she cocks her wrist and flicks the shirt at me. As I catch the jersey, I put it to my nose to breathe in her sweaty sweetness.

Ah, things are getting interesting.

I start to giggle at her over-the-top, come-hither looks. She presses a finger to her lips. And then she sits on the floor to take off her sneakers: first the left Nike and sock, then the right. These she thankfully doesn't send my way, but just leaves them where they lie.

Standing there in her sports bra, nylon pants, and bare feet, she starts to rub her hands all over her body in a teasing way—sliding up her torso to cup her breasts and then back down again. She licks her lips. She winks.

I know what she is doing. She is imitating the lacy, sexy femme in a scene from the lame cable movie we stayed up to watch last Tuesday. The fact that my wife is a tomboy jock in sweats makes her striptease both a turn on and an amusement.

But God, I love a woman in sweats! And *my* woman in sweats makes me so wet. That sexual response must have been imprinted on me the first time I saw *Flashdance* in my CYO-ball days. *Oh, what a feelin'!*

Now my true love has a thumb hooked into the elastic band of her black warm-up pants. She slides the crinkly fabric down to reveal skin on her right hip, mouths a kiss, then lets the fabric inch back up. Oh, and more hands on belly and breast, yes, rubbing, rubbing, *rubbing.*

Finally, both thumbs are in the waistband. She teases only a little this time as she dances around, lowers her sweats to her ankles and then kicks them my way.

She's wearing the black, silk boxers with the large baseballs on them! Of course, I prefer the pair with basketballs, but this will definitely do. It is too much to bear! I run to her like a hungry freshman getting her first minutes on the college floor.

As I slide my arms around her waist, our lips meet for the first time since I kissed her in our kitchen this morning. I close my eyes, and our tongues intertwine. I run my hands over the soft skin of her back and then down to the silky softness of her ample hips. I love her stocky, softball player build.

She grabs the base of my sweatshirt, and I lift my arms so that she can pull it over my head. As she kisses the nape of my neck, a soft *grrr* rumbles from my throat. I know that I am done in when she nibbles on my earlobes. I put my weight on my left side and try to kick off my right sneaker. It doesn't come, and getting it off becomes a priority. I kick again and again.

"Shh!" she whispers into my ear. "Patience."

On her way down, she kisses my stomach then slides her hot tongue into my belly button. Her hands run down my hips, thighs, then calves as she kneels to untie the laces. I shift my weight as first the left, then the right shoe comes off. Then the socks fall.

She rises up to my waist and hooks her thumbs into my nylon waistband this time. Our eyes meet courtesy of the soft glow in the gym. She drops my pants to the floor, and I kick them off.

"Ah, so that's why I couldn't find the basketball shorts this morning." She breathes into my ear and then nibbles the lobe.

I have them on, though hopefully not for long.

My hands slide from her hips down to her round softness. I squeeze those firm cheeks, pulling her into me. She exhales. She loves it when I do that. That knowledge comes with seven years of intimacy. But it is surprises like *this* that really keep the pistons sparking.

She kneels on the floor, and I join her there. We kiss again, and our hands roam everywhere. She laces her fingers into mine and, hand in hand, she pulls our arms out to our sides and then up as if we might be tipping for the ball...only with touching. The movie poster for *Love & Basketball* comes to mind. Why doesn't Wolfe Video make a hoops flick like that? I giggle, and she knows why.

"We have love and ball too, grrrl," she whispers.

I lower myself to the floor and lay on my back on the cold hardwood. She folds up my sweatshirt and puts it under my head. Then she lowers herself on top of me. I gasp at her presence. Tension rises from my center. I want her here, now. I slide my hands up her spine to the base of her sports bra. As I tug, she lifts her arms, and I remove the garment.

She balances above me, and I take her breast into my mouth. Ah, sweet heaven! I suck and suck as I rub the other breast with my hand. I can't get enough of her. As my heart flutters and my breathing quickens, I let go to take her sister breast into my mouth, sucking and licking circles around the areola.

It is her turn to be satiated. She motions to remove my bra, and I lift my body allowing her to do so. Her hands cradle my breasts, and she takes one into her mouth.

I think of how she sucks the lemon-water from the nipple of her water bottle during workouts. Watching her do that on the treadmill or between reps with the weights makes me so hot. Ah, but being in this moment is so much more fabulous! My favorite word; I whisper it into her ear.

"Hey, number eight, you are s-o-o-o fab-u-u-ulou-s-s-s!" She loves it when I use her former playing number as a pet name.

She laughs. "You're not so bad yourself, 33."

Her lips are still forming a smile as I arch up to take them in mine. Our tongues and legs are all in a tangle as I pull her into me. She starts to move slowly up and down on top of me. Her thigh presses into me, the silk boxers, now quite damp, cling to me.

Her right hand strokes my face, my breast, my hip, and my thigh. She glides ever so lightly over my mound, but then her hands fall to my hips.

"You are such a tease." I coax.

My baby slides down, fingers tugging on my boxers so I lift as she pulls them down over my ankles. She rises to her knees, and I sit up to tug at her baseball boxers. They slide down as she maneuvers to get them off.

I lay back and pull her down on top of me. She positions herself so that we touch...hot and wet on hot and wet. I gasp. She begins to slowly create friction in that delicate location. She licks the base of my neck and then blows softly on it. My skin tingles all the way to my toes.

Her lips are sucking my earlobe, tugging and suckling. Combined with the gentle rocking below, I feel like I could pass out right now from the shear pleasure of it all.

I want to say, "Oh, baby, I want you. I need you," but words fail me now. No matter, she knows what I want. She licks a finger, gliding just the tip from my lips, down my neck, around a nipple, down my belly, to my center. She separates my folds, rubbing the sweet spot gently; first up and down, then in artful circles.

She takes advantage of a beam from the safety light down the locker-room tunnel to look into my eyes. I feel like she is looking into my soul. My lover slips a finger inside me, and I gasp. Her finger makes a large stroke from my depths then up to meet my labia and back. I moan, and she adds another finger.

Our love, our bodies, our emotions are just too much for the moment.

A single tear forms in my eye, then runs down my cheek as my lover skillfully adds a third finger to the mix. Her thrust and technique are mind-blowing and, combined with our almost telepathic connection, my baby sends me right into orbit.

"I love you," she whispers.

My hips rise and fall to her touch. Rise and fall. Rise and fall.

As she strokes, brilliant colors form and flash behind my closed eyelids: purples and blues and greens. My breath becomes jagged. And the storm starts to swirl in my heart, my center, down deep inside me. *Ah, ha, hha, ahh, ha, ha, ha...uh, uh, uh, uh, ha, ha, uh, h-a-a-a...*

I exhale. My muscles release their grip.

Her hand stills. She stretches her body out on top of me again and lays her head on my heart. We embrace. I stroke her back, and we share the moment.

For a period, the only sound I hear is our breathing and our hearts pumping.

After a while, I speak.

"Not bad. Not bad. Way to hustle there, Coach," I tease.

She smiles and gives me her best studly wink.

Yet, there is still electricity to be made. My body aches for hers, as I know hers aches for mine. It's my turn to drive. I roll her over onto her back. Needling my fingers through her short, spiky hair, I spread her lips with my tongue, kissing her deeply.

Pulling back, I grab both of her wrists and pin them to the floor above her head. Then I kiss her again and again, pausing only to suck now and then on a nipple, earlobe, or lower lip. She moans and raises her body to mine, pressing up hard into me.

Finally releasing her wrists, I take both breasts into my hands and enjoy their shape and firmness.

"The softball team must be quite well-funded," I say, tossing the words into her ear, "because the coach works with such fine equipment."

"Yes, good equipment is important, but practice is key," she playfully retorts in her best "coach" voice.

Her hands guide my head lower until my face balances just above her wet core. Blowing softly, I use my fingers to separate her sweet lips. And then...and then...I use my tongue as the instrument of her pleasure.

I dart, I flick, I curl, and insert. All the while my baby moans and bucks and whispers, "Yes, yes" and "Oh, God." Somehow I know that God is here in the midst of our love and even in our expressions of love.

I drink in her warm, sweet wine as I again take her pearl of pleasure into my mouth. My steady strokes are working their magic, I can tell by the urgency in how she grabs my hair and in the way that her rhythmic hips rise to meet my touch. *It's time to bring her home,* I think to myself, and I don't stop. We're in the zone, and I keep up the rhythm and intensity.

"Mmm." A short moan escapes her lips. "Hmm...hmm...hmm," and then the stronger, longer moans come.

"Oh, baby, oh, baby. Yes, yes! Oh, you're so good. Yeah...yeah...God...Yeah. Oh, oh, oh, uh, uh, oh."

I feel her shutter start slowly and then burst into quick waves, and I darn near smile to myself. I love to make her come, to feel her tremble under my touch, to give her pleasure. I can almost imagine my heart expand right inside my chest with pride and love for her.

She exhales, and I hold her tight. She is my rock, and I am hers.

"Thank you," her whisper is low and throaty.

I slide up her body and spread my weight out on top of her. I gently kiss her lips and touch her cheek.

"So, Coach, how do you feel about your prospects this year?" My lover asks me in a voice that mimics that of the baby dyke reporter who covers women's athletics for the college paper.

"Oh, I'm feeling very optimistic. With our depth and talent there'll be no stopping us. I'm confident we can go all the way this year if we stick together and work our plan." I respond with a statement that I'm sure I've seen attributed to my baby in black and white somewhere.

"Thirty-three?" she inquires.

"Ya, Eight?"

"I love you."

at the almador motel

Jessie Fischer

Sylvia couldn't believe she'd lived to be 34 years old and had never been fucked with a dildo. She'd been gay at least half those years, and ever since she'd double-fucked those two strippers behind the Denny's in '93, she'd gained a rep among her friends as an insatiable sex fiend, someone who broke all the rules. But that was 10 years ago, and for the last four she'd been living the quiet life with Melissa in a sweet little home in the suburbs. Then one autumn morning Sylvia had woken up, looked around her, taken in all the "assembly life" crap from Pottery Barn and Williams-Sonoma and Crate & Barrel, and thought, *Who the fuck have I become?* Well, maybe it didn't happen that suddenly; for months Melissa's "Jeanette Sconce with Antique Beaded Articulating Wall Base" in the bedroom had been nearly sneering at her, making her want to dash into the kitchen and destroy all of Melissa's carefully organized back issues of *Martha Stewart Living.*

That was six months ago, and since then Sylvia had broken up with Melissa and secured a loft downtown, which she furnished eclectically. (Her one rule: Nothing could come from a catalog.) When she'd left Melissa, she'd had all sorts of fantasies about women pounding down her door; when word got out that the horniest lezzie in town was single, it'd be nonstop action, right? Well, not exactly: All the women who'd once crawled between the sheets with her on cold winter nights were now crawling between their own 100% Egyptian cotton sheets with their own girlfriends, in their own sweet little homes in the suburbs, making crafty centerpieces and ginger-laced hot chocolate and...making babies.

So Sylvia had gone the way of all desperate dykes and placed an online personal ad. Under "Relationship Desired" she had merely typed "Sex." And then the line, "First-timer looking for all-night strap-on action." She knew it sounded lame, but that's what she craved, right? Pure sex. No commitment. She yearned for those days when every weekend meant devouring a new and different pussy, taking in the smells and tastes of a hot femme or a stone cold butch or whoever the fuck she wanted.

She'd gotten some e-mails from a few duds—women who'd duped her with photos from 15 years ago, women who were really men, women who used to be men, women who wanted to watch her with a man, you get the picture. But the babe she was meeting tonight would be the one to rock her world, fuck her to oblivion— she just knew it. Sylvia had only gotten one e-mail from the woman—who went by the screen name "Dil-Master"—and it read:

Tomorrow night. Almador Motel. 9 p.m. Room 203.
I will fuck you to kingdom come.

And attached was a photo of a woman with the most piercing blue eyes, cropped silver hair, and a jawline more chiseled than that of Mount Rushmore's Mr. Jefferson himself.

The following night she spent nearly two hours in front of the mirror, blow-drying her silky brown tresses, applying and reapplying mascara, making sure her lip liner was just right. And then at 8:40 she jumped into her Honda Passport (the one aspect of Melissa's bourgeois lifestyle she couldn't part with) and made a beeline for the Almador. During the drive, she fondly remembered the night she'd driven the then-married-with-two-kids Joanna Inman to the same ramshackle establishment and turned her out on a scratchy, beer-stained bedspread. Joanna (well, "Jo") was a physical therapist with a flattop now.

The sky was cobalt and a silver crescent moon hung in the air when Sylvia knocked on the scraped lime-green door of room 203, car keys in one hand, pepper spray in the other. (You couldn't be too careful with those Internet liaisons. She'd read that in one of Melissa's *O* magazines.) The door opened to reveal the woman from the pic, who was even more stunning than she'd appeared in the slightly pixilated photo she had sent. She was wearing a black Tee and tight jeans, and a bulge the size of Toledo strained at her crotch, which instantly sent Sylvia's snatch into hysterics.

"First-timer?" the woman said in a sexy, low voice.

"Dil-Master?" Sylvia asked, realizing the cheesiness of it all, but what else could she say? She didn't know the woman's first name. And she preferred it that way.

137

Wordlessly, Dil-Master (or D.M. as Sylvia had nicknamed her) took Sylvia by the hand, closed the door behind them, and led her to the flowered bedspread. *This place hasn't changed a bit,* Sylvia thought, and as she did a chill ran from her spine straight to her cunt at the image of Joanna Inman flat on her back, her dripping wet pussy playfully pumping into Sylvia's insatiable mouth. But Sylvia was clearly with a pro now, not a virginal closeted housewife. This time Sylvia would be the one getting turned out.

Sylvia took in all of D.M.: her runner's body, her cut biceps, her strong thighs visible through the close-fitting jeans, and gave D.M. an approving nod. D.M. smiled in response, then positioned Sylvia on her back on the mattress and climbed on top of her. Sylvia looked up into D.M.'s steely blue eyes and saw a kind of wisdom there, a kind of experience, surely the kind of experience one can only get from having lapped at hundreds—thousands probably!—of hot, sticky pussies. D.M. began with gentle licks and kisses at Sylvia's widow's peak, an untamable tuft that had caused her endless taunting on the playground, but which now for some reason drove the ladies wild. *Funny how those things change,* Sylvia thought with a smirk, but not for long because D.M.'s expert tongue and teeth were now licking and biting the tender skin behind Sylvia's left ear. She thought she might come from that alone, but she held back, knowing the best was still to come.

When Sylvia emitted a moan—actually a cross between a chirp and a growl—D.M. pulled out all the stops, quickly slipping Sylvia out of her silk top and leather skirt. Sylvia dutifully assisted D.M. by whipping off her bra and panties. She flung her underpants across the room, which landed on a wall lamp that looked strikingly similar to her old bedroom nemesis.

Sylvia chuckled under her breath but quickly shut up when D.M. unbuttoned her 501s and unleashed a monstrous strap-on—the biggest, fattest dildo Sylvia had ever seen up close. (Actually, the only one she'd ever seen this closely had been on the Internet.) It was black and thick and long and looked nothing like a penis, for which Sylvia thanked her lucky stars. D.M. reached over to the faux-maple nightstand, pulled out a tube of lube, and greased up the slick cock with the gooey stuff. Just the sight of D.M. stroking her shaft sent Sylvia's hungry pussy into spasms.

With the tip of her dick, D.M. teased Sylvia, moving it in tight little circles around her pink bud, which grew harder by the second. Finally she poked the fatty inside Sylvia's gushing hole; it was just a little poke, like a child testing the pool with her toe, but it was enough to make Sylvia's entire body shudder with delight. *This is what I've waited half my life for,* she thought. *This is what that uptight Melissa couldn't give me. Sex without strings.* When D.M. realized the water was warm and welcoming, she plunged in deeper, thrusting slowly at first, then gradually increasing in speed. The roughness of D.M.'s denim-clad thighs against Sylvia's bare ones was delicious, almost dirty, she thought. They hadn't spoken a word since Sylvia had entered the room, and that was just how she liked it. The last thing she needed was someone asking her if she paid the gas bill through a mouthful of quivering twat.

D.M. was pumping full force now, Sylvia's big brown eyes fixed on D.M.'s baby blues. As D.M. slid her pole in and out of Sylvia's velvety snatch, she found herself unable to tear herself away from D.M.'s gaze. There was something intense there, she thought. Something profound and mysterious. Almost religious. She thought she might drown in their beauty, their wisdom. If there were a place one might find solace or God or Buddha or whoever or whatever holds our answers, this would be the place; Sylvia was certain.

But her pussy was a little more certain, and when she felt D.M.'s thick rod bump up against her swollen clit on its way out, then again on its way in, she closed her eyes tightly, savoring the fullness in her cunt, feeling the blood try to pound its way out of her body. When she opened her eyes again, she was instantly lost in D.M.'s gaze. *Surely this woman is a poet, a philosopher, a teacher, an advocate for the poor and helpless,* Sylvia thought. *How else could she make me feel so good?*

D.M. was pumping like a jackhammer now, and Sylvia's eyes practically rolled back into her head, the pleasure and slight pain driving her wild. Her cunt tightened with each thrust, gripping D.M.'s cock like there was no tomorrow. And just then Sylvia felt herself at the edge, as a million images swirled through her mind's eye and she heard John Lennon's "Imagine" playing gorgeously inside her head and her coming came in long loud waves and everything was perfect in the world and she cried "Yes!" so loudly D.M. thought the filthy wall mirror might shatter into a thousand glorious pieces.

Forget all those one-night stands and backroom quickies I used to have, Sylvia thought moments later, wrapped in D.M.'s strong arms. *What do I need those for when I've got this philosopher, this teacher, my beautiful silver-fox poet?* Sylvia knew she'd probably spend the rest of her life with this woman. D.M. obviously held all the answers to life's problems in those deep blue eyes; Sylvia just had to figure out which questions to ask.

"So what do you do for a living?" Sylvia finally asked a half-asleep D.M.

"Drive a truck," D.M. said. "For Pottery Barn."

sheds, spit and kisses

Mary K. Slavin

My arms are going numb, stretched above my head while I ratchet a bolt into a supporting 2 by 4 for my friend Kelly's woodshed.

"I just don't know what to do, Kel. It seems like I want people who do want me and I don't want the people want me, or I ruin a perfectly good friendship with attraction."

Kelly walks around the skeleton of the shed to face me. Her hand pulls at my heather gray T-shirt, releasing it from my jeans. Her hand disappears below the shirt, cold on my skin. Kelly grabs the front of my sports bra like a traveler grabs a suitcase. I am push-pulled backward, tripping over boards, ratchet flying from my hand, through a row of evergreen trees until my back thuds against a tall wood fence. I gasp and giggle nervously.

"Joan, you think too much." Kelly takes hold of the back of my head and pulls my mouth to hers. Her tongue plunges in. She swims in me, and I work just to keep up. The hand around my bra pushes me back against the fence. Her free hand tugs at my belt, freeing it from the loops. Kelly skillfully unbuttons the fly on my jeans. Her hand slips between boxers and skin, over orange fuzz and pink mound, and finds my cunt. I am already wet with the possibilities. One finger delves inside me, then another one. I inhale with each push from Kelly. She looks from my face to my crotch, and flashes a toothy smile.

"Oh, you ain't seen nothing yet," she beams. A third finger enters me. My legs want to collapse, want to fall on her hand. I whimper, but Kelly pushes me again into the fence. My shoulder blades burn.

Her hand emerges from my pants. Her fingers are sticky with me. She runs her fingers under her nose, smelling my wet and desire.

"Hmm, you smell delicious." She repeatedly breathes me in.

She must be done with me, I think. Wrong.

Kelly yanks at my jeans, pulling them down around my ankles. She slides her hand around to my ass, working my boxers down my legs. The tenderloin exposed, I feel hot and cold between the air and the rough fence. Kelly lets go of my bra and falls to her knees. I shudder when her lips touch my inner thighs with soft slow kisses. My legs want to tense, contract.

"Relax," Kelly growls. My legs are pried apart, drapes opening to an electrical storm. I feel Kelly's teeth, not biting but framing my cunt. Her hot breath tickles my skin. When her tongue laps at me, I moan, again feeling my legs wanting to collapse below me. I stretch my arms out, crucifix style, grabbing at the fence for balance. I pry my fingers into a hole in a board and hang on.

Kelly's mouth sucks at my clit, nibbles, licks, sweet-talks. My appreciation runs down my thighs into my boots. When she is done milking me, I am swollen and joyously sore. Again, I think I am done.

"Turn around," she says, tugging at my bare ass.

"I can't. I can't move." I feel my legs buckling. Kelly pushes both her hands against me to hold me up. The hole in the board won't release my fingers. The fingers are red, and I am losing sensation. Kelly stands and holds me up. She is soothing when she pulls my fingers out of the hole, kisses each one of them better. I am grateful and exhausted. I lean forward, resting my head on Kelly's shoulder.

"We're not done. Turn around," she scolds.

I moan in dissent but Kelly grabs one of my breasts in her hand, squeezing, pulling. I cringe and give up the argument. I twist around, raising my hands to my face to brace against the fence.

"Poor thing," Kelly says, her fingers massaging my ass. "The fence dug into you." A kiss touches each cheek. "How about I make that better for you?" Kelly's tongue licks at my wounds, slow methodical circles taking the sting away. A finger runs the length of my crack, and her tongue follows. She pulls apart my cheeks. Her breath tickles me. Kelly's tongue moves in slow circles around my rim.

"Inside," I moan, wanting more.

"No," Kelly says sternly, slapping my butt. A hot flush of shame rises on my face. Kelly goes back to rimming me. Knowing I can't get what I want stifles the enjoyment. Kelly stops, noticing that I've become still.

"Hang on," she says. One of her hands leaves. After a moment, her mouth returns to my body. I feel a tapping against my knee and I look down to see that Kelly has found a green-handled screwdriver used earlier. The handle is smooth and hard, with four vertical grooves about the circumference of my thumb.

"Yes." I want to spread my legs farther, but my jeans shackle me.

Kelly crawls between my legs, turns around, and sits with her back to the fence. She smiles up at me. She licks at the handle like it's a green lollipop. I smile and shake my head. Kelly points the handle at me, daring me to do a better job. I slide the handle into my mouth, suck it in slow long moves, run my tongue along the grooves. Kelly nods, chuckling. The handle slides out of my mouth.

"OK," I say.

Kelly crawls through my legs. Her mouth touches me again, licking more intensely until I feel soaked with spit and kisses. She wets the screwdriver handle one last time.

"Relax," she says. The butt of the screwdriver handle touches me. Kelly is gentle. She helps me take a few steps back, so I can bend over and open up. With a steadying hand on my lower back, Kelly works the handle inside me, little by little. I pull it into me, gasping as edges are negotiated. The handle turns inside me as it goes deeper.

Kelly pets my body with a soft hand, caressing me. Finally, her hand reaches my clit. My insides are set on fire. A few strokes of Kelly's fingers and I choke on orgasm after orgasm.

"Ahh," I moan, shuddering in the last bursts of passion as Kelly removes the screwdriver.

I cannot maintain any longer and crumple to the bark dust between the trees. Kelly unties a long-sleeved flannel shirt from around her waist and drapes it over my bare shivering backside. I lay my head in Kelly's lap. Her arms enfold me for a few minutes as I recover.

"OK, time to get up," Kelly says, releasing her grasp of me.

"Kel, no. I appreciate this but I can't go another round. That was enough."

"Babe, I'm not talking about that. You gotta get up and help me finish the shed."

double bill

Julie Mitchell

I am closing down the theater when I see Darlene—19, androgynous-sexy, and supposedly straight—watching me from the light booth. I quickly flick off the house and stage lights, climb the stairs two at a time, and stride across the tiny room to corner Darlene.

Palms flat against the wall on either side of her head, I breathe, "Are you absolutely sure you're straight?" into her mouth before kissing it. Not a tentative, should-we-be-doing-this kiss or a sweet, aw-shucks first time kiss, but an openmouthed, full-on, I-want-to-fuck-you kind of kiss.

Darlene grinds her crotch into mine in a way that a virgin who'd only made out with boys shouldn't know how to do. I laugh and pull away to look at Darlene's face—flushed, stunned, and less guarded than I've ever seen it. I take off her baseball cap and let her straight, blue-black hair out of its usual ponytail.

Running my short nails along her hairline, into her scalp, I twine my fingers in the thick mass and arch her head back. Even with her neck exposed, Darlene looks tough: angular chin jutting out, strong-veined fingers curled into fists. I'm a sucker for tomboys.

I lick from her collarbone to her jaw, run my teeth on either side of the sleek muscle of Darlene's neck until I hear her groan, see her fists melt.

I shift my thigh between her legs so the knobby seam of her Levi's is tight against her clit. Darlene's breasts nudge mine several times before I realize she's exploring being breast to breast with another woman. Her nipples are so taut I can feel them through her clothing.

I yank open her fly. *Snap, snap, snap.* Then I slip my hands beneath denim to separate Darlene from her Levi's, working them down to her ankles. I slide the slick material of Darlene's jersey over belly, breasts, and head. White Jockey underwear and sports bra frame a flat stomach, tan and muscular. Her cocoa eyes watch me watching her.

My palms traverse her cheeks and neck, across nipples and ribs, down to hips and ass. I pull Darlene's pelvis tight against mine, and she loops her arms around my neck, presses her tongue between my lips, and squirms against me. I want to cry because it's been so long.

The skin below Darlene's ass is silvery smooth, and I tuck a finger beneath the leg band of her underwear, trace a slow line from the center of her ass, around narrow hips, to the front crease of her legs. I feel downy tufts of fur on my fingertip, the swell of an outer lip. I hear Darlene's breath catch and stall. punctuated by little puffs of air against my ear.

Darlene's head is flung to the side, and I suck her earlobe between my teeth, touch my tongue along its edge. My finger meanders back and forth at the seam of leg and groin.

Erratic breathing, writhing hips, arching spine—Darlene's reactions tell me "more," "yes." The effect I've yearned, for three dry years, to have on a woman—even on one who's coming out with every teasing stroke of my finger, even a teenager who could be my daughter if I'd gotten pregnant at 14.

I merge my lips with hers to shut myself up, and kiss her relentlessly. Reaching behind her, I cup my free hand around Darlene's tight, round ass then dip my fingers inside her briefs. I knead her ass cheek to heighten the sensation of opening between her thighs.

Pausing between kisses, I lean away. Darlene's skin is flushed and mottled pink, as if she'd been jogging. Her mouth gleams, lips puffy from continuous kissing.

Lifting my hands from her underwear, I skim upward over each rib to the sides of her small breasts. My fingers make lazy circles around Darlene's erect nipples. They tap a Morse code of desire onto their material-covered tips.

"Take it off," I say, and Darlene wrestles her bra over her shoulders and head. My jaw drops when I see that Darlene's nipples are pierced with miniature silver barbells. I look from her breasts to the amazed expression on her face—eyebrows raised, bottom lip caught between her teeth—and throw my head back and laugh. *Straight girl, my ass.*

I trace decreasing spirals around Darlene's breasts until I'm encircling her puckered areolas. Careful to touch only metal, not flesh, I tug at her nipples, first softly, then harder. When they look ripe enough to eat, I flick my tongue across one nipple and then the other, until they're as shiny and solid as the silver piercing them.

Tucking my thumb into the crotch of her Jockey's, I pull down on wet cotton. I use my other hand to slip elastic over hipbones and ass, until her undies join her Levi's.

Darlene looks at herself, and I imagine that the blush blooming on her face is because her own exposed body turns her on. I lean in for a kiss then place my mouth to her left ear. "Keep your eyes open," I whisper, moving my right hand across Darlene's breasts. "Watch what I'm doing."

I roll the ball of my middle finger across her nipple, gently pinch the tip between thumb and forefinger, and rub my palm in circles across its erectness. Darlene's eyes flutter, and I remind her, "Keep them open," as I kneel to suckle her breasts. I savor the sensation of pliable tissue against unyielding metal, hot flesh against cool silver. Slitting my eyes to make sure Darlene is still looking, I lean back so she can see my lips and tongue as they wash over her seashell pink nipples.

My right hand reaches between Darlene's legs, caresses the pearly smooth skin of her inner thighs. I outline a triangle around Darlene's pubic hair—once, twice—then run my fingertips through the plush ebony fur and along her outer lips, where I apply subtle pressure to their swollen edges. After dropping into the cleft between outer and inner labia, I draw ovals, then figure eight's, around her clit and opening.

My teeth move along Darlene's nipples, clicking against the barbells. Darlene's breathing stops when I start to rub minute circles high on the shaft of her clit, drum as fast as I can on the rosy head so it vibrates, gather wetness from her pussy to glide in full-fingered strokes over the length of her clit. I match the rhythm of my tongue on her breasts to the rhythm of my fingers.

Gingerly, I slip my forefinger inside her, just to my first knuckle. Darlene gasps and clenches at the same time, relaxing when I use my thumb to massage her clit. As her arousal increases, I push in further, up to my second knuckle, and this time she gasps without clenching. I start to pulse my finger against her narrowness, rocking her open from the inside out.

Darlene's breath, now audible, quickens as I slide in all the way to my third knuckle. I brush my thumb side to side, feather-light against her clit, until her pussy muscles loosen completely. Then I begin to ride the hood of her clit over its tip while I fondle her deep inside.

With increasing speed, I move around until I feel her legs stiffen, then shake; hear her incoherent animal cry of pleasure; taste the salty sweat as it springs out of her skin onto my tongue; smell the musky scent of come mixed with the metallic tang of blood; look down to see a scarlet patina coating my newly liberated finger.

I stand up, blotting red on the black of my slacks, and hug Darlene. Her lips fumble against mine until she's kissing me, crushing my body to hers, her mouth supple and burning. I slow the kisses, run my hands along her sides in soothing strokes, and gradually disentangle our limbs.

"You're so hot," I whisper into her mouth, eyes boring into hers, "I could play with you all night." I shake my head. "But this is your first time. We should take it slow."

When Darlene starts to object, I place my finger against her luscious mouth. I wonder if she can taste and smell herself on me. "We'll have time, baby girl, don't you worry."

As Darlene saunters away down the sidewalk, I remember her first time at the theater. Trying to elicit her orientation, I had mentioned some queer events. Darlene sniggered, or maybe just giggled, at the word "queer."

"So, you're a straight girl?"

She looked up from the light board, said—deadpan—"Yeah."

"Uh-huh," I said, as if it were an indictment. "Uh-huh," I repeated, and walked away chuckling.

"What?" The word cracked behind me, as if it had two syllables. "What!" Darlene called again.

"If that girl isn't a baby dyke," I told the director, "my gaydar is broken."

Now, I turn back to lock up the theater—savoring feeling sated after years of being hungry—and notice I've left the dressing room light on. Halfway down the aisle, I see a shadow shift onstage. Stepping into the dusty light seeping from the dressing room, the shadow resolves into Carolina, the show's choreographer.

"Did you forget something?" I demand, angry at being startled.

"No," Carolina drawls.

"How long have you been here?" My eyes dart to the light booth. Carolina's grin spreads like butter across her face. "All the while."

I trot up the stage steps, brush past Carolina into the dressing room, then swing around, a foot from her face. "See anything interesting?" My mouth is thick with memories of Darlene.

"Oh, my, yes." Carolina inches forward so our breasts meet, hers small and high, mine large and low. "Quite interesting." A low-grade current electrifies her petite frame.

This woman is married, I tell myself, as she wraps her arms around my neck. *Happily married...to a man...* Her body melds with mine. *For 20 years...* She pulls my head down to hers. *With a teenage son.* If Carolina had gotten pregnant when she was 14, I could be her daughter.

Carolina's kiss—expert, heated, persistent—catches me off guard with its intensity. *She kisses like she means it.*

Carolina backs me into the dressing room, and I lift her to sit on the counter. She draws me in for minutes-long kisses—kneading my neck with her tiny, forceful fingers, encircling my torso with her sculptured calves. Carolina has the sexiest legs I've ever seen: ropes of muscle hugging bone.

"I had a dream about you," she'd told me shortly after we met.

"Oh? What about?"

"It was, you know, one of those kinds of dreams...erotic."

"Oh," I said, stupidly.

Later, I wished I'd come back with some witty repartee like, "And how was I?" or "Did you enjoy it?"

Arms around her now, I feel as if *I'm* dreaming. Carolina parts my blouse, her breathing shaky but her hands steady. I look down at the plump, pumpernickel-brown skin above the white satin bra that cuts a line across my breasts. My nipples are hard just from having Carolina's eyes on me.

Carolina traces my bra straps—from my back, over my shoulders and collarbones, to my sternum. She rubs her cheeks, nose, and lips against the swell of breasts, glossy satin, pointed nipples.

Undoing the bra, Carolina cups the weight of my breasts in her hands and moans deep in her throat, somewhere between a growl and a purr. Her fingertips graze the tender skin on the bottom of my breasts, her thumbs outlining my areolas. She nuzzles my cleavage, like a burrowing animal, parts her mouth to run dry lips along the fleshy parts of each breast.

My nipples, meticulously avoided, are full to bursting. Carolina lifts her head to kiss my mouth—hard, hungry. She takes my tongue between her lips and circles it with hers. My clit contracts in response. *This woman knows exactly what she's doing.*

Carolina's tongue teasing mine, I sense something brush the very ends of my nipples. I hum inside her mouth, feel a flood of warmth between my legs. Carolina flicks her tongue against mine as her fingers flick in time on my nipples: a counterpoint of pleasure.

When she stops, I am jarred senseless—as if I'd been dunked into a sensory deprivation tank. My clit had been pulsing to the same rhythm.

Eyes holding mine, Carolina removes her spandex tank top. There's no bra underneath, only Carolina's compact breasts: flat on top, round underneath, skin slightly loose around the nipples.

Carolina inches forward so our breasts touch. I shiver as she sways side to side, her dark pink nipples kissing my brown ones.

Carolina leans away, lifts my breasts with her hands, and wraps her lips around the tip of first one then the other breast. She suckles, kisses, and licks my nipples into aching tautness—devouring my breasts like an infant starving for her mother's milk.

Surfacing, Carolina snakes her limbs around mine in a fierce embrace, whispers in my ear, "I've always loved your breasts."

I flash back to the opening night party. I was talking to a dancer when I heard Carolina declare, "Women are beautiful, I'm sorry. No, I won't apologize. I love to look at women's bodies."

I whipped around, lifted my champagne flute, and shouted, "Hear! Hear!" We clinked glasses so hard I thought they might crack. Then we busted up. Those nearby who knew I was a dyke got the joke and joined in. The others smiled weakly.

Tugging on the waistband of Carolina's spandex dance shorts, I help her wriggle out of them. No underwear, Carolina's pubic hair is salt and paprika. I can smell her desire, sharp and sweet and glistening.

She unzips my slacks and they melt to the floor. Kicking off shoes, I step out of the pool of clothing. Carolina scoots from the countertop and pushes me so I'm propped against the wardrobe closet. She kneels down and works off my underwear with her tongue and teeth.

I watch, her head between my ankles, as she runs her short, reddish-gray hair along the insides of my calves, knees, and thighs until the fine strands tickle my clit. Carolina tilts her head up to press her hot breath into my cunt, slides her fingers up my thighs and around my hips, her thumbs kneading muscle, spreading me open, making me gush.

Carolina brushes her tongue along the ends of my pubic hair—a delicate, torturous tickling. Her nose bumps my clit, jolting me into hyper-arousal. Angling her head, she inserts her tongue between my labia.

My eyes flutter close and I brace myself with the closet. Carolina's tongue marks my edges—where my outsides and insides meet. She plunges her tongue into my cunt, and its slippery softness pulses in, out, in, out.

Carolina's hands spread my lips, and I slit my eyes open to see her glittering face peering between my thighs. Her tongue reaches for my enlarged clit.

When her lips encircle the sensitive mound, I can't hold out any longer. I release a long, low moan, knot my hands in Carolina's hair, and ride her tongue into orgasm after delicious orgasm.

When Carolina finally lets me go, my legs give way and I sink to the ground. Climbing on top of me, grinding her pussy against my thigh, Carolina shoves her come-soaked tongue into my mouth and French kisses me as if she could make my mouth come.

Carolina moves up so her breasts hang over my lips and places one nipple at a time between them. My hands run from her shoulders to ass, hips to breasts. I want to devour her, to swallow her frenetic energy.

I maneuver her up farther, so she's on her hands and knees above my face. I thrust two fingers into her wide-open pinkness, slide out slowly as she shudders, then push up and down in varying speeds as she drips onto my chin.

Abruptly, I stop, pull out, and hear Carolina's cry of protest. Grasping her ass, I lower her clit into my mouth, circling just around the tip until she cries out again, this time in frustration.

"Turn around," I order.

"What?" Carolina sounds intoxicated.

"Turn so you're facing the other way."

Carolina flips directions, and I have a full view of her engorged pussy. I spread my legs so my knees butterfly out, and guide her head between my thighs. She grunts when I enfold her clit in my lips, just as she touches my clit with her tongue.

Every time I feel Carolina's excitement build, I back off, letting my tongue circle the opening to her pussy or blow cool air across swollen tissue. Only slowly do I let the rhythm quicken, then slacken when it threatens to crescendo. I come again inside her mouth.

"Please." Carolina rests a damp cheek along my thigh. "Please."

I wrap my mouth around Carolina's clit and, with long strokes of my tongue, increase the pressure. With my right hand, I push three fingers inside Carolina's wide-open pussy and fuck her faster and faster.

Stimulating clit and pussy, I add the coup de grace and insert my pinky—slick from her juices—into the flowering bud of her asshole.

Carolina quakes once, then comes in tidal wave against my face and hand until I'm afraid my tongue and fingers might give way.

I look up between Carolina's voluptuous legs—at the mirrors framed by light bulbs; the tagged costumes hanging on their rack; the posters and stills from past shows.

There's no business like show business and, damn, do I love a double bill.

joy-jewel

Stephanie James

"You gotta see what I had done," said Lucia, lifting off her dress and pulling down her panties. As I knelt down before her, she parted her legs and showed me the jewel that she'd had pierced through her clit—a giant pearl attached to a gold hoop was dangling down from her juice-button.

"It's gorgeous," I said, as Lucia pulled my face forward until my lips were brushing against the pearl.

Just the merest touch of the pearl with my tongue was enough to make Lucia start to groan, since the newness of the piercing meant that it was still charged up to the max. With that in mind, I parted my lips, then swallowed not just the whole of the pearl, but also the whole of the gold hoop and the whole of my lover's prominent clitoris.

Lucia's fingers brushed through my hair as I began to tug on the pearl with my teeth, while pressing my lips up tight to the hood of flesh that surrounded her clitoris. The scent of her juices became more apparent as I gently worked the piercing. I pushed a hand against her cunt lips and felt the moisture on the surface, then pressed my hand through the gap in her thighs so that I could cup her left buttock within the span of my fingers. The lower curve of her plump left cheek seemed to fit perfectly into my splayed out fingers. I dug my fingertips into her flesh, lightly scratching the surface of her ass with my scarlet-painted nails.

All of a sudden, Lucia began to giggle. She told me that something tickled, although I wasn't sure if she meant the fingernails scratching her curvy ass, or the way that my teeth were tugging on the piercing in her clit. Her giggle was like a schoolgirl's laughter, suggesting that she was blessed with a youthful innocence that the piercing in her clit so clearly belied. I could feel the cool, metallic taste of the gold hoop in my mouth, as I worked it around in a circular motion. Breathing deep, I inhaled the fragrance of her pussy, getting sexually high on her heady perfume.

Her cunt was starting to bubble with juice, so I spat out the clit-pearl and pressed my tongue to her opening.

The familiar taste of sex juice struck my tongue with its usual powerful force, making me want to penetrate Lucia's gash as deeply as my tongue was able to. I puckered my lips around her orifice and stuck out my tongue like a spoiled child. Lucia's orifice was taut and unyielding, but still I managed to press my way an inch or so inside her body.

"Keep it right there," Lucia moaned, as I worked my tongue, lapping up the juices from her cunt. She gripped her hands around my head so that I couldn't move my face at all. I was being held prisoner between her thighs and something quickly told me that I wouldn't be escaping until my lover had climaxed.

It was a moment that I hungered for. I longed to feel Lucia coming inside my mouth, sharing her orgasm with me in the most intimate way imaginable. Her pungent sex juices would trickle from her cunt, like a delicate whisper from her lips—its secret message meant for me alone.

Desperate to hear that secret message, I gripped two fingers around the piercing and began to rotate the milky white pearl in semicircles. The clitoral stimulation had an immediate impact upon Lucia, forcing her knees to buckle. Her exhilaration had reached a level where she could no longer remain in a standing position. On the verge of orgasm, she flopped down onto the couch, instantly parting her legs wide open, so that I could resume without so much as a moment's pause.

The pearl's glow transfixed my eyes and I dived between my lover's legs and French-kissed her cunt lips. Lucia pressed her hands on top of the piercing, her fingertips making the pearl rock. It seemed to have the desired effect. A sudden spasm in Lucia's cunt muscles forced her orifice to shut up tight, expelling my tongue from the insides of her body. With the muscular contraction came a sudden gush of sex juice, which I caught within my gaping lips.

Pure, unadulterated bliss! I heard my lover repeatedly shout "Yes" as her body surrendered to a highly charged orgasm. Running my hands all over her thighs and her stomach, I could feel the goose bumps that had appeared all over her flesh.

Although the piercing had provided the focal point of the titillation, its potent sexual charge had dispersed itself throughout the entirety of Lucia's gorgeous body.

Moving away from Lucia's cunt, I took a long look at her pretty face, before planting random kisses all over her skin. Her eyes were tightly shut and her mouth had fallen open, as if the extent of the orgasm had taken her somewhat by surprise. Was it all thanks to the piercing? As I kissed her belly, her arms, and the lower arc of her breasts, it seemed to me that the metallic nature of the gold hoop pierced into her clit had electrified her entire body. A static electric charge seemed to be working its way through her nervous system, so that every point on her flesh became a pressure point, ready and waiting to be set off by the daintiest touch of a fingertip or the gentlest of kisses.

As I explored Lucia's body with my mouth, I savored the heartfelt tone and the depth of the groans that met each kiss that I placed upon her skin. Every groan was like a minor echo of the dominant cries of "Yes" that had signalled her orgasm. I kept that orgasm burning gently in her body by reigniting random pressure points on her flesh with gentle touches and strong kisses. No proper words were spoken throughout this time. Lucia communicated to me solely through the intensity of her groans.

Then she reached out to touch me. I felt her warm hands gently caressing my thighs as I zeroed in on her bosom and took one of her nipples within the compass of my mouth. I glanced up as I ran my tongue around the prominent center of her dark brown ring and noticed that Lucia's eyes were still shut. It wasn't until I bit into the nipple, that she opened her eyes wide and fixed me with a spaced out glare. The azure purity of her baby blues contrasted nicely with the reddened glow that had suffused her features during orgasm. I reached up to her face and stroked her cheek. She turned her head and kissed my fingers. Then she got me to lie flat out on the couch.

The warm glow of her orgasm was gradually fading and, with it, Lucia was slowly awakening, as if from some glorious dream. I parted my legs and let her climb between them, mounting my body in the missionary position. Her lips pressed up against mine for a fragment of a second, then she pulled back a little and stuck out her tongue. I figure that she had tasted her juices on my lips, because she then proceeded to slowly lick her way right around the circumference of my mouth. As she did so, her face lit up with total joy, so that even with her tongue sticking out, it was obvious that she was smiling.

Having licked her way right around my mouth, her tongue then darted between my lips. Next, I felt her arms reaching beneath my torso, as she hugged my body real close to hers. Our breasts pushed together, her prominent nipples easily discernible as they dug into my flesh. Lucia was holding and kissing me with a fervent passion that seemed to make our two bodies meld right into one. I returned her passion with an almost equal force, running my hands all over her ass, while squeezing my thighs around her torso.

Slowly but surely, Lucia began to buck her hips, moving her crotch on top of mine, so that her clit ring stimulated my cunt lips. She seemed aware that the pearl on the gold ring was positioned between my labia, so she used it just like a strap-on dildo, pressing it in and out of my hole. Although the pearl wasn't big and it didn't go far, it felt as though she was touching me deep inside when I closed my eyes and basked in the warmth of my lover's body. I didn't need her to fuck me with a nine-inch dildo. I was already high on the scent of her juices, the feel of her breasts pushed up to mine, and the way that her arms were wrapped so tightly around my torso.

For what seemed like an eternity, Lucia continued to kiss me, pushing her tongue in and out of my mouth exactly in rhythm with the bucking motion of her hips. The pearl kept on popping in and out of my pussy as she rocked. My cunt grew hot and clammy as the jewel repeatedly breached my orifice. As Lucia thrust forward it would press inside me, then it would pop right out when she pulled her hips back. Over and over again, I got to feel that initial burst of excitement that comes at the moment of penetration. No sooner would my cunt lips shut tight than the pearl would be opening them right back up again.

As the repeated penetration made my internal muscles start to spasm, I gripped my fingers hard into Lucia's buns. The sexual tension that I felt was truly exquisite, since my pussy could not quite come to terms with what was going on down there. My insides seemed to tauten in readiness for the deeper penetration that seemed likely to follow each time that the pearl pressed between my labes. But, unlike when Lucia used a dildo on me, the pearl went only an inch or so deep before pulling straight back out again. That left my cunt in a state of total paranoia. It didn't quite know how to respond to what was happening, so it just kept on tightening in spasms of ever-greater intensity.

Soon those spasms had reached fever pitch, and I found myself right on the verge of orgasm. Unable to contain the tension any longer, I broke away from Lucia's kisses and let out an ecstatic scream. Sensing how turned on I was, Lucia immediately increased the speed of her thrusts. I heard the slurp of the sticky liquid in my orifice, as the pearl pressed in and out of my cunt. My internal muscles were convulsing at speed. My lover had brought me to a triumphant climax.

My head spun, as I felt the all-pervading glow of my climax penetrating my extremities. All 10 of my toes curled back on themselves and the muscles in my fingers tightened. Lucia squealed as my nails dug into her ass cheeks, then once again she started to kiss me hard upon the lips.

Lucia's mouth twisted and turned on top of mine as I breathed my orgasm into her body. Excited by the burning passion in my breath, she kept on rocking, even faster than she had been doing before my climax. It wasn't difficult to appreciate why. As the pulsations of pleasure shot through my cunt, so the muscles in my orifice tightened their grip upon the pearl, causing the gold hoop to really tug at her clit. The stimulation that gave to Lucia swiftly brought her to a second orgasm. As she climaxed noisily, our crotches coalesced into a seemingly unbreakable mass of sticky, come-covered flesh. The come and the piercing glued us together with a permanence matched only by that determined by our love for one another.

"With this clit ring, I thee wed," said Lucia, kissing my lips between each word—our love and passion made eternal by a connecting band of gold.

the cerebral seduction

Brenda Whitehall

The Setting: Your place.
The Characters: You and Me. I'm wearing tight, faded blue jeans with a long denim shirt and ass-kicking cowboy boots. You are radiant in a breathtaking minidress that accentuates your amazing curves. You're wearing sexy, black fishnets with a garter belt and heels, and matching black lace bra and panties. We look simply delicious.
The Scene: Just a little sex.
The Action: We stumble through your front door, kicking it closed behind us, kissing and fondling each other wildly.
The Emotion: Animal attraction.
The Story: Goes like this...

You unbutton the fly on my tight-fitting jeans as I rub my body against yours, revealing a shocking bulge in my upper right thigh. Your breath deepens. My trembling fingers lightly caress your perfectly sculpted body, lingering for a moment at the side of each breast, enjoying your soft protruding flesh.

I slowly unzip your dress and it falls to the floor, unveiling such stunning beauty. Butterfly kisses take flight, showering your neck, shoulders, and chest with quick, tender pecks. My breath on your neck sends shivers down your spine as I nibble on your ear and whisper naughty secrets. Our hearts have synchronized into one pulsating beat. We share a long, slow, deep, wet, passionate kiss. Our tongues waltz to the rhythm of our hearts. We barely feel the ground beneath us.

I cup my hands to catch your voluptuous breasts as you release them from your sexy bra. I squeeze, caress, and kiss them gently. My thumb slightly circles your large, light areola while my mouth makes its way to your awaiting left nipple. I tease your nipple with the tip of my tongue and then suck it into my mouth; it becomes erect between my lips. I rotate from breast to breast, nipple to nipple. We both release light moans of excitement.

Our mouths reconnect for a hot and heavy kissing session. The sounds of the universe disappear. All we hear are pounding hearts and short sighs. Our bodies buzz with electricity. I feel a rush as you respond to my touch. My knees get weak. You take my face in your hands and direct it back to your well-defined cleavage. My head rests for a moment, feeling your heartbeat.

My hand reaches for one breast and my mouth takes as much of it as will fit. I place my other hand on your lower back, holding you close. I begin sucking, licking, kissing each heaving breast.

You know exactly what you want and take charge. You redirect my face to the center of your chest, pressing your breasts against my cheeks. I can hardly breathe, but you continue rubbing your breasts all over my face. One moist nipple lands in the crevice of my dimple—a perfect fit. I giggle, but you don't know why.

Our hands suddenly become uncontrollable and are everywhere! Our bodies vibrate with anticipation as you lead me to your bedroom.

You slide your panties down while I unclip your garter belt, but leave it on you. My hands caress, my lips kiss, my tongue explores your entire body. I drop to my knees and kiss circles around your navel, holding your hips with both hands. My hands ascend your sides reaching once again for your perfect breasts, stroking and squeezing them.

I tickle your tummy with flyaway kisses, both of us uncertain of where they will land. Your abdominopelvic muscles contract. My tongue's long, firm strokes coast from your groin to your navel—side to side, up and down—until I am dizzy with desire.

My hands continue their motion from hips to breasts, breasts to spine, spine to buttocks, buttocks to hips. You begin tearing off my clothes—that denim shirt, red lace bra, and cowboy boots—all flying in the air. My jeans are still in place, but unbuttoned. We share another passionate kiss. Your sensuous ruby red lips are magical. I break away to kiss your chin, suck on your throat and slide my tongue all the way down your body—

through your cleavage—past your navel, and finally resting my face on your Brazilian-waxed pubic mound. I brush my lips across your smooth skin while you run your fingers through my long, thick, silky hair. I ache to be inside of you.

You seductively part your legs, inviting me closer. My right thumb gently lifts your clitoral hood for a delicate, leisurely visit from my uninhibited tongue. I teasingly blow on your clit and then softly kiss it. You caress my earlobes and continue playing with my hair. My other hand reaches behind you, cupping your firm ass cheeks. My restless fingers yearn to enter your pleasure palace.

My tentative hand travels between your legs, caressing your inner thighs. I check for your approval. Your skin is velvety soft. I kiss and tease you with my starving tongue. I cup your satiny genitals in my hand. My body quivers as I feel your vulva swell with excitement. Your arousal thrills me. My fingers dance like ballerinas—graceful, assured, disciplined—touching every tender part of you. You are soaking with desire.

I quickly remove your garter belt, fling it across the room, and then use my teeth to peel the stockings from your long, sexy legs bit-by-bit. You lay on your bed, and I cover you with wet kisses right down to your tiny toes. I massage your feet with my strong hands. I lick and suck on each toe. You laugh when I simulate fellatio on your big toe, but it turns you on to see my luscious lips wrapped around it. I gently bite your arches while looking you straight in the eye. You're not sure what to think, but I think you like it.

I remove my jeans while you watch, licking and biting your sensuous ruby red lips. You laugh uproariously at my glow-in-the-dark boxer shorts, so I pounce on you in a moment of protest. We roll around on your bed tickling one another into near hysteria. Catching our breath, we lay side by side and sort out the tangled mess of hair we have just created. We hold each other and kiss. I love the way our tongues merge and the way your bare breasts feel pressed against my chest.

I slide off your bed, dragging my hands and cascades of long, flowing hair across your body. You spontaneously tremble. I signal your position with only my eyes. I'm kneeling at your bedside, completely at your service. You place your legs over my bare shoulders. Sitting up, you take my face in your hands, guiding my head between your legs. I kiss your labia and tease your clit with the sides of my tongue. As I take you inside my mouth, you lean back in bed, and I clutch your breasts.

I caress your gorgeous body, searching for every erogenous zone, but I don't liberate you from my mouth's embrace. My tongue jets inside of you as I suck on, lick and kiss you. I explore you from anus to navel, stimulating each nerve ending and sensing your muscles contract along my travels.

Long, firm strokes...gentle sucking...tender nibbling...swift tongue flicks...I'm lost in your loveliness. I carefully enter your warm, wet vagina with anxious fingers. I'm exhilarated just to be with you. I pause to savor the moment. You tightly grip my fingers, holding me inside you. I penetrate you as you release your clench—fast and slow, deep and shallow, circling and twisting—my fingers are dripping with your desire. I hungrily lick your juices from each digit, tasting and smelling your sweetness.

Your gyrating hips are driving me wild. They thrust to meet my fingers, pulling me deeper inside of you. My lips and tongue hold your clit hostage. My other hand is playing with your breasts—plucking your erect nipples, squeezing, groping, caressing.

I feel your body tense and release; you moan, your body tenses again. Your back arches. Your strong legs pull my shoulders closer. You moan. You run your fingers through my hair and caress my wandering arm. You moan. I continue probing, squeezing, sucking, licking, fucking. My thumb loiters around your anus, adding slight pressure and stimulation. You moan and gasp for air. You are breathless.

I take my sopping wet fingers out of you, replacing them with my tongue. Time has stood still. I completely devour your cunt— inside, outside, all around. Your writhing body energizes me. I can't stop. I don't want to stop. You feel and taste amazing. You are panting...moaning...groaning...begging for release...you call out my name as you come inside my mouth.

Your body still shudders with electric impulses as I draw the dildo through my boxers and climb on top of you. You are so incredibly wet that I easily mount and enter you. "Don't give me any of that slow shit, baby, fuck me hard," you order.

We kiss passionately and I begin riding you—really fast, alternating deep and shallow thrusts, just as you want it— bumping, pumping, and grinding outrageously. You tear at my back with your long, French-manicured nails while occasionally grabbing my ass to force me deeper. My black leather harness is a bit loose and the rapid pressure on my clit gives me a quick surface orgasm. I voraciously massage your breasts, suck ravenously on your nipples and return to your sensuous ruby red lips for deep kisses. Our passion and lust surpass all expectations.

We roll over and you ride me. It excites me to watch your bouncing breasts. I lick my luscious lips at the sight of your labia devouring my big dick. I hold your hips, pulling you closer, taking you deeper. You lean forward and pummel my face with your breasts. I latch onto your nipples. Pure paradise!

I turn sideways, we scissor, then we spoon for a while. You get on all fours and I take you from behind, ever so tightly holding your breasts. We jump out of bed and you lean against the wall. We fuck standing up. It's intense and sweaty. We can barely keep our balance.

We run back to bed. You yank down my boxers and undo my strap-on. You toss it aside. We hear a crash, but ignore it. I lay on top of you, skin on skin, no barriers. We tenderly kiss and caress. I gently spread your legs and you open yourself for me. One by one, we entwine our legs like an erotic game of Twister. I take my hand and part my labia, moving closer to put mine on yours. Our satiny genitals meet, saturated by our lust. We slowly begin gyrating our hips sliding in the silky wetness between us. We touch each other's breasts. I tightly hold onto your left leg for balance. I call you honey. You call me baby. I feel the tingling of another approaching orgasm.

I am lying on top of you again. You wrap your legs around my waist, tightening your grip. Our clits are touching and rubbing. We can barely catch our breath. Our hearts are pounding. We thrust; we wiggle—up and down, back and forth. Our bodies are so tense. All our senses have completely vanished. We have merged into one. We simultaneously explode with orgasm, equally aroused by one another's bodily convulsions. They continue, one after another after another. We are both exhausted.

We laugh. We gaze incredulously, but adoringly, into each other's eyes. We kiss. We wipe the sweat from our bodies and sigh. You snuggle in my arms. I pull up the sheets and kiss your forehead. We fall asleep, still smiling.

the seldom told story of a b-girl

Lovelybrown

I hate birthdays. I mean, I hated birthdays. No one had ever thrown me a birthday party, and the thought of growing older terrified me. Especially the year I was turning 25. But as my birthday approached, Nicole and Imani decided that they should do something special for me. They wanted this birthday to be different.

They took me to a WNBA game and out for drinks before I got too tired...and aroused. So we went back to their crib.

"Ah, Imani, can you massage my neck. I have a crook in it." I look at her, smiling. She positions herself behind me and starts to massage my neck.

"Nicole, when you are finished, come here. I think Caki needs some stress relief. She's kinda tense." I look at Imani, trying to read her face. It feels kind of good and Imani is looking nice. I can faintly smell that cologne that first caught my attention.

Nicole comes over to sit next to me. "You relaxing, ma? You looked bugged out!" she says, grinning at Imani.

What the hell are they up to? I probably was bugged out, because Imani had her hands all in my locks. And she had these hands that made me wet just from the touch.

"Check this out, ma, we gonna pamper you. Is that cool? We all friends here." There goes Nicole's smirk again. She starts massaging my feet, and I feel like I'm dreaming. I mean every girl has fantasies in the back of their mind, but to have someone actually do it... But then maybe I was being premature.

"We know what you need, Caki, so chill out. We your girls, remember, we said we had something special for you. We're gonna give you the platinum treatment." Imani gives me that smile again. She stops massaging my neck and heads toward the master bathroom. I hear water running.

"Nicole," Imani screams from the bathroom, "come here for a second. I need your help."

"What are y'all up to?" I ask Nicole.

"We're gonna give you a birthday you'll always remember. Yo, why don't you go into the bathroom, we have another surprise there for you." Dumfounded, I oblige, still curious about what those two are up to.

I walk down the hall into the restroom and there's a tub full of bubbles all ready for me, complete with a bath pillow. I take off my clothes and get in the water, noticing the candles illuminating the room, then settle back in the tub and relax.

I hear footsteps, and it's Nicole in a white terry cloth robe; she's smiling at me and carrying three champagne glasses. I look up to see Imani in the shadows. She is wearing a tight-fitted tank top that exposes the outline of her nipples.

"How's the birthday girl doing? We brought you some wine to make a toast."

Imani pops the cork and pours some in each of our glasses. *Here I am with two sexy-ass women, pretty much naked, and I feel comfortable as hell. I must be gone.* We drink and laugh a little and joke. Then Nicole just smiles and starts to wash my body, as Imani pours water in my hair and begins washing my hair. I can feel my body relax as these two women take charge of me. I hear myself moan.

All I feel is hands on top of hands touching me and caressing me. My eyes are open, yet they are closed. Imani rinses my hair and Nicole gets up and lets Imani take over where she had left off. Imani washes my back and caresses my breasts, as my nipples grow harder and tenser. Now she starts to kiss on my neck, and I find myself getting wetter and more aroused. Falling into a fog. Enraptured by something, I pull her face to mine and start to kiss her, feeling fireworks go off in the small of my groin. I'm feeling not only aroused but also excited. Nicole gets behind Imani and starts to kiss Imani's neck so that all three of us became one. I push Imani's face back. And gesture to Nicole to stop.

"Let's move somewhere else." My eyes are glazed and full of longing for something more, something deeper. Nicole takes a towel and wraps it around me as I get out. Imani, somewhat trans-fixed, sits on the edge of the tub to let the water out and tells us she'll join us in a second. I look at Nicole, questioning.

"It's OK, boo. We just want to treat you like you need to be treated, if you know what I mean." She smiles as she leads me into the master bedroom. I sit on the bed, not knowing what to expect, and she goes to the dresser and grabs some lotion. It smells fruity but subtle, and she slathers me all over. She stands and takes off her robe, and I have to catch my breath. Standing in front of me are two of the most supple, firm breasts I have ever seen. She casually places them in my face and starts to massage my scalp, gently pushing me back on the bed. All in one move, she manages to straddle me, and I feel her warmth riding me. The lights go down, and I hear soft music. Nicole gets up, pulling me with her.

I oblige and feel Nicole pressing against my back as her hands encircle my breasts. Then I smell Imani's scent as she comes my way. Imani gets on her knees and starts to suck on my nipples as Nicole feeds them to her. I moan as my legs get weak and I feel the lips on my vagina begin to swell.

Complete silence surrounds me. Imani, now only wearing boxers, goes to the bed and pulls me toward her. I'm lying on top of her, inhaling her as I kiss her full lips. While I am on top of her, I press my pelvis into hers until we start a rhythmic pattern of tension on my clit. I want her to touch it, my moans seem to whisper, as she kisses me and runs her hand along my back. I can feel myself getting wetter in anticipation.

I start licking her. At first I trace my tongue along her neck and then I arch my back so that my mouth is sucking her nipple. I smell her scent and start getting even more worked up as I feel my hands edge their way down to my spot. It's wet.

"Open your legs, ma." She says it so casually that my body moves before I can think about it. I feel Nicole's hands on the back of my waist, then her fingers, and then a soft, yet hard sensation. I gasp and raise my head, feeling Nicole but looking at Imani. She's smiling. Nicole is moaning. My ass is pointed up in the air and Nicole is entering me from behind, inch by inch. Pulling me faster and deeper on top of her strap-on. I join the rhythm and start to feel it, as Imani starts to kiss me again, driving her tongue in deeper.

"Can you feel me, Caki...does it feel nice?" I can't speak, so I acknowledge her with a moan. I feel myself going into a zone, and just as I start to climax Nicole pulls out of me and Imani gets up. They lay me on the bed, and Nicole lies down on her back and tells me to sit on it backward. I oblige and start riding her, with my ass checks bouncing on her pussy, wet from excitement. Imani moves in front of me and starts licking at my clit from the front. I start getting louder, falling into a frenzy of excitement as I feel Nicole pushing me deeper onto her.

I rise off of Nicole and position myself so that I can lie completely flat on the bed. I pen myself up to Imani so that she can ravish me. She opens my legs wider, places them in the air like a goalpost, and dives in, forcing every bit of energy into her tongue. I shiver. Both women are taking me to levels that I never thought possible. I feel my body jerk, and I feel the familiar sensation of a climax. I lose my breath and scream.

Nicole moves from underneath me and goes to Imani. Out of breath, I watch them embrace and kiss. Imani takes off Nicole's strap, gets on her knees, and goes down on Nicole as her head goes back in exhausted screams. I feel myself getting wetter watching the entire scene.

Imani places Nic on the edge of the bed so that she's in between my legs. She continues eating her as I watch Nicole moan and gasp. I look at her nipples and begin to play with them until she begs me to suck them. I oblige, but place mine directly in her face yet out of reach of her mouth.

I can smell our scents all fusing into one. Nicole arches her back, pushing her breasts deeper into my mouth. I suck harder and move my mouth along her stomach. Now I can feel her fingers entering my pussy, digging deeper, falling and sliding in my wetness. I gasp. Imani raises off of Nicole, allowing me to slide lower as I push my face deep into her warm soft brown. I gently lick her clit and suck her lips as her moans grow longer. I feel Imani's hand pushing me deeper into it. I moan as Nicole sticks her tongue deep inside of me.

Imani takes off her boxers and climbs on the bed. She sits behind me and starts to rub and slap my ass. I jerk out of shock and look back at her, and she says, "It's OK, baby. It won't hurt that much longer. Just keep doing what you doing, and let me handle the rest."

I go back to Nicole, then feel Imani reach into my mound to size it up. I bite down on Nicole's lips. Ahh...Imani enters me slowly from behind, going very deep from the start and then pulling halfway out. Quickly I become frantic, but Imani holds on to my hips and pulls me closer against her. I lose my concentration with Nicole, and she slides up from underneath me to become the voyeur. Imani keeps going deeper into me. Then she flips me on my back and looks at me with this intensity that seems faintly familiar.

"Baby, you are so damn tight. I've dreamed about this since I met you." Am I tripping, or is she sounding sincere? "Look at me, Caki...in the eyes...can you feel what I'm giving, what I want to give you?" She raises my legs higher and pushes her pelvis deeper and faster into me, all the while moaning and becoming aroused that she arouses me.

"Oh, Imani, baby...come for me, please. Oh, come on big daddy!" That's it—all of a sudden I feel her push hard and she screams so loud I think maybe she's hurt. But then she pulls out of me, takes off the strap, comes back toward me, and just closes her eyes, laying her head on my chest.

I awake the next morning not really believing it had happened. But then again, I'm in between Nicole and Imani. And I have a feeling that all three of us will be friends for a long time.

lap dance lust

Rachel Kramer Bussel

We pull into the shadowy parking lot in some corner of Los Angeles. I look around the deserted area, wondering where exactly we are, only half caring. Most strip clubs in L.A. are located in tucked away corners like this one.

I'm a little apprehensive as we walk around to the entrance and part the strings of beads to enter Cheetah's—a strip club, a real live strip club! I've been dreaming of just such a place for years, but have never worked up the courage to actually go. I'd heard that Cheetah's was "women friendly," and from the crowd I can immediately tell it's true. There are plenty of guys, but also a decent number of female customers who look like they're having a good time.

My three friends and I take ringside seats along the surprisingly empty stage and animatedly set about checking out each new dancer. Many of them are what I expected—peroxide blond, fake boobs, very L.A. and very boring. Some have a spark of creativity, and feign a glimmer of interest to tease out one of the dollars we hold in our hands, but many pass right by us or stare back with vacant eyes.

We watch as one girl after another maneuvers around the stage, shimmying up and then down the shiny silver pole, twisting and writhing in ways I can't imagine my body doing. It feels surreal, this world of glamour and money and lights and ultrafemininity. I look and stare and whisper to my friends. Though I'm having fun, the place starts to lose its charm when I have to get more change and still no girl has really grabbed my eye. I settle in with a new drink and a fresh stack of bills and hope that the next round of dancers won't disappoint.

Then the next girl walks out and I'm transfixed. She's the hottest girl I've ever seen. She's wearing cave girl attire, a leopard-print bandeau top and hot pants—all tan skin, natural curves, and gleaming black hair. She looks shiny, like she's just put on suntan lotion. She slithers along, making eye contact when she passes us, crawling back across the stage, putting her whole body into the performance. She toys with her shorts, thumbs hooked into the waist, before sliding them down her long legs to reveal black panties. I know that she's the one for me, that I really like her and am not just an indiscriminate ogler when I realize that I preferred her with her shorts on.

After her performance, I offer her a wad of dollars. "Thanks," she says. "I'm Gabrielle."

"Hi," I say shyly. "I really like your outfit."

"Me too," she giggles, then smiles before waving her fingers and gliding off the stage.

"O-o-oh, you like her. You should get a lap dance."

"Yeah, get a lap dance! Get a lap dance!'

My friends are practically jumping up and down in their excitement, making me blush.

"Maybe."

"No, no, you should get one. She's totally hot."

"I know, I know, but let me think about it, OK?" They're so eager for me to lose my lap dance virginity, I'm afraid they may drag me over to her.

I need to get away for a minute, so I go to the bathroom. To my shock, I find her sitting inside, casually chatting with a friend. "Oh, hi," I stammer. "Is this your dressing room?"

She laughs. "No, but it's almost the same quality." I smile and then go into the stall, nervous at having spoken to her. When I emerge and begin to wash my hands, she admires my purse. I tell her about it and then take out my sparkly lipgloss. She asks to try some, and I hold it out to her, watching as her finger dips into the red goo. We talk a bit more about makeup, and then she says, casually, "Did you want to get a lap dance?"

Did I? Of course! "Yes, I'd like that," I say.

"Great, just give me a few more minutes and I'll come get you."

I practically float out the door and back to my friends. *I'm going to get a lap dance, and I arranged it all by myself! Ha!* I feel like gloating. I wait patiently, trying not to let my excitement show in a big stupid grin.

After a few minutes, she emerges and summons me, leading me to the other side of the stage, against a wall where I've seen other girls pressed up against old men. She seats me on a plastic-covered couch, then takes a chair and places it a few feet in front of me. "So people can't look up your skirt," she tells me. I smile to thank her for her kindness; it never would've occurred to me. I give her some larger bills, and we talk for a minute or two before a song she likes comes on.

And then, quite suddenly, it starts. She pushes me so my head is tilted back against the wall, the rest of me pressed against the sticky plastic, my legs slightly spread. She stands between my legs, and then leans forward, pressing her entire body along the length of mine. She smells like sweat and lotion and some indefinable sweetness, and I breathe deeply. Even her sweat smells good, like baby powder. Her soft hair brushes against my face and shoulders; her breasts are pressed up against mine. Then I feel her thigh against my hand; she's climbed up on the couch with me. This is definitely not what I expected. I've never been to a strip club before, but I thought I knew the deal—I'd seen *Go*, right? You can't touch the dancers or you'll get kicked out. But what if they're touching you? What about her hand gliding along mine, the out-side of her smooth thigh touching my arm, her slightly damp skin setting mine on fire? The look she gives me is priceless: As her body moves downward and she's crouched near my stomach, I look and her hooded eyes are on me, her face a vision of pure lust, her mouth slightly open. I'm sure it's practiced, but it feels as real as any look I've ever received, and it enters and warms me.

I think I know what I'm getting into; I've read all the feminist arguments, the sex worker manifestos. This is just a job and I'm a paying customer: one song, one lap, and one transaction. But all of that background disappears, likewise my friends, my family, L.A., everyone else in the club. It's just her and me. Never mind the music; it's that look as she slides between my open legs. I swallow heavily. I can't move, and I don't want to, ever again. I just want to sit here and let her brush herself against me, as I get wetter. And then her hand reaches up, delicately turning around my Star of David necklace. It's the sweetest gesture, and something only another femme would notice or care about. She gives me a little smile as she does it, and I give her one back.

The song is almost over, and she gives it her all. Her body pushes hard against mine, pressing my chest, stomach, thighs. She's working me so good this huge bouncer walks over and glances at us suspiciously, but she turns around and gives him a look that tells him to move along. I like knowing that whatever she's doing with me is enough out of the norm to warrant the bouncer's attention. I feel ravished in a way I've never felt before; it's pure sexual desire, concentrated into whatever messages her skin and her eyes can send me in the course of a five-minute song.

When the song ends, I give her a generous tip, and she sits with me for a little while. She takes my hand in hers, which is delicate and soft, and I revel in her touch. It's tender and sensitive, and I need this, need to hear her sweet voice tell me about her career as a singer, her friendship with a famous musician, her upcoming trip to New York. I need to hear whatever it is she wants to tell me, true or not.

My head knows certain things; this is a strip club and that was a lap dance, this is her job. But inside, I know something else. I know that we just exchanged something special. It wasn't sex or passion or lust per se; it was more than, and less than. It was contact, attention, and adoration. Call me crazy, but I think it went both ways.

After we talk, I go back to my friends, but I feel a bit odd. I know they were watching, but did they see what really happened?

"That was some lap dance."

"Yeah, that was really amazing for your first time."

"She gave you her real name? That's a big stripper no-no."

"I think she liked you."

I nod and respond minimally, still in my own world. For the rest of the trip, whatever I'm doing, wherever I am, part of me is still sitting on that plastic-covered couch, looking down at her, breathing her scent, reveling in her look.

I haven't gone to any more strip clubs since, or gotten any more dances. How could they ever live up to her? I don't know if I want to find out.

retribution

Rakelle Valencia

She spread her legs wider, flattening their length to the mattress, thrusting her pelvis into the air, raising her ass checks off of the cool, cotton sheets. She squeezed her eyes shut, head thrown back, working faster at herself, in silence. Her girlfriend wouldn't appreciate it. Not that her girlfriend didn't know that she was always masturbating. But her packing, dyke girlfriend was due home any minute, and, like Archie Bunker to Edith, the butch would demand her dinner, or retribution.

It was worth the risk. Thinking of it made the brunet, computer geek wetter, her slippery juices drooling down along her crack to moisten an anxious anus. Oh, Becca could pop off right now, but she struggled to hold her orgasm at bay. Just a little more, that's all she wanted, just a little more heightening to the enrapturing sensations. With that teensy bit more she would go big. The nerdy, brunet beauty was pleading with her body for that mind-blowing come, slowing the circles, then stopping completely, then working them again, walking the edge with her fingertips.

"I knew you'd be in here."

The gruff voice made Becca go flaccid like a schoolboy caught beating off in the bathroom. Only she was no boy, a femme all the way.

"I knew what you'd be up to when I didn't find my dinner cooking on the stove." The butch dyke filled the doorway, hands on her leather-belted hips. It wasn't the way the butch, blue-collar dyke looked, but what she could do, that kept Becca around, convinced Becca to play into the old his and hers stereotypes.

The pale, cubicle-kept tech's buttocks collapsed back onto the mattress, the cotton sheets now feeling clammy, a musky sex odor rising up to fog the air. Half naked, missing crumpled khakis that were tossed on the floor in haste to lay inert between there and somewhere, Becca stared at Jo, but couldn't work up a sufficient fright. The prone, compromised woman's eyes scanned the big butch, blocky-built, squat woman filling out a larger frame, clad in a nondescript, navy button-down and newer, relaxed-fit 505 jeans. It was the bulge in the crotch of those Levi's that gave Becca what she desired. Unconscious of her actions, Becca licked her lips and squeezed her pussy tightly between sodden fingers.

"You've been naughty. Real naughty." Jo's words struck Becca as funny, but the intent didn't. Jo was in. It never took much.

Before Becca could think of any cheeky reply or stammer some adolescent excuse, Jo had the smaller woman flipped on her stomach.

Pale, frail Becca held on tight. The punishment would come swift. But the defiant girl still had one hand clenched to her twat, sinking thin fingers into the crease of her near-hairless lower lips, the other grabbing for cotton sheets, twisting them mercilessly in her small palm.

Whack. The sound from her fleshy ass cheeks seemed to reverberate from the thin apartment walls, gaining strength before stinging Becca's ears. It was the sound, the anticipation of that sound that the office geek wanted. The physical slap was only secondary and would only come into the forefront of the play when her ass was reddened to fluorescence.

"You've been very naughty, playing before your chores are done. Sneaking off to...to...what? What have I caught you doing?" *Whack.* "You would have me come home to this?" *Whack.* "After I have worked hard all day." *Whack.*

Becca was straining now. She didn't know if she could take any more. She had stopped stimulating her clit with those tiny circles, but just the pressure of grinding against her trapped hand with every openhanded blow from Jo would be her undoing. One more sound, one more smack, and she would go, losing to undulating waves of orgasm.

Maybe Jo sensed this, because now the butch woman was caressing Becca's buttocks in a soothing way like a cat playing with its prey.

"I know what you want. I know what you need now." The husky dyke pulled at Becca's legs, separating them until the nerdy girl's gleaming, sopping slit pronounced a greater redness and heat than did her chastised ass.

Jo sunk her finger slightly into Becca's hole then traced a moist line to her puckered anus. The dyke's slow, drawling finger met Becca's struggling digits clamped over a rigged clitoris. *Whack!*

"Yah, you do need a little something," Jo said.

Becca was already at the brink. Her eyes closed tightly, forcing salty tears to squirm from locked confinement. She was there, and she couldn't hold off any longer. And she knew it was all too soon for Jo.

Zip. The gritty sound alone drove the introverted tech over the edge. An image ripped through Becca's mind of Jo's thick, eight-inch, silicon, two-toned swirled dong plopping free from the 505s. "Ugh! Shit! Shit!"

"Bitch." *Whack.*

The mattress between long, stilted legs yielded to Jo's kneeling weight. Powerful hands clasped at Becca's hips. Strong arms lifted her rigid, bucking body to prop on pale, naked knees, ass flagging in the air.

For a moment, the computer tech felt Jo's smooth dong sliding along her wet crevasse, teasing her hungry hole with its slick, rubbery, mushroomed tip. And that was plenty if that was all there was to be.

Becca lost herself to the writhing of wave after wave, not noticing Jo's progressing dick-play—until the big dyke took hold of that rugged prick's base and rammed it home into Becca's pulsating, tightening cunt.

"Ohh..." The top of Becca's skull thumped the wooden headboard, but it didn't matter. The brunet hadn't felt a thing, even though somewhere in her mind she knew a growing lump would later plague her cranium. "Oh, yah. Yah."

Jo held a bear hug around Becca's thighs, keeping her prick thrust to the hilt as the bottom girl squirmed. The butch tongued the techie's lower back, nipping and sucking the quick-marking skin. "Are you done? My dick wants to fuck you, and I want to watch."

There wasn't much of an answer, and reply or not, Jo was determined. The butch dyke hauled herself upright from the waist, stroking her hands along white flesh, savoring the sight with eyes of a carnivore. She took a handful of hips again, sunk her dong in, and slapped her pelvis to Becca's fleshy ass, holding until the tails of her button-down and the unzipped 505s were soaked through.

Jo pulled almost all of the way out, watching Becca's hungry hole reluctantly release the eight inches. *Whack.* "Look at what you've done to my shirt. You've smeared creamy come on my good shirt and pants." *Whack.* And the brute of a woman pounded her dick to Becca for emphasis. "You've already slopped my shirt, but I will have my due."

She drew the silicon dong away as Becca squirmed toward it, following the exquisite, tormenting prong and emitting quiet, erotic moans of the very needy. "Don't you worry," Jo patted Becca's bare ass. "I'm going to fuck you hard, fast, and good. But I think you need a little something more."

The dong sprung out, bobbing with its weight as Jo sat back onto her heels, staring mesmerized into Becca's slicked crack. The butch stroked the shaved crease with the ball of her thumb, following a sunken line from cunt to puckered hole, wetting the pathway, spreading thick cream the entire distance. She rose up and thunked the tip of her dick onto Becca's darkened hole, watching the crinkled skin surrounding the opening contract at the teasing assault.

Then the dyke's prick slid in sloppy descent, as the butch woman's thumb further tormented the computer tech's tightened brown hole. At the same time, both projectiles were shoved home, knocking Becca flat to the sheets from her knees.

Jo stayed with the collapsing of the comp nerd, smashing her body atop, humping and thumping with her dick and thumb like a rogue jackhammer until Becca came again, this time harder and longer so that the slight brunet woman buried her face into the matching cotton-condomed pillows to stifle her obscene screams.

Jo climbed off Becca when the high-pitched obscenities turned to whimpering mewling, only when the body beneath was quieted except for the occasional aftershock.

"Now, would you get me some dinner?"

eva, surprised

Essa Elan Aja

It was some solo applause accompanied by flailing moans that awakened Eva in mass bewilderment. Her eyes spun and her ears stretched, wondering what the hell was going on in her condo at 5 A.M.

She finally pinpointed that the sounds seemed to drift from her roommate Irene's room. Frightened, Eva thought the worst. She'd gone to sleep knowing she and Irene were completely alone. The loud slaps and the way that Irene screamed made it obvious that something was horribly wrong. *Irene is under assault! Some masked attacker is smacking her around, beating her into submission so that he can have his perverse way with her!* Eva knew she would have to act quickly. Frantically yet quietly, she rummaged through her closet in search of a weapon. Finding a baseball bat, Eva crept like a cat to Irene's open door. She had approached ready to strike, but what she saw made her drop the bat and her defenses. Her roommate was alone, bent over on her bed, buck-naked before a mirror, one hand fucking her own pussy and the other one spanking her rear.

Irene was watching herself in the mirror as best she could between the thrusts and slaps. She had her whole hand inside herself, sliding it with super fluidity, occasionally retracting it from her dark infinity to tease her clit and outer lips. Simultaneous to this action, she mercilessly spanked her right cheek, bringing down a loud boom, bursting her capillaries only to rub the newly sensitized spot and then spank it again.

She was crying out in total abandon, oblivious to Eva's presence in the doorway, or even in the apartment at all. Or, perhaps she didn't care that she wasn't alone, since only her orgasm mattered.

Eva didn't make a sound throughout the bizarre scene. She never gasped in horror. She didn't even close Irene's door or run for coffee at the corner café.

The bright red spot on Irene's ass, the helpless recipient of her assault, mesmerized Eva. She allowed her eyes to follow the constant in and out of Irene's hand, the fingers gliding around the ridges of her pussy, the same fingers finding their way to Irene's gapping mouth, which was eager to taste her own juices, and momentarily muffle her moans. And all the while, Irene spanked that dazzling scarlet cheek.

Suddenly, Irene started twitching and shaking. Her body reverberated, dancing electric and free. All her nerves seemed hyper. Her ass was vibrating and resounding like thunder, and, without any warning, Eva found her own fingers touching her sex.

Finding herself already wet and swollen, Eva concentrated her fingers on the tip of her throbbing clit, propping one foot against the doorframe to keep from falling. Now her breathing was growing shallow and she was mimicking the low, deep moans of Irene's ecstasy. She continued to watch Irene spasm and slap until Irene threw her head completely back, her upper body falling like a leaf onto the bed, fully enraptured by her orgasm.

The sight sent Eva into fits as well and she moaned despite herself, loudly and conspicuously, until Irene, now a bit calmer, turned to find Eva standing in the threshold, caught in the act.

Unashamed, Irene gave Eva a slow, inviting smirk. But Eva didn't smile back. In fact, she was too shocked to speak. She'd never seen anything like that and she'd definitely never done anything like it. In silence, she picked up her baseball bat, turned from Irene's door, and purposely went back to bed.

angel

Julie Jacobs

Debbie put her glass down and placed her hands on both sides of my face, pulling me in for a kiss I'd waited nearly half my life for. Slow, sweet, sensual. Our tongues intertwined. I explored her with my curious mouth, my eager lips. She closed her eyes, and I kissed her forehead, her cheekbones, her chin, her neck. Softly, tenderly, with more love than I'd felt for anyone in my entire life.

I placed my glass on one of the end tables and lay on the bed. Debbie straddled me, sitting upright, her hands roaming the length of my body. "I can't believe this," she whispered. "I can't believe it's really you." She ran her fingers through my hair, traced my lips with her fingers, ran them over my face, down my neck, over my breasts. The mere touch of her fingers on my breasts sent shivers down my spine and flooded my mind with sweet memories of our summer nights together when we were teenagers. She continued to touch me like that, caress me through my dress, for quite a while. "Your body is so beautiful," she said. "So compact and firm. My God, you're gorgeous."

Somehow we wrangled ourselves out of our clothes—me out of my little black dress, Debbie out of her black rayon shirt and stylish gray slacks. We were still in our bras and underwear, but now we were skin against skin. Her curvy, smooth body felt like an old friend returning. I took Debbie's glasses off and set them on the end table. Her chestnut-brown eyes sparkled in the lamplight.

Debbie leaned over me and with her full lips placed tiny, gentle kisses on the part of my breasts that my bra didn't cover. She ran a finger down my cleavage. "So beautiful," she whispered. I reached around and took off my bra, and she just stared at me, taking me in like a long swallow of expensive wine. Then she put her luscious mouth to one of my nipples, circling it with her wet tongue, while kneading my other breast in her hand. The combination of her warm breath and wet tongue on my nipple drove me crazy. I quietly moaned, then whispered, "I love you."

Debbie looked up at me and smiled. "I know, sweetheart," she said, then continued down my body, caressing and kissing me, until she got to my panties, which I removed before helping her out of her lingerie. We were now both completely naked. Her skin was like alabaster. A lamppost outside sent light streaming in through the window and made her skin glisten; she looked like an angel. I put my hand between her legs and gently grabbed her short, trimmed pubic hair before spreading her lips with my fingers and running them lightly over her clit and vulva. She let out a small moan when I did this. She was so gorgeous, so loving, so clearly excited. I wanted to eat her up.

I covered Debbie with kisses from head to toe, touched her zaftig body all over, then spread her lips and buried my mouth into her crotch. I kissed her bright-pink outer lips, ran my tongue over them, tasted the tangy sweetness of her cunt. My mouth quickly found her clitoris, which was hard as a bead. I felt it swell and harden even more in my mouth. I alternately sucked and licked, pausing to circle the hood or lick the slippery entrance to her vagina. I inserted two fingers in her and slid them in and out as I continued my rhythm on her clitoris. "Just like that, baby, just like that," Debbie moaned.

I kept it up, my face wet and sticky now. "Faster," she panted. "Faster." I did as instructed and picked up the pace. Several times I thought about how although Debbie and I had had a sexual relationship in high school, we'd never gone down on each other. I guess it was a little scary for us back then, but now I was making love to her as a woman, and even though it was bringing back a flood of memories for me, I was making even more beautiful memories with her now, hopefully ones that would last a lifetime.

Debbie cried out in orgasm, her tender hands grasping my shoulders as I brought her over the edge. Her entire body shook, her face was flushed and sweaty, and she'd never looked more gorgeous than right then. I climbed up beside her and held her for a while. We didn't need words now. We had each other.

wet spell

Mona Johnson

I've chosen this location precisely because it's a piece-of-shit motel and because I revel in the irony of ending my six-month dry spell at a place called the Sahara Inn.

And now, just looking at Tasha's fat brown titties gets my motor revving; my panties are soaked. I can't wait any longer, but I need for her to want me. I'm no aggressor, not by a long shot. So I tell myself to calm down—all good things come to those who wait. I'm so turned on, but I can't move a muscle. I can't even believe I'm here, let alone walk over to her. Besides, I want her to pounce on me.

But my impatience gets the best of me. "Why don't you come over here, sweetness?" I coo, as I lie back on the bed and spread my legs wide open.

Tasha doesn't need to be asked twice; she's a smart girl. "That's what I was waiting to hear," she growls as she walks over to the bed and dives onto me, covering me from head to toe with licks and kisses. There's such an urgency in her actions. "Jesus Christ, you're so fucking hot," Tasha says between forceful rams of her tongue down my throat. "I want to fuck your brains out." She knows this is what I want: to be taken over, to be adored, to have someone want me like life itself.

I just nod.

Tasha removes my clothes, piece by piece, while she remains fully clothed. She focuses first on my nipples, dark brown and hard, biting and licking forcefully but with great care, with something that verges on love. Well, as much love as you can muster having known someone for less than a couple of hours. She kisses me forcefully, and her tongue is cold and sweet from the whiskey, leaving its taste in my mouth as she travels down to my snatch. She starts with butterfly flicks, little bites and teases, all the while saying, "Girl, your cunt is gorgeous."

I grab the back of her head and push her gently into my pussy as she sticks her tongue into my drenched hole. I guide her in and out of me, her long, thick tongue going in as far as humanly possible.

Tasha pulls back a bit. "What do you like?" she asks.

"Cocks," I tell her. "Big, fat cocks."

Tasha gets up, goes to her backpack, and pulls out a harness and two dildos, one medium-size the other one about 10 inches in length. She gives me a look that says, *ladies choice.* When I point to the larger one, Tasha grins wide, peels off her vinyl pants, and straps on the monstrous shlong. With a glob of K-Y in hand, she comes over to the bed and orders me on all fours. She's going to fuck me good and hard from behind. I do as told as she guides the cock in after lubing it up good and plenty.

She carefully inserts the rod into my hole and places both hands on my fat ass cheeks. My hands grip the rough carpeting below and she slowly goes in and out of me. It's a little painful at first, but soon we're matching each other's rhythm, and I cry out in sharp little moans. "Oh, Tasha. Oh, Tasha," I yelp. "Fuck, that feels good." My pussy is good and wet, and the cock slides in and out of me like a sewing-machine needle. Tasha grabs my ass cheeks harder, her nails digging in a little. I know she's getting off good, that the cock base is ramming up against her clit, because now she's moaning too.

All of a sudden a huge wave comes over me and I'm screaming nonsense and "Oh, fuck" over and over and over. And I feel chills up my spine as Tasha collapses on my back, her plump titties sticky against my sweaty back.

"Let's start all over," I tell her, because I don't want this to end.

another woman

C. J. Evans

We had the place to ourselves. I grabbed two beers from the fridge, and Joanna and I got comfortable on the couch.

"So you wanna finish where we left off?" I smiled.

I didn't even have to wait for an answer. Joanna pulled me to her and kissed me passionately. I put my hands on the back of her head; her short hair was fuzzy and tickled my fingers. I searched out her mouth with my tongue then nudged it playfully against her two front teeth, which had a small space between them. I bit her lower lip gently. Joanna trailed kisses down my face to my neck.

"Mind if I take this off?" She tugged at my T-shirt.

"Let's go into my room first," I said. "What if one of my roommates walks in?"

Joanna agreed, and we went into my room and shut the door behind us. She pressed me up against the door and kissed me again, this time a little more forcefully. "Let's take this off *now*," she said, and pulled my shirt over my head. I undid my black lacy bra and let it fall to the floor.

I turned on a small lamp by my bed and shut off the overhead light. We both got comfortable on my futon, me on my back and Joanna straddling me.

"Oh, baby, you are so beautiful," she said, kneading my breasts, and I was so glad to hear those words, especially coming from someone as hot as Joanna. My crotch was so wet I thought I'd soak the futon.

Joanna scooched down and started sucking and biting my breasts, slurping on my nipples like they were candy, circling over and over with her tongue. She made her way down my torso with her warm, wet mouth until she got to my belt. In a couple of swift motions she undid the buckle. Her quickness and agility were turning me on more and more by the second. After I helped her take off my jeans, she went in for the kill, sucking my red-hot clit through my damp cotton panties. The sensation was exquisite but pure torture: I wanted that tongue right on my clit. So I pulled down my panties and let her have it.

Now, I'd had guys perform oral sex on me many times, but they never knew what the hell they were doing. I was always like, "Um, excuse me, are you going to be done soon? Your head is blocking *Nightline*." When Ted Koppel is more interesting than having your clit sucked, you know something's amiss. But with Joanna it was completely different. She knew just how to please me, sucking my entire clitoris into her full lips, tonguing under the hood, flicking fiercely then gently, then teasing it with little licks. When she put two fingers inside me and continued to eat me out like crazy, I thought I was going to burst. My pussy was sopping wet with slippery come.

"You taste so good," Joanna said, and she pulled her fingers out and brought them to my mouth. "Here, taste."

She was right. But I'd bet my entire checking account *she* tasted better.

Joanna put her fingers back inside and added a third, thrusting me full force. She went back to tonguing my engorged clit, licking my entire vulva with her masterful tongue, around and around and around. My entire body started to shake as she brought me to the edge; chills flooded my skin as I cried out in release and ecstasy.

"That's it," I laughed. "Tomorrow I'm buying a monthly bus pass."

Joanna just laughed as she covered my face with kisses. We made love several times that night. And even though it was my first time with a woman, I knew how to please her—and brought her to orgasm several times—since I just did what I thought would make her feel good. And, as the saying goes, who knows a woman's body like another woman, right?

flea-market find

Jenn Hwang

Over the next few days all I could think about was Saturday night. In my head I kept replaying various sexual scenarios that I'd hopefully engage in with May: We'd do it on my kitchen floor, in my bathtub, up against the wall, etc. I even went to the mall to buy something sexy to wear: black leather pants and a tight black Lycra sleeveless Tee. Saturday afternoon I went to the grocery store and bought the best merlot I could find, a dozen white roses, and some lube.

It was nearing 8 o'clock that night, and I was psyched, waiting for May to arrive. Just then I heard the buzz of the intercom. I pressed the answer button and said hello.

"It's May. I hope you're ready not to disappoint me."

I just chuckled softly and buzzed her in. When I opened the door, May was wearing a long black leather coat, which was strange, considering it was the middle of August. I saw she had on her MOTHER/FUCKER T-shirt underneath.

"I see you've done as told," I said, pointing to the shirt. She came into my apartment and closed the door behind her.

"Yeah, well, I hope you don't mind a little artistic license," she said, opening the coat to reveal that she was *only* wearing the T-shirt underneath—as well as a pair of black high heels. Damn!

"Great minds think alike," I told her, and she was raring to go, because just then she pressed me up against the living room wall, mashing her full lips into mine. Her tongue was like an agile snake.

May pulled off her shirt, and I took off mine. Since I don't usually wear a bra, we were breast against breast, hot skin against hot skin. "Oh, baby, you're so sexy," she said. "I wanted you from the moment I saw you."

I chuckled a little, but May's hot mouth quickly shut me up. Then she grabbed my crotch and moved her hand up and down, kneading my cunt. "I'm going to make you so wet you're going to soak through this leather," she said. She slid her hand down my pants and felt how wet I already was. "Jesus," she whispered in my ear. "It's like a waterfall down there."

May slid her hand out, and then she helped me take off my pants and underwear. We were still standing against my living room wall. Then she got on her knees and buried her face in my pussy, lapping me up like cream. I squatted slightly over her while she sucked and slurped me into ecstasy. "I swear to God," she said, pulling away for a moment, "if I'm ever on death row and they ask me what I want for my last meal, I'm going to tell them 'pussy.' " Again I cracked up, but when May started tongue-fucking my hot hole, I shut my trap.

"Oh, you're fucking good," I told her. "You are a mother-fucking artist."

Just when I thought I couldn't stand it anymore, May brought me to the edge and I came in huge waves, my engorged clit feeling like it was going to explode. After the first time I came, she went back in for more. "Come for me, baby," she said. "Come on, let's make you come again." And I did...two more times.

But I was ready to please her now. "OK, you didn't disappoint," I laughed, "so now I won't. Stay here. I'll be back in a second."

I went into my bedroom, got the dildo I'd never gotten to use on Brian, put one of his condoms on it, grabbed the lube I'd just bought, and came back into the living room with my hands behind my back. May was sitting on the couch, legs spread open. "Like what you see?" she asked.

Jesus Christ, she was gorgeous. "Fuck yeah!" I said. "Do you?" I held out the eight-inch strap-on.

May's eyes bugged out at the sight of the mammoth cock, then a huge grin spread across her face. She helped me put it on, then asked, "How do you want to do this?"

"From behind," I told her, and she turned around, propping herself on the couch cushion with her hands. I lubed up the cock and gently placed my hands on her plump ass cheeks, then entered her pussy from behind, letting her take it in slowly.

"Oh, fuck yeah," she said, even though I'd hardly begun.

I built up speed, not thrusting full force yet, but getting there. As I did, I slapped her ass gently. May moved in time with me, meeting each thrust with her hot, juicy pussy, her beautiful ass meeting occasionally with the leather harness I was wearing. "Come on, baby...harder, harder," she cried. "Faster." I was pounding this hottie full force now, and eventually she screamed out in pleasure and rode a huge orgasmic wave.

May and I fucked many times that night, in between glasses of merlot and several cigarette and snack breaks. I lay on the couch and had May sit on my face as I ate her out; we had sex in the shower and on the living room floor; she fucked me hard and fast with the dildo, as I'd done with her. You name it, we tried it. By 4 A.M. we were wiped out and fell fast asleep.

I woke up with her tongue in my ear. "Hey, sleepyhead," she whispered. "It's almost 11. Wanna get some breakfast?"

"Yeah!" I said, then slid down and buried my head between her legs.

May erupted in laughter. As I said, I like a girl with a sense of humor.

May and I still sleep together semiregularly, but we're not monogamous. Sometimes we have three-ways with one of her more than willing female friends. She never fails to surprise me. I occasionally date guys, but I *refuse* to let them go down on me anymore. After all, you can't switch to SPAM once you've had caviar!

architecture of desire

Lisabet Sarai

She started to kiss me, but not in a tender or romantic way. Her tongue poked rudely into my mouth. Her lips were hard and insolent. That kiss stole my breath, liquefied my sex, and turned my knees to rubber. I would have stumbled and fallen against the steel shelving, if it hadn't been for her muscular arm around my waist. She used the other hand to assail the buttons of my blouse, tearing them open without regard for the delicate silk.

She had none of Marietta's refinement, none of that measured sensuality I had been missing so much, and I was grateful. I wanted her brash youth, wanted her fire to burn away my memories and my regrets. I was gasping when she finally released me. I could feel the hot blood in my cheeks, sense my smeared makeup. My clit was hugely swollen, throbbing with my racing pulse.

She pulled back and looked me over, hands on her hips. "You liked that, didn't you?" she mocked. "I knew you would. You've been nursing your drink at that corner table and watching me tend bar for two hours. You're dying to get into my pants. It's true, isn't it, Ms. Fancy Architect?"

A part of me wanted to slap her. The rest ached to throw myself at her feet and bury my nose in her denim-sheathed crotch. I stared at my hands, embarrassed by my need.

My blouse was still open, a button torn away. She reached in and brushed her fingertips across my lace brassiere. "Take it off," she said, a slight huskiness in her voice betrayed her own arousal. As I obeyed, my nipples tightened to hard little bullets. I carefully draped my blouse over the ladder behind me and stood barebreasted. *Do I look old to her,* I wondered, *flabby and overblown?* She grinned at my discomfort. Nevertheless she was a bit flushed and her breathing seemed faster than normal. I felt a tiny thrill of triumph.

"Now your trousers," she commanded. I removed my bikini panties without instruction. Her grin grew broader. I stood naked before her, reveling in her attention. I knew that she could see the moisture pearled on my pubic curls. I wondered if my engorged clitoris was visible.

She settled herself on a stack of Tanqueray boxes, reclining like a sultaness. "Show me how much you want me, Ms. Architect. Let me see what a raunchy slut you really are. And if I like what I see..." She trailed her hand languidly up the inside of her thigh. My eyes followed her every motion.

I knew what she wanted. I wanted it too. I slipped one hand inside my cunt, amazed at how swollen and soaked I was. Imagining that it was her hand, I worked my fingers in and out of my slick folds while my thumb strummed over my rigid clit.

Masturbation had been my only form of release since Marietta left, but even as my hands found their familiar rhythm, I knew this was different. My slender companion's eyes were riveted. Every few minutes, her tongue would flick across her parted lips. Almost absentmindedly, she slid her hand into the black satin bustier that made such a fine contrast with her torn jeans, and extricated one pale breast. Her fingers danced over her tawny nipple as I pinched and kneaded my own, sending bolts of electricity to my sex. Although she did not touch me—barely touched herself in fact—we were climbing the long hill together.

I closed my eyes, overwhelmed by the sensations building between my legs. In the darkness, I recognized the rip of her zipper, and my eyes flew open just in time to see her thrust her whole hand into her pants. Her gaze met mine, as she rubbed furiously.

"Your ass," she hissed. "I want to see you finger your ass." Her crudeness took me to new heights. I turned my back to her and bent over, thighs wide. I smeared my juices over my perineum and slowly worked my middle finger into that tight hole, continuing to frig my cunt with my other hand. I don't know what was more thrilling: the intense pleasure of the digit wriggling in my sphincter, or the knowledge that this little punk goddess was watching my every move.

An orgasm was welling inside me, rising higher with each hand motion. At any moment the flood would overflow and bear me away. The cluttered storeroom reeked with our mingled woman-scent. My breathing was shallow and ragged. An animal moan wrenched itself from her throat. The sound brought me to the very edge, where I teetered helplessly.

"Stop," she growled. "Come here." I turned to see her sprawled on her cardboard throne, bare thighs spread wide. "Make yourself useful," she said, pointing to her pouting cunt lips. I did not need a second invitation.

Her pubic hair grew rank and tangled, nothing like Marietta's neatly trimmed bush. Her labia and clit peeked out of this damp jungle, cherry red and glistening. Bending toward her, I inhaled her potent swamp perfume. Then I stretched out my tongue and delicately flicked at her swollen bud.

She writhed and moaned again. Encouraged, I traced the outlines of her outer lips, lapping gently at her juices, savoring the silkiness of her private places. A lick here, a nibble there: I took my time, trying to build her pleasure gradually.

Arching her back, she pressed her pelvis toward my mouth. Obviously she wanted more from me. I was happy to oblige. I opened her wide with my thumbs and repeatedly plunged my rigid tongue into her vagina. In between thrusts, I pulled back and raked my teeth over her clit.

She thrashed about wildly, bruising my lips. "Oh, shit, oh, yes! Oh, come on! Harder. Eat me, fuck me, oh shit, baby...!" Her flesh began to vibrate like a violin playing music too high to hear, a tremor running through the bowels of the earth. I sucked her feverishly, feeling my own sex tremble in sympathy. Suddenly she yelled out some obscenity and her whole body convulsed. Tangy moisture flooded my mouth. She slumped backward, every muscle relaxed. I continued to lap up her juices as her breathing slowed to normal.

I was more aroused than ever, but I felt no impatience. I merely licked my lips and basked in the satisfaction of having completed her pleasure.

After a few minutes, she sat up and grinned at me. There was a new gentleness in her expression, a hint of shyness. "Thank you...?"

"Judith." I answered her unspoken question.

"I'm Toby," she countered. "And I must say that even though you look as straight as Mrs. Beaver Cleaver, you do know how to eat pussy."

I couldn't keep the hint of sadness from my voice. "I had a good teacher."

"Well, Judith, I think that I should do something nice for you."

The mischief was back in her eyes, and I felt a twinge of apprehension. "Make yourself comfortable up here." I climbed next to her on the pile of boxes and leaned against the wall. "Spread your legs," she said, "and close your eyes."

"Is that necessary? I want to watch you."

"Don't argue, do it." Strange to find such a dominant streak in one so young. Her huge green eyes and cropped black hair reminded me of some anime waif. I knew that she would give me release, so I followed her instructions.

She bustled noisily around in the storage room, looking for something. Then in a moment she was back, standing between my legs. I could sense the warmth of her naked flesh. "Relax," she said. I felt her fingers carefully part my folds.

I trembled, my nervousness mingled with excitement. Suddenly there was a sensation I could not identify. Something smooth and cold slid deep into my cunt until it brushed against my cervix. Immediately she drew it out again, a polished roundness slipping over my drenched tissues, lingering at my opening. Heat flared in response to this icy invasion, and the flood waters of my climax swiftly rose.

She worked the frozen dildo in and out while I wriggled and twisted and did not think to wonder just what sort of devilish device she was using on me. Glassy and rigid, cylindrical and sleek, the instrument moved inside me, filling and emptying me, urging me on to that final crest. Toby ground the object deep into my cunt, pressing its hardness against my straining clit. I dimly heard myself screaming aloud, as the tidal wave broke over me as Toby laughed in delight.

She roused me by kissing me, a butterfly kiss that flitted across my lips and left me aching for more. "Well done, Judith," she whispered. I opened my eyes to find her sitting cross-legged beside me, wearing nothing but that bratty grin. She took a swig from a brown glass bottle; I noticed an empty one lying in her lap. "Want a beer?" she asked, barely stifling a laugh.

Embarrassment and wonder warred in me as she held my gaze. I felt an answering smile grow on my lips. "Sure, Toby. I'd love one."

who's the boss?

CeCe Ross

Andi closed the bedroom door and cornered me against the wall.
I clutched the collar of my coat with both hands. She had a look
in her eyes that made me gulp. I was immobilized.

"I really need to hang up my coat. For real...so can I just..."

"No."

I blinked at her. Her dark eyes held a terrifying tenderness. I
tried to move, but she had me pinned—physically and psychical-
ly. I felt warm. My breathing quickened. I thought, *She is loving
every minute of this,* and felt the heat coming off her as she moved
in close to kiss me gently on the cheek. She scooped me up in
strong, confident arms and carried me over to the bed. She
pressed my shoulders to the mattress. I still had the damn coat in
my hands. Her long body stretched out over mine, and she slowly...sank...down as if to let me enjoy her by degrees. *What arro-
gance.* She put her small pink lips to my sumptuous brown ones.
Definitely in control, she kissed the corners of my mouth then
circled my lips, appreciating their fullness. She kissed me passionately, her tongue making me dizzy; then she kissed me gently, just brushing my lips with her own.

When she was satisfied, she released me and said, "Now you can
hang up your coat."

I said, "Now I don't want to."

Andi and I took a bath in my clawfoot tub, kissing our nipples
together then pressing and sliding our lathered-up tits—so delicious. I had never bathed with another woman—let alone a white
woman—and, though I never thought of myself as racially naive, I
found myself exclaiming, "You're so pink!"

Buzz kill.

"Well, what did you expect?" she replied.

"I didn't expect you to look like a lobster."

It was a statement I regretted, because there was a bit of distance between us after that point. But by the time the two of us slid
between the sheets we had gotten well over it—and I actually think

it broke the ice some because we then felt free to murmur various silly things to each other, like when she told me I had a "berry mouth" like Horace Grant of the Chicago Bulls (which definitely made up for my "lobster" comment).

I wanted to please her so much, and I gently ran my fingers along her waist and tentatively kissed her breast. It was soft and pale and full and had a small red mole near the nipple.

"Yes, harder," I heard.

OK, bossy, I thought. So she knew what she wanted and wasn't afraid to ask. I liked that.

"Make me feel it," she said.

I sucked her nipple powerfully and felt it harden in my mouth. From that moment on, I tried not to be so tentative. But I did take my time exploring the subtle lines of her body. "Roll over," I whispered. When she did, I worked my tongue down the nape of her neck, along her long moist back, then kissed and licked her bottom as if it were a giant all-day sucker. Her nipples were tight and sassy—they felt *so good* pinched between my fingers.

Andi was spread-eagle on her belly when I entered her luscious pink pussy with my right hand and held her hips tightly with my left. I think my aggressiveness surprised her, because her lower back muscles tensed. But once I eased up some she relaxed and adjusted her elbows to help raise her ass and give her leverage to push back against my thrusts. She moved back and forth in a rhythmic motion as she buried her face deep into a pillow. As I fucked her, I ran the fingers of my left hand through her short brown hair, nipping her back and ass. Then I found a real hot spot. It drove her wild, and she growled and swiveled her hips rapidly. When she came it was like a handful of paradise—hot, wet, and wrenching.

I was covered in a thin layer of sweat. I fell with my face on her smooth, buoyant ass feeling her contract around my fingers, the spasms growing fainter and further apart.

Andi slowly pulled away and leaned over the side of the bed.

Zip. She was opening her backpack.

"What are you getting?" I asked curiously.

"You'll see."

Click. The sound excited me.

"Lie back," she commanded. Her face was flushed like a rose. "Ohh, m-m-m-m," I moaned. What is that? I like it." The slippery cool gel sent a chill up my spine and put a deep arch in my back. Her thumb was the first to disappear, and the other digits soon followed, slipping in and out and massaging gently, then more powerfully—I had never experienced anything like this. I felt open and full. I felt...like a cloud.

"I'm in up to my wrist," she murmured. "You feel so good."

Damn, this girl had talent.

"Oh, this feels nice."

"Yes, it does." Her voice was low and pleasing.

My body shook. I had just begun to explode when she suddenly—but painstakingly—eased her hand out. I wanted to cry. My cunt made a sound. Then, doing the splits, she eased right down into this crazy clit-in-cunt position. She found my rhythm and a series of exotic moans rolled out of her. Sure hands gripped my legs. Her pelvis shifted and rocked and ground her wet lips against mine. My clit throbbed, each throb like a drumbeat filling my head, slow, building, loud, louder...

"This is it, babe. Oh, yes, oh, yes, *ohh! Yes-s-s!*"

We lay in each other's arms, silent, our breathing synchronized. Without saying a word, we both knew this was the beginning of something real.

Finally the silence was broken. "Andi?"

"Yes?"

"That was incredible, babe."

"Yes, it really was," she murmured sleepily. "And it gets better."

the butch in the bathroom

Holly Franzen

I backed into the restroom, and Jenn walked in and locked the door. Immediately she leaned into me for a long, sexy kiss. Her sweet tongue made its way into my mouth with graceful agility. She had her strong hands on either side of my face, and occasionally she slid her right hand behind my head and through my long brown hair. "My God, woman, you are stunning," she breathed into my ear. "I've been wanting this since the first time I saw you."

I was speechless, so I just kept up with her, my tongue roaming her mouth as if it had a mind of its own. I love women so much, sometimes I think it does.

As Jenn continued to explore my mouth and nibble gently on my lower lip, she moved her hands down to my breasts and cupped them forcefully, kneading them through my T-shirt. I grabbed one of her hands and shoved it under my shirt, letting her know it was OK for her to get a little closer to the real thing. With that cue, she lifted my T-shirt over my head and unclasped my bra from the front, circling one of my hard, pink nipples with her tongue. She licked lightly at first, making little flicks, then put her entire mouth over my nipple, as though she were drinking me in. "So beautiful," she mumbled as she kept feeling me up. "So beautiful."

"You're the beautiful one," I said back, so turned on now I didn't care what I said. She had me in absolute heaven.

"Butches can't be beautiful. We're good-looking," Jenn laughed as she continued to lick and suck my breast.

"Nope. You disprove that theory 100%. Like it or not, you're a beautiful butch, baby."

Jenn just laughed again and made her way down my stomach with hot, wet kisses. She got down on her knees, tugged at my skirt, looked up at me, and said, "May I?" I assumed she wanted to go in for some honey, and I was raring to go. I was so wet and horny I wanted her mouth right on me. I just nodded.

Jenn lifted my skirt, and I held it up as she buried her face into my crotch. Through my panties she licked my clit, then moved her mouth up to nibble at the top of my panties where a few tufts of pubic hair stuck out. "Fuck! This is it! This is it!" Jenn said. "You smell so good. Now I want to see how good you taste." She pulled my panties down until they were at my feet, then shoved her face into my pussy. Graciously I spread my legs a little wider to give her some room to work her magic. She dragged her tongue over my lips and ran it over the hood of my clit. Just then she took my whole clit into her mouth and sucked and licked me into ecstasy. She fixed her warm, wet lips to it, and I felt her tongue lick gently under the hood. Man, she had a mouth made for sucking on a rock-hard clit. "You taste so sweet," she practically sang. "And you're so wet."

Jenn's cunt-lapping took on a new intensity as she built up in rhythm and speed. "Fuck! Oh, my God! Fuck! You're so good," I cried out, not caring if the whole county, let alone all the women in the bar on the other side of the door, heard me. Just then there was a knock on the door, and Jenn yelled, "Use the men's room!"

"Get a room of your own!" we heard a gruff voice bellow, and we both laughed.

Again Jenn buried her face into my hot, drenched pussy, and this time it was no-holds-barred cunt-slurping action. When she slid two fingers into my aching hole, I knew she was going to take me all the way home. In and out she slid, first slowly, then more quickly, as her tongue worked on my clit faster and faster. I felt my vagina contract at her touch, then clench her fingers. I felt the fluids inside my pussy pulsing, practically squirting out of me and onto her hand. When she hit my G spot, her fingers stopped sliding in and out, and she massaged it as she ate me out fast and furiously.

"You're so good, sweetheart, so good...Oh, god!" I cried out as I felt my knees go weak and wild electric sensations fill the entire lower half of my body. "Oh, god!" I said again, but this time it was a scream, one so high-pitched and loud I was sure it would break the bathroom mirror. Just then I rode the wave of a massive orgasm, and I felt my entire body go limp. I ran my fingers through Jenn's beautiful brown hair, and she looked up at me with a big ol' pussy-eating grin. When she stood up, she kissed my neck gently, then moved to my mouth and planted a long gentle kiss on my lips.

Her face was covered in my come, and I tasted myself on her lips. She was right: I did taste sweet, like honey from the hive. After a few minutes of kissing—which got me excited all over again—we got ourselves together and opened the bathroom door.

Well, who was standing there but Jenn's opponent from earlier in the night. From the huge smile on her face, it was clear she'd heard at least part of what went on. "Double or nothin' you can't make her scream like that again," she said, half-joking.

"I'll take that bet," Jenn smiled, then led me into the bathroom for more.

playacting no more

Heather Towne

My girlfriend and I were baking on the beach, when she rolled over and asked me to rub some suntan lotion on her back. "No problem," I said.

Beth and I were enjoying our summer vacation before we returned to college in the fall for our final year. And it looked like we might be going our separate ways once we graduated.

I squirted some lotion onto my hand and started rubbing it on her. She jumped when the cool, creamy substance hit her skin. "Sorry," I said, laughing. I rubbed the lotion into her back and shoulders and neck in long, slow circular strokes, and she sighed. Then she rolled over again.

"How about the front?" she said, grinning up at me. She tossed aside her bikini top and I stared at her huge, heavy breasts. Her pink nipples stared back at me—thick and erect.

"Uh..." I mumbled, and glanced around uneasily. There were no other people on our secluded strip of sand—a small beach that you could only get to by walking down about 300 steps.

"Come on, Julie, you remember how we used to play together when we were little. You'd be the daddy and I'd be the mommy."

I gulped some salty air. "We're not little kids anymore," I said. "I don't..."

She cut me off by grabbing my wrists and placing my hands on her breasts. "I've wanted you for so long, Julie," she whispered.

I couldn't believe my ears, or eyes, or sense of touch. I had watched Beth's body ripen into mouthwatering womanhood and had often fantasized about making love to her, but never dared to do anything about my feelings.

I was shaking like a leaf, but I managed to tentatively caress her breasts. As I grew bolder, I started to urgently knead and squeeze them. I bent down and kissed her full on her red lips.

"Yes," she responded softly.

I swallowed hard, rolled her nipples between my fingers. She groaned, threw her arms up over her head, abandoned her breasts to my loving hands and mouth. I squeezed her tits together, working them with my hands as I bent down and licked each of her nipples.

"Suck my tits," she moaned, her face lost in the silky strands of her long, blond hair.

I grew ever more confidant and aroused. I nibbled at her nipples, then flattened out my tongue and painted her tits with saliva. I licked and sucked her huge breasts for what seemed an eternity, the hot sun beating down on my back, the two of us oblivious to the outside world. I only heard the gentle lapping of the waves on the beach and Beth's moans of unquenched desire.

When she could stand it no longer, she pulled me down on top of her and pressed her lips to mine. We savaged each other with our mouths, years and years of frustrated yearning shattering before us. Her tongue bathed my lips before pushing inside my mouth. Our tongues danced together, the feeling hot and soft and dizzying, her breath becoming my breath.

I broke away from her wanton mouth and tore off my bikini. Then I frantically pulled off her own bikini bottom and covered her super-heated body with mine. We were mirror images of each other in our blondness, our full, ripe proportions and our lust. We pushed our tits together, rubbed our nipples back and forth—blossoming them to incredible hardness—then locked our mouths together once again.

"Fuck me, Julie!" she gasped, when I broke the seal on our mouths.

She spread her long legs apart, then lifted her left leg slightly so that I could rub my shaved pussy against hers, fucking her with my cunt. I ground my slick pussy into hers, my hips thrusting frenziedly, my tongue bathing her face and lips, our breasts jammed together in white-hot passion.

She gasped, and her body shuddered as an orgasm tore through. Her quivering body became mine, and my pussy tingled and then erupted in orgasm. I buried my face in her hair, pumping her cunt with my cunt, as orgasm after orgasm ripped me apart and sent my brain spinning off into oblivion. I screamed in uncontrollable ecstasy, and she clung to me desperately, our bodies ravaged by the reckless unleashing of our wildest desires. She moaned my name, and then I felt her tongue along my neck, licking at the sweat that dappled my body. We both shivered in the afterglow of our frantic lust.

We seldom left the beach the rest of that summer.

baptismal

S. W. Borthwick

Ariel entered the club just after midnight, crossing into my orbit like a stray moon wiping out the constellations. The white of her skin contrasted the black of her corset. The wine dark skirt matched her lipstick. Suddenly, nothing else in the S/M universe mattered but her.

The previous week, I'd seen her reduce a stone butch to tears with a cane. I watched Ariel intently that night, amazed at how she balanced severity with encouragement as she got the butch to take even more. Just when there seemed no limit to the punishment, the butch broke apart. And even a beginner knows that butches don't cry in public.

Perhaps Ariel remembered me watching that night, or maybe it was the black-velvet dress I'd worn this evening. Either way, she strolled over to me.

Without thinking of the potential consequences I asked her, "So what are you seeking tonight?"

Ariel, not missing a beat, replied. "What can you show me?"

What were the odds that this woman who was easily 10 years my junior, but who made up the decade with experience, would choose to bother with the likes of me? I hoped she wasn't just feigning interest so she could switch in the middle of the scene and thrash my ass like the butch. But what if she really did want to get topped? I'd never done it in public. How did she know if I was any good at it? What if I screwed up? She'd probably get pissed and word would get around that I was a fuck-up. Then no one in her right mind would trust me again. But she'd already challenged me, and backing down wouldn't do anything to build my reputation either. Plus she was stuffed so tightly into that corset that I felt it was my duty to let her out.

Improvising on the spot I said, "We'll use a color scheme. Yellow equals 'you're tickling me;' black equals 'stop.' Got it?"

She nodded with a coy smile. I couldn't decide if the smile was one of respect or one of derision and decided to act like she meant the former. "Take my bag to the medical room," was my first official command of the evening.

"Yes ma'am," she said like I was the new schoolmarm. She picked up my play-bag and trotted off ahead of me. Good thing she was in front and didn't see my knees knocking.

Inside the medical room, in front of a mirrored wall and having little to do with anything medical, hung a pull-down bar like the ones in a gym with leather cuffs attached. A long cable ran from the center of the bar up to a winch in the ceiling. I flicked a light switch on the wall that brought the bar down to where she could place her wrists in the restraints. I fastened the cuffs tight, and with a contrary flick of the switch she lifted up on to her tiptoes.

"I think you've seen enough." I said and took out a leather blindfold from my play-bag. She pulled back, hesitant to let me attach it, a healthy bit of caution on her part. Thinking back to how I'd seen her handle this type of thing, I said, "You know this is for your own good." She relaxed enough to allow me to cover her eyes. "And just so you don't get distracted by any loud noises," I brought out a pair of earphones usually reserved for shooting ranges. Now I'd transformed her into a strung up monument to sensory depravation. My heart raced with the prospect of impending blasphemy.

I unzipped her burgundy skirt. It dropped away like a rocket stage falling back to earth, exposing two sumptuous hemispheres. The white of her unblemished ass cheeks made my stomach contract. I put my hand against the curve of the left one, like caressing the curve of the moon. I could have held it all night. To refocus us both, I gave her left ass cheek a quick swat.

"Oh." she giggled.

I swatted again.

"Ooh." she said.

I got both cheeks red and warm to the touch. I moved around in front of her, put my arm around her middle, and drew her close, tangoing with my suspended partner to feel the caress of her cheek against mine. I untied her corset and let it fall away like the skirt, revealing her breasts, nipples already hard. I put my mouth on the right one and slowly brought my teeth together.

"Ah." She gasped.

Then I focused on her mouth. I wanted her tongue, but she made it shy. I settled instead for my bag of tricks..

"What's that?" she asked like a child hearing a noise under the bed.

"What do you think it is?" I said.

She shivered but didn't say anything. I draped the leash across her shoulder and fastened the dog collar around her neck. I half expected her to freak, but she stood rooted in place. I gathered up our stuff and I led her through the club blindfolded and naked. Spectators parted like the Red Sea to allow us through, every eye in the club focusing on us as we passed.

In a different room against a back wall stood the Catherine wheel. It resembled a huge imposing wagon wheel with six spokes, four of which had restraints. I lifted her blindfold to show her.

"Oh...I've never done that before." She looked wide-eyed at the wheel with a vulnerability that was hard to reconcile with the butch-tamer of the week previous.

"Excellent," I replied turning her around, undoing the collar and backing her up to the footrests at the base of the wheel. She stepped into the contraption, putting her arms out to be fastened. I brought the two crisscrossing straps across her torso and pinned her in place. And again, I lowered the blindfold.

I tilted her clockwise and held her at about at about 1 o'clock, just enough to wreck her equilibrium. I got a short cane from my bag and rubbed its cool shaft against her skin. She tensed. I removed it quickly. She winced in anticipation of a smack that didn't come. Instead, I tapped her opposite thigh. She jolted, surprised rather than hurt. I tapped her again and she squirmed. I tapped harder and quicker. The tempo increased and red stripes began to appear on her thigh. She took each successive swipe with a moan. I further tilted her from the 1 o'clock position until she was horizontal to the ground. "My turn," I said and exposed my left nipple, placing it against her lips for sucking.

"No biting," I cautioned.

"Yes'm," she answered, and took me gently into her mouth. A delicious bolt of electricity shot through my chest. This was really happening.

I righted her again. A couple of labia rings dangled between her legs. I tapped them lightly. A cry shot out of her throat. Checking that I hadn't gone too far, I asked her, "Do you remember your colors?"

"Yes ma'am."

"What color are we?" I inquired.

"Red."

"Red's a beautiful color."

I took her down off the wheel and brought her over to the adjacent leather examination table. She was so shaky on her legs I had to pretty much carry her. Out of the corner of my eye I noted that a crowd, mostly men, had gathered. I feared one of them would get lathered up enough to interfere with us, but they held their distance.

"Sweetie's doing real good. We're almost there," I said, guiding her up on to the table, the blindfold still covering her eyes. Spreading her legs wide as she sat on the examination table, I took in the sight of her exposed labia. They were swollen and slightly purple. I wanted to stop and just bury my face in her right then. I donned some latex gloves, deliberately snapping the latex so she would know what was coming next. She was so wet, she was soaking the table. I introduced her to my fingers, slowly exploring the inner ridges of her pussy. We hadn't discussed whether penetration was in or out. I must have communicated my hesitation because she smirked and said "Yellow!"

"I'll give you yellow," I said and pushed four fingers into her.

"Oh, sweet, yes."

Passion spite rose in me. I folded my thumb into the hollow of my palm and pushed to knuckle depth; her juice formed a tide line at the crest of my knuckles.

"So good...So big."

I was content to plateau there. This was more than I'd ever expected to have happen on a single night at the neighborhood S/M club. I was half expecting to get stopped by the owner because the club had a no penetration rule. But this wasn't a violation the straight crowd was expecting.

I felt a surge of pressure around my hand. At first I thought she was just shifting position, but then my hand disappeared into her. Her pussy swallowed me up to my wrist. I gasped, my heart dropped to my stomach like when a roller coaster crests the hill and drops down the other side.

"Give it to me hard," she shouted through gritted teeth.

I gave it hard, with equally gritted teeth. "You're getting it, baby's getting fucked." I summoned up my filthiest tone, putting all my shoulder behind each stroke.

"Gonna be all slutty for me, right?"

"Yes...Yes, mommy."

"Mommy's fucking baby."

"Oh, sweet mommy, sweet fucking mommy, give it to me hard!"

My hand felt like it was caught in some kind of pussy vice. Her vaginal muscles clenched so hard I had the fear that I might never get my hand back. I pounded and pounded, punch-fucking her pussy. As my arm started to ache, I felt a downward push from her as if she was attempting to force my fist back out, delivering it back into the world.

"Three fingers, three fingers!" She shouted as if she'd slipped off the ledge and was falling from a great height.

I backed out to three fingers.

"Oh, sweet...Yes!" she hissed.

A jet of water shot out from her, dowsing the table, the floor, and most of all me because it hit me straight between my breasts. It was like someone had turned on a garden hose. She slumped over against the wall, slack-jawed and sex coma-ed, but still blindfolded. I relaxed against the table like I'd fought a one-armed 15 rounder. Behind us, I was vaguely aware of applause.

Eventually I got her down off the table, gathered up the gear, and cleaned her up enough to get her back into her skirt and corset. We retired to the club's lounge area. People came up to us to comment on how hot we were together. I was too exhausted to do much more than nod.

As we left the club together, riding the elevator down to the street, I hoped she might ask to play again. She watched the floor numbers count off as if she were looking at something out beyond the confines of the elevator. I thought that maybe I hadn't done a good job. Then I touched the wet on my dress between my breasts and smiled. I walked her to the corner and hailed her a cab. She gave me a long kiss goodbye, and got in. I watched the cab disappear up Eighth Avenue. I thought it remarkable that you could be wrist-deep into someone, fingers buried into the core of her being, and still not qualify for a phone-number exchange. I couldn't complain because even if I didn't get her number, I did get a baptismal.

indigo

Nicole Foster

Slate had just undressed. Standing in the bathroom, she took a good, hard look at herself. Nice firm pecs. Great legs. Boxer's arms. She had a few lines around her eyes, but damn it, she was in the best shape of her life. She ran her fingers over her breasts, down to her firm abs, then slipped a finger inside her pussy. She was wetter than she could remember being in a long time—and she was damn horny. Slate shut off the lights and went into her bedroom.

She walked over to the TV-VCR combination perched on top of a couple of milk crates by her dresser, thumbed through a stack of videos—*30-Minute Butt Workout*, *VH1 Behind the Music: The Spice Girls*, and an A&E *Biography* on Amelia Earhart—then found her favorite: the bootleg Indigo Girls tape she and Lucy had made a few summers ago. Slate slid the tape in—that act of insertion alone was enough to bring her over the edge—and climbed under her down comforter.

She always fast-forwarded the first few minutes: Lucy in the driver's seat on the way to the Madison Coliseum, popping PEZ from an Incredible Hulk dispenser into her luscious mouth; teasing Slate about how she was going to sleep with Amy and Emily after the concert; saying "Surely, Shirley" over and over until Slate yelled, "For fuck's sake, cut it out!" Too many memories.

She stopped scanning until she could see Amy approach the mike to start Slate's anthem, "Romeo and Juliet." The words "A love-struck Romeo sings the streets a serenade..." spurred an all-too-familiar but glorious ache in Slate's loins. She slid her hand between her legs and circled her clit with her index and middle fingers. Her left hand traveled up to her small but taut breasts, a pinkish brown nipple perking under her touch. She looked up at Amy mouthing the words to her favorite song. Damn if that bitch wasn't playing to *her* that night. And God, just look at Emily, that devious smile on her lips, her blond locks falling over her gorgeous eyes, taunting Slate. This was Slate's secret indulgence, pining over these two unbelievably sexy, capable butches. She was gushing, in her heart and cunt, her slick juices rushing out with the splendor of the Girls' guitar chords, their sweet harmonies pulling heat out of her from deep within. With her fingers still circling her growing clit, Slate licked the fingers of her left hand and moistened her breast, building into a rhythm that matched that of Amy and Emily.

Just when she thought she could take no more, she reached into the oak night stand next to her bed and pulled out a dildo she'd kept ever since Lucy had left, hoping she might have the opportunity to use it on the dozens of femmes who'd be knocking on her door. *I might as well toss this out,* Slate thought, fingering the long pink sex toy. *What the fuck, just go for it.* Without a second's thought, she slid the dildo into her mouth, slowly, as if she were giving her own cock a hot and heavy blow, then withdrew it and pushed it inside her throbbing snatch. She'd only tried this once before—a few months ago—and couldn't get it in, but that night she'd been drunk on four bad Chi Chi's margaritas and had been dry as a bone. This time the cock slid in easily, the wide head spreading Slate's vagina, filling her. Slate moaned, envisioning the butch lover of her dreams— she had Amy's eyes and Emily's smile and Ellen's hair and Demi's body and Tracy Chapman's lips and Slate's own strong hands and...a sweat-stained UPS uniform.

Pleasure mounted in Slate's body, the dildo sliding easily in and out. God, she'd never even let Lucy touch her like this. But she was in control now, fucking herself, allowing herself to fantasize like she'd never had. Tonight she had opened a door and let the real Slate come out and play. She got up and kneeled on the bed, then pushed the cock inside her as far as it would go, its base pressing into the mattress. She rocked her torso back and forth, then slid her body up and down the pecker. "Fuck me, bitch. Pound me, you whore," she called out, fingering her wet, swollen clit, tongue-kissing her imaginary lover. Oh, God, this was good. Oh, for fuck's sake. She grabbed the bottom of the dildo with both hands, abandoning her clit, pumping and pumping until she thought she'd explode. All the women she'd never allowed herself to touch or love came flooding in her mind as a torturously powerful orgasm rolled in and out of her from a place she'd pushed down far too long, waves of warmth and come and heat and tears pouring from her body. And by the time the lyrics "You and me, babe, how about it?" shot out from the TV speakers, she had collapsed into her pillow, tears streaking her chiseled face.

business for pleasure

Eileen Finn

I was finally meeting her face to face after outrageously flirting with her over the Internet for the last year. I happened to be in her city on a business trip, and, on impulse, I called her and asked her to dinner. We met at a lovely Italian place, and we were enjoying ourselves immensely.

"I think I need a trip to the restroom," she said. "Are you coming with me? They say women only go in pairs."

"Sure, why not? Wouldn't want to break a stereotype," I said, sarcastically.

We both exited the booth and walked around the back to the restroom. It was one of those elegant, true "rest" rooms you only find in the best of places. The entrance was its own room with full-length mirrors on each side and one large mirror with a shelf underneath it in the middle. Continuing into the sink and stall area, there were counters with perfume, hair spray, combs in wrapped, sterile plastic, and other miscellaneous toiletries. No one was in there when we walked in. I excused myself and went into the first stall. She continued to the last stall, a handicapped one. I quickly took care of what I needed to do, washed my hands and waited. I didn't hear anything for a minute and thought she had already left when I heard, "This is embarrassing, but could you come here for a minute?"

I was puzzled as to what could have possibly happened, but I went ahead and walked back to the stall. As I went to knock on the door, she pulled it open and pulled me in.

"Thought you might want a live preview before the feature presentation."

I quickly learned that there was nothing wrong with her and that she was playing with me again when she pushed me against the wall and kissed me. My surprise in no way diluted the stirrings in my body, and I kissed her back immediately. The kiss was deep and passionate. I tangled my fingers in her thick black hair as I opened my mouth to her. She was pressing against me and pushed one leg between mine. I felt her thigh rubbing against me and realized how wet I was. One deep kiss, and I wanted her already. We continued to kiss, enjoying each other completely. Her hands were moving up and down my sides, alternately pulling me toward her and exploring my body.

I wrapped my arms around her and slid my hands under her shirt. I let my fingers lightly caress her bare back, and I felt her shudder. She pulled back slightly, never letting her lips leave mine, and unbuttoned my pants. She slipped her hand inside and her fingers found my waiting moisture. She teased my clit as her tongue explored my mouth. Soon, she pushed her finger inside me, and we both gasped from the pleasure.

I rocked against her as our kisses melted into one. We were both breathing hard, oblivious to our surroundings. I couldn't get enough of her tongue in my mouth. I licked and sucked it before running my tongue gently over and around her lips. Back and forth our kisses went as her finger moved inside me. I reached for her pants when I heard someone walking into the restroom. I could hear the woman's heels clicking against the tile floor as she walked. We both stopped, frozen with the fear of being discovered. We moved a little toward the back of the stall so one of us could get our feet out of sight.

I climbed on the toilet and half sat on the metal assistance bar. By this time, we were having a hard time controlling our laughter. The situation seemed so ridiculous. She leaned up to my ear and whispered, "Why stop now? Who cares if we get caught?" My pants were still unbuttoned and unzipped. She pulled them down. I kept trying to push her away. I was scared we would be heard.

She looked at me with an evil glint in her eye and yanked one more time. She almost pulled me right off the toilet, but I caught my balance by putting my hands on her shoulders. I was standing on top of the toilet now. Her face was level with my throbbing crotch. She pulled down my underwear, balanced me with her hands on my ass and slid her tongue between my legs. I thought I would scream out. The excitement of the situation was barely enough to handle, but the sensation she gave me almost put me over the edge.

She didn't seem to care that anyone else was there. She was

hanging on tightly to me as she slid her tongue over and around my clit. She let one hand go off my ass and reached around to the front of me again. With her tongue licking and sucking my clit, she slipped her finger inside me. I knew I was going to come soon, but I kept trying to hang on until the woman in other stall left. This stranger under me was relentless in her lovemaking, not caring what might happen. I think she hoped I would scream out with the woman still there. My breathing was so loud, I was convinced our visitor had to hear something. I was beginning not to care either. *Serves the bitch right for taking so long,* I thought irrationally.

All I could feel was tongue and finger, massaging my aching pussy. My hands were in her hair, holding her to me. She never stopped. Her rhythm was fantastic, giving me sensations through my entire body. I felt the build-up increasing, the heat spreading through me. As I felt the release beginning to come, I heard the water in the sink turn on. I let go and felt the rush of my orgasm flow through me. My body shook and my muscles gave out. I fell into her and jumped to the ground. As my feet hit the floor, the water shut off. I heard the woman pause as if to say something. Then I heard the door open and close. She was gone. I was still shaking, not sure if I should be grateful or pissed for the whole episode. My heart was beating fast enough for a fatal heart attack. I looked at her. She was smiling, then hysterically laughing.

"Oh, God! Oh, God! That was so great! Not only did you taste good, but I had an audience too!"

I couldn't speak. I wanted more of her, but there was no way I was going to be able to do it there. I looked at her amused face. She was having a great time. I grabbed her and kissed her deeply, tasting my own honey on her face. "I want you," I whispered. I could feel her heart beating fast, and I knew things were far from over.

"We need to get back out there. Our waiter will think we stiffed him," she said.

"But I want you! I want to taste you," I cried, almost whining.

"Then let's go out there, tell them to put our orders in a container, and we'll go back to the hotel."

"Yes! Let's go. I can't wait much longer."

I hurriedly straightened up my clothes, and we walked back to our table. The food was already there, so I had to summon the waiter and get him to pack it up. He gave me an odd look, but he took the food. We sat there impatiently waiting and not saying a word. I had no idea what to say anyway. All I knew was how much I wanted her, how my tongue longed to be buried in her sweetness.

After a couple minutes, he came back with the food. I left him a generous tip, and we practically ran out of the restaurant. The few blocks back to the hotel seemed much longer this time. We jumped on the elevator just as the doors were beginning to close, probably looking like two crazed women. The other passengers in the elevator were looking at us. We didn't care. All we could think about was being alone with each other.

Finally, the doors opened to my floor and we jogged down the hallway to my room. I fumbled for my keys. The excitement was overwhelming. I shoved the door open, put the bag of food right in the middle of the floor, threw off my coat and grabbed her. She was just wriggling out of her own coat when my arms wrapped around her and my lips were on hers again.

I couldn't get enough of her kiss. She had the perfect mouth: soft lips, a wide grin full of beautiful white teeth, and a tongue with obviously many skills. I wanted to smother her in my kiss. Breathing seemed to be secondary as our passion consumed us. We fell onto the bed. Our tongues were wildly caressing each other. I rolled her on to her back and straddled her crotch. I began to unbutton her shirt.

She was grinding her hips against me, and I could feel my own wet soaking my underwear. With her shirt open, I reached down and lightly touched her breasts. I let my fingers glide over the smooth skin, and watched as her nipples hardened. I pulled her into a sitting position and took her shirt all the way off. I reached around and undid her bra, gazing at her breasts as her bra fell away. She shook her arms from the straps as my hands reached to touch her.

I softly kneaded her breasts as I began to kiss and suck her neck. I slid my tongue the length of her throat on its way to those creamy breasts. The sensation of her nipple in my mouth made me want to take all of her immediately. But, because she teased me in her own way back at the restaurant, I was going to make her wait.

She lay back down and pulled me on top of her. I was still sucking and kissing her nipples, and she began to grind her hips against me again. I knew what she wanted, but I wanted her to wait a little longer. I moved back to her soft lips and kissed her slowly. As she tried to capture my tongue in her mouth, I pulled it back and ran it along the outside of her lips. It was beginning to drive her crazy. Her movements started to become more frantic as my kisses became more urgent. I was holding out as long as I possibly could. I found this sort of play to be agonizing, but extremely exciting.

She reached up and lifted my sweater. I pulled it the rest of the way over my head. I moved up a little and let my cleavage press against her face. I heard her moan as she began to kiss my breasts. I felt her tongue sliding all over me until I couldn't take it anymore.

I climbed off of her and pulled her up with me so we were standing next to the bed. I put my hands on her waist and pulled her to me. Our breasts met and our nipples rubbed together. It was an extremely erotic feeling as we moved against each other. We both allowed ourselves to get lost in the softness of the other.

I slowly slid my hands downward to undo her pants. They fell to the floor around her ankles. I knelt in front of her and pressed my face against her panties. She was so wet and so hot. I wanted to try and tease a little more, but my own excitement prevented anymore waiting. I yanked her panties down and saw her soft, dark hair glistening in front of me. I kissed her belly and began moving down with slow kisses until I was at the center of her heat.

I poked my tongue out and slipped it between her wet lips. She shuddered and fell backward on the bed. Her legs spread open for me, and I grabbed them and wrapped them around my neck. I buried my tongue deep inside her, reveling in her sweet juices. I was licking and sucking all the sweet cream from her lovely pussy. I let my tongue slide up to her clit and took it into my mouth. I sucked gently, and she began to rock against me. I heard her moan as my tongue played against her hot clit. I continued to suck softly and moved my tongue faster and faster against her. Her hips were keeping a rhythm as her climax began to build.

I listened to her breathy words of pleasure. I wanted her orgasm to be explosive, so I made her wait once again. I let her clit slip out of my mouth and I slid my tongue back inside her. Her wet was incredible. My face was covered in her sweet cream. I lapped up every bit I could as I moved my tongue in and out of her. Soon, I moved back to her clit. I felt her legs tighten against my neck as I sucked her in. This time I didn't hold back. My tongue was flicking furiously against her. Her body was rocking wildly and then she let out a scream. I felt her muscles tighten as the waves consumed her. My tongue was everywhere, catching every drop of her pleasure.

After she calmed down, I moved up the bed to kiss her beautiful face. She smiled at me and stroked my hair. Our hands were clasped together as we fell into the sweet kisses that only happen after lovemaking.

Within a few minutes, she rolled me onto my back and undid my pants. She pulled them off along with my underwear and threw them to the ground. She climbed on top of me and straddled my hips. I could feel her wet against my own as she began to move. Our pussies were rubbing against each other as we began to grind our clits together. I was so hot and so wet from the taste of her that I knew it would not be long before I'd come. She reached behind her and slid her hand between my legs. I felt her finger slip barely inside me. I expected her to push all the way in, but she chose to tease me.

I could feel the familiar heat covering my body and mind. She teased me with her finger, barely moving in and out of me. The wave rushing through me was enormous. I held my breath, closed my eyes, and felt the release crash through all of my senses. A second wave was beginning as I opened my eyes. My hips were still rocking against her, and I realized she was going to come again as well. I rocked a little faster, milking my own orgasm as I watched hers begin. The whole episode took my breath away. She collapsed on top of me and we held each other as we caught our composure.

We lay in each other's arms for a long time, stroking hair, kissing, caressing. I could have stayed there forever. I was already thinking of how I would arrange my next trip to her city. She looked at me with her brown eyes glowing and said, "Who said there is no pleasure in business?"

butch on butch

Carole Joseph

The first time I fucked another butch was in the parking lot of a seedy dyke bar in northern Vermont. She wore brown leather boots and smelled of wood smoke. She'd spent the entire evening tempting me from the corner of the bar.

I saw her as a challenge—an incredibly sexy challenge. I could tell she'd always been the one to make the first move, and she'd do it with a kind of self-conscious but unflinching assertiveness. I doubted she had ever been surprised by her own lust, but I quickly learned that she had always been aware of whom she was attracted to, and when, and why. Butchness came to her naturally and comfortably, as it did to me. She was good with a strap-on and knew it, just as she was good at chopping firewood and putting up drywall.

She knew I was watching her, and it made her uncomfortable—and interested. I could tell I had her attention when she fleetingly glanced down to see if I was packing. She noticed the bulge in my jeans and met my eyes. Her look was even and unwavering, not flirtatious in the least. I was younger than her, and smaller, although I nearly matched her in strength. She did not know why I was looking at her, but she should have; it was the same look she'd been giving the sleek femme in the corner all night. Or nearly the same look; I knew better than to evaluate her body so frankly. She would have turned her back in distaste, as I would have done. But it was her butchness I wanted, her strength I respected. It wouldn't do to threaten her sense of control, at least not yet.

The challenge was to seduce her without making her feel like she was being seduced. The opportunity arose sooner than I expected. Half a dozen women entered the bar, holding the door open long enough to exchange some of the smoky interior air for a fresh breeze. The woman in brown boots turned to look and stepped back suddenly, placing a horde of rowdy college students between herself and the door. Obviously she was trying to avoid someone; exactly whom I couldn't tell.

I crossed the dance floor and came around behind her. She was eyeing the women at the door, who were fumbling to get out their identification for the bouncer, and she didn't see me approach. I put my hand on her shoulder and said, "So, why don't you want to be seen?"

Without turning, she shrugged and took a sip of her beer. The women were now moving toward the bar, their backs to us.

"Come outside?" I asked, and she shrugged again, but she followed me toward the parking lot.

Outside, she lost some of her reticence. Her name was Toni. She told me she worked as a vending machine stocker. She asked what I wanted.

I knew that if I told her I wanted to fuck her, she'd turn and walk back inside. Not because she didn't want it too, but because even the words would be enough to cast doubt on her self-image. I had to make her realize it was OK to want me. The best way to do that was by showing her that I wanted her too.

She was holding a cigarette in one hand and a beer bottle in the other. We were standing between two cars, screening us from view of both the road and the bar's entrance. I eased the bottle from her hand, took a swallow, and set it on the hood of a car. It made a clinking sound against the metal. Then I slowly but firmly reached for her hand and placed it on my cock.

She didn't move for a second. I could feel her deciding what to do. She closed her eyes, opened them, and looked right at me. She took a long drag of her cigarette. Her hand was still on my cock.

"I know how to fuck you," I said. "I know how to fuck you like no femme ever will."

She absorbed my comment quietly. I didn't expect her to acknowledge it. But her silence was confirmation enough of her desire.

I led her to my beat-up blue van, the kind that police always suspect of being car bombs because they have no windows. The lack of windows was precisely what I knew would make her feel safe inside. No windows, and so no chance of being observed in a compromising position with another butch.

She looked at the van, noted the Nevada license plate, and pretended to be interested in my hubcaps. I crawled into the back, spread out an old sleeping bag, and waited. A minute later she crawled in behind me.

I gave her a moment to get used to the dim interior, but not long enough to start having second thoughts. Then I moved around behind her, slid my fingers through her belt loops, and suddenly pulled her toward me. Surprised, she took a sharp breath but caught herself before exclaiming. She was sitting, facing the door, and I was kneeling behind her, my chest pressed against her back. I loosened my grip on her belt and ran my fingers over her crew-cut hair and down the back of her neck. Her shoulders were strong but tense, her jaw clenched. She wore one silver stud in her right ear; I took it in between my lips and pressed against her.

She was wavering, unsure whether to let me continue, and I knew that my confidence was all that was holding her there. Her eyes darted around, looking everywhere but at me. Just as I sensed she was about to pull away, I released her and, taking her hand, shoved it down my jeans. She gasped but relaxed instantly, relieved to have something to do. She expertly undid my zipper and pulled out my cock. Holding it with one hand, she reached for my clit with the other. As her fingers slid over me, I felt a surge of wetness and involuntarily tightened my cunt. My knees weakened. My clit was burning already and I felt as if I'd come with just half a minute of her touch. But I didn't want to; this was her turn. I pulled away.

I was right when I'd hoped that letting her touch me, albeit briefly, would make her more relaxed. Her breathing became ragged when I reached between her thighs, kneading the rough denim of her jeans, but she made no move to stop me. Nor did she stop me when I unlaced her boots and, laying her back on the blanket, pulled off her pants. I could smell her warm scent mixing in with the pungent leather of her footwear.

She looked up at me guardedly, no longer trying to hide her lust but still uncomfortable; she wasn't used to being the one on her back while I knelt over her, cock in my hands. She could no longer control her breathing or the growing wetness between her legs. Her obvious unease made her all the more sexy. I ran my palm over the head of my cock and watched her shiver with anticipation as I moved toward her. Easing her thighs apart, I slowly entered her. No preliminaries.

A deep moan escaped her as she took me in. Her cheeks were flushed, her hair a dark outline against the orange blanket. My own heart was racing and I wanted to take her urgently, but I struggled to calm myself, wanting to draw this out as long as possible.

I guided the strap-on in and out of her with one hand and pressed down on her clit with my thumb. I could feel it hard and throbbing. She raised her hips slightly, wanting me to move against her clit. I pushed my cock into her harder and smiled. I knew what she wanted, and I intended to make her wait.

Her breath came hard as I moved in and out of her, my thumb dulling the sensation of her clit. Her strong thighs tightened rhythmically as she took me in. She was still wearing her T-shirt and her hands lay on top of it, protectively covering her stomach. I moved my hand on top of hers and rested it there for a minute, letting her wonder what I was going to do. She shivered and tried again to control her breath, but her excitement was increasing. Under her white shirt, I could see her nipples harden.

Suddenly I released her clit and, grabbing both wrists, pinned her hands roughly above her head. At the same time I moved my cock over her clit, finally giving her the sensation she'd been yearning for. She gasped and attempted, halfheartedly, to free her arms from my grasp. But I held her tighter. She glanced at my flexed muscles, saw my resolve, and backed down. We both knew she could get away if she really wanted to.

She had held women down like this many times, skillfully walking the line between fear and desire. Done well, it would make the woman relax into her dominance, entrusting her with complete control of the situation. Done badly, it would make her withdraw and freeze. I was sure she never did it badly, and neither did I. We both knew full well what game we were playing. What neither of us knew was how it felt to be on the end she was on now.

She didn't resist but closed her eyes and swallowed hard. That was her decision. I felt her relax into me and I responded gently, lowering my body onto hers and resting there, quiet and unmoving. My cock was still in her and I let her feel the solidity of it.

I wanted to touch her breasts, to feel her nipples under my tongue and taste her salty skin. I wanted to place my mouth over hers and feel her warmth inside me. I wanted to say fuck it to all the roles we've set up for ourselves, the roles that make us embarrassed to want each other like this. I did want her, not just for one night in the back of a beat-up van, but over and over again. I wanted to be completely in control, fucking her all night and making her cry out. But I had to make her feel safe enough to let down her guard. Equally, I longed for her—for someone—to do the same for me. But we couldn't without calling our whole butch identities into question. I knew she would never do that, and neither would I. So I made no move to kiss her or to reach under her shirt. It would be too intimate.

I also wanted to fist her. Somehow that seemed less intimate than kissing. I slowly withdrew my cock and replaced it with first three fingers, then four, and finally my whole hand. Her eyes widened and she bit her lip, distracting herself from the pain in her cunt, but she didn't pull back. I held still for a moment, letting her adjust to the pressure. I could feel the pulse inside her. Or was it my own pulse? I couldn't be sure.

Slowly she relaxed around my fist. I smiled reassuringly, trying not to let her see how much her trust meant to me—or how sexy it was to see her in front of me and feel her muscles clenching around my wrist. I didn't want to scare her by wanting her too much.

She looked back at me intently, searchingly. I wondered if she'd ever taken anyone in like this before. She looked almost overwhelmed.

The tension—both physical and mental—was becoming too great. I could hardly bear the throbbing in my own cunt as she began to move against me again. I bent down over her and moved my mouth across her stomach, touching her lightly with my lips. Then I slowly ran my tongue over her clit. She gasped and grabbed onto my shoulders. I moved my tongue faster and rotated my fist inside her almost imperceptibly, aware that even the slightest movement would send shock waves through her body. She let out a low, deep groan and dug her fingernails into my shoulder. For a second I thought I'd come just from the pure excitement of touching her.

I began to remove my fist ever so slowly. She responded with increased urgency, arching toward me and holding my head between her thighs. Her hands were sweaty and she was gasping for breath. I kept up the pressure on her clit but continued withdrawing my fist. She tried to hold me in, but I wanted her excitement to grow until it was almost unbearable. I wanted to give her no choice but to completely lose control. Her clit was still hard and I flicked my tongue over it quickly and unevenly, knowing that the irregularity was bringing her over the edge.

She came as my hand was almost out of her cunt. I felt the pleasure surge through her body, and she let out a deep, hoarse moan.

thirsty

Rachel Kramer Bussel

We leaned against the wall and against each other, heated and eager. We'd met only minutes before, but that didn't matter; it only took a few seconds to know that we'd found our match for the night. She glanced toward the bar for a minute, then back at me. I knew she was thirsty but didn't want to ask for anything. I signaled the bartender and for a glass of water and she quickly brought one over.

"Thirsty?" I asked with a smirk, holding the glass in my hands and taking a leisurely sip, letting some of it splash about my lips so they were wet and dripping. She answered with a little smile, clearly unnerved but utterly aroused. I held the large glass up to her lips and poured a little down her parched throat. I liked the way her neck looked as she strained to be ready for whatever amount I chose to anoint her. I knew she'd slaked her initial thirst, so the next tilt of the glass was for me. I held it just a few seconds longer than necessary, watching her unsuccessfully try to gulp it down, a trickle spilling down her chin and wandering down her neck.

I fished out an ice cube and trailed it along the path left by the water, her sweat making it salty. The creaky fan attempted to spread some cool air in the place, but the amount of bodies packed in there, dancing and rubbing up against each other, was getting it pretty hot. Her black tank top clung to her, and even though she could've used one, she wasn't wearing a bra. I could see her hard and insistent nipples poking through the fabric. I swirled the ice cube across her exposed chest, watching the water mix with her sweat. I couldn't resist bringing it a little lower, rubbing it along her breast and against her nipple, my hand easily slipping under her shirt. I brought it back up almost as soon as I'd started and pressed myself closer to her, angling my leg between hers. Her short, silky skirt rode up, draping itself over my thigh as I raised my leg to press against her. I brought my arm around her, pressing the last of the ice into her back, then sliding my wet hand down the back of her skirt. I cupped her ass and pulled her toward me, leaning down to lick the cold, salty moisture off her chest.

I didn't care who was watching or who wasn't; the hum of the room faded as I inhaled her scent, turning my face left and right, rubbing my cheeks against her moist skin. I started kissing her with small, delicate lip imprints, and then I got greedy. My tongue worked its way along her neck, boldly tracing a path designed to make her melt. By the time I got to her mouth, her nails were digging into my back as her hips pushed against me, begging for more. Her tongue was hot and probing, tangling with mine and sending tingles through my body. She pressed her entire body against me, and I felt her wet shirt and insistent nipples against me. She sucked on my lower lip, her eyes open and taunting as they stared at me.

I grabbed her by the hair and pulled back her head, tugging just a little more than necessary. She moaned as I exposed her neck and sank my teeth into the tight flesh, my hand still on her head in this battle of needs and wills, each of us pushing, pulling, grabbing, tasting. It was like a race to see who could get the furthest the fastest. But either way, we'd both win. I worked my way around her neck, licking along the sides and then pushing her head down to get at the back of her neck. I wanted to be everywhere at once—her lips, her neck, her breasts, her ass. I tried my best to touch as much of her as I could, but we were crammed against the wall and we knew we'd have to be creative to get what we wanted. I brought my hand up to her mouth, and she gave me a look that shot straight to my cunt, a look that said she was mine, tonight, and tomorrow, and the next day. That look said she'd take my finger and my body and anything else I cared to bestow on her. I slid two fingers into her slightly parted mouth, slowly, deliberately tracing every inch of her tongue. We stood still, stopped groping and grabbing, eyes on each other as she sucked my fingers into her and pressed her tongue against them, tickling me. I pushed farther in and then slid just as slowly out, keeping my fingers poised at the edge of her mouth.

Things had just gone from fun and flirtatious to deadly serious. I slid my hand slowly down while keeping my eyes locked on hers, then grabbed her hand and pushed it down her skirt. I stood in front of her as a shield and leaned forward to whisper in her ear, "Touch yourself for me, touch that nice, wet pussy that you were just pressing against my leg, work it until you can't stand it anymore, till you're ready to give up or cry out or grab me and beg me to fuck you. Keep going and don't stop until you come, I want to feel you come right here," I said. I heard her swallow and could feel the small movements of her hand and arm shifting gently beneath me.

"That's a good girl, I knew you could do this for me. If we were in a little more private area, I'd do it myself. I'd have my hands all over you, spreading you out, teasing you, sliding up and down your slit until you begged me to fuck you. And I'll do that, don't worry, I'll do that very soon, but I want you to do this right now." I ran my tongue along her earlobe and tugged on the soft, hanging flesh with my teeth, gently baring down and suckling. Her arm moved faster beneath me, and I sucked more urgently on her ear. I wanted to reach my own hand down my pants but that would have to wait.

"That's it, that's my girl, keeping going." I quickly crouched and got another ice cube out of the glass. It was almost melted, but there was enough for my purposes. I put it in my mouth and let my tongue get icy cold, then kissed her, pressing her against the wall with my body. I could feel every movement and knew she was close. She buried her head in my neck, her breathing quickening as her hand moved faster, and then she finally shuddered against me, collapsing as I held her. We stood against the wall for a few minutes, silent, simply breathing and holding each other until we could talk again. I stepped back and held her chin in my hand, forcing her to look at me when she tried to look down, a blush spreading over her face.

"Still thirsty?"

"For you—always," she said with that wicked grin. I signaled the bartender for another glass of water, and we started all over again.

sex, girlfriends, and videotape!

Therese Szymanski

"Yeah, and it's a piss-poor birthday when you're sober and have to drive yourself home!" I gave a last wave at the bartender and let the door slam shut behind me. Damn Joan. *How could she stand me up on my birthday?*

I never saw the two butches who fell into step behind me until their hands were gripping my elbows, propelling me deeper into the alley where I'd found a place to park my Mustang.

"Hey, what're you doing?" I said, fighting against their tight grips. I started to scream, but I was pushed against the wall, knocking out my breath.

"A nice, pretty blond," the butch next to me said. "Just what I was hoping for." She ran her hand down my cheek. Someone else gagged me.

Panicked, I looked around. Next to my Mustang in the dark, lonely alley were a few bikes with a band of masked figures dressed in black standing near them. I didn't need to look twice to realize they were all female.

A shiver of excitement ran through me.

One of them grabbed a stone from the ground and smashed out one of the few remaining lights nearby.

I was thrown onto the hood of the 'Stang, and hands spread me out across it. A woman walked toward me, stopping directly in front of me.

"Oh, this is very nice," she said. I recognized her voice: one of Joan's best buds. "That shirt is too much, though." She ripped it open, popping all the buttons on my expensive silk blouse.

I glanced around and recognized the thick chain one woman wore on her wrist. All of the women were wearing black pants, black shirts, and black ski masks.

As a woman snipped off my bra with a pair of scissors, I realized the scar across the back of her hand was Mel's. And over there was a woman wearing the shirt I'd just told Robbie last week I loved on her...

My breasts were exposed, my nipples hard in the chill night air. Fingers were at the zipper of my jeans. They would realize right away I didn't have any panties on. I'd shaved for Joan—she liked surprises. It made me wet when I realized they were going to see all of me.

"You like this, don't you?" Her fingers were working at the seams of my jeans after another undid my zipper. Involuntarily I arched up against her. I recognized her voice as well. Jenna.

They were all going to see me naked...naked and shaved and totally exposed.

But...

Were they all going to fuck me? Feel me up? Finger me? Be inside of me?

I gasped for breath, feeling the heat course through me as my pussy tightened.

I laid my head back against the hood. And I saw something move in the window of an abandoned building nearby.

"Cut them off," the first butch said, turning from me. Two butches walked up and pulled out knives. I felt the cold of the blades against my hips and recognized the knives as our new Henckels. The women were skillful with the blades, putting the blunt side against my skin so as to cut a painless line as the blades sliced through my jeans, splitting them open on the out-side of each leg.

A woman came next to me and grabbed my right nipple, twist-ing it slightly. I twisted toward her, but the hands holding me down didn't let me move much.

My shredded jeans were stripped off me. "I like a shaved woman," someone said, lightly drawing her hand across my crotch and down an inner thigh.

The first butch, whom I recognized as Jen, walked between my legs and looked right into my eyes. "You know what we're doing, don't you? We're gonna take turns with you. We're all gonna fuck you." She unzipped and pulled herself out. She was wearing a big pink one—very big. She stood with her hands on her hips and her dildo aimed right at me.

The women holding me pushed me down the hood, bringing my open cunt down toward her and that big, pink dick...

I squirmed, not wanting them to know how badly I wanted her inside of me, how much I wanted her to fuck me.

She stood between my legs, running her thumbs up and down the soft flesh there. Slowly she spread me, holding me open with her fingers while her thumbs caressed my clit, briefly pushing inside of me with just their tips.

She nodded toward the women holding me down. "Take the gag off. I want her to be able to breathe." She leaned down over me, her hands still on my cunt. She met my eyes. "Just know that it'll be worse if you scream."

I was glad they'd be able to hear me. I said, "I want to be naked when you fuck me."

They cut my shirt off me, still holding me open. I looked up—the light in the window was still on.

My legs were hanging over the front of the hood, Jen's dick less than an inch from me, her hands still sliding over me. "Hold her for me," she said to two women who weren't touching me yet. They reached between my legs, holding me open while she took herself in her hands and slowly pushed into me.

"Oh, God, yes," I moaned, "yes..." She went deeper and deeper until she was filling me, then she slowly pulled out.

And then she began to fuck me. I arched against her, trying to force her into me.

"Harder, oh, God, harder!" I squirmed beneath their ministrations, "My nipples, please, my nipples..." I looked at the woman on my right, "Sharon, please, squeeze it as hard as you can..." Then to my left, "Amy..."

"God, she's got nice tits...look at how big her nipples get!"

"Squeeze harder!"

"She is so wet..."

"Fuck me...hard...harder...oh...oh...God!"

I was still gasping for air when Paula let go of my ankle and switched places with Jen. Jen zipped herself back up, and I could just see her grin under the ski mask, which she had pushed up so she could breathe more easily.

Paula pulled her zipper down, pulling out an unbelievably large strap-on. I squirmed away from her, saying, "Oh, God, no." Joan had never used one so large on me. It would never fit.

"You want it, baby, and you know it," Paula said, liberally applying lube and rubbing up and down the thick length of it. Then she pushed it inside of me, just the tip at first, then more and more as I tried to squirm away from her...and it.

They held me in place, though. I couldn't get away and she easily fit it all inside of my wet, eager pussy.

When Paula was done with me, Sammy propped me up while Nicky fed me like a baby from a bottle of water. I was still being held spread out, even though it felt as if my legs were locked open. Wide open.

Steph took over between my legs. She rolled up her sleeve and rubbed lube all over her hand and wrist.

I didn't have the energy to even try to squirm away. No one had ever taken me that way before. No one had ever invaded me like that.

"Do you think you're warmed up enough yet?" Steph asked, leering down over me. "Are you ready for me?"

My only response was to gasp for air.

Steph leaned forward and the two women pinching my nipples released them so Steph could cup my breasts, then run her hands down my stomach and over my hips, leaving a trail of lube and my own wetness the entire way.

I moaned.

As one, Nicky and Sammy said, "Leave something for us, Steph."

Through my pleasure-fogged mind, I remembered all the times Steph had sat in our living room, talking about her latest one-night stand. She always waited until I went to the bathroom or to get drinks or munchies before she'd give Joan all the truly lurid details of exactly what she did and how she did it.

And I always eavesdropped and wished she'd do all those things to me.

Steph began stroking my clit while she put first one finger, then another, into me.

She had listened when I told her, years ago, about my fantasies. She knew I'd been listening all those times and I wanted Steph to take me like she took all her women.

"You ready for me?" Steph said, just before she shoved her entire fist into my sopping pussy.

I arched, bucking against the sudden force. I was filled with her. I could feel each of her fingers inside of me as she fucked me with that fist.

I felt as if I would burst from her, as if I couldn't take her. But she continued to slam it deep into me, then pulled it out and slam it again.

It started with my cunt, tingling upward and spreading down through my thighs so that I screamed as yet another orgasm thrashed through me.

I fell back against the car hood, struggling for breath, wonderful colors lighting behind my closed eyelids.

How many of them had had me now? How many of them were there? Heat coursed through me when I thought about the rest of the butches taking turns with me. Impossibly, I started becoming aroused yet again.

"Our turn," Sammy and Nicky, the twins, said together.

"Think you can stand, baby?" Nicky asked, lying down on the hood next to me. She looked around at the others who were still holding me down, spread open. She gave them a sign and they let me go. She helped me close my legs and she started massaging the top of my thigh, helping to relax the muscles.

Her sister lay down on my other side and started doing the same thing. "We need you to be able to stand," she said.

"We've always wanted to share a girl."

"And take her at the same time."

I felt drugged. I reached up and pulled off their ski masks. I tangled my hands in their identically short hair and pulled their heads down so they could suck on my tits. I glanced around at the rest of the women. "Take your masks off. I want to see you watching."

Sammy and Nicky trailed their hands up my legs, fondling me. My entire body was slick with sweat, and the cool night air felt good. Someone brought back the bottle of water for me to suck on, and then trailed chilled water over my excited body when I was done drinking.

Then Sammy and Nicky stood me up, holding me between them as they unzipped and pulled themselves out, and lubed up.

A shiver ran through me when I realized what they were about to do. I had always wanted Joan to take me from behind, but never knew how to ask for it. Now I felt my ass clench in anticipation.

"You're shivering, baby," Nicky whispered into my ear. "You want us to warm you up?"

Hours, maybe days later, they finished and laid me across three women sitting in my backseat.

Joan climbed behind the steering wheel and started the engine. She leaned over the seat to look at me, the video camera still in her hand. "Happy birthday, baby."

I moaned my response. Hands were still caressing me, searching all my most private spots.

"I've got some real nice home movies for us to show at our next party, baby." Joan looked around at her friends. "Took me a while to figure out what to give the femme who has everything," she said with an evil chuckle.

Her friends laughed with her.

buzzed

Kristina Wright

I was sitting on a beach in Key West, Fla., mourning the loss of an old love and an old friend and trying to blot it all out of my mind. I didn't want to think about tomorrow. I didn't want to think about anything at all except the beautiful girl next to me. A girl I'd known a few hours. A girl I wanted like I hadn't wanted anyone in a long, long time.

"Are you OK?" Georgia asked.

I nodded. "Yeah."

She didn't push. We sat hip to hip on the sand. It felt good. At some point, I leaned against her, my head dropping to her shoulder. She smelled like smoke and gardenias. Her braid pressed against my cheek, and I wondered if I'd have a waffle-mark against my face when I got up. I kind of liked the idea of being marked. I shivered.

Georgia turned her head toward me, maybe to ask how I was doing or to tell me her ass was getting wet from the water lapping so close to us, I don't know. But when her head turned, her lips nearly brushed mine, and I suddenly knew what I wanted. I leaned in the fraction of an inch that separated us and put my lips against hers. It wasn't a kiss, just a meeting of mouths. I held myself there, unsure how she would respond or if I could handle it if she pushed me away.

But she didn't go away. Her lips softened under mine, parting ever so slightly as she breathed her breath into me. We kissed, slowly, sweetly like the strangers we were, trying to learn each other's feel and taste. I slipped my tongue between her lips and she sucked on it. The sensation sent a zing of electricity to my cunt, and I moaned. She did it again, and I squirmed in the wet sand, hungry for her softness.

Georgia slid her hand up my waist and stroked one of my tits through my T-shirt. I pressed against her hand until she rolled my nipple between her fingers. I groaned, twisting toward her so I could return the favor. Her sweet tits were way more than a handful, and I wasn't complaining. I cupped and squeezed them, releasing her only long enough to tug at the buttons on her blouse. Her bra was next, popping loose to reveal the tits I'd been mauling. Dusky pink nipples capped her luscious, tanned breasts. I raised them to my mouth, licking and sucking each sweet nipple while Georgia dug her fingers into the damp sand and groaned.

"I want to fuck you," I said, staring into her eyes as I pressed her hands to my tits. "Let me fuck you."

She nodded and started to stand.

I pulled her down on top of me. "Here. I want to fuck you here."

I think she would have argued if my hand hadn't slipped under her skirt and zeroed in on her cunt. I could feel her wetness pouring out of her like heat off hot asphalt. It had been more years than I cared to count since I'd felt a rush of heat and need as strong as this. I thought she'd go off like a rocket in my hand. She clutched at my shoulders, quivering and whimpering as my middle finger made slow circles against her clit, my fingers pressed up against the tight curls on her mound.

"You're soaked," I murmured against her ear. "Does my honey girl like that?"

She nodded into my neck, her hands slipping down to squeeze my tits. I felt her fingers at the waistband of my jeans. She fumbled with the zipper and the material tugged, pulling up snug against my own juicy cunt. I groaned and leaned back to help her, never taking my finger from her clit. She was trembling by the time she'd stripped my jeans off me, then the panties that clung to my wet flesh. I jerked my shirt over my head with one hand. I was now naked in the sand, wet from the ocean and my own arousal.

She whimpered and buried her head between my smallish tits, sucking and biting my flesh like she couldn't get enough of me. We were rolling around in the sand, each of us pushing and straining against the other, both of us wanting to get fucked.

I didn't know what her reasons were, but I knew mine. I didn't want to be alone. I'd lost two people in my life and I needed her tenderness to soothe the ache. I wanted my honey girl to make me forget.

I snaked a finger inside her wet heat and she bucked against my hand. A few seconds later, I found myself flat on my back with her on top of me, one leg scissored between my own, her thigh riding high against my fevered cunt. She sank her teeth into my neck and pinched my nipples while I arched against the delicious weight of her leg. I squeezed a second finger into her, and she whimpered, braids smacking me in the face as she moved against me.

"I want to eat you," I said, voicing the thought almost as soon as I felt it. "Come up here."

She obliged, straddling my face like a buckaroo at the rodeo. I swiped my tongue over the wet, pouting lips of her cunt and was rewarded by her clamping her legs around my ears.

My world was reduced to the cunt over my mouth, and I couldn't think of anything better. I was oblivious to the water and foam splashing us as the tide came in. I wanted only what was within my reach: Georgia's sweet cunt drowning me in her juices.

I planted my hands on her thighs, holding her open so I could do the job right. My thumb glided across the small tattoo that curved over her hip bone. It was an inky shadow against her tanned skin, impossible to make out in the darkness. But I kept my thumb on it, stroking it like a worry stone even while my tongue stroked her clit.

She whimpered and moaned, arching her back and ass as my mouth devoured her. Her fingers found my slick opening and teased me with matching strokes until I delivered the goods and sucked her clit between my lips. Then she plunged her fingers into me—two or three, I couldn't be sure—and fucked me hard. I moaned into her cunt, hearing, seeing, and smelling nothing but her moist flesh and soft hair.

She froze, pressed against the flat of my tongue, every muscle in her thighs and stomach tensed. I knew she was close. I knew I only had to wiggle my tongue and she'd go over the edge. So I did, and she did.

She came hard and wet, groaning loudly. She kept grinding against my mouth as if she wanted me to eat her whole. I anchored her against my mouth and did my best to oblige, wondering if I'd ever get the scent of her off my skin.

Her fingers in my cunt stilled for a moment and I clamped my thighs around her hand in case she had any ideas of stopping. I shouldn't have worried. She was pumping my cunt again as soon as her orgasm subsided, fingers angling up high and hard, rubbing my G spot like there was no tomorrow. She kept her cunt raised a bit from my mouth. I knew she was too sensitive to take anymore, so I nuzzled her and whimpered as she fucked me.

She shoved another finger into me as my cunt began to contract, and I thought I would die from the fullness and need. But then I was over the edge, her fingers pumping into me as I rocked and jerked on the sand, legs stiffly spread out, water lapping up between my thighs to splash my quivering cunt.

I couldn't stop coming and I didn't want to either. I buried my face against her wet thigh and sobbed, rocking on her hand, letting her fill up the emptiness inside of me with something warm and hard.

Eventually her fingers slipped from me, and I felt empty. She stayed there, straddling my face, as the ocean lapped at our bodies. I was getting the worst of the tide because I was on the bottom, but didn't care.

"That was...Thanks," she whispered down to me, her face ringed by moonlight, her braids bobbing against her chest. "I hope you liked it."

I laughed against her muff. Sweet Georgia, worrying about me. I could get used to this. "It was my pleasure."

The moon peeked out from behind the clouds, and I had a better look at Georgia's tattoo. At first I thought it was a butterfly, it's wings outstretched over her hipbone. But the coloring was wrong. It was a bee—a honey bee.

The yellow and black stripes of the fat, fluffy bee hugged her knobby hipbone. I ran my thumb over it again as she eased off of me and stretched. I was shivering now, the tide coming in far enough for the water to cover my legs. I watched Georgia standing over me, stretching her lithe, tanned body and I knew I needed to get up. But I lay watching her, watching the bee undulate on her hip.

"Didn't that hurt?"

"What, this?" She rubbed the tattoo with her fingertips. "It stung a little."

I couldn't help laughing and crying all at once. A wave splashed over me, and I started choking on seawater, still sobbing.

"Rae?" Georgia asked, kneeling beside me, her braids draping over her body like damp seaweed. "Are you all right?"

I shook my head and tried to push her away, but she held on, propping me up and thumping my back hard. When I stopped choking, she sat back on her heels, her pale blue eyes dark in this light.

"Better?" she asked softly, smoothing a hand over my damp cheek.

"Better," I agreed, turning my face into her hand, dizzy from tequila and honey. "It just stings a little."

barfly

Mia Dominguez

I walked into the bar and took the first seat I found. Shortly after that, I turned to see who was walking through the door. Who else could it have been? She wasn't the most attractive woman I've ever lusted after, but there was something about her: something sexy and raw and animal. Something made me hot and uninhibited whenever she was around, and I wanted a piece of her. Gloria walked over to me. It was obvious that she had been drinking a little before she walked in.

"Hi, honey." She turned to kiss me on the lips. I made it linger a little longer and a little deeper than a friendly "hello."

"Hi, baby." I turned to look at her date. "Hey," I said, not waiting or caring to hear a response and turning my attention back to Gloria. "Wanna go dance?"

"Sure." Gloria took my hand, "I'll be back in a bit," she said to her girlfriend as I sped by her and onto the dance floor.

Gloria and I began to dance, or, should I say, I began to dance for Gloria, running my hands across her body as I wiggled my way down. She enjoyed looking down at me with my face inches away from her cunt. I danced my body close to hers, rubbing my tits softly across her chest. She smiled and I devilishly smiled back, knowing that her woman was looking at us and she'd probably get into big trouble when she got home. But I knew she probably wasn't going home tonight.

"You look so good, babe," Gloria whispered in my ear as she drew closer and closer to me.

"Good enough to eat?" I laughed.

"Oh, yeah," she replied.

"Then why don't you?"

"Now?

"Yes."

"Where?" she asked as she pulled me closer to her chest. By this time her woman was pissed off and ventured off into the patio to cool off.

"Take me home," I demanded.

"OK," Gloria agreed. "Just let me go tell Jamie I'm leaving."

"No," I demanded. "Fuck her. Just leave with me now and you can deal with her later."

"That's not cool."

"If you want me, we have to leave now."

Gloria looked bothered for a moment, but laughed it off. "OK, let's go." She took my hand, leading me out of the club in a rush, most likely, so as not to get caught.

Gloria opened the car door for me, closing it once I boarded, then rushed to the driver's seat to begin our little journey. The second Gloria entered the car, she turned to me, kissing me hard and desperately, running her hands across my body and up my skirt. My pussy grew wet as she searched for an opening that would allow her fingers to enter through my panties. Finally, she simply pulled them off to the side and rammed her fingers inside my hot, wet, throbbing pussy. Gloria started her engine, as mine was already purring, driving me closer to home at every stop, showing me how desperately she wanted me. Her car nearly collided with others several times before finally arriving in front of my place. We were so into each other nothing else mattered but getting her naked, into my bed, and onto my body.

She parked her car; I grabbed her arm and led her into my bedroom. Gloria stared me down, took my hand, and spun me around.

"Damn you look so fine." She held me close while rubbing herself on my ass. I bent over a little and rubbed my ass back at her as a sign of appreciation. Gloria slowly led me to the edge of the bed. I felt her warm lips kiss their way down my spine, and I absolutely loved it when her tongue bore its way into my tight hole. Gloria grew more intent on making me scream as she witnessed my increased excitement. She reached around to massage my clit while she licked me. I got hotter feeling my creamy come drench her fingers. Slowly, Gloria worked her tongue back up my spine, sending erotic chills thought my being. She turned me over on my back while caressing me in her strong, muscular arms. Gloria planted herself on top of me, grinding her pussy into mine. I felt her warmth more and more with each thrust.

"Take off your pants," I demanded.

"No," she whispered. "Not yet."

I became crazed wanting to feel her hot, wet pussy come on my own. I climbed on top of Gloria, bumping and grinding my hips into hers. I started to moan louder and louder, making Gloria even more persistent in her attempts to thrill every single inch of my flesh. I sat up on her and slowly pulled off the black lace dress that I wore to entice her. She didn't hesitate to reach out for my tits. Gloria massaged, kneaded, and squeezed me into a white-hot, passion-driven orgasm as she teased my hard nipples with her pierced tongue. It was a thrill to feel the cool metal of the silver stud tap firmly against my swollen nipples. I continued to moan aloud.

"I want you to scream," Gloria shouted as she bit down on my tits.

"If you want me to scream, you need to make me scream." Gloria reached down to play with my throbbing cunt. I came over and over while she taunted my delighted clit with her fingers, and then brought those fingers drenched in my sweet, lustful nectar to her mouth and licked them clean.

Gloria was so raw and bohemian in her eroticism I couldn't help but want her to fuck me knowing she had another woman waiting for her. I secretly got off on the fact that there was someone sitting at home as Gloria spared no energy or desire to pleasure me many times in several ways. I loved that she'd rush home that night with my scent on her breath and kiss her woman hello.

"Take me, Gloria."

"What do you want me to do for you?"

"Anything you'd like. Have your way with me. Fuck me with everything you have." I thought of my favorite song at the time and shouted, "Fuck me like an animal!"

Instantly, Gloria turned me around, buried my face into the pillow, and massaged my ass. Slowly, her fingers probed, until they disappeared inside. I backed up into her fingers, demonstrating my approval in her choice of methods to get me off: me, on all fours, and Gloria behind me, ready and willing to meet my every expectation and demand. It was climactic. Once again, Gloria rubbed herself into me. I felt the bulge on my bare ass and was excited to know that she remembered how much I enjoy toys.

"Do you still want me to take off my pants?" she asked while holding my ass down on her crotch.

"Yes," I replied. "Please take them off. I want you. I want you to fuck me."

Gloria quickly unzipped, and without pulling them all the way down, she whipped out her impressive appendage. Her strap-on was as strong and sturdy as she was and felt incredible as it brushed the outer edge of my asshole. I was frightened that she might hurt me, but that hurt disappeared into pure lust as she slowly entered me. Gloria was masterful in her sexual endeavors, and I was grateful to have someone so skilled, if only for one night.

I screamed every time she thrust that hard dildo into my ass. As much pain as it brought me, it pleasured me to no end to feel her body slap into my ass while she pulled my long hair back, exposing my neck to be bitten with long, painful, pleasurable bites. Gloria loved my reaction and she continued biting my shoulders, my back while I screamed. As long as I was not screaming for her to stop, she continued to fuck me like an animal, just as I'd demanded.

As Gloria slowly pulled out, I turned around to face her, unsnapping her harness and releasing it from her body. I lay on top of her, grinding my pussy into hers, wanting to prime her to receive my pleasure for me. I reached out to her with my tongue, brushing her pink clit with long, soft strokes. Gloria began to moan lightly as my tongue delved deeper and deeper, penetrating her warm lips. Slowly, as the tension welled up inside of her, she thrust her hips forward and back, grinding into my tongue with every forward thrust. To say I was excited would not give Gloria the credit she deserved. She was the finest lover I had enjoyed up to that point in my life, and how skilled she was: not only in giving pleasure, but in receiving as well.

After we concluded, we lay in bed holding one another, until she began to sneak away under the blankets.

"Where you going?" I asked.

"I can't stay, baby, I gotta get home. I have someone waiting for me, remember?"

"Oh, yeah, I remember. Well, lock the door when you leave because I don't feel like getting up." I turned around because I didn't want her to see me cry. "I had fun, Gloria." I managed to force out of my mouth.

"I did too, baby." Gloria turned and smacked me on the ass. "When can we do it again? I'm dying for you already."

"Call me."

the cleveland cleave

Peggy Munson

I am stuck on a repeating word that's like a gaping camera shutter.
The word is *hole* and she has said it three times. The word *hole* is
caught in the weir of my crazy muzzled mouth. She pours booze
into the word. She says, "I'm going to fuck each (word) you have."
The wretched ache of the word is so obvious. "I've got a boner
from here to Columbus," she says. "And you'd better believe this
state starts with *O*." The word is the noose she made to hang the
cheap piñata full of cheap candy she bought at a party goods store.
The word is a lavatory in a vortex in a cheap motel. The word is
resting on the other side of the Bible in the drawer, over the horizon where Revelations ends.

"Open your fucking hole," she says. She shoves the motel table
out of the way and hangs the piñata by its noose from the dim
chandelier. She opens up a plastic packet and pulls out a bootlace
and wraps it around my wrists behind my back. "Kneel down and
spread your hole," she says. I tilt my tipsy heels, and then her hand
pushes my shoulder down. She squats to position me, spreads my
knees apart so that my skirt fans out around my knees and lifts my
tits up so that my back arches. She raises my chin toward the light.
She grabs the wooden paddle that is oblong like a cricket bat, and
says, "Close your eyes." I hear an awful smack, but not on my ass.
Once the candy beats me in the face I realize what she's doing. The
pieces fall into my mouth, or bounce off my teeth, and they are not
hard candy, but chocolate kisses, unwrapped.

She picks up strays and begins feeding them to me as I let the
chocolate liquefy. The candy is so sweet that the force of her cock
being shoved in my mouth makes me gag and my eyes snap open.
"No you don't," she says, roughing up my hair as she rams her
cock into my throat. "Open your greed-hole because I'm going to
fuck every bit of hole you got." The bar in Cleveland where I met
her was mostly wall-to-wall carpet munchers, but I felt her bulge
against my ass when I slid through a pack of butches to get a beer.
She lit one cigarette end to the next in the Chevy cab as the radio

bent us slowly around a steel guitar, but that was the only fragment of intimacy. I thought we'd do it like a businessman and a mid-list whore, but I didn't think she'd fuck my mouth. I didn't think she'd do it like she didn't care if it was blood or spit running down my chin. My wrists were too tethered to fight, my provincial tongue learning French on the baguette. "Your lips are pretty around my cock," she said, as I started learning her groove, licking the tiny rut at the tip until my lipstick shamed her cock. Then she came so jerking hard and rough in my mouth that I almost fell backward onto carpet that was as defeated as a pressed corsage. "Holy Toledo," she said, her cock slamming my sounds back to their harmonicas.

I didn't know women could come like that. I didn't know come tasted like Pennsylvania chocolate, driven down a turnpike to the crosshairs of a rain-tamped field that ended in a door with a number full of beckoning hole. "Sweet mercy," she said, pulling her cock from the muted space. My pussy was dripping on the sandpaper carpet. When one hole closed, a new wind tunnel welcomed resistance. Her fingers grabbed at my cunt and they fumbled for my clit. She looked at me fiercely as the shoved three fingers in. Her lips formed a beatific grin. "When there's a hole in the clouds it's always heaven," she said.

hatchback

M. L. Renki

I saw her jogging my way as soon as I'd parked my car. She had no idea that today was her lucky day. I go to the park for two reasons: to look at the ducks and find pussy. I make sure to back into the parking space so that the wondering or interested ladies can easily spy the rainbow flag on the front of my SUV. She had and was.

"Running in circles? I can work you out in half the time."

"Is that a proposition?" she asked, trying to catch her breath.

"Nope, it's a promise."

I used the electronic key to unlock the hatch. There is just something sexy about the *tweep-tweep* sound the key makes. She was a bit giddy and smiled as she climbed in headfirst so I could see the shape of her ass in her sweaty, tight, jogging shorts. She sat and began to unlace her running shoes. I stopped her.

"Don't bother, you're not sleeping here. I'm just gonna fuck you and then you can go. Pull your shorts down and lay back." Her shorts were sticking to the back of her legs, and I watched her squirm out of them. Her scent filled the car as her shorts and panties simultaneously came off. She was wet from running and her pussy smelled salty and warm. It's hard to smell warm, but that scent is clear: wet, swollen, and ready.

I lifted her muscular, tanned legs that her clothes had shackled at her ankles and placed them over the back of my neck. I spread her legs apart at the thighs and moved my mouth in closely, licking the inside of her thighs along the way.

I wanted to see her. I wanted to see the personality of her mound, the curves of the pink, wet pussy that belonged to only her. I pulled the lips apart and saw her swollen, throbbing clit begging for my tongue's embrace. It had a long, slender shape like a stretched hourglass. It was one of those cunts that would lengthen from the bridge of your nose to your chin while you were deep inside.

I tasted her. Sweet, salty, and warm...I buried my face into her rich cunt. This is the moment I pine for: the first taste of a new woman, the smell and taste filling your face, your mouth. It is a perfect moment filled with little expectations that always give you more than you bargained.

She was already moaning and I had barely started. She had no idea what was in store for her. My two forefingers entered her pussy and pulled the lips apart to get my tongue deep inside. My whole mouth was wrapped around her cunt, sucking the wetness from her while teasing her clit with my tongue. Her legs and running shoes bore down on me, pushing me even deeper inside. There, I could feel her marvelously contracting around my tongue as her clit swelled. I was deep inside of her feeling the inner sides of her slit engulfing my mouth and cheeks. Lips surrounded by lips, feeding and eating each other. I felt her hair tickle the side of my face, and I was suddenly inspired to pull out.

"Turn over," I said.

"What?" she panted back, questioning my motives.

"Get on your hands and knees." The SUV jostled as our position changed. Only then was I able to see her ass. It was firm, beaded with sweat and positioned in the air for me. Her back was swayed and her head was resting on the leather of the rear seat.

I sat there momentarily, taking in her curves, the round apple shape of her perfect ass, while deciding just how it was that I needed to enter her.

"Hurry, fuck me before somebody sees us," her voice was earnest as she was beginning to realize that we were in a public place and starting to lose her focus.

"Oh, no, Flo Jo, I'm taking my time with you." Indeed she had a runner's body: tanned on her exposed limbs, but secretly pale untouched flesh on her back and ass. She was gorgeous and pungent with cunt juice dripping from her, running down her thighs. I licked the inside of her thigh, just to bring her focus back to fucking.

"Oh, fuck yes," she moaned.

I wasn't strapping that day, but I was packing. I pulled a 20-inch black double-sided dildo from the bag that housed both my jumper cables and my car-fuck gear. I took one end of the dildo and slid it between her legs so that it lubricated with her own juice. I hated lube; the way it felt and tasted took away from the natural juice that I craved. After the tool was slick, I pushed it deep inside her. I entered her hard and forced her open. She clenched her teeth and dropped her head, raising her ass. She looked back to see what I was using.

"Oh, a double. Are you gonna use it with me?" she asked.

I smiled. "No, this is all for you, now turn around."

I rose onto my knees and placed one hand tightly on her ass curve. I wrapped the other hand tightly around the rubber dick and began to fuck her hard. I wanted her to feel how badly she needed to be fucked. I rammed her harder and harder...

"God, I'm gonna come."

"You better not come before I get all of this inside you. You have to take it all," I warned her.

"I cant' take anymore. It's as deep as it will go. Please let me come...I need to come."

"Not until it's all inside you." I folded the dildo and shoved the other side on top of the other one already inside her pussy. It spread her beyond her imagination. I could see the pink pussy pulled apart and filled full with my cock. Her mouth was open, but she wasn't making any noise. She gripped the headrest of the seat and pulled herself closer to the back of the seat and waited for me to finish fucking her. Her teeth were clenched, her fists were clenched, her ass was clenched, and her cunt was full of my dick.

I dropped my pants while it was in her. I had to feel her. I was throbbing and I needed to come with her. I pushed my mound into her with full force. I wanted her to feel me; know I was the one fucking her. My cunt pushed against her, shoving the dildo further into her. I repeatedly ground into her, each time harder than the last. I was beating off on her ass and cock-filled pussy. I rocked her hard, I fucked her hard, and she was taking it all. She wanted it all.

"Oh, Jesus...I'm coming...Jesus, I'm coming."

She did come. She came so hard that the dildo pushed out of her cunt and against my stomach, dripping and wet. She sat still on her knees, panting, trying to catch her breath and to stop her hands from shaking.

I pulled up my pants, opened the hatchback, and climbed out. "You can pull your pants up now. Take a few minutes if you need, but close the hatch when you're done. I'm going to look at the ducks."

better to receive, then give
Heather Towne

My roomie and I were getting dressed for a night of bar hopping when she slapped my bare ass. "Hey!" I yelled. "Watch it, bitch!" We were standing in front of the huge mirror in our bathroom, nude and lewd. I glared at Holly, pretending like I was angry. She's a slight girl with a sun-burnished body, auburn hair, and a pair of heavy-duty tits that cry out, "Grope me!" I, on the other hand, am lean and long, with raven hair and small, firm tits. My body is shockingly pale compared to hers. We're both 18.

"I am watchin' it, girl," Holly said, staring hungrily at my ass.

I turned my butt to the mirror and looked at the red mark on it. "How'd you like it if I smacked *your* ass around, you little slut?"

She wrapped her arms around my chest, pressing her big tits into my back, her hands squeezing my own pert hooters. "What a great idea," she enthused. "You ever had it up the ass before?"

I blushed. Her busy hands worked over my super-sensitive tits, plucking at my nips until they were red, thick, and long. Holly's a wild one, but that's what I love about her—that and her fuck-me body. "Uh, I thought we were going out," I said.

"I didn't think you had," the sex-crazed kitten said, a smile on her pouty lips.

As we stared at our hot bodies in the mirror, I knew that the drinking and dancing were going to be put on hold. Holly wanted to try something new, and when that green-eyed cunt-licker wanted something new, I wanted it too.

She whacked me on the bottom again and stared fiercely at my reflection, the lust smoldering in her eyes. I held her eyes, my blood beginning to boil, the internal and external temperature suddenly soaring along with our mutual desire. She repeatedly slapped my ass, fanning our flames. She spanked one fleshy butt cheek and then the other, over and over, faster and faster. My butt and pussy tingled with her abuse, and I moaned as she walloped.

She grabbed a long, red dildo that lay on the counter—her

favorite toy. "Spread your legs, ho!" she commanded. "And your cute ass!"

I glanced at her reflection, hesitating, but she shoved me forward. "I'm gonna ass-fuck you, baby! Your anal cherry is mine, girl-friend!" Her face was red, her eyes frenzied.

I spread my hands on top of the counter, bent over slightly, and pushed my butt into the air. My pussy was drenched, my body quivering with the anticipation of shattering yet another taboo.

"That's more like it," Holly murmured, then stuck the eight-inch dildo in her mouth and sucked on it. When it was good and wet with her hot saliva, she pulled it out of her mouth and stuck it in mine, then rubbed it against my bare pussy.

"Yeah!" I gasped, my knees buckling. I swallowed hard and stared into the reflection of my feverish violet eyes. My long black hair shimmered under the lights, and my white, tight body seemed to glow, heated with equal parts anxiety and excitement.

Holly grabbed my ass and played the dildo over my crack. "Ready to be butt-fucked, sweetie?" she asked, her jade eyes flash-ing, her huge mounds heaving with excitement. She grinned wickedly at me, and I nodded.

She shoved the dildo into my moist cunt, and I jumped just as she began fucking me with it. "That's just to get it even more wet," she said, her breath hot against my ear. She plunged the plastic cock in and out of my cunt for a long while, then pulled it dripping wet out of my snatch and pressed it against my tight pucker.

My body quivered. "Yeah," I urged her, bending over further, standing on my tip-toes and abandoning my virgin ass to her wan-ton desires.

She pulled my butt apart with her left hand, her right hand clutching the dildo. I felt a short, sharp pain, and then, as the sex toy pushed through my starfish and plunged into my ass, a warm, heavy feeling of pre-ecstasy flooded my super-heated body. My legs trembled and my arms grew goose bumps as I watched Holly work the dildo up my butt. She was biting her lip, a look of intense con-centration on her gorgeous teen face, determinedly steering that man-substitute into a place where no cock had gone.

"Just a little more, baby," she grunted.

"Shove it all the way in, bitch!" I screamed, my passion bursting into flame. "Fuck my ass with your cock!" I was already teetering on the brink of a massive orgasm, the unexpected ass plundering rocketing me to the dizzying heights of towering ecstasy a whole lot quicker than I'd expected.

Holly sensed my gathering storm and slammed the last couple of inches of the pleasure tool in between my butt cheeks. "Your ass is mine!" she cried out, staring wildly at my ecstatic reflection in the mirror.

"About time," I groaned defiantly, sweat dappling my smooth skin. The hardened cock felt good in my ass, like it belonged there. I grabbed my left tit and squeezed, pulling desperately on the inch-long nipple. "Fuck me!" I gasped, finding it hard to catch my breath with that cock up my ass.

"With pleasure," Holly responded. She pulled some dick out of my butt, and then plowed it right back in. She quickly picked up a rhythm, her hand working furiously, and I closed my eyes and surrendered my body and my senses to the erotic, electric feeling of her anal intrusion.

She slammed the dildo, pumping my butt with it, her hand a blur, my mind a blank. She swatted my cheeks and it all became way too much for me.

"I'm coming, baby," I moaned. "I'm coming!"

She smiled grimly and drove my ass all the harder with her wicked cock-stick. She whacked my burning bottom and plundered my flaming asshole until my entire body was consumed by fire, and I erupted with a mammoth orgasm.

"Fuck, yeah!" I hollered, blindly dancing around in the throes of ass-centered ecstasy. My torso shuddered as orgasms tore me apart, my arms and legs shaking with white-hot joy as Holly's relentless ass banging drove me to the blissful precipice of near-unconsciousness.

I sank down onto the counter, my mind reeling, my body quaking, as Holly's eight-inch boyfriend continued to unrepentantly hammer me between my bouncing butt cheeks. "Goddamn it," I murmured into my folded arms, as a final orgasm churned through my wasted being and left me exhausted.

Holly eased up on the anal plunger then slowly slid it out of my stretched-out bum-hole. She swatted me one last time on the bottom, bent down and kissed and bit my ass, and then asked, "How 'bout givin' me some backdoor lovin'?"

I gazed at her teasing smile through bleary eyes, then cautiously stood up and turned around to face her. "Sure thing," I said quietly, my ass sore but content.

She tried to hand me the bitch-pleaser, but I brushed it aside. "I've got something better for your sweet little ass," I told her, and walked, stiff-legged, out of the bathroom and into the bedroom.

When I quickly returned with a strap-on fastened to my hips and pussy, Holly's eyes bulged with surprise. "Holy shit! When'd you get that?" she asked, her voice breaking a little.

"Oh, I picked it up a couple of days ago. As a surprise." I grabbed the 10-inch black cock that dangled dangerously between my legs and pointed it at her, stroking it. "Think your little ass can handle Black Beauty here?"

The sexed-up teenage vixen excitedly nodded her head.

"Good. But first, why don't you lube my monster cock with that talented tongue of yours?" I barely had the words out of my mouth before she had the dick in hers.

"Mmm," she moaned, on her knees, her mouth crammed full of cock. She sucked up and down on the prick prosthesis like it was the real thing. Her ultrapink tongue snaked out and bathed the underside of the cock, then teased the head of the ebony snake. She gave me the kind of suck-job that would've had me blowing plastic semen in under a minute.

As her head bobbed up and down on the ever-hard erection, I felt pressure start to build within my steaming cunt—the sight and friction of her dick gobbling was setting my pussy to tingling all over again. "OK, that's enough," I gasped, yanking the glistening rod out of her greedy mouth. "You're making me jealous." I pulled her up off the floor and mashed my mouth against hers.

She aggressively stuck her tongue into my open mouth, using it for something a whole lot more practical than cock polishing. We slapped our tongues together, twirled them against each other, and fought a ferocious battle that was interrupted only briefly when I sucked up and down on the slimy length of her taste buds, as she had done on my artificial manhood.

I gripped her massive tanned tits and squeezed, then bent down and sucked on her swollen brown nipples. I bounced my head back and forth between her gorgeous twin globes, feasting on the sensual ripeness of them.

"Suck my boobs, baby," she moaned, running her fingers through my silky tresses, desperately seeking fulfillment from my savage mouth.

But I knew just how sensitive my sexy girl's rubber-tipped mounds really were, so I soon broke mouth and tongue contact with her gigantic hooters and snapped, "Assume the position! Time for some payback."

She spun around and leaned up against the counter, waving her tight little ass around in front of me like it was a red flag, urging me to gore her with my huge black horn. "Fuck me up the ass!" she said unnecessarily.

I slapped her ass around, getting it nice and red and hurting, reveling in the squeals of delight my handiwork elicited. Then, when her butt cheeks were good and sore, I lubed up the waist-mounted pleasure pole and steered it toward her tight pink opening.

"Oh, my God!" she cried, as I stabbed the swollen black head into her resisting pucker.

"Here it comes, ass-whore," I gritted through clenched teeth, recklessly pushing the monster prick into her tiny bunghole.

I just about had the massive hood inserted into her anus when she suddenly thrust backward and buried half of the dick in her bum. Holly didn't like to wait for her pleasure. I grabbed her narrow waist and pushed my hips forward. The hardened cock slid into her ass like it had been there before and was anxious to return. I was quickly buried to the balls, splitting the little quim-teaser in half with my humongous tool.

"Fuck me!" she shrieked, her pink mouth hanging open, her eyes squeezed tightly shut.

There was no use being gentle—no fun in that either. I pumped my hips, and the black battering ram plunged in and out of her ass, slowly at first, then faster, until my thighs were cracking against her ass cheeks with frenzied regularity and my clit-extension was slamming her anus with an awesome intensity. I tore her bum apart with the giant cock.

Holly groaned, then snapped her mouth shut and hung onto the counter with grim determination as I rode her rump like a cowgirl rides a bucking bronco. I showed her no mercy, banging her butt with abandon, and my pussy responding with warm, wet feelings of its own.

Unbelievably, the ass-plastered Holly managed to yell "Fuck me harder!" and I desperately strove to double my already frantic efforts. I pounded her ass like a drum, ravaged her bunghole with my joy-toy until she cried out in uncontrollable ecstasy, and her body convulsed with the first of her multiple orgasms. "Come for me, baby!" I shouted, a maniacal grin on my face as I pile-drove her ass and watched her being torn asunder by spasms of blistering sexual ecstasy.

Only when the last of her many orgasms had thundered through her bronze and broken body did I ease the rock-hard rod out of her ravaged butt and tenderly spank her trembling bottom with it.

She turned her head to look at me. "You think that strap-on will fit me?" she asked softly.

"It just did," I replied playfully. "The question is: Will it fit me?"

the fisherman's wife

Urszula Dawkins

You're on the boat working, on the other side of an ocean, and I'm lying in my bed and thinking, *What do I want?* There are so many pretty people in the world, and the skeletons of admirers rattling around my cupboards. And I think, *You're my lover, and you're so far away, but so what?*

I write so often and don't write to tell you this: This morning my heart comes down to Third Street and doesn't care what happened in the past. From Third Street, my heart walks down that little side lane and into the potholed alleyway: I can see the dinghy tied up by your boat. So I send out a wave of myself: Something here is stronger than the pull of heavy seas. You know and come to get me. I come onto your boat, and we go below. You don't know what's coming.

I tell you to take down those grubby overalls so I can see you. You're gonna protest a little, maybe a lot, or get grumpy with me because you're busy; your head is somewhere else. But I'm 10,000 miles away and this writing can't disturb you unless you want it to—unless there is something in you that *does* want to hear me tell you to get those dirty overalls down around your knees. So I can see you again. So I can touch your shoulders there in that empty hull.

Let's fill it with something for a minute. With your body: your arms and legs and hips and neck and belly. Let me feel your shoulders and remember the shape of your breasts again with my mouth. Let me remember the nipples, rubbery hard, and the firmness of your chest. Let you not know how to sit or be comfortable in that state; let's get our feet wet with the bilge and not care while I make you lay back on whatever piece of wood or metal is lying there. With the pelicans plunging into the creek like they did when I was working on the deck beside you.

I want to look at your cunt, be eye to eye with its little pink eye, and let my teeth feel the cushion of the labia protecting you. I want to tug at your labia with my teeth, gently, selfishly, to remember the

251

flesh; all in that one place as though your whole body is encapsu-lated *there*, in that center. I want to feel them swelling, filling hard with blood, against my mouth. It's that little pink eye of you that I have my heart set on, tasting you, grasping at your hips, reaching to feel the firmness. Breathing nothing but your exhaled center, suffocating amid kerosene smells, and the smell of you.

It's been hard in me this morning, the need to bite you where the hardest little hairs grow, to run my tongue round that round hole, to start to feel the silky cunt murmuring. I need to feel it with my fingers, gradually knowing that pink stuff, that incredible sur-face, softer than anything, softer than any other part of you. I could run my finger around that little hole for minutes and long minutes, teasing you, telling you with my fingers that I want to enter there, get deeper into that velvet. That part where absolute vulnerability reigns while the muscle in that same place takes everything—it is the strongest and the softest place in the body, and I'm gonna put my finger there, experience it firsthand.

I'm beginning to sweat now, and it's all a mystery 'cause we did-n't fuck for so long. But somehow, if this thing is going to exist across oceans, the sex might as well be floating amid everything else. If the raft is still floating, the flotsam of our sex might as well be there to cling to.

I grip your thigh and slide my finger deeper. And I take you then; sometime soon is the moment of surrender, at which you can't protest, can't tell whether you're over water or on land again. You only know the sound of your own noises, wanting me, begging me to fuck you hard and finish you.

This is not just my cunt speaking: it is my fingers and tongue, it is my thighs and hands and the hand that reaches beyond every-thing and touches you inside. I want to feel the ridged flesh with-in, slow enough to read you in detail. I want to fuck you with the sound of the bridge clanging over with wheels, on my Saturday, your Friday. I want the boat to be rocking and your resistance to get weaker, I want your blond hair to be lying across old planks like seaweed on a dike.

I want everything that is old and weathered to be a part of what we do while I make you moan. And even that moan might be like wind in my ears while I stand on the top of that same dike watching you in the distance walking, so far off that I don't know if you're coming toward me or moving away. The fog of San Francisco enveloped everything, and the fog of Frisia covered the windmills; and even in Australia as we stood under the eaves looking up through the rain, the fog was swirling along the brim of the mountains, turning into clouds and dissipating upward in deep breaths.

Your toiling cunt takes whatever it wants in this dream. I want to give it to you, in the dark safety, the cavity of your vessel.

I cannot yet imagine the afterward. It's been so long I don't know what either of us thinks anymore. But when I'm here in my house and the dishes haven't been washed since Thursday and I wonder who loves me, and I find myself believing that you do, as though you are right here with me.

When my heart speaks like this it is louder than the oceans between us; and if I am already up to my neck and getting colder, there is nothing to lose by reaching for another piece of raft and holding tight. And perhaps it is like throwing a line to you too, floating wherever you are. There is desire even where no ship has been sighted for months. Somewhere remote where those creatures live that men have never seen, the giant octopus that sucks its pretty mouth around the fisherman's wife's fantasy. I seek those eight arms in you still, holding me where I cannot get free. And I struggle too, but live for these moments where it spouts up hard against you.

Rock-hard

R. B. Mundi

Last June I was driving with my girlfriend Charlotte from L.A. to Chicago, to see my family during my summer break from UCLA. We decided to take a detour and stop at Joshua Tree National Park. We were both horny and wanted to try something exciting and new. It was the middle of the afternoon, and the desert sun burned brightly. We parked the car and dashed behind one of the hundreds of huge reddish-brown rock formations that speckle the park like giant confetti.

I pushed Charlotte up against the hot rock and shoved my hand into her jeans. Her pussy was soaking wet, and her panties were drenched with sweat. It must have been 100 degrees outside; her thighs were sizzling to the touch. "Mmmm," she moaned as I grabbed her cunt and squeezed it like I was making orange juice. "I need this so bad."

I yanked Charlotte's jeans off and tongued the line where her black silk panties met the crease of her thigh. She let out a whopper of a sigh as I teased her, my tongue making tiny circles on her skin. I occasionally lifted her panties with a finger to lick her delicious triangle of flesh.

Charlotte groaned in delight when I pulled her panties to her ankles and she kicked them off. I placed my hands on either side of her on the molten rock she was leaning against. The heat was like a bolt of electricity that coursed through my body. She grabbed the back of my head and pushed my hungry mouth into her succulent cunt. I wanted her now more than ever as she urged me on with words like "now" and "faster" and "That's it, babe, that's it." I heard a car pass by—and I was sure Charlotte did too—but her sugary cunt was a dessert I'd been craving all day, and I couldn't stop gorging myself.

Charlotte's smooth, pale hips bucked as I curled my tongue around her rock-hard clit. It pulsed quickly, erratically as I enveloped it in my lips, sucking it like it was candy. I readjusted my angle so I could plunge my tongue into her tight hole, then fiercely lap at her walls. Charlotte's hands were planted on the back of my head, her long fingers grabbing at my dark sweat-soaked curls. Her pussy was a warm river as I buried my face in her cave, her sharp scent traveling through my nose then taking hold of my body. Shivers darted up my spine and through my shoulders as she moaned and pressed me harder into her voracious snatch.

I heard the roar of another car—no, this time I could swear it was a motorcycle—come closer and closer, then quickly die down. I heard voices too, but they were mere murmurs as Charlotte's heady scent and exquisite taste filled my nose and mouth. I was in seventh heaven; even if someone were nearby, there was no way I would cut my feast short. "Did you hear that?" Charlotte whispered.

"Yeah, but I'm not about to stop."

Apparently the thrill of being caught took hold of us both because my own clit was beating hard and fast, and I felt Charlotte's snatch tremble and vibrate faster in my ravenous mouth. I looked up at her for a moment; she was a study in beauty, with the face of goddess sculpted in marble, burning with desire yet completely in control. When she caught me stealing a glance at her, she licked her lips, and said, "I'm almost there. Keep going." But I didn't need any urging as I dove in for her sweet goods, licking her tight button, my tongue diving in and out of her fire-hot hole.

"Let's set up over here," came a woman's scratchy voice. "Can you get the cooler for me?" The voice was so close, the woman—and whoever she was with—must have been right on the other side of the large rock I had Charlotte writhing against.

My own pussy was crying for me to take care of it, so I balanced the weight of my body with one hand against the big rock, and quickly undid the button and zipper of my cargo shorts with the other hand. My tongue did cartwheels on Charlotte's clit as I fingered myself, my index and middle fingers hugging either side of my tight, hard knot.

"Do you want this over here?"

"What?" I said.

I looked up at Charlotte, whose eyes were closed tightly. She didn't answer me. The words must have come from whoever had arrived on the motorcycle.

My clit was beating like a drum, faster and faster, in rhythm with my tongue on my lover's sweet spot. Charlotte continued to buck her hips into my mouth; she was close to the edge, and I was right on track with her. My body quaked, fire danced in circles throughout my chest and pelvis. And then I came with a monumental gush.

I knew Charlotte's cunt was about to burst, and I knew she liked it rough and fast, so I flicked and sucked and lapped as quickly and diligently as I ever had.

"Want a beer?" came the voice again.

"Oh, fuck, yes!" Charlotte screamed, her hips and thighs and stomach melting into me in one incredible rush.

I didn't know how we were going to get out of this one, but I was sure it was going to be good.

contributors

Essa Élan Aja lives in Los Angeles.

Anna Avila is an office manager for a technology corporation in San Francisco. She is almost finished with her first novel, a romantic thriller titled *Open Till Nine.*

S.W. Borthwick is a writer-musician in New York. Her first story, "You Swallowed My Hand, I Followed You Home," appeared in the 2004 anthology *Up All Night.* E-mail her at St_Evie123@Yahoo.com.

C.L. Brown resides in Oakland, Calif., where she writes and manages environmental reports for development projects by day and dabbles in writing short, lesbian-focused fiction the rest of the time.

Rachel Kramer Bussel (www.rachelkramerbussel.com) serves as senior editor at *Penthouse Variations.* Her books include *The Lesbian Sex Book, Up All Night: Adventures in Lesbian Sex, Glamour Girls: Femme/Femme Erotica, Naughty Spanking Stories From A to Z,* and *A Spanking Good Time.* Her writing has been published in over 40 anthologies including *Best American Erotica 2004; Best Lesbian Erotica 2001, 2004,* and *2005; Ultimate Lesbian Erotica 2005, Awakening the Virgin 2,* and *Faster Pussycats,* as well as *AVN, Bust,* Cleansheets.com, *Curve, Diva, Girlfriends, New York Blade, On Our Backs,* Oxygen.com, *Penthouse, Velvetpark,* and *The Village Voice.*

Marla Carter lives in Santa Monica, Calif. She runs an online dating service for lesbian and bisexual women. In fact, that's how she met her soul mate, Daphne. They recently bought their first home and celebrated their fifth anniversary.

M. Damian recently moved from Staten Island, N.Y., to New Jersey, buying a house with her partner of six years, Amy. They are the proud parents of a beagle, Barney, and two young Yorkies, Pegeen and Blaise. Her lesbian detective novel, *I Don't Do Murder,* will be published in the near future, and she is also currently toiling away on a children's book and two more mystery novels.

Urszula Dawkins lives in Melbourne, Australia. Her stories have been published in Australia, the United States, and the United Kingdom, and she has performed her work in Melbourne, Sydney, Newcastle and Adelaide, Australia and in San Francisco.

Mia Dominguez resides in Los Angeles with her child and cat. She has previously been published in other Alyson anthologies— *Awakening the Virgin, Wet, My Lover My Friend,* and *Skin Deep*— and has also had work published in *Lesbian News, Tongues,* and *Philogyny.*

Nicky Donoghue is a St. Louis-based writer and visual artist. She lives with her partner, Sam, and her two adopted children, Sophie and Chloe.

C.J. Evans lives in Seattle, where she works for a nonprofit agency that assists the homeless. Four of her plays have been staged in Seattle and Portland, Ore.

Eileen Finn lives in the Chicago area with her partner, Kate, and their son, Adam. She is politically active in the area of GLBT rights and a member of the Human Rights Campaign. Her day job is in finance, but she has published other stories, poems, and articles in various publications.

Sarah Finster grew up reading too much Ian Fleming in the suburbs of Chicago. "Breaking the Girl" is her first print-published work.

Jessie Fischer is a singer-songwriter in Austin, Texas.

Holly Franzen lives life on the edge on the mean streets of Chicago, but she loves New York–style pizza. She's hard at work on her first novel, W*icker Park.*

Shanna Germain's writing has appeared in a variety of magazines and anthologies including CleanSheets.com, *Heat Wave, The Many Joys of Sex Toys,* Salon.com, and *Zuzu's Petals Quarterly.* She is the assistant fiction editor at the CleanSheets.com e-zine and the managing editor of both her partner and her cat. For more see www.shannagermain.com.

Sacchi Green has published work in five volumes of *Best Lesbian Erotica,* four volumes of *Best Women's Erotica, The Mammoth Book of Best New Erotica 3, Penthouse,* and a knee-high stack of other anthologies with inspirational covers. Her first coeditorial venture, *Rode Hard, Put Away Wet: Lesbian Cowboy Erotica,* is scheduled for release in 2005.

Andrea Herrmann is a writer, poet, and independent business owner who currently resides in Rhode Island. She presented at and coordinated the Annual Symposium on Lesbian, Gay, Bisexual, and Transgender Issues at the University of Rhode Island while completing both her undergraduate and graduate degrees. You can reach her at aherrmann76@aol.com.

Jessi Holhart brings to her writing a long history of sexual exploration and education: membership in PSSST, Outcasts, LINKS, etc. She is currently living happily with her wife of 12 years in Baltimore.

Jenn Hwang is an antiques dealer in Silver Lake, Calif., and holds an MFA in creative writing from the University of Wisconsin-Madison.

Debra Hyde's fiction can be found in *Best Lesbian Erotica 4, Naughty Spanking Stories From A to Z, Spurred On,* and a whole host of other anthologies. When she's not writing erotica, she maintains the long-running Web log PursedLips.com. And when she's not writing, she engages in the kind of activities that inspire erotic stories.

Julie Jacobs lives in Los Angeles, where she's a producer for reality television as well as a screenwriter. She lives with her partner, Debbie, a stay-at-home mom and online entrepreneur.

Stephanie James was born in the seaside town of Lowestoft, England. Her sex stories appear in a variety of top-shelf magazines, including *Penthouse Variations, Forum,* and *For Women.* Stephanie relaxes by acting out the sexual fantasies from her writing. Her long-suffering partner, Lucy, gets very little sleep—Stephanie writes on average four stories a week and every one of them has to be re-created in full!

Lynne Jamneck is a writer and photographer from South Africa with a penchant for women, strong coffee, and guns. She is still accepting suggestions on how to combine the three. Her fiction, nonfiction, and photography have appeared in various markets in South Africa, the United States, the United Kingdom, and Canada. The first book in her Samantha Skellar mystery series is available from Bella Books (February 2005). Lynn is the creator and editor of *Simulacrum—The Magazine of Speculative Transformation* (www.specficworld.com/simulacrum.html) and currently lives in New Zealand.

Mo Jensen is a tomboy lesbian who loves sports, lesbians, and butch women who wear boxer shorts. "Coach-able Moments" is her first anthology submission. She extends special props to a certain sport-writing mentor who continues to inspire her and so many others. Mo lives near Washington, D.C.

Mona Johnson lives in Northern California, where she owns a landscape design firm. She's single and looking!

Melinda Johnston is a Vancouver, Canada writer who has been published in *Xtra West, Outlooks,* and *Hot and Bothered 4.* She usually writes stories that she can't show to her mother—and is proud of it!

Carole Joseph was born in New England but raised in the Midwest, where she spent the next 20 years trying to figure out a way to return to Vermont. She now lives, happily, near a river and two streams.

JT Langdon is the Buddhist, vegetarian lover of chocolate responsible for the erotic lesbian novels *Sisters of Omega Pi* and *For I Have Sinned*. Despite numerous requests to leave, some made with pitchforks, the author continues to live in the Midwest.

Lovelybrown is a writer and spoken-word artist born under the sacred zodiac of Scorpio. Originally from Louisville, Ky., she has spent the past six years of her life in Atlanta. She has published works on Kuma2.net and in *Queer Ramblings*. In August, she self-published a book of poetry with an accompanying CD entitled *Trying to Get This Lesbian Shit Right*. Currently, she resides on the East Coast, where she is attending graduate school.

Julie Mitchell, born and raised a city mouse in the megalopolis of Los Angeles, happily became a country mouse when she moved to the rural Big Island of Hawaii in 1998. She lives next door to Kilauea, the most active volcano in the world and home to the fire goddess Pele. A freelance writer, she contributes regularly to the *Hawaii Island Journal* and coordinates the writing program for the Volcano Art Center. Her writing has been published in *Love Shook My Heart: New Lesbian Love Stories* (Alyson Books), *Lesbian Review of Books,* and *Feminist Bookstore News* among others. Her essay "Creature of the Air" was selected as a finalist for the 2003 Penelope Niven Creative Non-Fiction Award. She is currently working on short fiction, creative nonfiction, and a novel.

R.B. Mundi's writing has appeared in *On Our Backs* magazine. She lives in Los Angeles.

Peggy Munson has published erotica in 10 editions of the *Best Lesbian Erotica* series as well as in *On Our Backs: The Best Erotic Fiction, Tough Girls, Best Bisexual Erotica II,* and *Genderqueer*. Her poetry and fiction have appeared in *Best American Poetry 2003, Blithe House Quarterly, Lodestar Quarterly, Margin, Spoon River Poetry Review, The San Francisco Bay Guardian,* and elsewhere. Visit www.peggymunson.com for more information and updates.

Barbara Pizio is the executive editor of *Penthouse Variations* magazine. Her writing has appeared in *Ultimate Lesbian Erotica 2005, Naughty Spanking Stories From A to Z,* and *Penthouse Forum.*

M.L. Renki spends a great deal of time reading and writing erotica. A connoisseur of sorts, Renki finds it important to portray the real side of lesbian sex, which means its passion, intimacy, and grittiness. She and her partner live in Nashville.

Jean Roberta teaches English at a Canadian prairie university and writes in various genres. Her true coming-out story appeared in Alyson's *Up All Night.* Her erotic stories have appeared in *Best Women's Erotica* and *Best Lesbian Erotica* as well as numerous other anthologies, magazines, and Web sites. Her book reviews appear in her column, "In My Jeans," on the Web site BlueFood.cc.

Teresa Noelle Roberts, when not writing, is a Middle Eastern dancer, a gardener, and a member of the Society for Creative Anachronism. Her erotic fiction has appeared in *Best Women's Erotica 2004* and *2005, Ripe Fruit, Down and Dirty II,* and other publications and Web sites. Teresa is half of the erotica-writing duo known as Sophie Mouette. She is also a fantasy writer and a widely published poet.

CeCe Ross is the pseudonym of an overworked Hollywood TV producer. She resides in Studio City, Calif., with her domestic partner, two beautiful sons from Cambodia, and a pair of teething shar-pei puppies.

Lisabet Sarai is author of the erotic novels *Raw Silk, Incognito,* and *Ruby's Rules.* She is the coeditor of *Sacred Exchange,* which explores the spiritual aspects of BD-S/M relationships. A collection of her shorter works, entitled *Fire,* is scheduled for publication by Blue Moon Books in 2005.

Dawn Sitler lives and works in Tulsa, Okla. with her loving and supportive partner. "Silicone Pony" is her first published story.

Mary K. Slavin was previously published in *Early Embraces* (Alyson Publications, 1996). Mary lives in Portland, Ore. where she gets paid for technical support. In her free time she writes, teaches herself how to DJ, and bartends for her friends.

Therese Szymanski is the Lammy-nominated author of the Brett Higgins Motor City Thrillers, editor of *Back to Basics: A Butch/Femme Anthology,* and one-fourth of the team behind *Once Upon a Dyke: New Exploits of Fairy Tale Lesbians* (and *Bell, Book and Dyke: New Exploits of Magical Lesbians*). Her stories have appeared in about a dozen anthologies. She believes in maximizing the erotic content of life.

Heather Towne's writing has appeared in *ssspread, Options, Hustler Fantasies, Leg Sex, Newcummers, Variations, Forum, 18Eighteen, Abby's Realm,* and the anthologies *Skin Deep 2, Mammoth Book of Women's Sexual Fantasies, Wicked Words 9,* and *Ultimate Lesbian Erotica 2005.*

Rakelle Valencia's stories have appeared in *Best Lesbian Erotica 2004* and *2005, Best of Best Lesbian Erotica 2, Ride 'em Cowboy, On Our Backs, Naughty Spanking Stories From A to Z, Best Lesbian Love Stories 2005, Ultimate Lesbian Erotica 2005,* and www.sextoytales.com. With Sacchi Green, she is contracted by Suspect Thoughts Press to produce the anthology *Rode Hard, Put Away Wet: Lesbian Cowboy Erotica* for 2005, and by Alice Street Editions, The Haworth Press Inc., to produce the anthology *Dykes on Bikes: Short Story Erotica.*

Brenda Whitehall's journalism career began in the working-class steel town of Hamilton, Canada. She has directed music videos, produced records, booked and promoted concerts and festivals, written and produced radio documentaries, and has been published in numerous magazines and newspapers across North America. Currently residing in Vancouver, she is focusing her creative energy on scriptwriting and short stories.

M.J. Williamz, raised on the California coast, was living in a small college town in Northern California when she realized her true callings—as a lesbian and as an author. Now living in Portland, Ore., M.J. is working on her first novel.

Karen Dale Wolman is an accomplished fiction writer and the founder—executive director of Lavender Writes, an organization for gay and lesbian writers. Her first novel, *Rites of First Blood,* achieved local best-seller status two days after its release in Los Angeles, and her second novel, *The Ancestor,* sold out at its publication party. Her most famous short story, "Telling Mom," has been published six times. She has been granted honors, awards, and fellowships from the Florida State Arts Council, the University of Southern California, the Helene Wurlitzer Foundation of New Mexico, and *Ibelle* magazine. She is the first literary artist to be awarded funding from the Broward Cultural Council in Florida.

Kristina Wright's erotic fiction has been published in numerous anthologies including *Best Women's Erotica 2000, Best Lesbian Erotica* (*2002, 2004* and *2005*), *Bedroom Eyes: Tales of Lesbians in the Boudoir,* and *Ultimate Lesbian Erotica 2005* among others. Her writing has also been featured in the nonfiction guide *The Many Joys of Sex Toys* and in e-zines such as Clean Sheets, Scarlet Letters, and *Good Vibes* magazine. Kristina is a full-time writer and part-time graduate student living in Virginia with her very patient husband and a menagerie of wayward pets. For more information about Kristina's life and writing visit her Web site, www.kristinawright.com.